PRAGUE SPRING

Also by Simon Mawer

Chimera
A Place in Italy
The Bitter Cross
A Jealous God
Mendel's Dwarf
The Gospel of Judas
The Fall
Swimming to Ithaca
Gregor Mendel: Planting the Seeds of Genetics
The Glass Room
The Girl Who Fell From the Sky
Tightrope

PRAGUE SPRING

SIMON MAWER

Little, Brown

LITTLE, BROWN

First published in Great Britain in 2018 by Little, Brown

1 3 5 7 9 10 8 6 4 2

Copyright © Simon Mawer 2018

The moral right of the author has been asserted.

A CIP catalogue record for this book
is available from the British Library.

Hardback ISBN 978-1-4087-1114-9
Trade paperback ISBN 978-1-4087-1115-6

Typeset in Sabon by M Rules
Printed and bound in Great Britain by
Clays Ltd, Elcograf S.p.A.

Papers used by Little, Brown are from well-managed forests
and other responsible sources.

MIX
Paper from
responsible sources
FSC® C104740

Little, Brown
An imprint of
Little, Brown Book Group
Carmelite House
50 Victoria Embankment
London EC4Y 0DZ

An Hachette UK Company
www.hachette.co.uk

www.littlebrown.co.uk

For Sophia and Olivia,
two more of the next generation

I

1

It started in a pub. Not unusual for a journey. Phileas Fogg started his at the Reform Club in London, but then James Borthwick was not Phileas Fogg, and this pub was the nearest thing to a club that James knew. And this journey wasn't round the world, which these days you can probably do in less than eighty hours and never leave aircraft or airport. So, a pub, a student pub full of noise and laughter and spilt beer, with photographs of rowing eights on the walls and signatures of oarsmen and rugby players on the ceiling and even an oar hanging over the bar. Yes, one of those pubs that anxious tourists enter during the vacations in the vain hope that they are going to witness that ephemeral will-o'-the-wisp student life, when all they find is indifferent bar staff, flabby beer and flabbier meat pies.

'Do you really think it makes any sense at all?' James asked, feeling, for a moment, emboldened. He was sitting at a small, round table, opposite a rather ragged-looking girl, leaning towards her across the table so that they could catch each other's words amidst the noise. James was feeling nervous because it wasn't every day that he got this close to someone like Eleanor and he didn't want to be wafting beery breath all over her in case that should blow her away. Also because, let's face it, they came from opposite ends of the undergraduate spectrum. She was reading English while he was a scientist of a kind, and she was in her second year whereas he was a fresher. Furthermore – there's more, we're going further, into the murky world of class – furthermore, and despite her scruffy appearance, there was something decidedly superior about Eleanor that was noticeable when she spoke, a certain manner of enunciating her consonants, hitting the Ts and Ls and sculpting the vowels, that put her in a social class above James. His voice was vaguely Northern; hers was county. It doesn't really matter which county. Perhaps even Oxford, although the Oxford voice, with its hooing and its cooing, was really a thing of the past. But the most decided difference between them was not accent or even social class but the plain biological fact that he was male and therefore one of many thousands, whereas she was female and therefore, within the university, as rare as a nun in a monastery. Perhaps that's a surprise, considering that nowadays women outnumber men by the fraction that superior intelligence and unwavering work habits give them, but in those days it was so: lots of men, few women. Furthermore, those two contrasting versions of the species lived very separate lives for the simple, adminis-trative, historical, insane reason that the colleges were still single-sex. Thus Eleanor belonged to St Hilda's, all the way down the High and over the river. Turn right, away from the medieval glories of Magdalen, and you'll find the rather lesser nineteenth- and twentieth-century glories of St Hilda's college just there. No tourist bothers, ever. Whereas James lived in the Renaissance glory of one of the old colleges in the city centre, where tourists bother all the time.

Coming from such different worlds, they might have drifted past each other without even passing the time of day had it not been for one of those chance events of university life: they were acting together in a college play.

'Of course it doesn't make sense *in the way you mean*,' Eleanor replied, leaving James to wonder which way he did mean and, furthermore, what kind of sense it might make in any other way. Thus instead of reducing his uncertainty, Eleanor had actually succeeded in increasing it. Typical of an arts undergraduate. The subject in question was the play that had brought them together both at a series of rather awkward rehearsals in rooms in college and more immediately on a stage in a hall somewhere in Walton Street, she as a female cripple in an old-fashioned pram and he as the witless male condemned to push pram and female around the rather limited universe of the playwright's imagination. This unlikely duo was searching, so the storyline went, for the city of Tar. Although why they should wish to get to Tar was never made clear. Sub-Beckett, James wanted to say of the play, but lines like that were dangerous when you were talking to someone who was reading English, especially when you were reading science.

'I suppose not,' was what he replied, which appeared to cover all possible lines of attack. 'Do you want another beer?'

'I haven't finished this one.'

'No.'

She was smoking. James didn't smoke because he didn't like it, but she smoked, rolled her own, in fact, because ... what? She did like it? Or did she feel that rolling her own made her seem closer to the working class whose virtues she extolled? He wondered other things – did she smoke pot, perhaps? That was the term in those days. Pot, hash, grass, weed. Shit, if you were feeling very edgy. Probably others that he didn't know. Anyway, did she? And another, much more disturbing question: did her mouth taste of cigarettes? Disturbing because her mouth was itself disturbing. Full, with a slightly heavy upper lip. And very red. Somehow not exactly English. And he knew – for a fleeting moment as he tried to think what else to say – that he would love to kiss it, cigarettes or no cigarettes.

'So what exactly are they searching for? Fando and Lis, I mean.'

'They aren't *exactly* searching for anything.'

'Of course not. So what are they approximately searching for?'

That made her laugh. It was lovely, that laugh. Despite the cigarettes, her teeth were very white and the inside of her mouth coral pink. In contrast her skin was quite pale, and her hair – a curly cloud – straw-coloured. He would never have admitted it to anyone, but just being there at the table with her, watching her laugh, brought the beginnings of an awkward erection.

'You're so funny,' she said, which, laughter being the great aphrodisiac, made the erection worse.

'I suppose for fulfilment,' James suggested.

'What on earth do you mean, *fulfilment*? That's a weasel word if there ever was one. I thought you scientists were meant to be precise.'

'Well . . . ' he hesitated. 'Love, perhaps.'

'God, you'll be calling them hippies next.'

'Or maybe they're just looking for a youth hostel.'

It was then, following a further little bout of laughter, that she asked, quite casually, *apropos of nothing* (as she might have said), the question: What are you doing in the long vac?

Vac. Inwardly James cringed. He hated terms like this. Rugger and cuppers and scouts and other stuff. Soccer as well. And he hated the prospect of *long vac* for what it was, a desert of nothing to do that stretched aimlessly from Trinity to Michaelmas and was both a purgatory and a wasted opportunity. Trinity and Michaelmas. More of those bloody terms. Terms for terms in this case, Trinity being spring term and Michaelmas being autumn. I mean, what did they *mean*, for Christ's sake? Trinity, an atom-bomb test. And Michaelmas, a daisy. 'I dunno, really,' he answered her, wishing he had something more impressive to say. 'Got to get a job, I suppose, but what I really want to do is travel. I had thought of going to Europe. Hitching. But . . . '

'But what?'

'I was going with a mate but he's had to cry off. So . . .' He hesitated, not wanting to go into too much detail. It wouldn't sound cool, two guys going round battlefields. Because that's what it was. A friend from home, like him an enthusiastic war-gamer. Not something to admit to freely. Like trainspotting or stamp collecting, it seemed a silly, childish interest. Board games and that. Ludo, Cluedo, Monopoly, all the crappy amusements of childhood. Except that it wasn't the same, really. It was an attempt to reconstruct the past, to relive it and learn from it. But to explain all that to Eleanor would have just made things worse – she'd have looked at him with that knowing look and made him feel foolish and naive. Better just keep quiet.

'That's weird,' she said.

'Why weird?'

'I had the same idea. But my friend decided to get married instead.'

'A guy?'

'*To* a guy. She's a girl. We were going to retrace the Sentimental Journey. Do you know it?'

'I remember my parents dancing to it in the sitting room. With Workers' Playtime on the radio.'

Her laughter was so loud the hearties hushed their voices for a moment. 'Not the *song*, you idiot. The *book*. By Sterne.'

Stern? He knew *The Principles of Human Genetics* by Curt Stern, but he doubted it was the same author. And of course there was the physicist Otto Stern, who must have published a great deal on quantum mechanics, but it wouldn't be him. That was the trouble with science – it wasn't the matter of ordinary discourse. You could get sconced in Hall for talking about bond energies, but you could never get sconced for talking about Shakespeare. *Sconced*. Another of those terms he hated, this one involving being challenged to drink too much

7

beer out of one of those large silver tankards that graced the dining tables on special occasions in Hall. Punishment, of a kind. But Eleanor was going on. She'd clearly mistaken his ignorance for another of his jokes. 'Oh, you should read it. It's brilliantly funny, although not as important as *Tristram Shandy*. You *have* read *Tristram Shandy*, haven't you? Anyway, we thought of taking it along with us as a guide – *Sentimental Journey*, I mean – although Sterne never gets beyond Lyon and the sequel, written by a friend after his death—'

'The friend's?'

'Sterne's, you fool. This friend tried to continue the book but his effort just isn't up to the original. Anyway, that idea's all finished now because Jenny's gone and got engaged.'

'Shame.'

'So now I'm wondering what to do with myself.' She took a sip of beer and looked at him thoughtfully. 'What about going together?'

The oarsmen had started up again and were making such a song and dance about things that James couldn't even be sure if he had heard right.

'*What did you say?*'

She drew on her cigarette and blew blue smoke up towards the nicotine-stained ceiling. 'I said, what about going together?'

The singing stopped. At least that is what it seemed to James, sitting there nursing his beer and his erection. 'Sounds all right.'

'I mean, just as friends, of course.'

'Of course.'

'The idea was mainly to sleep rough. In railway stations, public parks, you know what I mean. Hostels and *pensions* at a pinch.'

'Could be dodgy for two girls.'

'That's what my parents said. But it wouldn't be as dodgy with a guy, would it?'

'No,' he agreed.

'So what do you say?'

He tried to take a calm swig of beer, but somehow it got caught up in his tonsils. Spluttering, he apologised.

'Of course, if you've got other ideas ... '

'No, really.'

'It was just a thought ... '

He looked at her, wondering. She wasn't pretty, not in any ordinary meaning of the word, because she wasn't ordinary-looking – she was striking. That wild, uncontrolled hair, those bold features, her cheeks dotted with faint freckles, her mouth designed with anger and amusement, her eyes alight with a green fire. And she had a reputation that was largely political, although it did extend, in some whispered conversations, to the sexual. She was a member of ORSS, the Oxford Revolutionary Socialist Students, and she had been manhandled – literally, although you could prove nothing; maybe his hand had just slipped – by the Oxford City police during a student occupation of the Clarendon Building. Subsequently she had spent a night in gaol and had been charged with disturbing the peace and fined two pounds. Worse than that, she had been threatened by her college with rustication. Rustication was another of those words that James loathed. What was wrong with 'suspension', for Christ's sake? Anyway, that little incident had made her political reputation. Her sexual reputation, on the other hand, was more obscure. Gossip had it that there had been a man who was no longer around. She had been in love with him but was now off men – a natural but temporary state, James surmised, for someone who had been crossed in love.

'Are you *serious*?'

'Of course I am.' She giggled.

'What are you laughing at?'

'Nothing. Just a thought, that's all. No, *don't say it*—'

But he already had, and realised his mistake as soon as the words were uttered: 'Penny for them.'

She finished her beer. Maybe the suggestion she'd made was a terrible mistake.

'Well?' he insisted.

'Let's go, shall we?'

'*Are* you serious?' he asked again, convinced that he must be the butt of some kind of tease.

'About going? Yes. I've got to meet someone who's going to review the play. For the *Oxford Mail*, no less.'

'I meant, about this summer.'

'Oh, *that*.'

They climbed the steps up to the daylight of the Broad. Another of those terms. 'The Broad.' 'The High.' Why was the word 'street' left out of the equation? 'Well, *are* you?'

'Maybe, maybe not. *Not* if you talk in clichés. "Penny for them", indeed. Look, I must rush. See you later.'

And she'd gone.

2

Then came the performance itself, with its intensity of experience, its focus on the two of them – James and Eleanor, Fando and Lis – as they meandered across a creaking stage before the gaze of a hundred invisible faces. The play, with Lis tied up and dumped in an old pram and swearing love and devotion for her captor. The play with fear and fright and catharsis – Eleanor's word – both in the script and in the minds of the players. The play, with Fando's sudden raging temper and equally sudden collapses into recrimination and apology. The play with its inconsequential dialogue – 'sub-Beckett', wrote the reviewer in the *Oxford Mail*, stealing James's unuttered line – and hopeless outcome.

'They *loved* your Mancunian accent, darling,' the director told James at the party after the opening, draping his arm round his shoulder.

'It's Sheffield.'

'Whatever. Northern, that's what it is. Gritty, darling, gritty. You should seriously think about the Royal Court.'

At the curtain call, Fando had carried Lis to the foot of the stage as though she really was disabled, and there were those in the audience who were fooled, one of them coming up to them next day as they walked together in the Cornmarket, on their way to a photo shoot for the student newspaper, to say how brilliant it had been and how she'd assumed that

Eleanor actually *was* handicapped, so convincing was her performance.

After that encounter with fame they went to his rooms in college, in the Old Quad, with the Tudor gatehouse visible through the windows and the two-bar electric fire turned on to provide a focus of warmth before which the figure of Eleanor could disport itself, as careless but more articulate than Lis. She was wearing a red skirt and black tights and a black top. The skirt was a novelty, presumably intended for the photographer. Normally, when not dressed as Lis (whose costume had been a tattered and grubby nightdress), she wore jeans and assumed a vaguely military look. But now a photogenic skirt. Thus clad she set to toasting crumpets on the fire by hanging them on the grille with hooks made from paper clips. The hooks were James's suggestion. 'Typical scientist,' she said, but he detected a hint of affection behind the mockery. 'Do you often have crumpets in your rooms?' she asked. She was on all fours before the fire. A small shriek of pain as she dropped a crumpet onto the plate and sucked her fingers.

'As often as I can persuade them to step over the threshold.'

Laughter, edged with something more than amusement. Appetite, perhaps. She rearranged herself on the rug – a length of gleaming black thigh – and began to apply butter. James poured tea from the brown teapot he had brought from home and that Eleanor had declared 'very ethnic'. By mutual agreement they sat side by side, on the rug, facing the fire, hot butter on their lips and fingers. By mutual agreement they turned to look at each other and then leant forward and kissed. There was a little exploratory engagement of buttery tongues and the mingled taste of each other's crumpets and Eleanor's cigarettes.

'Mmm,' she said, as though to take the agreement one step further. Then she pulled back, took a puff from her cigarette, sipped her tea and might as well have been sitting in the café in the covered market. 'We were going to talk about the summer vac,' she said in a faint tone of admonishment.

'The summer,' he repeated, thinking more about this spring, the here and now, and wondering exactly what had just happened.

'We've got to have some idea of what we're doing and where we're going, haven't we?'

'Are we going then?'

'Of course we are. Aren't we?'

'If you want to. I want to.' He had feared she might prefer to go to Paris or something, to dig cobblestones out of the Boul' Mich' and throw them at the battle lines of the CRS. But no, she'd already done that. Pavé was passé. Now she just wanted to explore Europe, Italy especially, and maybe even make Greece and see what conditions were like there where the Colonels reigned supreme. 'Fascists,' she said disdainfully.

Alarm bells went off in his head. 'You're not planning—'

She laughed. 'Don't worry, I won't get you into trouble. It's just that I've never actually been to a Fascist dictatorship. Except Spain of course, but that doesn't really count any longer, does it?' And then she touched his wrist and said he looked terrified, but assured him that she would be as good as gold, which was not an element he was familiar with except to know that the only thing good about it, apart from its cost, was the fact that it was virtually inert. He doubted Eleanor would be inert.

They went on to talk about what they'd need to take with them, how much money, what clothes. Eleanor treated the whole thing as though it were a joke – 'I can always sell my body if we run short of cash' – and yet there was a bedrock of seriousness about the discussion, as though they really were going to do this. So James talked about sleeping bags, a couple of changes of T-shirt, a second pair of jeans. Washing things and changes of underwear, of course. What else? And he suggested his tent. 'It's okay for two at a squeeze,' he added. He knew about these matters from weekends spent in the Peak District and the Lakes.

'Your *tent*? At a *squeeze*?' She had never slept in a tent.

'Never?'

'Well, not since my brother and I pitched one on the front lawn. That was ten years ago.'

'Front lawn? You camped on your front lawn?' To James *front lawn* implied *back lawn* and dragged along with it *kitchen garden* and *orchard* and probably, just probably, *paddock*. With a pony.

'Yes, you know – one of those green things. Or don't you have such things up North?' She bit into another crumpet and told him the story. He was happy to listen, intrigued for the moment by lawns, front or back, as well as by the movement of her lips as she spoke and the butter that glistened on them. Apparently she and her brother had pitched the tent before having supper in the house and kissing their parents goodbye as though they were setting off for the South Pole. Darkness had descended on the garden and the tent. Inside, brother and sister had wriggled and fidgeted and tried to get comfortable on what had once seemed soft grass but now revealed itself as a bed of nails fit to try the patience of a fakir. Thus they had spent four sleepless hours before fleeing back indoors, her brother terrified because he had heard noises, Eleanor smugly triumphant because she had made them. 'So, I am *not*,' she concluded, 'sleeping in a tent, and certainly not *squeezing* into one with you.'

'That's all right. I'll sleep in the tent and you can sleep outside.'

That prompted a punch, not very effective, which landed on James's upper arm. He responded by grabbing her wrist. Another punch, another wrist held. There was a brief struggle in which elbows and knees were involved before they were kissing once again and Eleanor was saying, through teeth and tongue and lips, that perhaps this was not a good idea, that she just wanted to be friends, that there was someone else in her life and that was the trouble.

There was an awkward rearrangement of limbs and clothing. She smoothed herself down. 'I'm sorry,' she said, more than once.

'There's nothing to apologise for,' James insisted, although there was, in fact, a great deal.

'It's just . . .' she said.

'Just what?'

'I mean, it's difficult.'

'It seems rather easy to me.'

'Maybe it is for you. You're a man.'

'Is it easier for men? Men have feelings as well, you know.'

'Do they? I thought they just had erections.'

He made no reply to that, understanding when it was pointless to continue. 'You know when we took that curtain call? When I carried you to the front of the stage and showed you to the audience?'

'Of course I remember.'

He nodded, picking up the remains of her crumpet. 'I think it was then that I realised how much I like you.'

Like you. A euphemism used in a time of hardship. There was a pause while he didn't dare look at her.

'That's very sweet,' she said. 'But at the time I was a cripple wearing handcuffs.'

3

After the awkwardness of the afternoon tea and two more performances of the play, James and Eleanor settled into some kind of unspoken compromise. It involved a certain degree of physical contact – holding hands, kissing, perhaps a hesitant hand on a reluctant breast – but would go no further until . . .

'Until what?' James asked, emboldened.

Until she sorted herself out.

'That sounds very bourgeois.'

Once again sitting in his rooms in college, talking in that rapid, articulate manner she could adopt, she denied it. Her emotional difficulties transcended all matters of class. They could belong to someone from an impoverished Irish family in Liverpool or Birmingham just as well as someone like her with her moneyed upbringing and her private schooling. Whichever way you looked at it, it was just nuns and priests.

'Nuns and priests?' Comprehension dawned slowly, for this was just another of those Oxford things – a peculiar ritual that might have meant something in the past but was now an irrelevance. So much of Oxford seemed irrelevant. 'You mean you're *Catholic*?'

'My parents still are, in their different ways. My father treats it as an elaborate legal code and my mother tries to wash her guilt away in a mixture of consecrated host and gin.'

'You mean you believe all that stuff?'

'Of course *I* don't. I gave it up a long time ago. But it's like being a Jew. You never entirely get rid of it.' She opened her hands as though to demonstrate her helplessness. Even James, brought up in a godless household, saw a weird significance in the gesture. As though she might be demonstrating – what was it they called the wounds of Christ? – her own personal stigmata. 'Wounds may heal,' she said, 'but the scars remain. With guilt still embedded inside like bits of grit.'

'What's there to be guilty about?'

'You wouldn't understand. You don't have to be guilty of anything in order to feel guilt. That's the secret.'

'That's daft.'

'Daft it may be but that's how it is – original sin. The most oppressive thought control anyone has ever invented. George Orwell's Thought Police, centuries before he ever wrote about it. The Catholic variation is that you are the police as well as the criminal.'

'But if you no longer believe it, where's the problem?'

She looked at him, head on one side. 'You don't understand, do you? That's what I like about you. You see life in simple terms.'

'It *is* simple. It's you who's screwed up. You shouldn't spend so much time thinking about things. Just let them happen. Religion's no different from studying literature – you spend all your time obsessing about fictitious people and imagining they're real.'

'You sound,' she said, 'just like my father.'

'He sounds all right.'

And eventually, there they were, at her house in Surrey, in the stockbroker belt, with Leatherhead on the one hand and Esher on the other and Sheffield as far away as Patagonia. And he was about to meet both her mother and her father. Mummy and Daddy.

The father was a daunting man – big, loud, with a sharp look and a quick tongue. A lawyer, apparently. A barrister, a QC in fact, although James barely understood the difference between one type of lawyer and another except that barristers wore gowns and wigs, which always seemed bloody silly. Yet somehow he could see that Mr Pike would not look silly in gown and wig, would not ever look silly in fact, but would be well practised in the fine art of making others both look and feel immensely foolish. 'So you're the latest, are you?' he boomed. A bittern, James thought. A bittern booming. The same posture, hunched over his utterance, grasping his lapels, glaring at the witness.

'The latest?'

'Eleanor's latest.'

She stood close to her father, hugging his arm. 'Daddy, I keep telling you, he's just a *friend*.'

Daddy's gaze never wavered. 'Well she would say that, wouldn't she?' he boomed, and James laughed, recognising the line in the way that one might recognise a Latin tag, with amusement but also with the faint sense of having passed some kind of test.

'Actually, what Ellie says is true, sir. We *are* just friends. Unless she knows something I don't.'

Daddy liked the 'sir'. It showed an appropriate measure of deference. He liked the recognition of his quotation, liked the humour of the response. 'It is my experience,' he said, in the portentous manner of the judge he would doubtless soon become, 'that a woman almost always knows something that a man doesn't.'

Dinner that evening was a ritual fraught with the possibility of solecism. Her mother was a pinched woman with heavily applied makeup and suspiciously brassy hair, whose eyes settled on James like two iridescent beetles, watching him carefully to see how he manoeuvred his knife and fork, how he used his napkin, how he broke his bread and which way he tilted his soup bowl. 'That's an interesting accent you have,' she remarked when he dared speak. 'Do you come from Manchester?'

'Sheffield.'

Her mouth compressed, as though he might have got it wrong. 'Eleanor said Manchester.'

'I *suggested* Manchester, Mummy, ages ago.'

'Sheffield is in Yorkshire, isn't it?'

'That's right. And Manchester is in Lancashire, on the other side of the Pennines.'

'The Pennines,' the mother repeated, as though he might have said the Urals or the Carpathians. 'And what do your people do, James? On their side of the Pennines.'

Your people. As if he came from one of the great families of the North, Percys or Nevilles, wild people leading bands of kerns and gallowglasses and for ever waging wars against their neighbours and the Picts over the border. 'Both my parents are teachers.'

'Oh, indeed, are they? Amble forth?'

James looked blank. Amble forth? Was that what she imagined Northerners did? Did she think they ambled forth into the Peak District or something, like the ramblers on Kinder Scout in the 1930s? He felt that he had been put to a further test and this time had failed. 'I'm sorry, I . . . '

'Friends of ours have children there. The Remnants.'

'Remnants?'

'An old recusant family. Obviously not.'

James looked even blanker. It was safe to say that he had not understood a word of that particular exchange. Remnants? Recusants? Ambling forth? The woman seemed to live in an alternative linguistic universe.

'Mummy, James's parents teach at a *grammar* school,' Eleanor explained. 'Not bloody Ampleforth.'

'A *grammar* school? Where they teach—?'

'Grammar,' said James.

It was with some relief that he accepted the barrister's invitation to join him in his study after dinner to try his favourite malt whisky. You couldn't argue that the family stinted on alcohol. Before dinner it had been G&T; during the meal they had consumed three bottles of a red wine called Aloxe-Corton which had been quite good; and now it was a malt whisky that had lain in casks in a dank cave in Scotland since before James was born.

The barrister sat in his large, leather wing-back chair while James pressed himself defensively into the corner of a button-back Chesterfield. Once they had dispensed with the formalities of sipping and exclaiming and agreeing that this golden elixir ranked amongst the finest experiences a man could have, the barrister regarded James with beady and judgemental eye. 'So are you two sleeping together?' he asked.

'I'm sorry?'

'My daughter. Eleanor. Are you sleeping with her? It's a plain enough question.' How to describe the expression on his face? Bleak? Accusatory? Adversarial?

'No sir. Of course not.'

'What's "of course" about it? Doesn't every young man want to sleep with every young woman? According to the papers the younger generation does that kind of thing all the time, apparently to the exclusion of everything else except smoking pot. Surely all the journalists can't be wrong.'

'I can't answer for my generation.'

'But you can for Ellie and you.'

'What I said before: we're just good friends.'

'Ha! You sound as though you've just been caught in her bedroom with your trousers round your ankles.'

'But it's true.'

'And is that the limit of your ambition? Mere friendship?'

The barrister's eyes, James decided, were considerably less blurred with alcohol than his speech. He was probing with intent, edging towards some kind of judgement about James's suitability as company for his daughter or, more probably, manoeuvring into a position to warn him off. *You're not worthy, are you, young man?* Something like that. *You don't have the right background, the right accent, the right parents and prospects.*

'Well, I'm very fond of her, of course. But there's another man around, isn't there? Kevin, I mean. He sort of gets in the way.'

The barrister smiled knowingly. 'Ah, yes. Kevin.'

'Ellie still seems a bit in love with him.'

'Does she, indeed?'

'And I think it better to let her get over that.'

The barrister sniffed. Perhaps at his whisky. 'Do you want some advice? No, I don't suppose you do. The young never want advice from their elders and betters, at least not until they're on remand and trying to convince a judge that they are of good and upright character and should be granted bail. But I'll give you some nevertheless.' He sipped and savoured for a moment, contemplating the texture of his words. 'Women are fantasists. That makes them good historical novelists and bad witnesses. Love them as much as you want, but don't ever make the mistake of believing what they tell you. Especially anything that my daughter says.'

It was a joke. James laughed to demonstrate his acute sense of humour. Ellie's father frowned.

'I'm not joking, young man. Believe me. She always lived in a fantasy world as a child. Dragons and elves. Hobbit stuff. Tolkien. I used to go to his lectures before I saw the light and changed to law. Bloody idiotic, all that elvish nonsense. Most children grow out of it, but not Eleanor. Wouldn't take

21

my advice and read law. Instead she wanted to wallow in Romantic poetry and feed her imagination with all sorts of nonsense. And then there's the politics. Another fairyland. From each according to his ability, to each according to his needs. Pah! So don't believe a word she says about Master Kevin. Or anyone else. She's a delightful girl but she's a fantasist.' He reached for the decanter and poured James a further two fingers of the precious whisky. 'Now tell me about yourself. A scientist of some kind, aren't you? I like scientists. They make good witnesses. And defendants.'

It wasn't until after midnight that James won his release and made his way quite shakily upstairs to bed. The women had long since retired. The upper floor of the house was dark and silent. He crept to the spare room and climbed into bed, thankful for his freedom. Five minutes after he had turned off the light and was beginning to drift into unconsciousness there was a scratching at the door like the sound of a mouse in the wainscot. Dimly he was aware of the door opening and a shadow slipping into the room. For a dreadful moment – in silhouette their figures were not dissimilar – he thought it might be Mrs Pike. It was only when the shadow whispered, 'James, are you awake?' that he recognised Ellie.

He felt her climbing onto the bed, pushing his feet aside. He scrabbled for the bedside light and when finally he found the switch, there she was, cross-legged, at the foot of the bed, elf-like, wearing a long cotton T-shirt and apparently nothing else. His eyes went up and down her figure, and hesitated where matters were most difficult, where the hem of the T-shirt was stretched tight from thigh to thigh and there was a dark triangle of shadow. Possibilities crowded in on him. Lis, he thought, remembering moments during the play. She could do that trick, the actor's trick, of assuming personalities at will.

'So how was cross-examination by my beloved father?'

'I think I passed.'

She considered him thoughtfully. It was disturbing to see vague and uncertain reflections of her father in her face, almost as though he was a hideous caricature of his daughter. 'I think he likes you. He likes scientists. They make good witnesses, that's what he always says.'

'And he asked if we were sleeping together.'

She sighed. 'How very forensic of him. What did you reply?'

'I told him the truth, that Kevin gets in the way.'

That seemed to silence her. She looked down, picking distractedly at the duvet. Finally she raised her eyes and looked at him. 'That's what I wanted to talk to you about. I haven't told you all about Kevin. Not really. I think I should.'

'Not if it's going to make me jealous.'

'Envious,' she corrected sharply. 'You're jealous of what you already possess, envious of what someone else has.'

'And Kevin has you?'

She pouted. It was a good pout, with a strong French accent. He could imagine her in Paris, throwing rocks at French policemen and pouting.

'Kevin and I were engaged, you see. I haven't told you this, have I? I mean really engaged, a notice in *The Times* and the *Telegraph*, the church booked – yes, church, for God's sake. Nuptial mass. The order sheets had gone to the printers. Reception at his college. It was all planned.'

'I'll bet your mother loved the idea.'

'She did as a matter of fact. But it all fell apart. Differences, I suppose. Of character, of ideas. It was all a bit traumatic. Anyway, we decided at the last minute to call the whole thing off. Except it isn't, really . . .'

'Isn't over?'

'I went up to London last weekend.'

'To see him?'

She looked miserable. Maybe, he thought with aston-ishment, she was about to cry. 'We did it,' she admitted quietly. 'You know what I mean. We'd broken up and the idea was to meet up for lunch like old friends, to wish him all the best with his new job ... and it sort of happened. In the afternoon. In his new flat that he shares with a couple of other guys. And there we were, shagging in his bedroom while they were watching football in the sitting room.' There was silence. They sat at either end of the bed watching each other and experiencing all the agonies of behaviour in a time of transition, when love was meant to be free but actually was merely denominated in a new kind of currency. What did she owe the wretched Kevin? What, if anything, did she owe James? And what did she keep in the bank for a rainy day? She turned her attention back to picking at the quilt. 'Don't you mind?'

'Not yet.'

A wry smile. She crawled up the bed to kneel beside him and plant an artless kiss on his cheek. 'You're very sweet, you know that? And funny.'

'Funny'll do, but I'm not sure I want to be sweet.'

There was something infinitely appealing about her face just a few inches from his, mouth part open, as delicate as a flower. He bent forward and touched his lips against hers. This was about to be, he felt sure, the moment – of truth, of consummation, of catharsis, of something. He wasn't quite sure of the words. There was that familiar presence of her against him that he recognised from the play, when he, Fando, had had to carry her, the crippled Lis, on the road to Tar. He knew the angle of her bones, the roundness of her joints, the flesh and the sinew. And the smell of her, an amalgam of things that included soap and shampoo, but other, nameless scents as well. His hand went downwards, beneath the T shirt and down the front of the underpants he discovered there, the sort of groping he knew, back row of the stalls stuff, that he had done with one or two other girls. Then she twisted away.

'What's wrong?'

'Nothing. I'm fine. It's just, I don't want that now. I'm sorry, but I don't.' She slipped off the bed. 'It's not you, James, it's all sorts of stuff. Kevin, of course. But other things as well. The parents, everything.'

'*Everything?*'

At the door she paused, looking back with a bright and positive expression. 'Tomorrow we set off,' she said. 'How's that for exciting?'

And then she slipped out into the darkness of the upstairs landing and the door closed behind her.

II

4

Sam leaves the bed, crosses over to the window and draws back the curtains.

How does one end up here, he wonders, in this wooden-beamed room with its painted ceiling and arched windows and, beneath the floorboards, the soft tick of some beetle that will ultimately destroy everything? Of course he can provide a literal answer to all that – languages in the sixth form at school and then that Russian course at the Joint Services School for Linguists during his National Service, which gave a callow youth a taste for things Russian that he could never shake off. University followed as a matter of course, with an upper second in Slavonic languages and the foreign service examination in which his academic weaknesses were easily outshone by his sharp, clipped mind and ability to synthesise an argument from a plenitude of facts. And his knack for thinking on his feet. And the fact that he could actually speak Russian pretty well, where all the others could conjugate and decline and analyse and parse but they couldn't actually *feel* it in the way he did. But none of that is quite what he means as he stands there looking out on the squat fifteenth-century towers, the grey bridge decked out with statues, the river that everyone knows from Smetana's musical homage, Vltava.

Vltava; Moldau.

As always, a German name stands like a gothic shadow

behind the Czech – Praha, Prag; Malá Strana, Die Kleinseite; Vltava, Moldau – just as German history looms behind Czech history, occasionally reaching forward to tap it on the shoulder and remind the Czechs that they only occupy a narrow Slavic salient thrust into the heart of the Teutonic world.

'What's the time?'

He glances at his watch, then back at the bed. 'Six o'clock.'

Stephanie regards him through a blur of sleep. Her small face has the precise features of fine porcelain. Pretty. 'I'd better get a move on.'

'You haven't got a train to catch.'

'Still.' She gets out of bed on the far side, with her back to him so that she preserves her modesty as much as possible. She dislikes being seen naked. Her slender figure flashes white across the room, seeking the sanctuary of the bathroom. When she emerges, three-quarters of an hour later, her public persona is in place – a faint blush of makeup, hair hitched back and gathered in a chignon, her crisp white blouse buttoned to her neck, her navy skirt as perfectly pleated as her mind. They have breakfast, barely speaking. It seems like the awkward silence of a funeral, mourning the loss of something permanent, whereas all they are doing is anticipating a temporary separation.

'You could have gone by air.'

'You've already said that a dozen times.'

'It's just—'

'I know what it's just. It's just that there's no way I would have left Ringo behind.'

'Or waited so that I could come with you.'

'You know I couldn't do that.'

After breakfast he carries her bags out to the car and they stand together dejectedly, looking at her Volkswagen parked in the small square outside the building. As she has teasingly told him many times, the VW, purchased duty-free when she first came out eighteen months ago, is her real love. The name *Ringo* is discreetly painted on the bonnet. Ringo is Steffie's favourite Beatle, although God knows why, because he is, as Sam has remarked, an ugly bugger. 'I like ugly buggers,' she replied.

'So where does that leave me?'

Stephanie turns to face him. She is disturbingly lovely like that, standing there in her navy skirt and sky-blue linen jacket. White boots. A little black beret. The very antithesis of the Slav looks one sees in the girls around the city. They have strong bone structure and wide cheeks, but Steffie's look is that of a Dresden shepherdess, her precise features composed into what she does best – an ironic little smile. *Aren't I pretty?* it seems to ask. And, *isn't it all a bit of a sham?* 'We've talked it over a million times, haven't we?' she reminds him. 'We know what we're doing. Giving it a rest for a bit. Trying to get some kind of perspective on the whole thing.'

'You know what perspective has? A vanishing point.'

'But that's where parallel lines meet up. So who's to say?'

'You mustn't *do* that.'

'Do what?'

'Leave questions hanging.'

She composes her smile into a little pout. 'Who cares?' Then glances at her watch. 'Look at the time. It'll take me hours to get to Jenny and Jeremy's. I must go.'

'Be careful.'

'You know very well I'm as tough as nails, and so's Ringo. By this afternoon we'll be with Jen in her cosy little married quarters in Munching Gladbark or whatever it's called. Anyway, it's you who must be careful.'

'Me?'

'Of Eric's wife.' Eric is Head of Chancery. His wife is French, acquired during a posting to Paris a decade earlier. There was some story about his having prised her away from her first

31

husband who was a *fonctionnaire* at the Quai d'Orsay. The affair created something of a diplomatic incident, but in general everything worked in Eric's favour – in the corridors of the Foreign Office it was considered quite a triumph to have one of ours steal a Frenchwoman from her husband while playing away from home. Like winning a test match in Australia.

'Madeleine? She likes bigger prey. An ambassador here, a minister there, perhaps a film director, perhaps a writer.'

'She also likes little snacks now and again. She'll try to get you into bed as soon as my back is turned, you just wait and see. We women can tell these things. You poor men are little more than grazing gazelles when the female hyena is on the prowl.' It might have been rabbits and vixens, but Steffie always likes to emphasise her African background – Zambia when it was still called Northern Rhodesia, where her father was something to do with copper.

'You're mixing your metaphors.'

'As long as you don't mix your affections.'

'You don't show *affection* for Madeleine. You might feel lust towards her, or loathing, or perhaps even love, but nothing so dangerous as affection.'

'Oh, shut up.' She raises herself up on her toes and puts her hands on his shoulders to kiss him. He catches her scent, the perfume she always wears, the one that he claims ought to be banned for indecency, for its name alone, never mind its smell: *Youth Dew*. Her kiss is hesitant, as though each time were the first and she isn't quite sure how to do it. He puts his arms round her and feels her narrow fragility. 'I'll miss you,' he tells her.

She laughs. 'I'll fly out and see you once things are settled at home. And remember my warning. Beware the hyena.'

Another tentative kiss and she climbs into the car, allowing him a glimpse of stocking-top and narrow, white thigh before she adjusts her skirt and slams the door. The vehicle starts with that familiar clattering that is more like a washing machine than a motor car, and then she is gone, the particular, personal fact of being Stephanie in her Beetle called Ringo translated into an anonymous Volkswagen stuttering out of the square, turning the corner and out of sight.

Once she has gone, Sam goes to his own car and drives across the river. He feels a bit disconsolate but also strangely liberated. On his own again. He wonders whether it is true about Madeleine Whittaker, but more immediately there is the question of whether he will be late for his appointment, and if he is, will the man wait? On balance, probably yes. An opportunity to talk to a First Secretary (Chancery) from the British embassy is not the kind of thing one turns down these days. Everyone is trying to get hold of an audience willing to listen to declarations, manifestos, opinions, promises, threats, hopes, all those things that go to make up the startling political life of the country at the moment. A little while ago the place was the usual depressed Soviet satellite, the kind of post that people at the Foreign Office would rather risk malaria in West Africa to avoid. But now everyone wants a tour of duty basking in the sun of Dubček's socialism with a human face.

He drives along Resslova, through the sparse scattering of vehicles that passes for traffic in the city. Eric Whittaker always explains it as Soviet equality made manifest: cheap beer and trams for the masses; champanski and Tatra automobiles for the *nomenklatura*. The result is wide boulevards with barely a car in sight, and the guilty pleasure of exclusivity.

The meeting is in the New Town, in a café full of the noise of talk and the smoke of cheap cigarettes, with Marta Kubišová's earthy voice over the speakers, belting out her version of 'Walking Back to Happiness'. He stands on the edge of the crowd and watches for a while, trying to ignore the music and

33

follow what is being discussed. The talk is all politics – not the comatose politics of the last two decades but the new, anxious, outrageous politics of the present. It's like a new religion, a new creed that people believe might achieve some kind of earthly paradise. Passion lives in uneasy alliance with logic, neither emotion familiar in the political discourse of the country until the last few months. Appropriately enough, the man conducting the meeting, the man he has come to see, has the look of a prophet about him, the pinched features of an ascetic, the gaze of a visionary. Sam is reminded of Tom Courtenay playing the scar-faced Strelnikov in the film of *Doctor Zhivago*: a starveling face and the staring eyes of a messiah. But this particular man's name isn't Tom, it's a distinctive Zdeněk; and his wife – brittle, energetic – is Jitka.

After the meeting breaks up – there are questions, statements, arguments, laughter, groans and catcalls – he comes over to Sam and grabs his hand with surprising strength. 'We bring freedom to Czechoslovak people,' he announces. 'Freedom will be compulsory.'

'That's a good line.'

Jitka glosses her man's English with a quiet urgency: 'He means, not the freedom of Dubček's party, not communist freedom given out like sweets to children. But real freedom, of heart and soul.'

Zdeněk speaks quickly to her in Czech, so fast and colloquial that Sam only gathers the odd word. Amongst which *americký* and *kapitál*. 'And not American freedom either,' Jitka explains. 'We will not be slaves to capital any more than we will be slaves to Marxism. We are ready to forge a new instrument. We are, you see, the children of communism. We were born in the socialist state and that is all we have known, and now we are demanding something different.'

People have gathered round, listening to what is being said, eager to put their point of view. Word has got out that

34

Sam is from the embassy. 'When will the Americans help us?' someone asks.

'We don't want Americans,' another interrupts. 'Americans are bad as Russians. We want our own future.'

'You come to our public meeting tomorrow,' says the Strelnikov character, leaning forward and speaking urgently into Sam's face. 'Can you do that? Can you?' Once again he takes hold of Sam's hand to emphasise his point, the urgency of it.

'Of course I can. Just tell me where.'

Driving back through the Old Town, Sam is reminded of the protesting students back home. He saw them on a visit to his mother in Oxford a few months ago. They were occupying the Clarendon building, playing politics as though it were a parlour game dreamed up for a bit of entertainment. *Deanz Meanz Feinz* had been chalked on the walls of Balliol, alongside *Je suis Marxiste, tendance Groucho*. The Czech students might look no different from the Oxford ones – the same worn T-shirts and bomber jackets, the same faded jeans, the same unkempt hair, the boys barely differentiated from the girls – but this lot aren't playing a game. At work he sees the intelligence briefings. He knows of the thousands of Russian troops within the Czechoslovak borders, still there after military exercises in the spring; and he knows of the hundreds of thousands more waiting just outside the borders in neighbouring, fraternal, East Germany, Poland, Hungary and Ukraine. Soldiers and tanks, the full panoply of the Warsaw Pact poised to crush one of its own member states. Unlike British students, Czech students won't be able to run home to Mummy and Daddy if that particular axe falls.

That afternoon he tries to phone Steffie's friends in Germany to see if she has arrived, but he can't get through. 'You can book a call,' the operator informs him. 'It will take five hours.'

5

The meeting next day was in a deconsecrated church in the new town. It was part of Sam's job to attend as many meetings like this as he could, and since the first student protests the previous year he had got to know many of the leaders. Stephanie used to come with him whenever she was free — somehow she made his presence less obvious, although he never tried to conceal what he was doing there. 'I'm at the British embassy,' he'd say if asked. 'I'm not a spy or anything. Just interested in what's going on.'

This time the group was new, the Strelnikov character was new, and who could say what might become of it or him? The meeting was all to do with forming a new political movement. *Svobodná strana* or something; the Freedom Party.

When she caught sight of Sam, Strelnikov's wife, Jitka, raised her hand in acknowledgement. She was one of a little gaggle of activists milling around in the place where the high altar had once been, fixing microphones and speakers and arguing about where the chairs should go. He went over and said hello to her and the preoccupied Zdeněk, shook a few hands, exchanged a few words. They were students, mainly. One of the helpers turned and smiled at him. Blue eyes and Slav cheekbones and careless hair. Jeans and a leather jacket. A complexion that wasn't flawless like Stephanie's and features that weren't as perfect. But strong. Face not quite beautiful. Hair not quite blonde. If features betray character, then these suggested strength and a certain amused indifference. They hovered on the edge of beauty without doing anything so obvious as stepping over the borderline. 'Lenka Konečková,' she said, her eyes holding Sam's at the same time as her hand grasped his. 'I saw you at meeting before.' Good English, which was rare. 'I remember you.'

'I'm afraid I don't—'

'You don't see me. Of course not.'

'I can't think why I didn't.'

A wry smile. And that look, a communication that moved at the speed of light, that *was* light, nothing more, crossing the gap between them and carrying with it a message that needed no deciphering but made things happen inside him – a swelling, a weakness, a fluttering running through his viscera as though something had come loose. He hadn't expected this, really he hadn't.

'Samuel Wareham. I'm from the British embassy.'

'They told me. You speak good Czech. A bit Russified but good.'

'Russian was my main language at university.'

A beguiling laugh. 'Tainted, then.'

'I'm trying to purge it. Look ...' Sam hesitated, looking round, trying to work out if there was anyone else with particular claims on this girl – what was her name? Lenka? – but it seemed she was on her own. He thought of Stephanie somewhere in West Germany, chatting happily to Jenny – her old school chum – about life on the other side of the Iron Curtain, about Prague and her job, and, presumably, about Sam. Saying what? That they were sort of engaged. An understanding, really. Imagine being a dip's wife! But the relationship wasn't always easy ... 'Do you want to come for a drink when you're finished here? So we can have a chat. In Czech.'

She shrugged. 'And I can tell you how you go wrong? Sure.'

And then the rest of the meeting, the voting, the passing of motions, the arguing and the applauding, and all the time the girl called Lenka sitting on the other side of the nave from him, taking notes some of the time but also glancing across at him. The occasional conjunction of eyes. The suggestion of a smile. At the end of the speeches a young girl mounted the rostrum, carrying a guitar. People applauded as this approximate Joan Baez lookalike stood there in the crossing of the ex-church, looking faintly diffident, slightly dishevelled, watching the audience with something like embarrassment. 'We've even got an anthem,' she announced into the microphone. Lenka glanced across at Sam with a deprecating smile while the singer fiddled with a capo and then struck the first chord. It was all predictable enough: 'We Shall Overcome', sung without the evangelical fervour that seemed to characterise it in the West but with something that only central Europe could manage – a kind of bitter irony. We shall overcome some day, perhaps, but surely not now. No one sang along but at the end, everyone clapped. And standing there beneath the dome of the deconsecrated church, Lenka Konečková looked directly across at Sam and smiled. As though there was a joke to be shared.

He smiled back, wondering about Stephanie beetling around the German countryside in her Beetle. What would she think of the look that Lenka Konečková was even now directing back across the church at him, a blend of amusement and curiosity that brought with it disturbing possibilities? Surely this encounter was entirely innocent; but innocence could so easily spill over into guilt.

After the meeting they went to a well-known *pivnice* a few streets away where, it was said, Bohumil Hrabal would come in for a glass of Pilsner most days. 'They say that about every pub in the city,' was Sam's view. 'He'd be pissed as a newt if it were true.'

Pissed as a newt. Lenka laughed at his attempts to provide a translation. They found an unoccupied alcove where they could talk. Beer came. They drank a bit, looking at one another all the time, finding out how things were as much by glance and manner as by words. Lenka was at the university, doing a master's degree in English. Why English? That shrug. Because it's not Russian. He laughed. And she did some writing for one of the literary journals that had sprung up like mushrooms feeding on the rich humus of free speech. And the occasional piece for Czechoslovak radio. She was twenty-five years old, which made Sam feel almost fatherly; but she knew things far beyond her two and a half decades, he could see that. The conversation soon veered away from the personal to politics. Politics were on everyone's lips, how things had changed since censorship was abandoned and where things might go next. What would happen when Dubček and his supporters confronted Brezhnev and the rest of the Soviet Politburo. 'So what does Mr Samuel think will take place?' Lenka asked. 'All we want is to continue with free expression. Freedom to say what the hell we please and do what the hell we please. Will they let us?'

'Depends what you say and what you do.'

'We don't know in advance. That's what makes it so exciting.'

Sam considered the matter carefully, as though he had been asked it by the Head of Chancery. 'The Party has made its decision, hasn't it? Abandoning censorship was the point of no return.'

'They could try to bring it back.'

'Difficult to put the genie back in the bottle.'

'Maybe the Russians will force them?'

'I don't think the Soviet Politburo really knows what to do at the moment. They've got troops left here since the spring manoeuvres and they don't know whether to withdraw them or not. There are various currents within the Kremlin itself, although Brezhnev himself is a hawk and he's the one who really matters. But there are other issues to consider, like the other Warsaw Pact countries, the fraternal allies. Romania, for example. What will Ceauşescu's position be? And Hungary's? Kádár needs to be brought on board. I imagine a lot of his sympathies are with Dubček. So any final decision is balanced on a knife-edge. But of course the main players are the Russians.'

Lenka laughed, running fingers through her hair. 'You know what I think? I think, fuck Russians. And fuck the fraternal allies.' That frank wide-open gaze. He had that feeling again, clotted at the base of his throat, like a sudden growth.

'What about lunch,' he suggested, not wanting this encounter to die. 'I must get back to the office now but what about tomorrow? Let me buy you lunch tomorrow. I've got a meeting at the foreign ministry in the morning. And then ...'

She took a moment to consider, as though assessing him and the implications of his invitation. When she answered, her tone seemed almost indifferent. 'Why not?'

Masaryk

The Černín Palace guards its secrets as assiduously as a bank guards its vaults. Home to the Czechoslovak ministry of foreign affairs, the building sits across the ridge of land outside the gates of Prague Castle, the Hrad, as though blocking the way from the Castle to the West and freedom. Not for nothing had it been the seat of the *Reichsprotektor* of Bohemia and Moravia during the Nazi occupation. But the biggest secret of all, hidden within the walls of this monstrous, monotonous building, was the one that stood prominently in Sam's mind whenever he had an appointment here. It concerned the fate of Jan Masaryk, son of the first president of independent Czechoslovakia, Tomáš Masaryk, and it came down to the question: did he jump or was he pushed?

By March 1948 Masaryk, who had spent the war in London with the Czechoslovak government in exile, was foreign minister of the Czechoslovak Republic. More than that, he was the only non-communist minister not to have resigned in protest at the communist power grab of February. He was also middle-aged (sixty-one), lonely (a divorcee), mentally fragile (bipolar disorder) and disillusioned (who wouldn't be?). In the early morning of 10 March his body was found lying on the paving of an inner courtyard of the Černín Palace. He was wearing pyjamas and lay forty-seven feet directly beneath the open bathroom window of his official apartment on the third floor.

Did he jump or was he pushed?

Two decades later, Sam Wareham walked over to the window of the anteroom and looked down on that selfsame courtyard. Bright sunlight dissected the space with sharp diagonals of shadow. Small ornamental trees. Basalt paving stones. Somewhere down there Jan Masaryk's body had lain on that cold March morning.

Did he jump or was he pushed?

Outside the anteroom, in the corridors of the ministry through which Sam had been led by a uniformed flunkey, was the kind of chaos one expects in a beehive threatened by a bear. People hurried from office to office clutching files. Phones rang the second the receiver was replaced. Meetings were scheduled and rescheduled, then broken off because something more important had just cropped up. Oblivious to all this, Sam stood at the window and wondered.

Did he jump or was he pushed?

The popular feeling was, of course, that Masaryk had been pushed. Such a *tidy* man, they said with bitter irony, he had even made sure to close the window behind him.

That was the joke.

On the other hand, a number of friends and most of his relatives refused to accept this idea. Appalled at the political situation of the country and the dilemma in which he found himself, they said, Jan Masaryk took the honourable way out. Even his sister believed this. Yet the question remained, unanswered when Sam Wareham waited for his meeting, unanswered now, unanswered presumably for as long as vital files locked away within the former KGB archives in Moscow remained hidden from public scrutiny (which could be for ever): did he jump or was he pushed?

Prague is famous for its defenestrations. The first was in 1419 when a Hussite mob broke into the New Town Hall and threw a baker's dozen of burghers to their deaths; the second was two hundred years later, when two imperial offi-cials and their secretary were tossed out of a window of the Hrad. The first led to the fifteen-year Hussite Wars, the second to the devastating Thirty Years War. Both were about religion. The third defenestration was that of the liberal, saddened, dis-illusioned minister of foreign affairs, Jan Masaryk.

What did his defenestration lead to?

The man Sam Wareham was to meet, a harassed and con-fused *apparátník* who had somehow kept his job throughout the upheavals of the last year, apologised for having kept him waiting. 'We are, as you can see, at the eye of the storm.'

Eyes of storms were, as far as Sam knew, places of great and sinister stillness, but there was no time to unpick mixed metaphors. Instead they could only deal with the matter in hand – an imminent visit to Prague by a British trade union group. There was this factory tour that had to be curtailed, that meeting which needed to be rescheduled.

Sam nodded and noted. 'I'll let His Excellency know of the changes.'

'You know how it is, Mr Wareham, don't you?'

'Of course I do.' Which wasn't really true, but it was not too difficult to put himself in his opposite number's place. After all, the Russian bear was right outside the hive. While all the little bees were panicking you could hear his heavy breathing. And yet ... and yet at the end of the meeting he, Samuel Wareham, a First Secretary at Her Britannic Majesty's Embassy to the Czechoslovak Socialist Republic, could walk out into the sunshine of Hradčaný and stroll down the road into Malá Strana with the thought of what the Russians might or might not do no more than a distant irritation. This city might be rendered drab by the dead hand of communism, but still it remained, quite simply, the most beautiful in Europe.

His apartment was in a seventeenth-century building tucked in between the river and the great geological mass that supports the Castle. It was edged by cobbled alleys and faced on a square where, it was said, public executions were once held. He unlocked the outside door and went up to his apartment on the first floor. Only the week before, security had been round to sweep the place to see that it was safe, devoid of listening ears. 'Clean as a whistle,' the man from security had said. 'As far as we can see, at any rate. Difficult to get bugs through these old walls, so anything they manage to plant will be superficial, within the plaster, or behind pictures and in light fittings. That mirror, for example. Anyway, at the moment, zilch.'

Zilch? Where had he got that from?

Sam picked up the phone in the hallway and dialled through to the embassy. Dorothy answered his call, as impatient of his irregular habits as ever. 'I've been trying to find you. Mr Whittaker was asking where you were.'

'And what did you tell him?'

'That you were out chasing girls.'

'That I was out at a meeting in the ministry.'

'That you were out at a meeting in the ministry.'

'And I'm afraid I'm still tied up.' He paused. 'She's very keen on bondage.'

He could hear the outraged laughter in her voice as he put the phone down. But did Dorothy even know what bondage was? He tried for a moment to imagine her tied up and gagged, but failed. She, surely, would be doing the tying up, and the whipping. Glancing at his watch he went through into the sitting room. From the windows there was that view of the squat Gothic towers which had sat on the end of the bridge like warty toads for the last four hundred years. Heads had been stuck there during the Thirty Years War, a dozen Protestant heads like the victims of a Stalinist

44

purge, perhaps Slansky and his associates in 1952. He put some music on – an obscure piece of Janáček that he had discovered – and sat at his desk to type a memorandum summarising his meeting at the ministry. Three-quarters of an hour had passed before he glanced at his watch again. The damn thing would have to wait. He went to the bathroom, brushed his teeth, combed his hair and adjusted his tie. Five minutes late. He had offered to pick her up from home, but she'd demurred. 'You'd never find it,' she said, which perhaps meant, 'I don't want you to find it.' He went out, closing the door carefully behind him and, as always, leaving a tiny scrap of fluff wedged in the jamb.

There was what passed as a crowd on the bridge – tourists from the neighbouring countries, mainly. You heard German and Polish and occasionally the impossibly incomprehensible Magyar. Sometimes Russian. Almost never English, and when you did it was invariably strained through an American voice box.

At one of the statues an imitation Dylan was strumming a guitar and singing *Časy se Mění*, 'Times They Are a-Changin'', which was true enough in so many ways. Halfway along the bridge, at the statue of Saint John of Nepomuk, there she was, just as they had arranged.

She was different, metamorphosed from the casual, slightly dishevelled creature of their first encounter into a moth of various hues – a green, calf-length skirt, a navy blouse that was knotted beneath her bust and would have displayed her navel had she not been wearing a T-shirt underneath. Her face wore a touch of pale lipstick and a smudge of eyeshadow. Her hair was gathered up in a deliberately untidy chignon. They shook hands and he caught a breath of perfume: floral, slightly cloying, and something underneath – her own scent. 'Do I look all right?' she asked. 'Lunch at Barrandov ...?'

45

As though she was unsure of what exactly was involved. He felt a sensation that he had not experienced for a long time, a pulse of anticipation and excitement just above his diaphragm. Somewhere in the further reaches of his brain a small alarm of warning went off.

Talking about each other as you do when you are standing on the brink of intimacy, they walked to his car. She was sharp and blunt at one and the same time, asking probing questions but then driving the nail home with heavy blows: if you are a diplomat, why are you taking me to lunch? What's in it for you? How is this in the interests of the British government?

Sam laughed. 'Even a diplomat can have a private life. Although sometimes he has to be careful.'

'Careful? Why careful? Are you married?'

'No, not married.'

She turned to him almost accusingly. 'But you think I am a spy?'

'Actually, I don't, but suspicion reigns high on Eastern European postings. Supping with the devil, you need a long spoon.' He wasn't sure how to put it in Czech, but she seemed to understand, even made a joke about it. 'Well, it's lunch we're going to now, isn't it? Not supper. And I'm not the devil.' She looked at him knowingly as he held the car door open for her. 'But I'm not an angel either.'

The restaurant was in the south of the city, perched on cliffs overlooking the river. There was an observation tower and projecting terraces like the bridges of a transatlantic liner. Below the terraces, in what might have been an old quarry, a swimming pool gleamed like turquoise set in tarnished silver. Splashes of laughter rose up to the diners. The tables were crowded with people from the film studios nearby – middle-aged men with loud voices, girls in short skirts and beehive hairdos, boys with longish hair and button-down shirts. Dark glasses were worn like a badge of office. The scene might have been in Hollywood, except there were no palm trees, no pink Cadillacs and a fraction of the money. Lenka tried not to gawp, but her eyes were alight with excitement as an obsequious waiter led the way to their table on the edge of the terrace. For almost the first time, she seemed her age, looking around and trying not to stare but spotting the stars nevertheless. 'There's Iva Janžurová. And Menzel, that's Jiří Menzel.' There were other names that Sam didn't recognise. Apparently Lenka was something of a film buff, and for a while that is what they talked about. What had Sam seen of Czech film? What did he like? What did he admire? Like and admire were two different things, weren't they? She was insistent on the point. You could like something such as *Ben Hur* without admiring it. Or admire *A Report on the Party and the Guests* without liking it. It was all a matter of the critical faculty, wasn't it?

Sam was sure it was. He managed to move the conversation away from such matters on to the personal. What might she do once she'd finished her studies? Travel abroad, improve her spoken English, perhaps in London. There were possibilities now the shackles of the past twenty years were being thrown off.

Sam tried to picture her in London. What might she ultimately become? A writer? An academic? A full-time journalist? That kind of thing was imponderable, whereas Sam's fate was altogether clearer: he would soon enough be Head of Chancery in some forgotten ex-colony, married to Steffie, with two children and a mortgage on a house in Surbiton that would be suitable for the retired ambassador he would inevitably become. Maybe he'd even acquire a K: Sir Samuel Wareham. Terrifying how quickly the options closed down. One moment the world seems your oyster; the next you see it for the mollusc it really is – an octopus that has grabbed you with its tentacles and will not let go.

'At least now I'd get an exit visa,' Lenka said. 'Now things have changed for the better. You see, with my background I was lucky to get to university.'

'Why lucky?'

Her mouth twisted in distaste. 'Politics. Now everything may be different, but however hard they try to rewrite it, they can't change history.'

'What history are you talking about?'

'My family's.' She attempted a smile, that ironic, Iron Curtain smile that Sam had long ago come to recognise. 'Let's talk about other things. Maybe I'll introduce you to my mother sometime and then you can find out. But not now.'

So they talked about other things, and it was easy enough – the new freedoms, the freedom to write what you liked, report whatever concerned you. Food came and went. They had a bottle of Moravian wine which was not as dreadful as usual, and she wanted to know about London, swinging London, Carnaby Street, the Rolling Stones, the Beatles. Hippies. Hash. And then himself. Why exactly was he taking her out to lunch? He'd never said, the first time she asked.

'Because I find you attractive. That's not a sin, is it?'

'It all depends. You say you have no wife.'

'No.'

'And is there no girlfriend?'

He hesitated with the tense. 'There was. She's called Steffie. She works for the Service, although she's not a diplomat.' He tried to pretend it was of no importance, but there was the snake-like slither of guilt running up his spine. He'd had a letter from her that morning, a brief but heartfelt missive enclosing a postcard of Cologne cathedral. *Having a lovely time, wish you were here*, was scrawled on the card. The letter said the same thing, but without the irony: *Perhaps I shouldn't have been so hasty*, she had written. *It's being apart that makes me understand how good we are together.*

'She was posted back to England.'

'And your heart is broken?'

'We didn't break up exactly. It's just ...' Momentarily, he felt himself floundering beneath her steady, interrogator's gaze. Blue eyes, narrowed against the light. 'It's always been a difficult relationship. When you are on post, when you meet such a limited range of people, things are always difficult. Artificial, I suppose.'

'And now?' It was a challenge, and he deflected it.

'Now you must tell me about yourself. That's only fair.'

'What do you want to know?'

'No boyfriend?'

'There has been. Not recently. Not serious, anyway.'

'What's serious?'

'If they matter to me. One did. He played in a group. You know? Guitars, pretending to be The Beatles? We were together a couple of years. Since then ...' She let her voice trail away into silence.

For dessert they had the inevitable *palačinky*, pancakes, with a sharp cherry filling and too much whipped cream. Sam glanced at his watch. 'Look, I'm sorry but I've got to get back to the office. People to see, minutes to write.'

'Of course.'

'Perhaps I can see you again?'

'Why not? There is – I do not know if you are interested – there is a concert coming up. My flatmate is in the orchestra so I get tickets. You met her – Jitka.'

'Of course.' He thought for a moment, riffling mentally through his social diary and deciding that no one would notice if he didn't turn up to the reception at the Swiss embassy to celebrate what? Their national day, presumably.

Madeleine would notice but she could go hang. 'Yes, that's fine. Where? What time? Maybe we can get something to eat afterwards.'

Again that shrug. 'The House of Artists. At six. On the steps. There will be others there. Friends.'

6

The concert. A scrum of people going up the steps into the auditorium, and Lenka grabbing Sam's hand to lead him through a side entrance and up stairs to one of the balconies. 'You're with the poor students now, Mr Diplomat,' she said. They shuffled sideways into narrow seats. He was introduced to some of her friends, faces that were familiar from the political meeting – the Barboras and Terezas, the Mareks and Pavels. There was a buzz of excited conversation as they peered down on the audience in the body of the auditorium. 'There's Smrkovský,' someone said, and everyone craned to look at the tough-looking man taking his seat in the stalls.

'Do you know who he is?' asked Lenka. It was hot up there just beneath the ceiling. Her forehead and upper lip were beaded with sweat.

'I'm political, remember? Of course I know him. I've even met him.'

'You've *met* him?'

'Talked with him. For about three minutes.'

'So what do you think of him?'

Sam considered for a moment. Far below people were pushing and shoving to get a moment's contact with the man. He smiled round, shaking hands. A pugnacious, genial face, a short brush of grey hair. A member of the Central Committee of the Party, he was one of Dubček's closest associates. 'I think

51

you're looking at a man riding a tiger. You know about riding a tiger?'

'Hard to get off?'

'Exactly.'

People applauded. The applause began close to Smrkovský and spread out like a wave in a pond until everyone in the auditorium was clapping, from the stalls to the gods, until the man was settled into his seat. More applause greeted the orchestra as it filed on stage. Lenka pointed. 'There's Jitka. Second violins, next to the bald-headed man. I rent a room in her flat.'

Down amongst the penguins Jitka seemed transformed from the febrile woman of the political meetings into an elegant lady in a black evening gown. There was the sense of her beauty, even at this distance. But then, you so often had a sense of beauty with Czech women, at whatever distance you might choose. After a few minutes the conductor appeared, bobbing and weaving like a footballer through the ranks of players. He bowed to the audience and turned to the orchestra, holding out his hands to calm the storm of clapping. Then, when a perfect silence had been achieved, he raised his baton and unleashed the first crashing, portentous notes of *Blaník*, the sixth and final of Smetana's cycle of tone poems, *Má Vlast*. It wasn't on the programme, that was the point. The programme, on a roneoed sheet handed round amongst Lenka's friends, had Dvořák's *Slavonic Dances* and Martinů's Sixth Symphony, not pieces of music that would have stirred Sam's interest very much. But here, without warning, were the familiar tones of *Blaník* sending a pulse of excitement through the hall.

Má Vlast, My Homeland. Patriotism without kitsch, an almost impossible trick to pull off. *Blaník* tells of the legend that Václav, Good King Wenceslas of the Christmas carol, a kind of Bohemian King Arthur, waits beneath the Blaník mountain with a company of knights, ready to emerge and save the Czech people at their moment of greatest need, when they are threatened – legend has it – by four hostile armies. We may savour the bitter irony of that now, but then, on that hot summer evening in Prague, the music seemed a clarion call to the nation. The Russians, the East Germans, the Poles, the Hungarians would all be defied. Holding hands, the Czechs and the Slovaks would move forward into the sunlit uplands of freedom and prosperity. Socialism would show its human face to all mankind.

The audience listened transfixed throughout and, at the crashing end, stood as one to applaud. Lenka's eyes were bright with tears. There was sweat certainly, sweat and tears mingling on her cheeks. Sam dared to put up his hand to brush them away and was blessed with a wry smile.

After the concert they all went – Jitka the violinist and half a dozen others – to a place on the river where a quartet was playing cool jazz. There were tables outside under the trees and food was served till late. Laughter, argument, beer in the warm night, the kind of thing one dreamed of even in social-ist Czechoslovakia, especially in socialist Czechoslovakia now that it was finding this thrilling, novel freedom. They were joined after a while by the Strelnikov character himself, Jitka's husband Zdeněk. He greeted Sam with enthusiasm. 'My Englishman. I like my Englishman,' he said. The talk was a blend of practical politics and speculative philosophy. Names were bandied around – Lukács, Marcuse – and con-cepts that bore names like *reification* and *alienation*. Sam felt old, an emissary from another generation. 'What do you think?' they kept asking him, hoping for an optimistic answer. He did a great deal of shrugging, verbally and literally. He had exhausted this kind of talk when he was at university, and working for the Foreign Office had killed any residual idealism there might have been. Where do our best interests lie? was the watchword of the diplomatic corps: pragmatism elevated to a political philosophy.

'Mr Wareham is a cynic,' Lenka warned. 'He doesn't understand the power of an idea.' She was holding onto his arm, tethering him to their earnest conversation as though otherwise he might float up in the warm air and go sailing away over the river and the city like a golem, back to the West perhaps. It pleased him, this display of ownership, this assumed knowledge of the workings of his mind.

'I'm a realist,' he said.

They laughed at that. 'You haven't lived here long enough,' Zdeněk said. 'No one can live in this place for long and still believe in reality.'

One of the group had a camera. While they talked he moved around them taking shots – close-ups, figures seen through beer glasses, candid shots. They laughed and made faces and got him angry because they weren't taking his art seriously. When Sam produced his own camera – a neat little Japanese compact he'd bought duty-free in Berlin – there was even more laughter. 'Tourist!' they called, as though it were an insult. But he managed to get them to pose more or less sensibly for one shot. The flash gave its milliseconds of brilliant, zirconium flare and held the group in stark immobility on the retina of any watchers and on the film itself.

When it was time to go – the musicians had packed their instruments away, the waiters were stacking the chairs – the group of friends broke up, as such groups do, with promises and exhortations, with kisses and embraces, with awkward last-minute discussions on the pavement of the embankment. There was a moment when Lenka might have gone with Jitka and her husband, but then the moment was past and the couple had gone and Sam and Lenka were alone, walking together towards the bridge. He said something about his car and driving her to Jitka's flat, wherever that was, but nothing was decided. Holding hands, talking about not very much, they walked across the river, over the Charles Bridge between the two rows of grimy statues that made it seem like walking up the aisle of a church. Ahead was the altar of the nation, *Hrad*, the Castle, lifting its shoulders to blot out the night sky. Lights were on up there, officials at work in the engine room of the ship of state, desperate to avoid the icebergs ahead, while down here two people were negotiating the first moves in a relationship. In the secluded cobbled square in front of his apartment building he stopped, keys in hand, beside his car. 'My flat's just here. Do you want to come up?'

'Yes,' she said. 'Of course I do.' The 'of course' was curious. He unlocked the outside door and led the way upstairs. Why should this be so easy? With Stephanie it had taken weeks, circling round each other like animals as likely to kill as to love; but this was so straightforward. They both knew where they were going and why.

'Nice place,' Lenka remarked when he opened the door to his apartment.

'Goes with the job.' He showed the way through to the sitting room. 'Do you want anything? A beer? Coffee?'

'A glass of water,' she said. 'And the bathroom.'

'Of course.'

Why was everything 'of course'? Was it all so obvious, preordained and inevitable? Ineluctable. One of those words with no antonym, no 'eluctable' to make things easy to get out of. Maybe the word should be invented, for the benefit of diplomats.

When she came back there was something scrubbed about her face, as though she had stripped it of all artifice. Perhaps she had just taken off her makeup and brought her appearance back to how she'd been when they'd first met. It gave a vulnerable cast to her expression, made her look rather plain but somehow more attractive. Wide jaw and high, Slavic cheek-bones. Pale blue eyes. A face that had come a long way, out of the Asian steppe thousands of years ago to end up here in his living room with the view of the bridge out of the window. He knew this was fanciful nonsense but the conceit pleased him.

They kissed, gently, thoughtfully, exploring each other's taste and texture, eyes watching. Steffie had always closed her eyes when kissing. She'd seen it done like that on the films, but Lenka watched him closely all the time, as though measuring him up, assessing what his intentions might be. 'You don't have to get back to Jitka's?' he asked.

A small smile. 'Are you looking for an escape? I have my own key.'

He put some music on – that Janáček piano music seemed appropriate – and led the way into the bedroom. They undressed, rather shyly at first, watching each other cautiously. If he had expected passion and frenzy, that was not what he got. Instead they lay on the bed touching very gently, moving slowly, watching each other's eyes, sensing how things – heartbeat, expression, breathing – change. How bodies can be measured and vibrant, as though under a great tension, like the strings of a cello.

Afterwards, they dozed, touched each other again, dozed, kissed, dozed again. Sam realised, amongst many other things, that he felt unconscionably happy. It cannot last, he thought.

And then he slept and so, presumably, did she.

7

When he came back from the bathroom in the cool light of dawn Lenka was awake. Her face seemed blurred with sleep, the features ill-defined, her hair a chaotic cloud across the pillow. 'What's the time?'

'Six-thirty.'

'It's early. Come back to bed.'

He stood, looking down on her. Already regrets were coalescing in his mind. What did a night like this mean? What did it mean to her? What did it mean to him? He knew how dangerous it all might be. Diplomats were warned about it time and again, warned of blackmail, warned of beautiful women who will flatter a man's self-image and wheedle information out of him. Swallows, the Soviets called them, swallows, with its hints of what they might do to you, and, correspondingly, what you might do as a result – swallow them hook, line and sinker. It was worse if you were queer – they'd find pretty boys who'd suck your cock while the film cameras whirred away behind one-way glass mirrors. Look at Vassall. A clerk in the naval attaché's staff in the British embassy in Moscow, he had been famously set up by the KGB, famously photographed pleasuring and being pleasured, and was now famously languishing in Wormwood Scrubs. Of course, Sam told himself, he was running nothing like that kind of risk. No wife to worry about. No heavy-handed policeman to arrest him for indecent behaviour. As Eric Whittaker, his boss, had memorably observed, 'If you're going to blow your nose, for God's sake make sure that the handkerchief is clean.' Well, Sam's handkerchief, folded and pressed, had certainly been clean enough up to now because Stephanie was British and worked at the embassy. The worst that might have happened was a raised eyebrow from the ambassador's wife and a suggestion from the ambassador himself that Sam make an honest woman of the gel. Which would have meant Stephanie resigning her job, the archaic ways of the Foreign Office insisting on the spinsterhood of its female employees. But that hadn't happened. The ambassadress had said nothing, while he and Stephanie had spent three months more or less together before she got that posting back to London that she couldn't turn down because her mother was unwell and she was needed to help her father deal with the problem. Aged parents, an only child. It wasn't easy. The intention was to keep in touch and catch up when Sam got back to London, which would be in eighteen months.

In the meantime, what would happen to their oblique, tense relationship, based as it was on emotions never fully expressed and intentions never fully articulated?

Half-smiling, Lenka looked up at him from the bed. Nothing tense or oblique at this precise moment. He reached down and pulled the sheet aside to expose her to the cool light of dawn. Steffie would have cried in protest and struggled to cover herself. Lenka didn't move, just lay there beneath his gaze, imperfect and erotic, and so unlike Stephanie as to belong to a different gender altogether. Lenka had a body; Steffie had a figure. Lenka had a scent; Steffie had perfume. Steffie's perfume was alluring enough – something floral, hints of jasmine and citrus and sandalwood – but Lenka's scent was different. Ripe and dark. Something sour, astringent. Mammal, organic. He recognised it from someone else, the first woman he had ever loved when he was young and naive. She had been a generation older, a strange, wayward woman who had taught him passion but not constancy. Standing over Lenka, he felt that familiar stirring. Lust? Love? Something beyond words, expressible only by actions.

'Do you want?' she asked. She could see that he did. There was no disguising what was happening. But time was pressing. 'I've got a meeting at nine.'

'It's Saturday.'

'Her Majesty's envoys work tirelessly to protect the realm.' He didn't know how to do that in Czech or Russian without it coming out like a piece of Stalinist propaganda rather than the irony he intended, so he said it in English, which meant Lenka rather missed the point. He sat on the edge of the bed and put out a hand to touch her, just her face, the line of her chin, almost as though to define it.

Where, he wondered, do we go from here? And then he turned the thought into words before he had a chance to censor them. 'Where do we go from here?'

She sat up, pulling the pillows behind her, unashamed of her nakedness. Her gaze was narrow, as though she was trying to see right through his eyes and read what was going on in his mind. 'You're worried about your girlfriend?'

'Not only.'

She reached for a cigarette from the pack on the bedside table. 'Ah, you think maybe I am an informer. Maybe I work for the *StB*?'

He smiled. 'I doubt it, but you *might*. Diplomats always worry about that kind of thing. Should I be doing this? Is it a set-up? In the proximity of women we're worse than priests.'

'If you're a priest, then I'm a nun.'

Was that a joke? It was difficult to tell. Her manner was strange, oblique at times, startlingly direct at others. Perhaps it was just her unfamiliarity with spoken English. She put her cigarette to her mouth and lit it. A skein of grey smoke appeared between her lips. He had already discovered many of her tastes, and that was one of them, the faint, acrid flavour of tobacco on her mouth.

'You can't be a nun. Nuns don't smoke in bed.'

She laughed now, real, smoky laughter that took a moment to disperse. 'So, if I am not StB, you ask where do we go from here? But it is not *we*, is it? It is *you*. Where do *you* go from here? Because you are thinking of your girlfriend whose name you have not yet told to me.'

'Steffie. Stephanie, actually.'

'That is Štěpánka in Czech. It is beautiful name.'

'Better in Czech. To me it sounds very English.'

'And is she very English?'

'Very.'

'But I am not, and you are wondering about the difference. Did Stephanie sleep with you the first evening you spent with her? I expect she did not. So, does that make me, what? A prostitute?'

No misunderstanding there. One of the universals. *Prostitutka* in both Russian and Czech, and probably every other language under the sun. 'Don't be absurd. I don't think like that at all. We both did it, me and you together. Our choice.'

'But that is how men are, you are thinking. And women aren't. They should be saving themselves, like Štěpánka did.'

They were hovering on the edge of their first argument. 'Rubbish. You're putting words into my mouth.'

'Ha! Then everything is all right. If we want to stay together, we stay together. If we want to go to bed together, we go to bed together. If we want to go away, we go away. Is that all right?'

'It seems logical.'

Logic appeared to satisfy her. Logic was good. She sat there in his bed, on his side of the bed, looking as prim and determined as it is possible to be when you are entirely naked. 'So, are you going to tell me about Štěpánka?'

He tossed the sheet over her knees to cover the disturbing sight. 'Some other time. Now I must get a move on. Make yourself some coffee if you want. There's stuff for breakfast. Cereal, toast, anything you find.' He went to the bathroom to shower and shave and clean his teeth, trying, and failing, to rid himself of the thought of her. When he came back she was in the kitchen, laying out breakfast things, pouring coffee. She was wearing her shirt from yesterday and nothing else: bare legs, faintly dusted with golden hair, bare feet and, as he discovered as she reached up for something from a top shelf, bare arse. She'd made toast. There was butter in a dish and she had discovered a pot of Frank Cooper's Oxford Marmalade. 'This is very English breakfast, isn't it? But I cannot find sugar.'

'The maid hides it. She thinks there may be shortages and we should keep it hidden.' He opened the cupboard under the sink and took out a carton of sugar.

Lenka had stopped what she was doing. Her expression was transformed to that of angry primary school teacher – a frown, lips pursed. 'You have *maid*?'

'Goes with the job. Like the flat itself. She only comes one day a week. To clean the flat and take my laundry. '

'That is very bourgeois.'

'We *are* pretty bourgeois in the Foreign Office.'

'I'll bet this *služka* she works for StB.'

'She probably does. It's better always to keep your enemy close, where you can see him.'

'*Close*? Do you fuck her? Once a week?'

'Certainly not. They tried an attractive one but I had to send her packing. She didn't know how to iron shirts.'

'So what is this ugly one's name?'

'Svetlana.'

'There!' Her tone was triumphant, as though the matter was certain. 'You cannot get any more Russian than that. She is maybe KGB.'

Half an hour later he let her out of the flat, making her take the back way, out through the courtyard and the abandoned garden at the back of the building, where there was an ancient wall twelve feet high with an anonymous door that gave on to one of the alleys running down to the river. Once she had slipped away, Sam strolled through the Malá Strana to the palace that crouched warily beneath the Castle and housed the British embassy.

8

In the secure room deep within the embassy, an exclusive little group took its seats at the conference table. The secure room was not a cheery place. Windowless bare white walls, bleak fluorescent lighting, metal and plastic furniture. It was known as the mortuary.

'Heard from the lovely Stephanie?' the Head of Chancery asked Sam. Eric Whittaker had that knack, bestowed on high-flying diplomats, of being able to talk trivia while preparing for matters that matter. 'So sorry to see her go.'

'I had a card from her – Greetings from Cologne, wish you were here sort of thing. She was staying with friends at Rheindahlen but she should be crossing to England by now.'

'We'll miss her. Easy on the eye. You two still' – a moment's hesitation – 'together? Madeleine always said you were perfect for each other.'

'I used to think so too. Steffie has always had doubts.'

'Frightened of becoming an embassy wife?'

'Enough to put anyone off.'

Whittaker laughed, glancing round the meeting. There was a distinct feeling of Saturday morning. One member of the group was even without a tie. Whittaker coughed in that apologetic manner of his, to bring the meeting to order. 'I'm afraid,' he announced, 'that H.E. cannot be here this morning – hobnobbing with the Yanks, I believe – so I'm in the hot seat. And' – he glanced at the papers before him – 'hot it certainly is.' He tapped the paper. 'So, what is this place, Čierna? Never heard of it myself.'

'Čierna nad Tisou,' someone said. 'Eastern Slovakia, right on the Soviet border.'

'Anyone been there?'

The fluorescent lighting of the secure room hummed thoughtfully. People waited for someone to contribute. Rather diffidently, Sam offered his own experience. 'I have, as a matter of fact, Eric. Back of beyond, really. Little more than a rail terminus.'

'Rail terminus? What on earth were you doing there, old chap? Trainspotting?'

There was a stir of amusement at the table.

'If you remember, Eric, you sent me on a fact-finding tour of Slovakia when I first got here.'

'Good God, I'd quite forgotten. What on earth had you done wrong?'

Laughter. Sam inclined his head, as though acknowledging applause. 'But the rail terminus is actually rather interesting. It's one of those forgotten corners of Europe, close to the point where Ukraine and Hungary meet with Slovakia – I believe geographers call it a tripoint – and there's this enormous railway terminus with over nine hundred sidings. Makes Clapham Junction look like Adlestrop.' He looked round at his audience. 'I'm sorry, am I boring you?'

'Not yet,' Whittaker said, 'but I bet you're going to.'

There was further laughter. 'I fear I already am. The problem is, Russian railways have a broader gauge than the rest of Europe, which means that every single trainload that crosses from East to West or West to East – goods, passengers, even politicians – has to trans-ship from one gauge to the other at Čierna. It makes for the most fantastic bottleneck, so much so that a few years ago they even built a broad-gauge spur over a hundred miles into Slovakia, just to bypass Čierna and ferry Ukrainian iron ore to the steelworks at Košice.'

The military attaché felt the need to contribute. He was a major in his final posting before retirement and was always conscious of being out of place amongst the diplomats. Perhaps he thought that Sam was trespassing on his territory. 'It is worth pointing out that Russian armed forces have to do exactly the same thing when moving westwards – tanks, armoured cars, all materiel, in fact, has to be brought to Čierna nad Tisou, offloaded and either transferred to road or to another train. Wipe out Čierna and you block the way to the West for the Red Army.'

Eric raised his eyebrows in that infuriating manner he had when spotting a red herring swimming through the pond of his meeting. 'But we're not talking about *war*, are we David? At least, I hope we're not. We're talking about Dubček and his partners in crime being summoned to a meeting with the entire Soviet Politburo at this godforsaken railway station. Why on earth, one wonders, choose this place?'

Sam said, 'I think the Czechoslovaks are most reluctant to meet outside their own borders at the moment. If you're riding a tiger you don't want to ride it into the tiger's own den.'

'To stretch a metaphor.'

'Beyond its breaking point, I fear.' More amusement at the table. He and Eric were good together, Chancery putting on a show of irony and self-deprecation, qualities that had once been a stand-by of such people through centuries of empire and now seemed equally well adapted to Britain's lowered status in the post-war world. 'At the same time, Comrade Brezhnev appears a little nervous about being seen in Czechoslovakia. I understand the Russian train is due to be shunted across the border to Čierna in the morning for talks, and then, in the evening when the discussions are over and they've had a jolly dinner with the fraternal comrades, they'll be shunted back to Russia for the night. That's what we gather.'

'You're not serious? They're *frightened* of spending the night in Czechoslovakia?'

'Something like that.'

They digested this piece of news in silence before Whittaker spoke again. 'We can only await developments, I suppose. And hope that common sense prevails. In the meantime, I would like to draw your attention to a report that comes, unattributed and unattributable, of course, from the Friends.'

The Friends, everyone knew and no one mentioned, were those enigmatic individuals who rooted around in the shadows of events like dogs raiding dustbins in a back alley, and came up with what they called, oxymoronically at times, intelligence. They were an inferior species to the true diplomats, inferior yet somehow enviable. It was hard not to have grudging admiration for the rather stout fellow who was their particular Friend, a man of no apparent consequence and even less significance, but who was here or hereabouts all the time, pretending to be responsible for cultural affairs while reporting not to His Excellency, Her Britannic Majesty's Ambassador to the Czechoslovak Socialist Republic but rather to a man in Century House on the Thames in London, a man who was head of an organisation so secret that even its true name was secret, a man who himself was only ever known, in the manner of the worst spy thrillers, by a single letter – C.

'This is, of course, most secret,' Whittaker said, adding in one of his familiar parentheses: 'I do so hate the word "secret". It always sounds like an invitation to tell all.'

The stout man remained impassive. Others round the table smiled knowingly. 'Just a straw in the wind, really, Eric,' the man said. 'Nothing to get too excited about. It seems that SIGINT has detected attempts by Russian forces to cut telecommunications from Prague to the outside world. Just brief moments of blackout. Probably trials.'

The little group, couched in its sealed room, was silent. Whittaker raised an eyebrow. 'SIGINT?'

The man looked crestfallen. 'An acronym, Eric. Sorry. Signals intelligence.'

'Ah. An Americanism, no doubt.'

'I fear so.'

'But not really an acronym *sensu stricto*. More an abbreviation.'

'I'm sure you're right, Eric. Anyway, it seems possible that these blackouts are some kind of rehearsal. If the Warsaw Pact forces were to intervene—'

'—invade.'

'They would wish to move in beneath an electronic blanket.'

Whittaker nodded wearily. 'So that is the background against which the Czechoslovak presidium is meeting with Brezhnev and his henchmen at' – he glanced hopelessly at the papers in front of him – 'Trainspotters' Delight.' There was more amusement round the table, the laughter of relief. 'How do you divine the mood on the streets, Sam? You seem best equipped to give us the low-down. To use another Americanism.'

Sam thought of Lenka and her friends. 'There's a kind of bloody-minded insouciance about the activists. If they do invade, so what? Armies cannot defeat an idea whose time has come. That seems to be the general feeling.'

'Sounds like flower power to me,' the major said. 'Armies cannot defeat a crowd of hippies. Unfortunately it's not true. There could be a lot of blood.'

'Somehow, I doubt it. The Czechs ...' Sam hesitated. It was the kind of statement that you made with caution. You needed to phrase it exactly right. People might quote him. '... are pragmatists. It's not for nothing that Good Soldier Svejk is

their hero. They know when not to kick against the pricks –
but how to deflect them instead. Look at what happened in
1938. Or rather, what didn't happen. Had they fought, the
country would have been destroyed and this city would have
been left in ruins.'

'Not got the stomach for a fight,' the major said briskly.

Sam turned on him, still thinking of Lenka, but now
imagining her lying in the street with blood on that elegant
Slavic face. 'Look what happened to the ones who did fight.
Look what happened in Warsaw during the war, or East
Germany in fifty-three or Hungary in fifty-six.'

Whittaker sensed tempers rising. 'Let's hope common
sense prevails,' he said pacifically. 'As always we must hope
for the best and prepare for the worst. And to that end, I
want to circulate this proposal for how we might look after
the best interests of families and auxiliary staff in the event
of a Soviet' – he hesitated – '*interference* in local affairs.
Contingency planning, that's all. Just in case. Naturally, I
wouldn't like this information to get out of these four walls
lest it cause more upset than circumstances deserve ...'

The typewritten sheets went round the table. There was a
hasty scanning, some suggestions, nods of approval. 'And in
the meantime we have our Members of Parliament doing the
rounds. Where exactly are they now, Sam?'

'I believe they are in Pilsen this morning. This afternoon
it's a glass factory.'

'It's always a glass factory.'

'And then in the evening there is an informal party hosted
by your kind self. And Madeleine, of course.'

After the meeting Sam searched out the stout little fellow who
was everyone's Friend. Harold Saumarez. Could he have a
word? In strictest confidence?

Of course he could. Perhaps a breath of fresh air in the

garden? Where, it was understood but never mentioned, they would be out of the hearing of any hidden microphones. So they strolled across velvet lawns where the ambassador held a summer garden party, assuming the weather was kind, to celebrate the QBP, the Queen's Birthday Party, symbol of British insouciance abroad.

'Just a word in your ear, Harold. In strictest confidence, of course.'

'That's the second time you've said that.'

'Shows how important it is, doesn't it? There's a name I'd like to have checked out, you see. Someone I've met recently. One Lenka Konečková.' As they walked they tried to keep their faces averted from the balustrade of the Castle high above where, so the rumour went, expert lip-readers attempted to oversee conversations in the gardens of the British embassy below and interpret what was being said. He even put his hand to cover his mouth as he spoke the name. 'Twenty-five years old. Calls herself a student. Does some journalism, occasional work for the radio, so she says.'

Harold raised what were, by any standards, heavy eyebrows. 'Personal interest?'

'Professional.'

'It's hardly my job, you know.'

'Of course it's not, Harold. But you know as well as I do that security doesn't know its arse from its elbow. Mr Plod the policeman, retired. Whereas our dearly beloved Friends ... '

Harold sniffed, torn between wounded pride and flattery. 'I'll see what I can do. You don't have a photo, do you?'

Sam produced the film cartridge and tucked it into the man's top pocket as he might have tucked a cigar. 'In there, right at the end. Perhaps your chaps can have it developed. I didn't have any time. There'll be a few snaps of little consequence – Steffie and me doing something silly – but the last one should show her. It's a group photo, gathered round a table, late evening. Taken with a flash, so I've no idea how it'll come out. Some of them will be making faces, but not her. She'll be on the far left.'

Harold removed the item from his top pocket and secreted it elsewhere about his person, as though there was a correct place for such things. 'I'll see what I can do.'

'I'd be most grateful.'

9

The Whittakers had a rooftop terrace. This elevated their apartment to a level appropriate to Head of Chancery. One reckoned one's progress through the service by measures like that – the quality of posting, of housing, of furnishing – until finally you reached ambassadorial level and might live in a palace surrounded by furniture and artworks fit for a museum, at which point the time came for your K and subsequent retirement to that dull and unfamiliar bungalow in the Home Counties. But for the moment, as he showed his guests onto the terrace, Eric Whittaker was heedless of that. 'Two messages are inherent in this apartment,' he was explaining in his best academic manner. 'One is *that*.' He made a theatrical gesture to demonstrate what was obvious, the view before them, across the rooftops of Malá Strana to the river and the Charles Bridge. Beyond the river were the imposing buildings and pinnacles of Staré Město, the Old Town. On one building a red star glowed like a single, malevolent eye. 'From that view you may appreciate that we are amongst the elite, rising above everyone else in the city, except' – he turned in the opposite direction, backstage, to where a massive bastion rose up from the terrace like a cliff, blocking out half the night sky – 'that lot up there.'

Up there, looming over everyone, was the Hrad, the Castle, where the president of the country resided and Kafka reigned supreme.

'That,' he said, 'is the second message.'

The visitors laughed dutifully but nervously. They made up the parliamentary delegation come to convince itself that Socialism With A Human Face really was possible even behind the barbed wire and tank traps of the Iron Curtain. They'd spent the morning at the Škoda works in Pilsen and the afternoon in a glass factory, where each member of the party had been presented with a piece of abstract Bohemian glass resembling something you might find in the waste bin of a hospital operating theatre. Now it was an informal dinner at the Whittakers' with carefully selected guests.

'What dreadful, dull people,' Madeleine whispered. She was tall and dark and vindictive towards things that did not amuse her. The MPs' wives did not amuse her. Having spent most of the day showing them the sights of Prague (the wives not deemed serious enough to deal with the Škoda factory), she now considered her duty done and had enticed Sam into a secluded corner of the terrace where she could give vent to her spleen. 'In France *tout le monde* understands that you must imitate the arbiters of good taste even if you 'ate what they admire; but these people seem to think that taste is a matter of *opinion*. Worse than that, they appear to think that it is a matter of *démocratie*.'

She'd had the foresight to put some music on the record player, and the cool voice of a soprano saxophone drifted out of the speakers. Sam knew what was coming next. She would suggest they dance and she would press her hips against him and get him aroused, and he would picture Steffie's face twisted into a little scowl of 'told-you-so'.

'I think you ought to get your guests dancing,' he suggested.

'Pah!' It was astonishing how dismissive an innocent exclamation could become when manipulated by a pair of French lips. 'Those clod'oppers,' she said. 'There is nothing worse-dressed and worse-mannered than a British socialist. And nothing worse at dancing. So I want to dance with you, Sam, and find out how you are doing without the virginal Stéfanie at your side. Is celibacy already beginning to get you down?'

'She's only been gone a few days.'

She laughed. 'Do you know what President Kennedy once told me?'

'When did you meet President Kennedy?'

'When Eric was in Washington. You don't believe me?'

'It all depends on what he said.'

'He said, "I get terrible headaches if I haven't had a new woman in three days."'

'I don't believe you.'

'But it 'appens to be true.'

'And you replied?'

'"Do you have a headache now?" And he said, "Ma'am, I sure do." To which I replied, "Well, Mister President, if you come with me we'll see what's in the medicine chest."'

She laughed and took hold of him, moving with the music exactly as he had predicted, sinuously, pushing her hips against him, a rather expert movement that might have been mistaken for a tango. One of the visiting MPs laughed. There was a smattering of applause. Sam heard Eric's voice saying 'French' to one of the guests, as though by way of explanation. Another couple joined them in the dance, with nothing like Madeleine's snake-like immodesty but with a degree of regimented competence that spoke of hours of practice in Northern ballrooms.

Her mouth close to his ear, Madeleine whispered, 'Steffie has entrusted me with looking after you. To ensure that you don't suffer from Kennedy 'eadaches and go looking after lovely Czech ladies.'

'Steffie asked you to do that? It'd be like putting the fox in charge of a chicken.'

A little breath of laughter, carrying with it the scent of Chanel No. 5. 'Are you a chicken, Sam?'

Eric's voice came from across the terrace. 'Sam, put my wife down. You don't know where she's been.'

Gusts of laughter. These Foreign Office boys, the laughter seemed to say: nothing like as stuck up as they seem.

Madeleine's voice continued in his ear, 'Or are you just a tiny bit queer, like so many of you public school boys?'

'Grammar school, I'm afraid. Altogether more normal. And duller.'

She laughed with him and detached herself from his arms to do a little pirouette. 'So show me.'

To Sam's relief the record changed. Something more upbeat, with a heavy bass riff and an organ wailing protest. Madeleine detached herself from him and began to dance in the middle of the terrace, her arms above her head, hips gyrating in time with the insistent beat. 'Gimme some lovin',' a raucous blues voice demanded. One of the MPs began to jig around opposite Madeleine, leaving Sam to make his escape to the drinks table.

As he poured himself a whisky a Northern voice spoke over his shoulder. 'So what's your role in all this, young man?'

He turned to find one of the delegation at his elbow. The man was short and stout and would have fitted well enough into the Party Praesidium during Gottwald's reign – ill-fitting grey suit that shone like beaten pewter, a shirt collar as tight as a garrotte, a glance that hovered between unease and malice. Before the delegation had arrived in the city the diplomatic staff had been briefed to treat members of the group with extreme caution; most of them were well to the left of almost anyone in Dubček's government and all of them considered the Foreign Office little more than a sinecure for ex-public school boys. This particular example was one such, a trades unionist who was mainly renowned for having brought his own particular branch of industry to its knees through a series of wildcat strikes. 'My role in this *what*, exactly?'

'In Her Britannic Majesty's embassy to the Czechoslovak Socialist Republic. Aside from dancing with the boss's wife, that is.'

'I'm political.'

'Are you, indeed? And where do your politics lie?'

'Wherever the current government tells me they should.'

The man laughed humourlessly. 'Ever the diplomat, eh?'

'That's what people keep telling me.'

'I'll bet you're a Tory.'

'I wonder if you'd find any takers amongst those who actually know me.'

'So what's your view of the politics here?'

'I think I know too much about it all to have a single view. I have many views, each one calling the previous one into question.'

'Typical Foreign Office response. Come off the bloody fence for once. Admit that Dubček's a working-class hero. He's showing how socialism should be. And you Tories are just as pissed off as the Russians.'

Sam looked at the man pityingly. 'Actually, the Office doesn't consider hero-worship of foreign leaders to be in our best interests. And whatever you may see now, it's worth remembering that Dubček and his merry men all came up through the ranks during the Stalinist era, during which they accepted all kinds of horror as though it was the will of God. Now they're standing on the brink, wondering whether to jump into the unknown or turn back into the familiar arms of Mother Russia. When push comes to shove, they're likely to turn round and beg Mummy for forgiveness.'

'And when will that be?'

'It's probably happening now, at their meeting in eastern Slovakia. No doubt the fraternal comrades are toasting peace and happiness at this very moment.'

'Have you met the man?'

'Dubček? Once, at a reception. The ambassador was in London and Eric Whittaker was ill, so the lot fell on me.'

'What's he like?'

'Courteous, amusing, intelligent. As far as one can tell from hello goodbye.'

The man hummed a bit, his bluff, aggressive humour dampened for a moment. 'Speak the language, do you?' he asked unexpectedly.

'Czech? Well enough. My Russian is better.'

'At least they've posted you to the right place.'

'Pure chance, I can assure you. I might just as easily have got Ouagadougou.'

Wry laughter. Did the man even know where Ouagadougou was?

It wasn't exactly clear what brought the evening to an end. Probably the arrival of cars to take people back to their hotel. There was much handshaking and a bit of two-cheek kissing, which rather surprised the parliamentarians. And then the terrace and the house below was empty of all but the hosts and Sam was making his belated farewells. Madeleine managed to get him alone for a moment, which was what he had been dreading. She took hold of his shoulders and kissed him full on the mouth. 'Sam,' she said, 'will you go to bed with me?'

'Did Steffie suggest you ask me that?'

'More or less.'

'Well tell her the answer's no.'

She laughed. 'Is that because you're being faithful to her, or because you've got someone else lined up?'

'Mrs Whittaker, you're drunk.'

She was doing that thing, fiddling with his tie as though to make him look respectable. 'And you are boring.'

'Boring is what I should be, under the circumstances. Can you imagine what Eric would say if the First Secretary in Chancery was shafting his wife?'

'Eric doesn't mind. When he took me on I warned him that sometimes I'd have a little fling and he wasn't to mind about it. It was my first husband who minded, and look what happened to him.'

He took her hand and lowered it to her side. 'Was he pushed or did he jump?'

She thumped him gently in the chest. 'I began to push,' she said. 'He thought it easier to jump.'

It was a short walk to Sam's flat through the maze of alleys. As he reached the little square in front of his building a figure detached itself from the shadows and accosted him.

'Did I give you a fright?' the SIS man asked.

'Not at all, Harold. Nothing gives me a fright in the Malá Strana. Safest place in the whole city.'

'Ghosts, I thought. No amount of security can guard against them.'

'Are you a ghost, Harold?'

'Spook, maybe. But I've always thought of myself as a kind of golem. Occult powers, if you know what I mean. No, I won't come up. Safer to have a quick chat out here.'

'I'm sure my flat is clean.'

The man laughed. 'Is that what Mr Plod the policeman tells you?' He reached inside his jacket as though going for a gun, but all he brought out was a plain envelope. 'I thought you'd like the photo. Nice little souvenir. Don't bother looking at it now. I just wanted to say that she has form. Your young lady, I mean.'

'Form? What kind of form?'

'Interesting, really. A few years ago – sixty, sixty-one – she was having an affair with a member of the Party. Respectable chap, married, three children, house in Vinohrady, you know the kind of thing. Destined for the Presidium, by all accounts. So we got to know about his little peccadillo with this particular girl – don't ask me how – and we had him lined up for a bit of gentle blackmail.'

'Charming.'

'We are, Sam, we are.'

'And what happened?'

'Total bloody failure. As soon as he was approached by us, he dropped her like a hot potato, confessed everything to the wife and told the StB. Our own chap had a difficult time extricating himself from the deal. He was working under diplomatic cover, thank God, but they declared him *persona non grata* and we had to get him out in a hurry.'

Nothing could be more normal, Sam told himself. Young girl falls for older, successful, married man, then gets thrown over when the affair threatens to go public. Yet nothing could be more abnormal than having Harold and his spooks sniffing around your private parts. 'But she wasn't actually *working* for us, was she? It wasn't – what do you lot call it? – a honey trap?'

Harold glanced sideways at Sam. He was hoping, oh, surely he was hoping, that he looked like Orson Welles in that scene in *The Third Man*. Not as he was in the later scenes – not running through the sewers, and certainly not clawing at the grating of the manhole cover. But the one where Harry Lime appears for the first time, standing in the shadows of the doorway. 'I'd say she was a not-so-innocent bystander caught in the crossfire.'

'Not so innocent?'

'Apparently your girl was only fifteen when she started with this fellow. Quite a little titbit.'

Sam felt something snap inside him. Nothing dramatic, just a small palpable rupture. Trust, or something. '*Fifteen?*'

'That's what it seems. Been with him for three or four years when we caught up with it. There's a theory going around the files that we were trespassing on another operation. That she was set up by the East Germans. Who knows if that's true or not?'

'So she might have been an East German agent? At *fifteen*?'

'Not saying so, old chap. Just a rumour.'

There was a pause while Sam digested this possibility. 'Sure you won't come up?' he asked. 'A nightcap?'

'Quite sure, old chap. Must be getting along. Work all hours these days. I do hope I haven't put the kibosh on the start of a lovely friendship.'

'Nothing of the kind, Harold. And thank you for the information.'

In his sitting room Sam opened the envelope Harold had given him and tipped the photographic print out along with two strips of negatives. He examined the print. It was the kind of thing you took on holiday – a group of strangers gathered behind half-empty beer glasses, frozen by the flash and backed by shadows. Faces were white and staring, grimacing with laughter. One of the group had put his hand round the back of his neighbour's head to give him an antenna of two fingers. In the centre was the violinist – Jitka, that was her name – and her husband. On the left of the group was Lenka. The others laughed, she smiled.

What, Sam wondered, was she smiling at?

III

10

It's raining. Scudding clouds like damp rags hung out in the wind. A boy and a girl, laden beneath rucksacks, climbing out of a Land Rover and taking up position on the roadside. The Land Rover drives off in a plume of spray and laughter.

'Daddy doesn't believe we'll get anywhere,' Eleanor mutters angrily, and it's only defiance that stops her fulfilling her parent's belief. Her anorak hood is letting in water around the neck, it's too damp to roll a ciggie and she's having second thoughts about this venture.

Lorries, cars, buses, splash past. They seem indifferent, not even inhabited by human beings, just steel boxes of varying size and design and colour careering past as though on a conveyor belt. 'What do we do now?' she asks. She feels hopeless and angry, above all angry at James for bringing her here.

'We walk on a bit.'

'*Walk on?* I thought the idea was to bum a lift off someone.'

James is wearing a smug expression that says this is what he knows and she doesn't. He's the expert here. 'First rule,' he says. 'Only hitch where there's a place the driver can pull in. No one's going to stop in the middle of a main road.'

'What's the second rule? Give up and take a taxi?'

They shuffle through the drizzle as far as a lay-by. 'You may as well start,' he says, plonking his rucksack on the grass verge. 'Shouldn't be difficult. I'll stand back a bit. They'll stop for a girl.'

'For a *girl*?'

'Come on, stick your thumb out.'

'I don't want that kind of lift.'

'It won't be that kind of lift. It'll be a lift.'

'It's like hustling.'

'It's only hustling if the customer thinks you're a tart. But they'll just assume you're hitching. Now stick your bloody thumb out.'

She does so, like someone trying in vain to plug a leak. Cars splash by.

'You want to look the driver in the eye as well. Make it personal. That's rule number two. You're a girl, so take advantage of it.'

'I told you, I don't want that kind of lift.'

'Come on, Ellie. All he'll want is a grope.'

She turns on him, but at the very moment that she's about to loose a stream of invective, a van slithers to a halt in the lay-by. 'Hop in,' the driver yells through the window, and James is opening the door and shoving Ellie and the rucksacks across the seat before she can utter a word. 'Dover,' James says across the sodden, furious figure sitting in the middle of the bench seat. The driver, a callow youth with prominent Adam's apple and rodent teeth, slams the vehicle into gear and accelerates back into the stream of traffic. He's chewing gum and smoking and scratching his groin, all these things at the same time as driving. It takes concentration, a degree of slick skill. 'You going abroad then?'

'France, Germany, Italy. Maybe Greece.'

He grins at them. 'And you've had a row already?'

11

'About last night,' she says. They've bought tickets, had something to eat in a greasy-spoon café and then boarded the ferry and waited for it to depart, all without broaching that most delicate of subjects. Now they are on deck looking back over the ship's wash to where low-lying cloud throws a wartime smokescreen across what might be the white cliffs of Dover fading into the night. The lounge they have abandoned is like a refugee encampment, littered with squalling babies and arguing adults, dominated by a large, loud American extolling the virtues of the latest film to anyone who will listen and many who are trying not to. 'You've gotta see it,' he is insisting. 'It's just ace. This little guy Hoffman. He's a real star.'

Out on deck it is quiet and cool. The rain has stopped.

'What about last night?'

He senses rather than sees her indifference. 'I'm sorry, that's all. Just . . . I don't want to rush into anything.'

'Bloody Kevin again.'

'Perhaps.'

There is silence between them but not around them. Around them, beneath them, is the sound of the ship and its way through the water. It pitches and shudders like an old lady confronted with something not altogether pleasant. Deep in its bowels is the rumble of machinery. He wonders what she thinks of him, while she wonders what he thinks of her. Neither offers the other much in the way of clues. Should he take her hand? It seems mad. They've kissed a bit, and now he doesn't know whether to take her hand or not.

'Strange, isn't it?' she says. 'Tomorrow morning we'll be in France—'

'Belgium, actually. Zeebrugge, remember?'

'Only because you insisted, because it was cheaper.'

'My mother brought me up to be careful with money.' He waits. 'You were different with your parents, you know that? From what you're like at Oxford.'

'Different how?'

He can't quite say. A hint, a feeling. 'Obedient,' he suggests. 'Wanting to please.'

'That's why I try to get away from them. Isn't it the same with you?'

'You'll have to come oop North and find out.'

'That depends on whether we survive this trip.'

We, he thinks. What exactly is this collective? Does it even exist outside the limits of this journey? And in the spirit of scientific exploration he decides to attempt to find out, turning towards her and taking that hand and ducking down to kiss her on the mouth. There is a moment's hesitation, just the fragile touch of her lips, and then she moves towards him and her mouth opens and for a moment there is the vibrant dance of her tongue against his.

She pulls back and moves away, turning back to the sea, her face in profile.

'What does that mean?' he asks.

'It doesn't mean anything. It just is.'

'Isn't it a signifier?' The word seems to startle her. Maybe he isn't meant to know things like that.

'What on earth have you been reading? Derrida?'

'Some crap about semiotics.'

'Well, if anything it's a floating signifier. It means everything and nothing. What you want it to mean.'

'I want it to mean you really fancy me.'

'But maybe that's not what it *does* mean.' She laughs and gives him a little consoling nudge in the chest. 'Come on, we'd better go inside and find somewhere to sleep.'

12

A Flemish dawn insinuates itself into the early morning. Ellie peers, bug-eyed from lack of sleep, through the salted window of the lounge. There's a smear of sea and vague shapes of coastline and harbour. 'Where in God's name are we?' she wonders out loud.

'Zeebugger,' says James. They take turns to guard their rucksacks while the other goes to wash in the overcrowded bathrooms. The ferry docks with a clanging of steel and a blast of ship's siren.

Outside on deck the air is cold. It has a different quality from the air they left behind at Dover, a strange hint of foreign, a sense that they are on the edge of a continent that stretches to the Mediterranean, to the Urals, to Finisterre. No longer marooned on an island, encompassed by an island's limitations. Here, anything is possible. But is that sensation just an illusion? After all, there's nothing much to see, just the industrial desert of Zeebrugge that lies all around the docks like children's toys abandoned across a concrete playground. Could be anywhere. Thames estuary. Merseyside. Tyneside.

Ellie huddles against him for warmth, which is good. He puts his arm around her and smells her hair. A warm, maternal scent that doesn't quite match the girl herself, who is brittle and filial. Below deck engines are being started. On the quayside men are waving instructions. Foot passengers begin to file off the ferry like the infantry of an invading army, each trooper bowed beneath the burden of his or her backpack. All that is missing is the weaponry.

'Foreign soil,' James says portentously as he steps down off the gangway. Not really true. Foreign concrete, more like. 'The first time,' he adds.

'The *first*—?'

'—time abroad. That's right.'

'I don't believe it—'

'We 'aven't all got t'brass you 'ave,' he says, putting on his phoney Yorkshire accent to amuse her. They stump along a quay, past vehicles are already queuing to drive on once the ferry had been emptied.

'Look,' Ellie says pointing. 'Ringo.'

'Ringo?'

'There.' In the queue of cars is a VW Beetle bearing the name on the bonnet. A face watches them from the driver's seat as they walk past. A pretty little girly face. Blonde and blue-eyed and rosebud-mouthed. 'Ringo. For a Beetle. Now is that funny, or just naff?'

'What's naff?'

Ellie affects surprise. 'Don't you know anything? *You* are, my dear, you are. So where do we go now?'

'South,' he says, not caring if he is naff, feeling, for the moment, like Ernest Shackleton but without the icebergs – an explorer making his first, tentative steps in unexplored territory, although a slow plod through the purlieus of Zeebrugge, passed by overloaded cars bearing GB stickers on their rear ends, doesn't quite match Antarctica.

'Why's no one stopping?' Ellie demands petulantly.

'Because they're bloody full. Can't you see? And they're English, which means they're on holiday, which means they're not going to pick up hitchers in a foreign country.'

They pause to examine the map that they bought in Dover.

'We're here,' he says, pointing. 'And that's where we want to be, at the Ostend to Brussels road.'

Ellie launches into a silly game, ratcheting up her accent to sound like an army officer in a 1950s war film, stabbing the map with a spiky finger. 'We are he-are and Jerry is they-are.'

'Piss off,' he tells her. She sulks. He folds the map away and they plod on through the early morning, Ellie stumping on ahead as though she isn't with him. He watches her, liking her and loathing her at the same time; a strange combination of emotions. Spoilt brat, is what he loathes. What he likes is more difficult to explain – something about the sharp flights of her mind, her knowledge and her self-confidence. On the ferry she told him something about the weeks she spent in Paris last May, sleeping on someone's floor, going out during the daytime to throw cobblestones at the CRS and spending the evenings at a student bar with music and beer and hash. She was even arrested and spent a night in a police cell with half a dozen other girls. In the morning she was let go because she was British and they didn't want the bother of dealing with the embassy. That Ellie seems like an emissary from another continent, far from Yorkshire, far from England even.

The countryside south of Zeebrugge is flat and dull, smeared with rain, named with Zs and Ks: Dudzele, Zuienkerke, and the hip Koolkerke. Only 'Bruges' is familiar. 'Let's go to Bruges,' Ellie calls over her shoulder. 'I've heard it's lovely.'

'I thought we were going to Italy. If we stop off at every place that—'

'All right, all right.'

Cars pass by full of smiling families off on their continental hols, but the one that does stop isn't one of them. The driver is on his own, an undistinguished man as grey as the morning. He winds the window down. '*Autostop*?' he asks.

'Er ... no,' James answers.

'Yes!' shouts Ellie, running back. 'Yes! We're doing *auto-stop*. *Autostop* means hitching, you idiot.'

'I thought it meant our car had broken down.'

Gratefully they clamber into the car.

'Where you go?' the driver asks.

'To Italy. And Greece.'

He laughs, as though Italy and Greece are figments of the imagination, like the land of Cockaigne. 'I only go to Oostkamp. I drop you on the Brussels road. Maybe there someone take you to Italy.'

In the car they examine the map again, Ellie leaning over the front seat and reaching out to trace a line past Bruges, past Brussels towards Luxembourg and the Rhine. She looks up with a sudden grin, as though a single lift of no more than a few miles has made all the difference. Her face, rubbed plain by lack of sleep, is suddenly immensely desirable. Not a spoilt brat at all. 'Hey,' she says, looking at James with that intensity of gaze that she has, 'we're on our way. And you're really not naff.'

Throughout that morning they move through the Flanders landscape, elated by their successes, stunned by tiredness, and, in James's case, thrilled by the novelty: foreign road signs, foreign place names, foreign cafés and shops. Even the design of houses. How could you make something different out of a row of terrace houses constructed of bricks and mortar? Yet the Flemish had achieved that very thing.

On the outskirts of Brussels they take a tram with a conductor sitting behind a desk just inside the door, dealing out tickets with a mangled stump of a hand and complaining about life to anyone who will listen and many who won't. Around them people talk in a blizzard of French, and, to James's surprise, Ellie talks back at them. 'Skiing holidays,' she tells him by way of explanation. 'And summers in Juan-les-Pins.'

'Sounds posh.'

'How could I help it?' she asks, as though it had been some kind of indignity that her parents subjected her to.

They leave the tram at the end of the line and walk through the last, characterless suburbs. On the south side of the city, other hitchhikers stand like anglers on the banks of a river waiting for a bite. Some hold up cards with their intended destinations, as though these might attract their prey. James knows what to do here – walk upstream and take whatever is coming just to get away from the crowd. And soon enough Ellie lands a catch, a Peugeot driven by a young man in a grey suit who might be a travelling salesman. 'Namur?' he asks.

'Namur *ça va*,' Ellie replies because it is okay; almost anywhere in the general direction of south is okay. They clamber in, triumphant, and set off. Dull, terrace houses, a supermarket and a filling station give way to farmland. A sign announces Waterloo and shortly a great mound rises like a Neolithic tumulus out of the farmland ahead. People are gathered at the summit beneath the statue of a lion. 'You want to see?' the driver asks.

He parks the car amongst the tourist coaches. There's a memorial stone telling anyone who bothers to read that *La Butte du Lion* was constructed by some king or other to celebrate the fact that his son, Prince someone or other, was wounded during the battle.

'Typical imperialist crap,' Ellie decides. 'No one gives a shit about the slaughter of common soldiers, but they built a bloody great monument like this because Prince William got knocked off his horse.'

'You're judging the past by the standards of the present.'

'No, I'm not. I'm judging it by the standards of the Enlightenment and the French Revolution.'

'So you'd bring the guillotine back?'

'Some people deserve the guillotine.'

Arguing, they climb the steps up the side of the mound while people coming down push past. Up on the top, in the shadow of the pedestal, a cool breeze blows. An information board gives the layout of the battle. It is weather-beaten like the battlefield itself, the colours faded, the names – Napoleon, Wellington, Blücher and all the others – partly worn away. They look from the board to the landscape before them, to the shallow slopes of farmland that at the time meant such a lot. A mile deep and a couple of miles wide, that's all; a few square miles of open fields and scattered woods, with an occasional farm. James tries to picture the chaos of an early nineteenth-century battle: drifting palls of musketry smoke; the scythe of canister shot; comic opera uniforms; horses plunging and whinnying. Europe tearing herself to pieces, as she always seems to do.

They go back down, arguing the merits and demerits of Napoleon. Was he a little Hitler? Or a great civiliser of Europe? Revolutionary or dictator? About Wellington Ellie has no doubt: duke, prime minister, reactionary bastard. He'd have gone to the guillotine, and deserved it.

The driver listens to their argument as they drive back to the main road. 'Who gives a shit?' he says.

13

Namur. Bastions, ramparts, the slippery flow of a great river. Beneath the city walls they stop to buy a newspaper and write postcards. James notices that Ellie's postcard home is addressed solely to her father. A bleak missive: *We're fine. Hope Mother is OK. Love, Ellie.* The newspaper runs stories about the war in Vietnam, about disturbances in France, about dictatorial colonels in Greece. A long editorial asks whether Russian forces will invade Czechoslovakia as they did twelve years ago in Hungary.

Beyond Namur the countryside changes. No longer the dull flats of Flanders but now a crumple in the continent's mantle that gives rolling hills and woods. Their lift drops them in the main square of Marche, an ordinary little town where they find a brasserie with tables outside under the trees. They sit in the afternoon sun and drink dark, slightly sweet beer. The map shows that they have done almost one hundred and fifty miles.

After buying bread and charcuterie they set off in evening sunshine along the road to Bastogne. The countryside has a mellow, timeless quality to it, spacious and open, as though no one could do it any harm. Towards seven o'clock they stop at a farmhouse and Ellie is pushed towards the door to communicate with the natives. '*Bonsoir, Madame,*' she says to the woman who answers her knock. '*On fait l'autostop vers l'Italie. S'il vous plaît, avez-vous un endroit où on peut mettre la tente?*'

The woman's face is stolid as a potato. She turns and calls to someone inside.

'What did you say?' James asks.

'Is there somewhere we can pitch a tent?'

The woman turns back. '*Une canadienne?*'

James is indignant. 'Canadian? No! *Je suis* English. *Anglais!*'

This brings laughter. 'Shut up, James,' Ellie says. '*Oui, Madame. Seulement une canadienne.*' There's a brief discussion, a waving of arms and a pitying smile in James's direction accompanied by laughter from the woman. At that moment a little girl emerges from the shadows of the house and, with great solemnity, leads them round the back. '*Voilà la cerisaie,*' she announces in a piping voice, pointing beyond outhouses to where there's an orchard, placid in the evening sunshine, the trees laden with fruit. Cherries. A cherry orchard.

Ellie dumps her rucksack on the ground. 'How very literary,' she says. 'Or is that lost on you?'

'Everything's lost on me. What was all that about being Canadian?'

'A *canadienne* is a tent, you berk.'

'How the hell do you know *that*?'

'Camping,' Ellie admits reluctantly. 'With the Guides. We went to a jamboree in Vence in the south of France.'

'You were a *Girl Guide*? For fuck's sake! And you told me all that crap about camping on the lawn with your brother.'

'That was true. The tent on the lawn was true.'

'But you never mentioned the Guides, or jamborees or anything like that. What were you? Brown Owl?'

'That's Brownies.'

'It's all the same. Bloody silly games. How does a Girl

Guide light her fire?' He dumps his rucksack beside hers and looks at her questioningly. 'Well?'

'I don't know. How *does* a Girl Guide light her fire?'

'She rubs against a Boy Scout.'

'Ha ha.'

He unrolls the tent in the long grass beneath the trees: a strip of bright nylon with rings and cords and zips attached.

'Orange,' Ellie observes disparagingly, as though orange is a colour that has long been out of fashion in the tentage world. Naff, maybe.

James tosses a small bundle of aluminium poles onto it. 'Go on then – show us how you do it.'

'You think I can't?'

'Show me.'

In a few minutes, beneath the grave eyes of the little girl and with disconcerting skill, Ellie has the tent pitched. Cautiously she unzips the entrance and peers in. 'Am I meant to get in *there* with *you*?'

'Wasn't it like that with the Boy Scouts? You get inside the tent and they get inside you.'

'Don't be so crude. I didn't sleep a wink on the bloody ferry, and now this.'

'This is all right. You can sleep like a baby, in my arms.' He pulls out his sleeping bag and unrolls it inside the tent. Called by the woman, the little girl has disappeared. They are left alone with their paltry meal and their tent. Fando and Lis. On the road to Tar.

'We haven't got anything to drink,' Ellie complains.

James pulls two bottles of beer out of the side pocket of his rucksack. They have foil round the neck, like miniature champagne bottles. 'Here you are. I got them on the ferry.' He glances at the label. 'Stella Artois. Never heard of it. Not the kind of thing a red-blooded Englishman would be happy with, but beggars can't be boozers.'

'If I want a pee?'

'I thought you were a Girl Guide. Just wander off into the cherry orchard and commune with nature.'

'Sounds like Chekhov.'

'Easier in those days.'

'Easier?'

'Long skirts and no knickers.'

'They wore knickers!'

While they are arguing about that the little girl returns, silently bearing a large paper bag full of cherries like an offering to the gods who have blessed her with their presence. '*Merci beaucoup*,' is all that James can manage, which seems paltry under the circumstances. '*Merci, merci. Très bon*,' he adds despairingly.

The little girl laughs and runs off to tell her mother about the strange man who can't really talk properly. Ellie is delighted with the gift. Perhaps it fits in with her idea of the generosity of the peasant class. 'How kind. And it saves us having to steal them.'

So they sit together at the opening of the tent and eat their supper of bread and rillettes with cherries to follow. It is almost idyllic. Mainly Ellie talks, that quick, energetic talk, of what she thinks and what she intends, of how the day has gone and how she doesn't really care about sleeping in a tent. 'Actually,' she concedes, 'it's quite fun.'

They take it in turns to wash at a tap on a nearby outhouse. Teeth are cleaned, armpits self-consciously splashed.

'Now what?' James asks. He blows up the airbeds, light-headed with the effort, then pushes them into the tent and stands up. The sun is setting, brushing peach and apricot into the cherry orchard. It is beautiful in the way that the ordinary can be beautiful. Just somewhere nondescript in Europe, in a cherry orchard amidst farmland where armies once tramped. And the tent is there between them, something between a double bed and a single coffin lying beneath the trees. Ellie dives inside. 'I'll tell you when,' she calls from within.

He waits. Noises come from inside the tent, of movement, of things being taken off and stowed away. 'Come,' Ellie says, peremptorily. He unzips the entrance and peers in. She's sitting cross-legged at the far end of the space, bathed in light strained through the fabric of the tent, shades of ochre and amber. She's wearing a T-shirt and underpants and a smile; before her is what's left of the bag of cherries and a tin of Gold Leaf tobacco.

'Welcome to the tent of ungodliness,' she says.

He crawls in to face her. What, he wonders, is expected of him? He struggles to take off his jeans in the confined space, and when he has finished and has sat himself opposite her she opens the tobacco tin. Rizla paper and mossy shreds of tobacco. The scent of something other than tobacco seeps into the close air, mingling not unpleasantly with the smell of socks and sweat. A pungent, earthy amalgam. He watches as she rolls the mixture into an expert cylinder. Her tongue emerges from its lair to moisten the margin of the paper.

'What's that?'

'A smoke.'

'I don't smoke.'

'You'll try this, though.'

Understanding dawns. 'You brought *that* with you? Through customs?'

'Relax.' Her smile is part amusement, part contempt, wholly challenging. A match flares and she takes a drag. Her inhalation isn't perfunctory as with a cigarette. Instead she pulls the smoke in and holds it, breath suspended, eyes closed. The smell spreads through the narrow space, dark and fierce.

'You're mad.'

She laughs. 'You're a virgin. Here.' She holds the thing out, damp at one end, smouldering threateningly at the other. 'Let me take your virginity. Have a couple of tokes and then ...'

'Tokes?'

'Drags.'

'Then what?'

A faint giggle. 'Then we'll see. Go easy. Don't want you to puke. Not in here.'

He takes the proffered joint, puffs at it and coughs. The smoke bites his throat. He feels his heartbeat rise. 'This is stupid.'

She shakes her head, taking the joint back. 'It just *is*. Trouble is all the adjectives we use. Adjectives kill things. Good and bad, moral and immoral, stupid and clever. It just *is*, James, it just is.'

The thing, the joint, the spliff – neither good nor bad, neither stupid nor clever, neither moral nor immoral – goes back and forth, briefly to James, rather longer to her because, she repeats, laughing again, he is just a virgin and shouldn't take too much. His head starts to swim. His throat burns and he feels both sick and happy at the same time, a strange, disjointed sensation. Within the tent the orange light glows more vivid, as though the two of them exist within the compass of something organic, pulsing with blood. 'Is that good?' she asks and he agrees that, yes, it is good in its own, unusual way.

'You see?' she says, and he does see. He sees things very vividly, the precise shape of her sitting there a few feet away from him, flushed orange. Eyes wide and black. Lips black. A pout that is somewhere between surprise and amusement. Her bony knees up against her chest and the scribble of hair on her shins. The form of her toes that are unlike any toes he knows, which isn't many, to be frank, but hers do seem unusually long, as though they might be able to grasp at a branch. Prehensile toes. A lemur, with those toes and those wide, black eyes. He laughs and coughs and the joint burns

99

down and she produces a small pair of eyebrow tweezers in order to hold it to the bitter end. 'There,' she says as she takes her final puff, as though she has proved something by the whole exercise, something about his naivety and her wisdom and experience. Smiling vaguely – is there a joke that she might share with him? – she puts the tweezers away and closes the tobacco tin. Then she lifts her hips and slips her underpants off. 'Now,' she says in a matter-of-fact voice, lying down and parting her legs.

All he knows is things that are entirely physical – a swelling, a pulsing, the sensation of imminent explosion, a cloud of something like ecstasy filling his brain. Is this real? Is he, James Borthwick, really there? Is Eleanor Pike really there, stretched the length of the tent, longer laid out than her height when standing, the shadowy ochre of her legs and belly almost filling the whole crepuscular space? Or is she just a figment of his imagination? He touches her as though to make sure, feeling the dense texture of her skin, exploring the hard edge of her pelvis, stroking the silken plume of hair. His finger slips in. He tries to say something but she hushes him to silence. 'Just that,' she whispers, 'just that.'

So he crouches over her while she pivots slowly on the axis of his finger, turning and twisting, lifting her hips up and down, even, at one point, issuing instructions – 'Slower, slower, keep it slow' – but mostly just emitting small exhalations that are almost musical in their pitch and intensity. And after a while – a long while when measured by the indolent clock that ticks inside his head – the music begins a crescendo, tempo and volume rising until she is convulsing and crying out like someone in pain. Then the pain or the pleasure or whatever is over and there is only grief left, grief and tears as he climbs on top of her and she twists her hips away, holding him and moving her hand so that he reaches his own paltry climax on her belly and has to scrabble for a handkerchief to clean up the mess. She turns away from him and his apologies and after a while there is the blessed palliative of sleep.

In the morning they barely speak as they pack up the tent, as though insults have been traded and arguments left unresolved. When he asks if she is upset, she pretends indifference. 'I'm fine.'

When all is ready and their little camp is no more, they knock at the farm door to thank their hosts. The farmer's wife invites them into her kitchen and offers them coffee with fresh bread and butter. They laugh and joke with her, or at least Ellie does; while James watches with something close to jealousy, that this unknown woman should be able to talk to Ellie whereas he cannot. That he could share the closest intimacy and yet can barely exchange pleasantries. Then they pat the little girl on the head (had she listened to the noises in the night?), say goodbye, shoulder their packs and set off on the road to Bastogne.

They pass occasional tanks on the roadside, old Shermans, painted the colour of shit and mounted on concrete plinths as memorials to what happened here a quarter of a century ago, the Ardennes counter-attack, the Battle of the Bulge, the last ferocious assault by the German army on the advancing Western Allies before the Rhine. Rolling hills and scattered woodland rise ahead of them, a mellow landscape that is difficult to imagine in winter, in the cold and fog of war. Now it's a lacklustre summer Sunday, with the few cars that pass full of families out for a meander round the countryside. No lift seems likely.

'Where do we go from here, Ellie?' James asks.

'Luxembourg. Isn't that the idea?'

'That's not what I meant and you know it.'

'It's what you asked. Where do we go from here? You asked it.'

'I mean us.'

'Ooz?' She says it with a faux Northern accent.

They walk on. He knows the danger of pleading. Instinct warns him. 'It's just that after what we've done ...'

'What *have* we done? I was stoned, you touched me up, I gave you a wank. Does that make us married?'

Cars pass by. Frustration rises with the temperature of the day. 'You know your trouble, James?' she says. 'I thought you were honest working-class but actually you're just bourgeois like everyone else.'

'I'm not working-class or bourgeois. I'm just a bloke.'

'A bloke? Being a bloke is as bourgeois as you can get.'

14

Luxembourg. One of those privileged city statelets that European history has allowed to survive amongst the big boys. Monaco, Andorra, San Marino, Liechtenstein, Luxembourg, cunning dwarfs who have succeeded in getting by in a world of giants, this one perched on rocks above a gorge. From towers, walls, bastions, bridges it regards two sweating hitchhikers with regal indifference. Lifts are few, shops are closed, businesses suspended, the Luxembourgeois are living up to their name, being both *luxe* and *bourgeois*, by going to church *en famille* and afterwards eating vast lunches that undoubtedly involve pork and potatoes. Ignored by them all, Fando and Lis climb up into the old town and find a pavement café where they dump their rucksacks and sit under a plane tree and drink beer. James unfolds the map. The German–French border, a fault line in the structure of Europe, meanders its way south from where they are. They debate the relative merits of left or right, east or west, Germany or France, Saarbrücken or Metz. It is like playing snooker, trying to think ahead, trying to judge where you should be one shot after the next. For the moment Ellie seems content as she traces the possible routes. When she is happy it is wonderful, like the sun coming out.

'Let's toss,' she suggests. 'I've always liked the idea of running your life by the toss of a coin.'

'Or a dice. Throwing a dice.'

'A die. One die, two dice.'

'Pedant. Anyway, we all die.'

'It's a good idea for a novel. Using dice to govern your life. And at the end, you die.'

'Called what?'

She thinks for a moment, frowning. '*Alea iacta est*. The Die is Cast. No, The Dice Man Cometh.'

'The Tosser,' he suggests, and wins her laughter. She is, he decides for the hundredth time, entirely lovely like that. No makeup, her hair in disorder, her features strongly shaped, giving her a look that is a fraction older than her real age. Unusual in a girl. He feels like a younger brother at times, which is not what he wants.

'Well, go on then. Toss.'

He takes a coin from his pocket, a half-crown that still lies there amongst the Belgian and Luxembourg francs he has already collected. He holds the coin poised on his curled forefinger, his thumb cocked beneath.

She stops him. 'Wait, there's another possibility.'

'What?'

'It's Sunday. Crap hitching, you said so yourself.' She looks round the little square. 'We could stay the night here.'

'Where?'

'Not in your bloody tent. A hostel perhaps, or a *pension*.'

'Heads we stay, tails we move on.' The coin rings out, flickering in the sunshine, and comes up heads.

The *auberge de jeunesse* is in the ditch below the city ramparts, down by the river, with a railway viaduct looming over the roofs. It's an ancient, dank building that might once have been a factory of some kind. 'Looks like one of the Yorkshire mill towns,' James decides, which pleases Ellie. She seems to derive a certain satisfaction at the idea of living amongst the proletariat. But the only proletarians here are the transient occupants of the hostel, a disparate collection of Americans, Australians, New Zealanders, leavened with German, French and Dutch. Everyone smiles naively across the various language divides, exchanging mispronounced words of greeting but little else. Banality is the order of the day. 'This town is so *old*,' one of the Americans exclaims. 'And amazing. I mean, who's heard of *Luxembourg*? And here it is – walls and towers and stuff, and real cute.'

Ellie becomes a focus of attention and James feels angry at the loss of her, annoyed that she has enthusiastically embraced this kind of communal living, even laughing and agreeing with the American about the age and cuteness of the town. She flirts with an Australian youth who wants to know all about Paris, argues with another American – or is he Canadian? – who is insisting that de Gaulle is once again the saviour of France. And he understands, with a sudden shock, that she might just as well decide to go off with someone else to somewhere else; that there is little keeping the two of them together. At least Lis had been bound to Fando by bonds of dependence.

That evening they eat an impoverished meal with a dozen others in the gloomy refectory. The talk is all the Vietnam War and the approaching American election and what a shit LBJ is but thank God he's going and how two of the Americans are evading the draft. Afterwards someone produces a guitar. That was the curse of those days – someone always had a guitar and the ability to strum a few chords and all of a sudden it ain't me babe and we're no longer thinking twice about whether there's any real talent because it's all right. At eleven o'clock an argument breaks out with the warden over whether too much noise is being made, and the group breaks up. Ellie goes outside with the Australian. James follows.

'A smoke,' she says, seeing accusation in his face. 'That's all.'

The Australian grins. His name is Declan. 'Hey,' he says, 'I don't want to get in anybody's way.' He has blond hair and scorched skin. James can imagine him at a Pacific beach, surfing or wrestling sharks or something else requiring much muscle and little brain.

'It's just James,' Ellie tells him. She has her Gold Flake tin open and is rolling a cigarette with great concentration. 'You're not in his way.'

'Aren't you two together?'

'That's right, we aren't together. Just friends.' She strikes a match, lights the cigarette and blows smoke away as though dismissing the very idea of friendship.

'For fuck's sake.'

'Hey, don't get riled, mate.'

There is a moment when James considers staying and arguing, with Ellie, not with the Australian. But he knows it would be pointless. Ellie is best left alone when she is in this kind of mood, so he just turns away and goes off to the men's dormitory to sleep on a top bunk and wonder what she is doing apart from flirting with the Australian and smoking her home-rolled ciggies.

He drifts off into a disturbed sleep. Trains rattle overhead throughout the night. In the men's dormitory, lying in racks like overgrown fruit, they groan and complain in their sleep. A couple – is the female voice Ellie's? The sound is too indistinct to identify – argue for hours in the street outside the hostel. Morning leaks light through veils of grey cloud and James feels he hasn't slept more than an hour or two.

'You look like death warmed up,' she remarks. She herself is bright with energy, her eyes glistening, her mouth, that could be so sullen, drawn into that summer morning of a smile. Is it the presence of the Australian in her life?

'Where is he?'

'Who?'

'Declan.'

'Oh, him.' She grimaces. 'As thick as a plank. He can't understand why they don't speak English here in Luxembourg.'

'Why should they?'

'Because they do on the radio.' She pauses. 'He was, my dear, thinking of Radio Luxembourg.' She laughs and James laughs with her. That was the trick. Laughter. Whatever she finds in other men, she'll find laughter with James. And laughter is a powerful weapon to wield in the tortured world of male–female relations.

After breakfast they pack their rucksacks under the critical eyes of Declan and a couple of others. 'Where are you off to?' Declan asks.

Ellie looks up at the Australian with complete indifference. 'Don't know yet. Toss of a coin.'

'Toss of a coin? You serious?'

'How we make all our decisions.'

'Cool.'

They sling their rucksacks and straighten up, feeling like two warriors setting off into battle.

'Well, go on, then.' Declan's tone is challenging. 'Let's see you toss your fucking coin.'

'That,' Ellie says, 'has to be done in private. At the moment of choice.' Her tone is prim, as though tossing a coin involves physical intimacy. With James following, she leads the way out of the hallway of the hostel into the grey morning. He's feeling absurdly happy, warmed by her unexpected inclusion of him into her world. Coin-tossing has been elevated to a shared personal philosophy. Thus connected by tenuous bonds of familiarity and companionship, and the promised toss of a coin, Fando and Lis are still together.

*

The coin is finally spun at the roadside in the southern outskirts of the city, where signs point left to Remich and Saarbrücken and right to Thionville and Metz. It falls heads down, which means Germany and the Saarland. They walk to the left-hand fork, Ellie sticks out an arrogant little thumb and a car stops almost immediately. Spirits lift.

IV

15

Sunday lunch with Lenka and her mother. He wondered why he had agreed to the idea and what the implications were behind it, but she had seemed so pleased that he had accepted the invitation. 'She'll understand,' Lenka insisted. 'Someone from the British embassy whom I found at one of the meetings. She'll be interested.' A knowing smile. 'And she will like you, I think. Your *šarm*.'

Perhaps it was that assurance that made the whole expedition all right. He was good at 'sharm'.

Her mother lived in one of those concrete apartment blocks – *paneláky* – built on the outskirts of the city after the war, part of that halo of concrete that forms a hideous modern setting to the jewels of old Prague. Her allotted portion was a sixth-floor two-room flat with thin walls and the sound of the neighbours having a row next door. Her mother was a florid woman in her mid-forties who still showed hints of a beauty that her daughter had inherited. Kateřina Konečková was her name: 'Katherine, possession of Koneček', whoever Koneček might have been. She stained the tiny apartment with her presence, with the smell of cigarette smoke and a clinging and rosaceous perfume that she wore. When she shook Sam's hand it was with caution, as though mere contact might be dangerous. 'What are you then, a spy?' she asked, and to show it was a joke – which it wasn't – she attempted a smile. Perhaps it was his ability with the language that made her suspicious. Foreigners didn't speak Czech, not even bad Czech. They spoke Russian, maybe, or German.

'I've told you all about Sam, Maminka.' Lenka's tone was impatient. She was a child again, doting on her mother yet at the same time apprehensive, as though fearing what she might say or do and what impression she might make.

'Not a spy,' Sam assured her. 'I'm a diplomat.'

'There's a difference?'

'One tells lies and pretends they're the truth; the other just tells lies.'

The woman gave a bitter, rasping laugh. 'Which is which?' She wasn't what Sam had expected – there was more than mere shrewdness in her look, there was a sharp intelligence. 'And you expect me to feed you, do you?'

'We offered to take you out to lunch, Maminka.'

'You know it'd be dangerous to be seen with a foreigner in public. Especially one from the British embassy.'

Lenka sounded exasperated. 'I keep telling you, Maminka, things are different these days. Things have changed.'

Her mother snorted derisively. 'You have no memory, that's the trouble with the young.' She looked at Sam as though for confirmation, thus placing him squarely in the company of her generation. 'They think they can do everything now. Freedom and love and all that rubbish. What will they be saying when the Russians invade, I wonder.'

'They won't, Maminka. Dubček will come to a compromise, you'll see. We'll give a bit and get on with things as we want.'

'Dubček is no different from the others. He just smiles, that's all. What does Mr Diplomat think?'

'Mr Diplomat thinks it is time to prepare the lunch.'

She laughed, a throaty, sarcastic sound. 'Conciliation

without answering the question,' she decided. 'Typical of his kind.'

In one corner of the living room was a kitchen area where they unloaded the bag they had brought. A large tin of shin of pork. Cabbage, potatoes. Two bottles of a Nuits Saint-Georges. Her mother watched with wonder as they stacked the things on the narrow shelf beside the cooker. 'Where the hell have you been?' she asked. 'Tuzex?'

'We can get things through the embassy,' Sam said.

'We?'

'I can.' Sam was adept at sensing mood. Picking up vibrations, Stephanie would have said. He could sense vibrations from Lenka's mother now – vibrations both good and bad. Jealousy and envy on the one side and the faint bat-squeak of curiosity on the other. The way she looked at him. What, he wondered, did she know about Lenka's previous adventures? And where – because Lenka had said nothing about her father – where was Mr Koneček?

'So you are not an optimist?' he asked, once the pork was in the oven and they had opened one of the bottles of wine. 'About what will happen to the country, I mean.'

They were sitting on upright chairs round the narrow dining table. The older woman smoked and drank and considered him with something that resembled contempt. 'I know what happens to idealists. People like Lenka. They are just as their parents were twenty years ago. Just like I was.'

'You were?'

'Oh, yes. Twenty years ago I believed. I was a Party member just like my husband. A true believer. When they arrested Milada Horáková I believed she was guilty. When she was on trial, I even signed a petition calling for her execution. When they executed her, I cheered.'

He knew about Horáková, of course. You couldn't read up about the country, as he had for the six months he was on

113

the Czechoslovak desk in London, without knowing. Milada Horáková. One of the emblematic figures of twentieth-century *Mitteleuropa*, encompassing in her life all of the tragedies of that time and that place.

'And then?'

The woman looked at him with cold eyes. 'And then they came for us.'

Horáková

It's difficult to know where to begin with the story of Milada Horáková, but not difficult to know where to end: on a rope in the Pankrác prison in Prague on 27 June 1950 at five thirty-five in the morning. She was just forty-eight years old.

How do you measure heroism? How do you describe it?

Before the Second World War, in those distant, heady days of Czechoslovak liberal democracy, Horáková was a mother and a wife, a prominent member of the Czech Socialist Party, an active lawyer and a powerful advocate of women's rights. After the Munich Agreement and the subsequent annexation of the Czech lands by Hitler's Germany, she became a member of the Czech resistance. Along with her husband, she was arrested by the Gestapo in 1940 and eventually imprisoned in Theresienstadt concentration camp. Later she was moved to various German prisons and eventually came to trial before a German court in Dresden. She was found guilty and condemned to death. This sentence was subsequently commuted to life imprisonment and she was moved to the women's prison in Aichach in Bavaria from where she was freed by American forces in 1945.

Is that enough?

The thing about Milada Horáková is that she never gave up. After her liberation she returned to Prague, to her husband who had also survived imprisonment, and their daughter, who, in the absence of her parents, had been looked after by relatives. Immediately Horáková rejoined the Socialist Party and was elected to the Czech National Assembly. She argued, as she had always argued, for freedom, for women's rights, for decency.

Once the Communist Party grabbed the reins of power in 1948, Horáková was forced to resign her seat in the national assembly. Nevertheless she refused to be silenced. An outspoken advocate for freedom and democracy, she remained a thorn in the side of the leadership. On 27 September 1949 she was arrested by the secret police once again, only this time it was the Communist StB (State Security) rather than the Gestapo. Along with a dozen other friends and associates she was subjected to the first of the communist regime's show trials, facing the charge of being part of a counter-revolutionary conspiracy to overthrow the new government. She was offered clemency if she signed a confession of guilt, but she refused. During the public trial, while the other accused read out confessions that had been prepared for them by the prosecution, Milada Horáková refused to admit any guilt and spoke out for the truth. She, along with three others, was condemned to death.

Is that enough? The measurement of heroism is so difficult that sometimes we find ourselves gainsaying it. Even Milada Horáková herself wondered about what she had done, writing in the very last letter from prison to her daughter:

one day, when you grow up, you will wonder why your
mother, who loved you and treasured you, managed
her life so strangely. Perhaps then you will find the right
answer to this question, perhaps a better one than I
myself could give you today.

It was after she wrote that letter that they took her out and hanged her from a hook in the ceiling. There was no drop.

According to the official report, Milada Horáková took fifteen minutes to die, by strangulation, hanging on the end of the rope.

Is that enough?

It's not a competition, is it? But by any standards Milada Horáková must rate as one of the greatest heroes of the twentieth century.

16

Lenka's mother opened a drawer in the table and took out a photograph, a snapshot of a young couple sitting on a rock. The pair were wearing hiking boots. The woman – a version of herself, an earlier, happy, clear, vivid version (a version, too, of Lenka) – was laughing at the camera, but the man was doing nothing more than smile, a little ironically, as though he already knew there was little to be amused by.

'There we are, in our Marxist-Leninist dawn,' the woman said. 'Weren't we beautiful? We saw the future as something wonderful to imagine. Certainly not this.'

'This' meant the narrow, two-room apartment with thin walls and grey plaster, and the sensation of being in some kind of concrete storage tank. 'This' meant Horáková dead. 'This' meant Soviet troops on Czech soil and a summons from Moscow to the Czech leadership to attend an emergency meeting at a railway junction on the border of the Soviet Union. 'This' meant her whole world. She replaced the photo with care.

'So what happened?' Sam dared to ask.

The woman drew on her cigarette, considering him through the smoke. 'Do you know about Slánský?'

The name sounded like a cymbal struck. Of course he knew about Slánský. He knew about Horáková; he knew about Slánský. Slánský was a Party hack, the kind of man to dismiss bourgeois freedoms with a derisive sweep of the hand, the architect of the communist coup of 1948 and, thereby, the man who became the right hand of the Party leader, Klement Gottwald.

'The Party was like a monster,' the woman said. 'First it consumed its enemies – Horáková and her kind – and then it turned on its own members. What was the name of the Greek god who devoured his own children?'

'Cronus.'

'That's right. So, like Cronus, the Party devoured its own children, Slánský, Clementis and the others. How many in all? Fifteen, sixteen? Espionage on behalf of Western capitalist powers, counter-revolution, all kinds of trumped-up charges. What do they call it? *Show* trial. Like something you might put on in the theatre. That's what it was, the theatre of the absurd.'

She nodded in Lenka's direction. 'She was only a baby. She remembers nothing about it. Have you heard of Margolius? Rudolf Margolius?'

Was she testing him, seeing how much he knew and therefore how much he was worth? 'He was a Czech trade representative,' Sam said, 'dealing with Western countries.'

The woman nodded, drawing on her cigarette as though sucking in courage. 'Well, Rudolf Margolius worked with my husband. They were part of the Czechoslovak delegation in London, trying to set up trade deals that would benefit the country. Trying to earn hard currency for the country, that's what they were doing. The ministry of foreign trade. And that was why they were arrested, along with Slánský and the rest. They'd been abroad, so they must be guilty.'

She talked some more, eager to explain to someone who would listen. Her husband was a clever man, too clever for his own good. If you were stupid then you got on. You did what you were told and nothing more. Don't show any initiative,

119

don't show any imagination, above all, don't show any intelligence. That was the way to progress. It's not much different now. 'He negotiated with Harold Wilson,' she added. 'Do you know Mr Harold Wilson?'

Sam tried a smile. 'Not personally. He's a little above my grade.'

The woman didn't smile back. Instead she made a face, as though she had eaten something distasteful. 'My husband didn't say much about his work but he told me about this man, Wilson. So when my husband was in prison, I wrote to Wilson for some kind of help. It seems futile, doesn't it? But what else could I do? I was helpless, powerless, just an irrelevance as far as the Party was concerned. My husband was on trial for his life but I could go fuck.'

'Maminka!'

She waved Lenka's protest away. 'I thought, maybe this Wilson can help. Does that sound crazy? But I was crazy. I wasn't allowed even to visit my husband in prison. Just one letter a month, and nothing in it about what was happening to him. So I thought about what Lukáš had told me about his visits to London and I got this Wilson's title exact so that the letter would reach the correct person: President of the Board of Trade, that was it.' She said the title in some kind of English and looked at Sam for approval, to see if she had got it right.

He nodded.

'I wrote the letter myself and had a friend translate it into English. I begged this Wilson for help, asked him to write and explain to the judge that my husband was an honourable man who never did anything other than try to get the very best for his country in the negotiations. And surely, being a fellow socialist, this Wilson would be able to confirm that this was so. Wilson is a socialist, isn't he?'

'Of a kind.'

'So, a kind of socialist. A bourgeois, Western socialist. I got someone to smuggle the letter out of the country because you couldn't just put something like that in the post.'

'And what happened?'

She gave a wry smile, as though disappointment was only to be expected. 'Nothing happened. I never heard from him.'

Sam felt a moment of shame. 'Wilson should have replied. Something. Anything.'

'But he didn't. And now he is your prime minister.' She got up and went over to the cooker to check the food in the oven, talking all the time. Perhaps it was a sign of the liberalisation in the country that she felt she could tell the story. 'They were Jews, you know that? Most of them were Jews.' The Czech word *židi* rang round the room. 'My husband's parents were Jews but he was an atheist, a communist, a good communist. But they treated him like a traitor and a Jew.'

'Mother, please,' said Lenka. 'This was meant to be a happy occasion. Sunday lunch. A family thing.'

'We have no family,' her mother snapped. 'Two people isn't a family, it's just survivors clinging to the wreckage.' The oven door slammed shut. Sam tried to step around the obstacle that lay in the path of further discourse. 'Weren't they all' – he struggled for the correct word – 'made good in 1963?' That was all he could manage: exonerated, absolved, acquitted, exculpated. All words beyond Sam's vocabulary in Czech.

Kateřina laughed. It was the kind of laugh you heard often enough in Prague, the laughter of contempt and resignation. 'What good was that to me? By then he was ten years dead.'

Lenka was still holding the snapshot of the couple sitting on a rock. Perhaps to her the world of that snapshot seemed too far away, another time in another country of which she knew nothing. Perhaps that faintly smiling figure who had been her father was a creature of myth. Yet for an adult, for her mother, it was a mere sixteen years.

'He doesn't even have a grave, do you know that? I don't know what they did with his body. They just told me of his death by letter. It took me a year even to get an official death certificate. And now—'

'Now?'

'A few months ago they sent me a medal, his medal. The Order of the Republic.' She made a sound that was halfway between a laugh and a cry. 'And now they say they want to give me compensation. But I don't want their medals or their money. I want my husband back.'

That was the moment when Sam feared she might weep. But she didn't. There was something hard and dry about her face, as though the tears had long since drained away like water through the limestone of the Moravian karst.

'I not only lost him, I even had to lose his name. He was Vadinský, Lukáš Vadinský. I was Kateřina Vadinská. But someone, a friend, advised me to go back to my unmarried name, so that was what I did. Konečková.' She smiled bitterly. 'Another betrayal.'

'It's the past, Maminka,' Lenka said. 'Things have already changed. And they are changing still.'

Her mother ignored her words. She began to lay the table with ill-matched plates, cutlery that you might find in a cheap café, a cruet set of Bohemian cut glass, two stemmed wine glasses and a tumbler. She shook her head. 'The past,' she said, 'is all we have. It just repeats itself.'

'She liked you,' Lenka said.

They were outside, walking between the *paneláky*. There was a Sunday sense of lassitude about the place. Kids were kicking a football around on a worn scrap of grass, but that was the only real activity. A bench of four old men argued about something. No doubt their wives were at home washing dishes.

'I thought she was cleverer than that,' Sam said.

His car was parked round the corner, next to a Trabant and a row of chained bicycles. Someone had written *Umyj mne*, wash me, in the dust of the rear window. One of the kids, no doubt. They drove away, avoiding the footballers.

'Your mother is quite a force,' he said, but Lenka felt the need to apologise on her behalf. 'She shouldn't have talked like that, she said. 'She should keep private matters private.'

'She needed to talk,' Sam said. 'She's a brave woman.'

The girl was silent. He knew she was looking at him. Those eyes that were the most intense cerulean blue. He wondered what she was thinking, whether she was measuring him up for something. If so, what?

17

He took an afternoon off and they went swimming. They decided on a place out of the city, on the river where Sam had been with Steffie once or twice. He hadn't told Lenka that bit. A place he knew, that was all he told her. She'd like it.

So they packed picnic things in his Mercedes and set off, and it wasn't long before he spotted the car following. In the last few months this sort of thing had grown rarer, as though even the security services had been tainted by the infection of liberalisation, but there it was, plain enough, an anonymous Škoda on his tail, like a faithful dog tagging after them, turning where they turned, slowing when they slowed, remaining all the time about one hundred metres behind. They made their way south of the city and after a while took a rough road that led amongst wooded hills close to the river's edge where you could park the car easily enough. The Škoda didn't appear. Perhaps it was waiting somewhere out of sight, knowing that there was no other way out.

He turned the engine off. Silence rushed into the enclosed world of the Mercedes. 'How's this?'

Lenka's expansive smile, a gleam of naked gum. 'It's lovely.' He felt that torrent of desire and affection, a dangerous complex of emotion over which he had no control. He leant towards her and kissed her, tasting the cigarette she had been smoking and the coffee she had drunk earlier, as though kissing her was to snatch a small part of her quotidian life and make it his as well.

They got out of the car and took their things from the boot. Not far away was a settlement of those small wooden cabins that Czechs use as country retreats – *chaty*. They were like beach huts on the English coast: the same clapboard constructions in vivid primary colours, the same defiant sense of pride. But these didn't have uniformity. They might be put together out of anything: offcuts from a timber yard, corrugated iron, tarpaper, panels from an ancient car, barrels from a brewery. An old man watched from his garden as they carried their picnic things down through the trees to the water's edge. The air was hot and still. The water flowed over stones and around spits of gravel with Smetana's scurrying rhythms. Things moved in the woods that bordered the space. Birds sang. An egret, sinuous and chalk white, stood in the water on the far side, keeping one cautious eye on the intruders.

Sam took up his camera and snapped some photos: Lenka tossing her hair, Lenka holding up a hand to keep the camera off her face, Lenka smiling, Lenka frowning. 'I will swim,' she declared in that matter-of-fact tone she adopted when speaking English, as though everything were a statement of fact and the subjunctive never existed. 'And no photos.' She shook loose her hair, pulled her dress over her head and dropped it at her feet. When he'd been here before, Stephanie had struggled beneath her towel and finally emerged in a modest one-piece bathing costume. Lenka was made of sterner stuff. As unconcerned as if she were in the bathroom at home, she tossed her brassiere aside, stepped out of her underpants and stood for a moment contemplating the river. There was something hieratic about her narrow, pale body, like a figure from Slavic myth, a *rusalka*. He'd seen the opera with Steffie the previous autumn at the National Theatre with Milada Šubrtová playing the title role of the water nymph who falls in love with a human. It's the age-old problem of a demigod getting tied up with a mortal, and you know it's never going to work, however eloquently Rusalka may appeal to the moon.

Sam took up the camera again, quietly, so as not to disturb his prey. If he thought of their escort, he didn't really care. The dirty buggers could peer at her through the trees with binoculars if that pleased them. Play with themselves if they liked. He'd not mentioned their presence to Lenka because he didn't want to spoil the day. The camera shutter gave its little secretive clap of satisfaction. Apparently indifferent either to the camera or to anyone else who might have been watching, Lenka the water nymph stepped forward onto the pebbles, then on into the flow. The camera snatched at successive images. The water rose from ankle to calf, to thigh, over her pale buttocks and up to her waist, as though she were being assumed back into her natural element. The egret stretched its legs and flew away. Sunlight glittered on the water all around. Finally Lenka launched herself into the stream, her hair floating free on the surface like weed.

'You aren't coming in,' she called back. Was it a question or a statement of fact? He hid the camera away, stripped off hurriedly and joined her in the water, conscious of his own bony, angular masculinity that seemed only graceless and maladroit beside her loveliness. She laughed and splashed. White masses wobbled and shimmered beneath the surface. He felt cool flesh and rough hair and wet lips and suddenly, drifting in the current, they were doing, more or less, what they had done before only in the cloistered privacy of his bedroom – a bohemian act in the middle of rural Bohemia, surrounded by her woods and fields, enveloped by the waters of the Vltava. Rusalka.

'You are not ashamed, are you?' she asked when, quite suddenly, it was all over.

'Rather overwhelmed,' he admitted.

'Don't worry, you will not drown.'

Later they towelled themselves dry and lay in the sun. A breeze had got up to bring some kind of cool to the day. They ate sandwiches and drank beer and talked, and when they'd finished eating she lit a cigarette, one of the American ones he had given her, blew smoke away into the warm air and asked about Štěpánka. She called her Štěpánka, not Steffie or Stephanie. Štěpánka, as though Lenka were subsuming her into the Slav world.

'Why do you want to know?'

'I want to understand.' A knowing smile. 'She is perhaps competition.'

He reached out and took the cigarette from her mouth. He could feel the dampness of her saliva on the tip as he put it to his lips. 'She works for the foreign service. I told you that. Not a diplomat. A secretary. And she's just gone back to England. Posted. Our relationship is on hold, do you understand? Paused. A cooling-off period.'

'Was it hot before?'

'Lukewarm.'

She didn't know the word. He explained – tepid, between hot and cold – and she lighted on the Czech word with delight: '*Vlašný*! So is Štěpánka a beautiful, *vlašnou* English rose?'

'I suppose she is.'

'And are you going to get married?'

'We've talked about it.'

'Diplomatically?'

'Very diplomatically.'

She laughed at the possibility of Sam contemplating marriage to this lukewarm English rose. 'That means you have made no decision. Diplomats never make decisions, do they? They always refer back to their masters.'

'But this time—'

'There is no master. And you cannot make up your mind. Of course she is not your first girl. There have been many others. So by now you should know.'

He laughed. She had a wonderful capacity for making him laugh. Whether this was intentional on her part he wasn't sure.

'So tell me about these other girls who have made you so without decision.'

'*All* of them?'

'Will it take too long? The first, then. Tell me about the first.'

So he told her. A brief outline of part of the story: a friend of his mother's, older than he by some years. Ten, twelve years, maybe. A brief, chaotic affair that lost him his virginity and gave him, what? some kind of understanding of what devotion might be. Love? He wasn't sure. 'It was just before I went to university. She made a great impression on me.'

'And what happened to her?'

'We ... lost touch. She went away. Abroad.' He shrugged off that part of his life that had meant so much at the time and was now consigned to the scrapheap of memory. 'Now you tell me,' he said, as though it were a game. Confessions, a kind of Chinese whispers, the message being passed from one to another and mangled in the process. 'Now it's your turn.'

She took the cigarette back. 'You remember what Zdeněk said that evening?'

'Zdeněk?'

'Jitka's husband. The composer. He said that here no one can live very long and still believe in reality. It is true. You have to remember it. Perhaps now for the first time we are beginning to live reality. It is like waking up from a bad dream. Suddenly all those things that were impossible during the bad dream become possible. We can say what we like, go places

128

that we want, we can even try to forget the bad dream. If the Russians come with their guns and their tanks, then we will go back to the bad dream again and reality will disappear, but for the moment ...'

She paused, smoking, looking away across the river to the woods on the far side. Of course he wondered what she was thinking, but there was something inscrutable about her expression that made reading her difficult. After a while she seemed to make up her mind. 'So, in the dream – the bad dream – there was a party official, *aparátník*, my mother knew. I think he had known my father. Anyway, he was my mother's friend. The usual thing: she gave him what he wanted, he used his influence on our behalf. What do the Americans say? A deal. I used to go to play with friends when he came to call. "Good day, Comrade Rovnák. What a shame, I was just going out." That kind of thing. It was through him that we were allowed back to Prague.'

'Allowed back?'

'That is another part of the bad dream. After my father's conviction we were not allowed to live in Prague. So we lived in Pardubice, and this *aparátník*, he found her a better job, back in the city. Cleaning an office rather than cleaning the streets. His office, in fact. And he got us the flat. Actually, I think she quite liked him. Of course he had a wife and children, but she was on her own and there he was, a man who would look after her a bit. Comforting, I guess.' She stubbed out the cigarette on a stone. 'And then he turned his attention to me. I was fifteen. He waited, you see. Until I was old enough.'

'*Fifteen?*'

'That is the age here. But the thing was, I wanted him. I think ... oh, I don't know. Jealousy, perhaps. I was jealous of my mother. She had her man and I wanted him. The funny thing was, like my mother said about herself, he was a believer. He believed in *socialismus*, the path towards a communist heaven. Often he would tell me about his family, his wife and his two children, what a good socialist mother she was, how excellent the children were in the Pioneers. You must be like that, Lenička, he would say to me. You must be dutiful and loyal to the Party. This is when we were in bed, after we had fucked.'

Sam thought of the SIS man called Harold Saumarez, with his access to secret records, his collection of sins and deceptions and betrayals. 'And what happened?'

She looked round at Sam with a little smile. 'One day he told me that he was very bad, that we shouldn't be doing what we were doing, that he couldn't betray his wife any longer and he would have to stop seeing me. I was heartbroken and he was heartbroken. I think someone had got to know. The StB, who knows? People are always watching and whispering. Anyway, he promised me that he loved me and that he would see that I could get a place at university – because otherwise, because of my father, as Lenka Vadinská, I was banned. And he did all that.' She gave a little laugh. 'You see how good and bad can be mixed up together? Was he good or was he bad? I never managed to work it out, and it worried me until I decided that there is no good or bad, there is just what hurts people and what doesn't hurt people. He didn't hurt his wife because she didn't know about me. He hurt me but only a little because I was young and could learn from my experience. And he didn't really hurt my mother because she was happy enough to let me take over. And he got me into university.'

'Doesn't that make him quite good?'

She made a face. 'You see, you use that word. Good. It is very bourgeois. He didn't hurt too much, that is what I think. You are always going to hurt a bit, someone. Maybe you will hurt Štěpánka, maybe she will hurt you. Just make it a little hurt if you can.'

'And what about me and you? Will we hurt each other?'

There was a silence, not the dreadful silence of the safe room at the heart of the embassy, which had the kind of artificial silence that seems to suck the hearing out of your ears, but instead one of those country silences that is never quiet, filled as it is with birdsong and bee sound and the scurrying of animals and water. 'I don't think I am easy to hurt,' she said.

Reluctantly they carried their things back to the car. Contrary to popular rumour, paradise is finite. The old man who had watched them arrive was no longer to be seen. The wooden huts were closed and locked. The slamming of the car boot seemed a hideous intrusion on the quiet of the afternoon. He started the engine and they drove further along the track, just to see where it led, that was the idea. And to try and shake off the mood of anonymous threat that had descended on the afternoon. But after a mile or so through birch woods the way forward was blocked by a military vehicle, an armoured car of some kind, the colour of mud, ugly as all such vehicles are.

Sam brought the car to a halt. 'What the hell's this?' He reached beneath his seat for the camera.

'What are you doing?' There was an edge in Lenka's voice that he had not heard before. As though it were fractured and might fall to pieces at any moment.

'A photo, before anyone appears.'

'You are a spy!'

'Just my job. Any opportunity.' The vehicle sat there dumbly, like a prizefighter asleep. It was four-wheeled, with a boat-shaped hull and sloping superstructure capped with a machine gun. He propped the camera on the dashboard and snapped a frame, wound the film on and took another shot. Then another.

'What is it?'

'Czechoslovak army? Who knows? No markings.' He

131

pushed the camera under his seat and began to edge the car forward.

It was at that moment that a soldier appeared from behind the vehicle. He wore khaki trousers and a striped sweatshirt of the kind that French fishermen wear in comic films. There were no distinguishing marks of any kind on his clothing, no rank badges, no insignia; and nothing comic. Sam wound down the window and leant out. 'We want to go through.'

The man stood and watched, as though he hadn't understood. Beyond the vehicle other soldiers could be seen. Some of them carried weapons. They'd been doing something in the shallows of the river. Just visible through the trees was an inflatable boat with an outboard engine.

Sam climbed out of the car.

'*Stůj*!' the soldier called. Halt!

Sam smiled uncomprehendingly, walking towards the soldier with his hands outspread and talking a mixture of Czech and English and ignoring Lenka calling out from inside the car, calling for him to come back. 'We just want to go swimming, you see? Me and my friend. *Plavání. Plavání.*' He even made the gesture of the breaststroke, just to make things clearer.

There was panic in the soldier's eyes. He called something over his shoulder. Sam could make out the words 'Comrade Lieutenant.' And then he understood what he had really heard – not the Czech *Stůj*! but the Russian *stoy*! Not the Czech *soudruh* but the Russian *tovarich*. An officer appeared from behind the armoured car. He was wearing a shirt with rank badges that Sam recognised as Czech. His face was wooden, the face of authority, prepared, under any circumstances, to deny whatever was being requested. 'You can't come past,' he said in Czech. 'Military zone.'

Sam the idiot looked blank. '*Nemluvím Cesky*,' he said. '*Promiňte.*' And then, in English, making sweeping gestures with his arms. 'I've been here before, with my girlfriend. Swimming.'

The man frowned. '*Anglicky?*'

'Yes, *Anglicky*. Diplomat.' He pointed back to the car. 'You see? Diplomatic plates. *Diplomatická*. CD.'

The lieutenant snapped his fingers beneath Sam's nose. '*Dokumenty.*'

There was a suspicious examination of passport and diplomatic pass, as though all such things were forgeries. '*Pojď*,' he said.

Sam glanced back to the car, at Lenka's anxious face peering through the windscreen. He gave a little sign of confidence – a grin, a brief thumbs-up. Then he was following the officer round the back of the vehicle where a sweaty soldier was crouched over a radio transmitter and another man – small, malevolent – sat reading a typed report. He wore khaki uniform but, again, without distinguishing marks. His battledress was tightly buttoned despite the heat. There was a brief exchange of words between him and the lieutenant, of which Sam was the subject. His papers were examined once again, with similar disdain.

'You English?' the malevolent man asked, in English.

'Yes,' Sam said. He smiled benevolently. This he enjoyed. He felt the cast-iron protection that his diplomatic status gave him, spiced with a hint of risk, a shiver of apprehension. His only real worry was Lenka, sitting anxiously in the car, with no diplomatic insurance and only the flimsy protection of association with himself. But what he knew now made any risk – surely small enough – worthwhile. 'I'm here with my girlfriend. We were going swimming. If you like you can ring the British embassy. Or the ministry of foreign affairs. They will confirm my accreditation.'

Malevolent seemed to find this amusing. 'You have no business swimming here, Mr Diplomat,' he said, and Sam recognised the accent, from long days spent at the language school in Cambridge. Not only the words but the intonation, the cadence, the timbre. It was part of his psyche. Russian.

'Well, maybe we should go somewhere else.'

'Maybe you should.' The man thought for a moment, then looked past Sam to the lieutenant. 'Bring the girl.'

'Hey, that's not necessary—'

Malevolent raised his hand to silence him. The soldier went and a few moments later a car door slammed and the sound of Lenka's voice was raised in some kind of protest. Protest had become a new habit amongst her generation. They felt they ruled the streets and the meetings. They could answer the police back, snap at officials, demand rights they never even knew existed. She came round the corner of the vehicle flushed with anger. Anger and fear, a dangerous combination. Sam gestured her to be quiet but it was Malevolent who achieved that. 'Shut up!' he demanded, and she did exactly that, startled by his peremptory command: *Sklapni*! The lieutenant took her papers and glanced at them. 'Student,' he told Malevolent, as though that explained everything. He passed the evidence over.

Sam took her hand, willing her to be silent, pulling her close to give her some kind of comfort. Her hand was damp with sweat. He seemed to feel her fear, crawling beneath his skin like the scurrying of insects.

'And at the moment Miss Konečková is studying English, is she, Mr Diplomat?' Malevolent said.

'I help her with her English, yes. And she helps me with my Czech.'

'I'm sure she does. And with your swimming.'

'And with my swimming.'

'Once upon a time a comrade had to report any contact made with a foreigner, you know that?'

'Things have changed now.'

134

'Yes, they have.' He seemed to consider the changes, for good or for ill. Finally he handed Sam's documents back. 'But some things do not change. This is an exercise of the Czechoslovak People's Army and you may not pass. I suggest you go home now how you came, to good cuppa of English tea. You are lucky – understand this clearly – you are lucky I do not arrest you for spying.'

Sam nodded, as though the point was fair. He turned to Lenka. He could see sweat glistening on her brow, beads of moisture on her upper lip, trapped in the faint blonde down. 'We'd better go.'

'My papers,' she said.

There was a moment of stasis. Malevolent pondered the matter, tapping Lenka's identity card in the palm of his hand and looking at the girl. You could see the conflict in his expression – he knew his power over her and his weakness in the face of Sam's diplomatic status. The radio jabbered something and the operator hastily put his earphones on. Finally Malevolent nodded, passed Lenka's identity card to the lieutenant, who dutifully handed it back. 'Comrade Konečková should think herself lucky,' the lieutenant said.

She was about to reply. She was about to explode with anger at being talked to like that. Sam took her arm. 'Discretion,' he murmured, 'is the better part of valour.'

'What?'

'It doesn't matter. Just walk away.'

Holding her tightly he measured their steps round the armoured car and over to the Mercedes. Sam held the passenger door open for her. By the time he got round to the other side, her anger had abated, along with her fear. He started the engine and screwed round to back the car up the track. 'I thought they would arrest us,' she said quietly.

'They don't arrest diplomats. Not unless they want to cause an international incident.'

135

'Me, then. Why didn't you just turn away right at the start?'

'Because I wanted to see for sure.'

'See what? That soldiers are shits? That if you put a reasonable man in uniform he turns into an ape?'

They reached an opening off the track where he could turn the car. 'Didn't you notice?'

'Notice what?'

'They're Russian.'

'*Russian?*'

'You heard what I said. They're Russian. There's that Czech officer as a front man but the others were Russian. No insignia on their uniforms, nothing. A Red Army reconnaissance unit of some kind. That guy spoke near-perfect English, but his accent was Russian. Whoever heard of a middle-ranking Russian officer speaking English? He's GRU.'

'What's GRU?'

'Soviet military intelligence.' They drove on in silence, bumping over the rough track the way they had come, before turning onto the tarmac road. 'Where are we going?' Lenka asked.

'Back home.'

'Why?'

'Got to see a man about a dog.' He attempted to render it in Czech but met, as he expected, only bewilderment.

'A dog?'

'It's an English saying. Rather old-fashioned. Means I don't want to talk about it.'

'It's about the Russians, isn't it?' And she nodded an answer to her own question. 'It's always the fucking Russians.'

Back in his flat he offered her some records to play. Steffie's *Sergeant Pepper* or something by the Incredible String Band. He wasn't really sure of her taste. Janáček, if that was what she wanted. Or anything from the small collection of classics that he had. Mozart, surely she'd be happy with Mozart. There was the Prague Symphony, or was that too obvious? Then he shut himself in the bathroom to develop the film. It didn't take long. He was practised at fiddling around in the changing bag, rolling the film onto the spiral by feel, before shutting it away in the developing tank secure from the deadly intrusion of light. Then the solutions, that little bit of alchemy that always fascinated him – developer, fixer, wash, each carefully measured and warmed to 20°C, each procedure timed with the clock brought in from the kitchen. It was the chemistry he had missed out on at school, a few simple chemicals turning blank acetate into tiny negative shadows of past moments: light rendered dark, black painted white. From the sitting room came silence as Lenka changed a record before the blaring trumpets of Janáček's *Sinfonietta* broke the peace. He waited while the brass sounded and the clock ticked out the seconds and the developing solutions performed their magic. When the time was up he extracted the film from the tank, unwound it from the spool and hung it over the bath just as Steffie had once hung knickers and stockings. A plastic squeegee took the wash away. He held up the film to the light and examined the negative images: Lenka sitting on the rug; Lenka smoking and laughing; Lenka frowning; Lenka standing naked in the river, white trees in the background, her flesh dark, her buttocks almost black. If you caught the negative at the right angle to the light, you could achieve the small miracle of glimpsing it in reverse, in positive, just as it would be when printed. A ghostly effect that vanished as soon as you changed the angle. He'd print them when he had time, but for the moment he took scissors and cut off the last three frames. These were not for private contemplation. Not for his memories.

'A stroll in the garden, Harold,' he suggested on the phone. 'Got something that might amuse you.'

*

In the embassy garden, surrounded by the bushes and the trees, Sam passed over the small fragments of film. 'Some more pictures for you, Harold. Developed it myself this time, but no time to print.'

Harold didn't deign to look at the negatives, merely sequestered them in his pocket. 'What do they show?'

'Nothing particularly exciting, I'm afraid. Not like the Sukhoi I got for you last year. Just an armoured car. But here's the thing – it's got no markings and neither had the crew. No unit insignia, no rank badges, nothing. They were trying their best to be Czech, even had a Czechoslovak liaison officer with them. But they were Russian. GRU, I guess. Special forces reconnaissance team. What are they called? Spetsnaz.'

'Where was this?'

'Upriver from here.' He gave the place. He could show him on the map if necessary. 'They're *here*, Harold. Little more than half an hour's drive away. A nasty bugger speaking almost perfect English—'

'You *spoke* with them?'

'Of course I did. I'm a diplomat. Diplomats speak to people. It's what we're good at – in fact it's almost the only thing we're good at. And all they saw was a bumbling dip, out for a bit of hokey-pokey with his Czech girlfriend.'

'That was your cover?'

'Hardly cover, old chap. The plain and simple truth. By the way, quite unprompted she told me everything about her dalliance with the minister. More innocent victim than Mata Hari. You can rule her out as an agent.'

Harold made a small grunt of scepticism. In the bushes the dog crouched in that strained and slightly self-conscious way they have when relieving themselves. 'That's H.E.'s dog, you know that?' he said. 'Surely they shouldn't let it shit in the embassy gardens.'

'If he's the ambassador's dog, I presume he can shit wherever he pleases.'

Harold sniffed disapprovingly. 'These Russians. How can you be sure?'

'I'm a Russian specialist. You know that. I know my Tolstoy from my Turgenev, and I certainly know a Russian *stoy* from a Czech *Stůj*.'

'The whole country has been crawling with Red Army. Those so-called spring manoeuvres. Why should your encounter be anything special?'

'Precisely because the last Soviet units were meant to have returned to base by now. Wasn't that part of the agreement at Čierna nad Tisou? And because they were pretending not to be Russians. As I said: no unit badges, no insignia, with a Czechoslovak liaison officer positively flaunting his. And the fellow in charge, the fellow I spoke to. Excellent English. You tell me what the chances are of finding a random Russian officer who happens to speak good English. Zero. So, GRU. '

The secretary appeared, calling for the dog. 'Come on, Rumpus.' The dog came, but only because she was holding out a treat for him. As she led the animal away towards the embassy building, she waved at Sam. 'Have you heard from Steffie?'

'A few days ago.'

'That's good. We had a postcard from somewhere in West Germany and Angela got one from Henley or wherever she is. But nothing more. Give her my love when you write.'

'Of course I will.'

A curious concept: love as an asset to be packaged in an envelope and passed on to a third party. Linda sends her love, even though she lets the ambassador's dog crap in the flowerbeds.

But does Sam also send his?

'Write it up,' Harold told him. 'For my eyes only. Everything that happened – it's all grist to the mill. Shame you didn't get more photos.'

'Someone,' Dorothy said when Sam got back to the office, 'has got to do a bag run.' She looked up at him over her spectacles, as though he might be able to organise such a thing even if her boss couldn't. 'There's all this stuff to go.'

'Nuremberg?'

'Munich. The consulate-general.'

'I'll do it.'

'I thought you were ever so busy.'

'I am, but I'm prepared to make a sacrifice to get you out of a hole.'

She blushed faintly. 'Do I book you a hotel for the night?'

'Surely you're not suggesting that I can do there and back in one day.'

V

18

It's the random element of hitchhiking that appeals. Like the tossing of a coin, your progress depends on the workings of pure chance. Perhaps it's a metaphor for life, then – random encounters, random occurrences, random partings on to which you try and impose the logic and thrust of a narrative. Thus they reach the border at a bridge where the River Saar converges with one of its tributaries and where they move from Germany across the border into France as much by the machinations of chance as through any conscious choice. A cursory examination of their passports on the German side is followed by a sharp, officious one on the French side where the uniformed official handles their documents with the manner of a health worker handling clothing contaminated with anthrax. He asks, 'Where are you going?' as though staying put was certainly not a possibility.

Ellie plucks a name out of the air. 'Strasbourg.'

'Paris,' he suggests.

'*J'ai dit Strasbourg. On va à Strasbourg.*'

He sniffs. He knows their destination is Paris, where they will cause mayhem on the Boul' Mich'. Turning to James he demands his rucksack, and for a few minutes rummages through the chaos of things inside, finding nothing more offensive than old socks and worn underpants. Then he points to Ellie's pack, flipping his middle finger upwards in a gesture that is almost, but not quite, obscene. '*Ouvrez.*'

Ellie unslings her rucksack and begins to take out her scant possessions – rolled T-shirts, folded underwear, a wash bag, the battered tin of Gold Flake, a couple of paperback books, a small towel, not much else – and lay them out. The policeman prods them thoughtfully before tapping the Gold Flake tin. '*Ouvrez.*'

James's heart lurches. Ellie does as she is told, levering open the lid to expose golden, mossy shreds of tobacco and a packet of cigarette papers. The policemen raises the tin to his nose and sniffs while Ellie smiles beatifically at him; only James recognises the true message behind that smile. It says, as plain as a raised middle finger, 'Fuck you.'

Thoughtfully, the policeman hands the tin back and contemplates the pair of them with distaste. Then he cocks his head dismissively. '*Allez, filez.*'

And so they move on into the vasty fields of France – Eleanor's quotation, of course – and go where the lifts take them. But lifts are rare. The road is their world, the verge their environment. There are wild flowers amongst the grasses – peas, vetch, catchfly. Bees hum around them, butterflies flicker in the sunlight like scraps of foil blown by the wind. It is a kind of idyll, despite their rucksacks and their sweat-stained shirts and blistered feet. They feel both free and captive, trapped by their straps and the load of their packs and the distance they can walk, yet unburdened of all other encumbrance – parents or work or any obligation except to themselves. And gradually – this is the absurd thing – James comes to feel an enormous gratitude towards Eleanor for bestowing on him this sensation of detachment and contentment. Just the delight of being there in the midst of this vast and peaceful countryside without any bonds between himself and home. It is as though he has been transformed into something entirely new – ageless, careless, indifferent.

'You know what?'

'What?' They sit on the verge watching an empty *route départementale* stretch away into the distance in either direction. She is lying back against her rucksack. Her eyes are closed and the sun has caught her face, smacked her cheeks pink, given her a dusting of pollen. Her T-shirt is splashed with a tie-dyed sunburst, damp with sweat in the armpits. He thinks, because he is an incorrigible romantic, that she looks entirely lovely. And, although instinct tells him how dangerous this thought is, how vulnerable it leaves him, he thinks also that he may be in love with her.

'I feel really happy.'

She opens her eyes and smiles. 'How sweet,' she says. 'Naive, but sweet.'

So there they are, Eleanor and James, by the roadside in the midst of the peaceful and bucolic delights of a countryside, a country, a continent, apparently, although not actually, untouched by political dispute. Fando and Lis on the road to Tar, Lis at the moment unfastening the waistband of her jeans and reaching her hand inside her underpants to pull out the stash. Fando watches in fascination as she rolls, with that fluid-fingered dexterity, a joint, lights it, drags meditatively on it, holds the smoke inside her head and then slowly, reluctantly, like someone surrendering to the inevitability of death, lets it out.

'Here.' She hands the joint to him. And he wonders, as he takes it and draws the cloying smoke inwards, whether there is going to be a repetition of what happened two days ago in the cherry orchard. Could it happen even out here in the open air, his hand pushed down the front of her jeans where she hides that other, infinitely delicate, infinitely supple and surprising stash?

You never know your luck.

Lying side by side they smoke, passing the joint back and forth, watching the sky and the hills. Slightly zonked out, slightly high, laughing at things that probably aren't really that funny, he imagines, remembers, sees shapes in the clouds that remind him of—

She leaps to her feet.

'Hey, what you doing?'

'A lift, you twit.' She yanks out her thumb. The vehicle – a battered van, one of those ugly Citroën things that looks like a pig – grows larger in the perspective of the tarmac, flies past them at some speed, before skidding to a halt fifty yards down the road.

Ellie pinches off the glowing end of the joint, snaps the dead remainder away in her Gold Flake tin, grabs her rucksack and gives James a kick in the side. 'Come on, shift your arse.' He shambles to his feet and struggles after her, fighting a vague hilarity within, the sense that this doesn't matter, this striving after progression, feeling instead that *things* are what is really important – the flowers buzzing in his brain, the ant crawling up his arm, the clouds gathering in the sky above, the warm declivities of Ellie's body that have gathered in his imagination.

'This is fucking silly,' he calls out as he runs. His brain seems to undulate within his skull, as though it were on gimbals. Suddenly he feels sick. 'Why don't we just—?'

'Hurry up!'

The door of the van slides open. She has thrown her backpack inside and is urging him on. He runs, stumbles, trips, feels the taste of smoke in his gut and an abrupt sensation of rebellion immediately below his diaphragm. And then the flavour of vomit, sour and bilious, erupts into his mouth. He turns, bends forward and heaves the scant contents of his stomach into the ditch.

'Come *on*, James! For Christ's sake!'

For a moment he's on his knees, eructating. And then he's unsteadily on his feet once more, staggering towards the van like a soldier under fire running for the helicopter. He flings himself into the vehicle and lies prostrate, submitting himself to Ellie's ministrations, which mainly consist of a few sips of water and rough sympathy: 'It happens like that, sometimes. Just a reaction. You'll soon get over it.'

'What's the trouble back there?' the driver calls. They're moving, the engine clattering, the van lurching from side to side as they breast curves.

'Something he ate.'

'Not you, I hope.'

Laughter. The voice, the laughter are American. Faces turn within the shadows of the van. Teeth and hair, lots of teeth and lots of hair; the glint of a pair of granny spectacles. There are two in the front, another two figures in the shadows of the back, where are piled loudspeakers and guitars, a keyboard, electrical gear, shapes that might be drums. And sleeping bags and cooking things, all muddled into the complex smell of food and sweat and the cloying scent of smouldering joss sticks. James feels his stomach heave once more. 'Where you folks headed for?' the driver calls over his shoulder.

'Strasbourg.'

'We'll take you to Strasbourg. You going to Strasbourg, we'll take you to Strasbourg. Fuck it, why not? There's a bridge across the Rhine there, isn't there?'

'Yes, there is.'

'Sounds like a fucking war film. Bridge Over the River Rhine. We're headed for Prague. That's where it's at, man. Got a gig there in a few days. But we'll take you to fucking Strasbourg if you wanna go to fucking Strasbourg.'

They are, it transpires, a rock group called the Ides of March, on what they laughingly call their European tour. 'Name's classical, man. It's like March fifteen in old Roman. But it's also where we come from – March, Idaho, founded March fifteen, eighteen thirty-six by this one guy called Isaiah

March. How's that for cool? This guy, March, creates this place March, on the Ides of March.' There is incredulous laughter, as though this has only just occurred to them. 'But folks just call us the Ides 'cos it's easier to recall.'

James sits silent, propped against the side of the van, nursing his swimming head and trying to calm his rebelling stomach. There is an exchange of names: John, Phil, Archer and Elliot. John is the driver, rhythm guitarist and leader of the group. Elliot and Phil are the guys in the back lying amongst sleeping bags, one the bass player, the other, Elliot, the lead guitarist who writes the numbers that they sing when they're not covering the Beatles and the Rolling Stones. He has long hair, a rodent face and an empty grin.

'D'you wanna hear?' John the driver asks. 'Give 'em "Rubicon", Elliot. Elliot and Ellie – hey, you two should get together!'

'Rubicon?' Ellie says, attempting to deflect the idea.

'Yeah, it's like a river that Julius Caesar crossed, ain't that right, Elliot? He knows stuff. He was majoring in classics before he dropped out.'

'Where was that?'

'In Italy, that right, Elliot? It's a river in Italy that Caesar crossed. It meant he was going to become emperor or some shit.'

'Not the river. The university that he dropped out of.'

'Oh, man, got yah! Yeah, that's real comic. You mean one thing, I understand another. UCLA. That's right? UCLA.'

Elliot grunted some kind of acknowledgement. UCLA it was.

'So give it to them, Elliot. Come on, man. "Rubicon".'

With little enthusiasm Elliot takes up his guitar and begins to pick at it. The dead, unamplified sound is barely audible above the engine noise. His voice is rough and almost tuneless:

Let me cross your Rubicon,
Let me hold you tight,
Let me cross your Rubicon,
Girl, it's gonna be all right.

The others sing along, adding 'yeah, man' and 'it's gonna be a'right' as they think fit. Archer beats out the time on the dashboard. The second verse, encountered as one might stumble into something in the dark, is not unlike the first.

I went down to her Rubicon,
I bent to taste it fine,
I crouched beside her Rubicon,
It had the taste of wine.

Then they repeat the first verse and that seems to be it. Ellie applauds. Elliot grins at her, white teeth and white eyes gleaming from the shadows of the van. He speaks in a whisper, almost as though he has an obstruction in the back of his throat. 'It's pussy,' he murmurs. 'The Rubicon. Know what I mean? Her pussy.'

'I think I'd sort of understood that.'

He reaches out and touches Ellie's shoulder. 'You wanna make out?'

'No, thank you.'

James dozes, barely noticing what is going on, his head swirling, the line *Let me cross your Rubicon* going round and round in the vortex. The words seem important, as though bearing a significance as great as any biblical text. It is Ellie's Rubicon he wishes to cross, and not really cross but dive into it and splash around. *Alea iactum est*, he remembers.

'*Alea iactum est*,' he says out loud, seeing the coincidental significance of it.

'*Iacta*,' Ellie says, throwing the correction over her shoulder as she argues with the guitarist.

'What's that, man?' the driver asks. 'That French?'

'Latin,' James mumbles, surprised at his own knowledge. 'The die is cast. It's what Julius Caesar said when he crossed the Rubicon.' But he's more interested in the quiet, suppressed argument that Ellie and Elliot are having. He hopes it is not her Rubicon they are discussing. 'Right,' Elliot says. 'Sure.' And gropes around in the bag he carries and pulls out money.

'Hey!' James exclaims. He intends a sharp interjection but the sound comes out more like a yelp of surprise.

'Cool it, man,' Elliot says. 'Just let it be.'

The van slows abruptly and they begin to snake through the narrow streets of a town. Horns blare, in French. The gears of the van grate. 'Son of a bitch!' John shouts from behind the wheel. 'Not used to a manual shift,' he explains to his passengers. The road begins to descend into the wide flood plain of the river Rhine. Whatever has been going on between Ellie and Elliot is concluded. Elliot sags back into the sleeping bags while the rest of the Ides sing, Archer the drummer beating time on the dashboard, Elliot strumming vaguely at his empty guitar. They sing 'Mr Tambourine Man', 'Yellow Submarine', 'Light My Fire', anything that comes to mind. Something called 'White Light White Heat'. And, of course, 'Rubicon'. Perhaps the Rhine will be their Rubicon – they have been booked to play in Prague by someone they met in Paris, a Czech who told them about the music scene in his home city. 'The Czechs are, like, crossing a Rubicon, aren't they?' John suggests. 'Saying fuck you to the Soviets. Hey, maybe Elliot can write us another verse.'

Elliot grunts and ponders the proposal. 'We're *gonna* cross the Rubicon,' he sings:

'We're going to be free
We're gonna cross the Rubicon

And choose democracy.'

'How *about* that?' cries John, hammering his fist on the steering wheel. 'That'll drive the Czech kids wild.'

'Or maybe,' Elliot adds vaguely, 'the other way round.'

Ellie has moved away from him and closer to James. She holds his hand in a rare demonstration of affection. 'You OK?'

He shakes his head. The whole world moves.

'It'll soon wear off.'

They come to the outskirts of Strasbourg, the supermarkets, filling stations, small factories and warehouses, a brewery, all the detritus deposited by a modern town around itself, like an animal shitting round its own nest. Then the buildings crowd in and the road dives beneath railway lines and over water and reaches the centre, part timber-framed, part a local sandstone the colour of bruised flesh. The timber is painted in a variety of colours, like an old lady tarted up with eyeshadow on her eyelids, lipstick on her impoverished lips, rouge on her cheeks.

'Looks a real cool place,' John the driver decides, peering through the windscreen.

'Yeah,' agrees Archer. 'Old.'

'Cute,' Ellie offers.

'Yeah, cute.'

'Look, you can put us down anywhere. Just here'll be fine.'

They pull over at the edge of a square. A sign points towards *Le Rhin, République Fédérale d'Allemagne.* John turns round. 'Hey, guys, you sure you don't want to come on with us?'

'Go on, man,' says Elliot. He grins at Ellie and mouths the word *Rubicon.*

'Thanks, but no thanks,' she replies. 'We'll get off here. Going south, you see.'

Elliot leers and points. 'Down south?'

'Italy.'

'Right, Italy.' He nods vaguely. There are plenty more Rubicons in the lives of men. Ellie slides the door open and

151

leaps out, dragging her rucksack after her. Dutifully, a little unsteadily, James follows, pursued by cheers from inside the dark cave. Archer, the drummer, leans out of the front window and beats a paradiddle on the side door. There are whoops and yells as the van pulls away in a squeal of tyres. Pedestrians stare.

James feels relief, as though some kind of danger has been overcome. 'Let's find somewhere to stay,' Ellie says. 'We passed a *pension* a couple of streets back.'

'We can't afford a *pension*.'

'We're not going to pitch your bloody tent in the middle of the town, are we? Anyway, Elliot's paying.'

'Elliot?'

'I sold him the grass.'

'The *grass*? For God's sake, why?'

'Don't want you turning into a pothead, that's why.' There's something approaching affection in her expression.

'Why should I?'

'I could see it in your eyes. My advice? Stay clear. Keep clean and simple like you were. It suits you. You don't want to end up like that cretin.' Which is something of a relief, because, in his befuddled state, he almost fancied Ellie and Elliot as intertwined as their names, crossing and recrossing each other's Rubicons. Now she marches on alone, slight and indomitable, down a narrow street where an ancient sign announces *Pension Alsace*.

The hallway of the pension is narrow and dark brown and smells of mould and vinegar. A framed print of women in traditional costume hangs on the wall nearby but the Madame in charge of the place has long ago abandoned any decorative dress in favour of what appears to be a nut-brown sack. At Ellie's peremptory ringing of the reception bell, she emerges from somewhere in the back and regards the two new

152

customers with a mixture of contempt and suspicion. '*Oui?*'

Ellie smiles. She can do that, smile warmly to disperse all doubts. She is small and sharp and able, while James feels large and clumsy and incompetent. Her language helps, the French she learned at school, polished on holidays in France and finally, James has subsequently discovered, buffed up with a six-month exchange with a family in Bordeaux. So the two ladies smile at each other and trade polite greetings and icy compliments while the visitors' passports are examined as thoroughly as by any border policeman. The woman looks up and says something to Ellie in which the words *mariés* and *épouse* seem to feature, along with the word *catholique*. Ellie's smile is like a razor cut. *Bien sûr*, she replies. *Notre lune de miel*, she insists. *Étudiants*, she explains. The woman ponders the matter for a while before squirrelling the passports away in exchange for two forms to be filled in with enough details for a job application. '*Ça va*,' she agrees grudgingly once the forms are completed, and hands over a key with a brass label inscribed with 301. '*Seulement une nuit.*' As though more than one night might lead to moral complications she can hardly tolerate.

'What was that all about?' James asks as they climb the stairs – there is, of course, no lift. 'Are we—'

'Married, yes.'

'*Married*? What the—?'

'If we weren't married, there wouldn't have been a deal at all. Madame is a very devout Catholic. At least that's what she claims. So if we weren't a newly-wed couple she'd have insisted on separate rooms. And I wasn't going to pay for two.'

The room is on the top floor, crouching beneath the eaves. It's halfway between an abandoned attic and a dormitory, a twisted, asymmetrical space divided with wooden beams and posts, with a double bed at one end and two single beds halfway down. There's a washbasin but no bathroom. The bathroom is off the landing, shared with whoever occupies the other room up there under the roof tiles.

'So here we are,' Ellie says, contemplating their little retreat. She seems awkward, as though she hasn't really been expecting this. Somehow a shared room is more intimate than a shared tent. 'I'm going to have a shower, and then we'd better get something to eat.'

Which is putting off all the awkward implications. Married, even. And a shared bed will be necessary evidence. James the scientist thinks these thoughts amongst many others as she darts off to the bathroom and comes back with hair somehow more ordered – that vivacious cloud of pale gold – and T-shirt changed (the old one washed and laid out on the tiles outside one of the dormer windows) and even – is this possible? – a dash of lipstick on those eloquent lips. They go out, taking Madame's recommendation, to a small bistro round the corner that serves local food at a good price, where they share a *pichet* of Alsatian wine, and then another when the first – faintly sweet and scented – disappears with silken ease. Ellie laughs, relaxes, smokes, seems altogether different from the sharp and prickly woman she can be. Her eyes glisten. Her lips shine. Or is it the other way round? She even bums a cigarette off the men – a trio of builders – at the next table. Does she want to join them for a beer? No, she doesn't, although it was kind of them to ask. She is with her fiancé, thank you.

He can come too, if he wants.

Actually, they are on their honeymoon. *Lune de miel.*

Much ribald laughter and understanding.

Back in their room – *their* room; the sexual thrill of that collective pronoun – she stands beside the bed, looking at him with that strange, out-of-focus look she has. The only illumination is a single bedside light – the other one doesn't work

154

and the ceiling light is a harsh, bare bulb that she turned off with a shriek of horror as soon as it came on – so her figure is blurred, like something sketched in charcoal, thrown into relief and shadowed with grey. 'So,' she says, giving a little smile and pulling her T-shirt over her head. She has nothing on underneath. He knows that, of course. He has watched her at length, already observed the fluid shifting of things beneath the cotton, but despite the strange intimacies they have already shared, this is the first time he has seen her breasts. When she shakes her hair out they move loosely, pale in the half-light. He tries, and fails, to avert his eyes, but why should he bother? She appears heedless of his gaze, dropping her jeans round her ankles, kicking them away and slipping under the bedclothes with blithe indifference. He sits on his side of the bed to try and keep things to himself.

Then what happens? These things get forgotten over time, the details lost, merged into other moments, blurred like the charcoal edges of a smudged drawing. But it goes something like this: he lifts the bedclothes – some kind of limp eiderdown – and slides beneath. She snaps off the light so that the only illumination comes through the threadbare curtains from street lights outside. He rolls over in the bed to face her and they lie there between the sheets, a foot apart, a whole confusing concatenation of lusts and inhibitions apart. In the half-light he can make out the whites of her eyes and the secret gleam of teeth. She breathes softly.

'Ellie,' he says and leaves her name there in the narrow shadows between them.

'What?'

Moving closer he touches his lips against hers. Her lips are closed, as though opening them would open a window on her soul through which all manner of things might be revealed. But she doesn't stop his hand, which crosses the divide and touches her breast and the small nub of her nipple.

155

Doesn't that signify arousal? He doesn't know. Acceptance? He doesn't know anything, really.

Still she doesn't move.

'I don't understand what you want, Ellie.'

'Why should you?'

'Because of what happened in the tent.'

A breath of laughter in his face. 'Messy, in more ways than one.'

'But we did it. And now I want to make love to you. Properly.' He says it almost without considering, as though to surprise himself as much as her.

She looks steadily at him, her head on the pillow, mere inches away but a whole world apart. 'You've been very good, you know that? Not pushy, not protesting your devotion or anything nauseating like that. You've not really used the L word at all, except just then – that horrible expression "making love".'

'What's wrong with it?'

'You don't know? And you a scientist. Haven't you read *The Naked Ape*? Of course you have. Well, we're just animals, aren't we? We mate, promiscuously, most of us. We grunt and sweat and get all wrapped up in each other's fluids and we call it by the same word as we use for our relationship with the eternal creator of the universe. Love. Not very convincing.'

'So what do you want to call it? Fucking?'

'That's what it is, isn't it?'

'So, are we going to do it? I mean, if it's just some physical function—'

'But it's not, is it? Not *just* some physical function. That wanking thing, maybe. But not fucking. Not your sticking your penis inside me.'

James has never had a conversation like this before: he has never really heard the word 'fuck' mouthed by such articulate and feminine lips. A part of him to do with chapels and

156

Wesleyan Nonconformism and pure Northern prudery is profoundly shocked; while another part, to do with biology and, in particular, the organ between his legs, is profoundly excited. He wants her to be clinging to him and whispering that word in his ear.

'I mean,' she continues, 'it *signifies*, doesn't it? It's not called intercourse for nothing. And it also brings with it the other things – childbearing, motherhood, procreation.'

'I don't think we're quite ready for that.'

He'll remember that laugh. He likes making her laugh. It is the principal weapon he possesses. 'Don't worry about that. I'm on the pill, although I did miss one in Zeebrugge. But I like an element of risk.' She pauses, as though struck by a sudden idea. 'You're not a virgin, are you?'

'Of course I'm not.'

'Of course?'

'Did you imagine I was?' He hopes he sounds worldly-wise, but in fact his previous experience of sex is limited to one partner, a girl called Muriel, known, because she hated the name, as Mu. Mu was a fellow pupil at his grammar school but she left before the sixth form for reasons that were never quite clear, and went to work behind the counter in Boots, selling, amongst other things, condoms to grown men and blushing boys. It was to Mu that he happily lost his virginity, although he was fairly sure that she had mislaid hers long before, and in the same careless manner with which she conducted much of her life. After his first term at university she had dumped him because she said, despite his protests, that things were no longer the same between them, were they? 'As far as I'm concerned,' she said, 'you've become posh.'

And here he was now, phoney posh lying in bed with proper posh in a cheap hotel somewhere in the middle of France; and she was saying fuck to him without turning a hair.

'Anyway, you did agree that we wouldn't have sex,' Ellie pointed out. 'When we talked about it, you did agree.'

'You agreed, with yourself. I said nothing.'

'So it's up to me?'

'Of course it's up to you.'

She considers him, head on one side. 'Well, I've decided that you're quite nice and we're quite good together and so if you like we can ...' She doesn't say the word. He waits for her to say it but she doesn't.

In the event, nothing much. She lies beneath him and lets him in and he feels that eloquent slide, that momentary sensation of danger and delirium that is like slithering over a cliff and discovering you can fly. But quite soon the flight comes to an abrupt end in a paltry climax and he slips out of her almost surreptitiously, vaguely aware that he should do something for her despite the fact that she doesn't seem to want anything, having turned away from him almost immediately and composed herself for sleep.

'Was that all right?' he whispers over her shoulder.

'Fine,' she replies. 'Fine.'

Reaching over he kisses her cheek and finds it damp with tears. 'Are you all right?'

Her voice mutters into the crook of her arm. 'Go to sleep. I told you, I'm fine.'

Tears. Enigmatic things. If you ever doubt the concept of mind over matter, then think of tears. The most effluent manifestation of grief, but also of nothing at all. Almost as contagious as a yawn.

So what were Eleanor Pike's tears for?

Next morning she's up early, too quick to allow a repeat of what had happened the evening before. She doesn't allude to it either as they pack their things and go down to the reception desk to pay. Whatever it was might never have been.

'I want to look round,' she tells him as they leave the *pension*. 'I want to see the city.' She says it as though she is pitching for an argument and expects him to object. So they spend the morning like tourists, winding their way through the medieval streets of the Grand Île, peering round the ancient gloom of the cathedral, even taking a boat trip on the canals that intersect the city. They have lunch at a table on the pavement and share another *pichet* of Alsace wine and for most of the time Ellie seems happy, distracted by the sights, content to forget what happened the evening before and might happen again; but over lunch there is a change. 'Let me tell you,' she says and then leaves the telling hanging in the air.

'Tell me what?'

She looks at him with a little twisted expression then glances down. 'About last night.'

'What about last night?'

'You know what I mean.'

'I'm not sure I do.' He wishes he hadn't said it like that, the tone all wrong, making the neutral expression almost an accusation. She fiddles with things on the exiguous table, the salt cellar, her wine glass, a spoon, almost as though to distract his attention. 'I wasn't very good, was I?'

'*You* weren't very good?'

'I didn't . . . oh, I don't know, react. Not as you're meant to.'

'As you're *meant* to?'

'Look, if you're going to repeat everything I say—'

'I'm sorry, I'm trying to understand.'

'There's nothing much to understand. I don't enjoy it. That's it, really. I've never, you know, enjoyed it. I can't . . . let myself go. That's what you've got to do, isn't it? Let yourself go. Ecstasy, religious or sexual. All much the same. Both involve letting go. But I can't. Not with Kevin, not with anyone else. And now, not with you. Whom I trust.'

159

Words and images stumble round his brain, bumping into each other like drunks in the dark. He feels overwhelmed by the concept of trust.

'It's my parents. Everyone accuses them, but it's true. My mother, really, not my father. I love my father, worship, perhaps, which can't be healthy. But my mother . . .' She gives a little laugh, empty of all amusement. And then she tells him. Sitting there at the pavement café in the summer sunshine, she tells him about her mother and what she did with somebody or other. An uncle? A cousin? Both? Going off for long, belligerent, adulterous, alcoholic weekends or something, leaving her father shut away in his study, needing comfort, which Ellie, a devoted daughter, offered.

'Comfort?'

She looks at him for a moment, then away across the square at the shifting tide of anonymous tourists. 'He seems a strong man, doesn't he? But he's not. Not weak but . . . ' She hesitates, considering. 'Vulnerable. I adore him. And he adores me.'

'What comfort?'

'There were bitter arguments when my mother came home. Rows, fights. I tried my hardest to protect him. It seems ridiculous, doesn't it? A child trying to shield her own father? My brother was away at boarding school, so there was just me, crushed between the two of them. You know what happens to something when you crush it? Either it breaks up into little pieces or it becomes hard.' She laughs faintly. 'I've done both.'

The waiter appears and asks if they want anything else. More wine, perhaps? A dessert? Perhaps that interruption is a good thing, killing the question he has tried to ask and she has avoided: what comfort?

When the man has gone, she continues, almost as though the answer has already been given. 'And then she'd do the religious thing, go off to some bloody convent to confess her sins and become a holy little wife again. Until the next time. The

160

eternal grind of sin and confession and absolution. Of course I reasoned it all away as I grew up – I could just shrug it off, break away, find another version of love and affection. Except I didn't. Couldn't, in fact. I couldn't let myself go, ever. Not with Kevin, not with half a dozen other boys before him. And then you came along, and I thought, yes, why not. Maybe with him. You see' – she glances up at him for a moment – 'you're so fucking *nice*. That's why I'm telling you this.'

James was suddenly aware that niceness was something one shouldn't be. 'No, I'm not.'

'But you are. You can't help it, but you are. And I thought maybe it'd be different with you.' She looks directly at James and he recognises the pinched, sorrowful expression that Lis wore throughout the play. 'But it isn't.'

'In the tent ...' James leaves the rest unsaid. In his mind is an already confused memory – a suffusion of orange light, pale ochre limbs moving, heat, a cry, a moment of ecstasy.

She shakes her head. 'What's that? Neurones firing, synapses activating, you ought to know. It's just a bit of biology. But there's no connection. Don't you see how right Forster was?'

'Forster?'

'E. M. Forster. You know? You must know. *Howard's End.*' A fractional pause to gather her thoughts. 'Only connect the prose and the passion and both will be exalted and human love will be seen at its highest. That's what I can't do.'

The quotation gives it away: it has become one of those Oxford conversations he has learned to despise. All theory and no fact. Head in the clouds and feet at least six inches off the ground. He can't do anything to stop her now. 'It's Forster's metaphor,' she continues. 'Well, Margaret Schlegel's in the book, but it's Forster himself, of course. Prose is here and now, you sitting there across the table, me here, us talking together, being friends, being happy in each other's company. And passion is that moment of ... what? Ecstasy?' She frowns, correcting herself as though it matters: 'Human love will be seen at its *height*. Height, not highest. That's what Margaret Schlegel thinks. You connect the two, the prose and the passion, with love. But I cannot.' She opens her hands as though to display their emptiness. 'Don't you see, I want to love. You or someone. Anyone. But I just cannot. I live in fragments, that's the trouble, small, hard fragments.'

There is, at that summer holiday pavement bistro, with its easy indolence, its chequered tablecloths and blackboard chalked with the *plats du jour*, a pause. James doesn't know what to say. As far as he's concerned it's all nonsense, this self-examination. It's the nonsense of psychology and the nonsense of philosophy. All we are is animals – complex animals, of course, but animals nevertheless. And what we do is what we do and what we feel is what we feel and the important thing is just to get on with it. So it's Ellie who steps into the pause and makes it hers. 'You know why Kevin and I broke up?' She answers her own question before he has any need to guess. 'The real reason, I mean. It wasn't his politics. Compared with this, I couldn't give a fuck about politics, and anyway he isn't the fascist I've said he is. He wanted love, that was the trouble. Although he never put it in those words – he'd never read Forster in his life – he wanted me to build that bridge, and when he found I couldn't he just got angry. Told me I was frigid. Shouted at me, called me an emotional cripple, said he wanted someone who could show love for him, real love, not some intellectualised version of it.'

Anything James might say will be wrong. He knows that. This girl who seemed so self-assured is as fragile as an eggshell. Yet there were no tears, that was his thought when he reflected on this conversation later. Such a moment of high emotion but no tears. Her expression appeared inverted, as though she was looking in on herself and finding nothing there. 'I've never told anyone all this. Except you.'

'Does that make me special?'

She shakes her head, as though to toss the question aside. 'I wanted to explain, that's all. You seem ... worth explaining it to.'

'More than Kevin?'

'Kevin would never have understood. I'm not sure that you do, but at least you're sympathetic.'

But perhaps he is wrong – perhaps there are tears in her eyes. Not flowing down her cheeks or anything too dramatic. Just glistening. He reaches out across the table to take her hand, and for a moment they sit there, holding hands across the table like any young couple who have just become lovers. Then she withdraws and blinks and the eyes seem dry once again. 'That's the problem,' she says. 'I live in fragments. I've tried to put them back together but I can't. The pieces no longer fit.'

19

They leave the debris of that conversation at the bistro table and walk into the Place Kléber where, amongst the tourists and beside an antique carousel, they examine their map and the possibilities. Another coin. Heads to Germany, Austria and the Brenner Pass, or tails to Switzerland, the St Gotthard and Milan. Ellie laughs. The spinning coin delights her, like a child placated with a new toy. It rattles on the paving stones and lies head up, glinting in the sunshine – 'heads' in this case being a wistful woman striding across the obverse, casting seeds in her wake.

So they sling their backpacks and set off towards the river, towards another approximate border control, with Ellie apparently purged of her nightmares for the moment, talking and laughing and being once more the girl with the acute mind that he worshipped from afar and now cherishes from close to. On the German side of the river they get a lift in a van going south towards Freiburg, and from there they take the road into the Schwarzwald, the Black Forest, the home of cuckoo clocks and cherry cakes and, Ellie points out, the Nazi philosopher Martin Heidegger. Afternoon turns into a gentle sunlit evening. Dark, foreboding hillsides are mitigated by the warm valley. They walk along an immaculate verge past meadows of trimmed velvet where perfectly groomed cows ruminate on a benign future of grass and cud and milk.

Little traffic passes and there is scant prospect of a lift, but James doesn't mind. This is a kind of heaven in which the word transport takes on a different meaning. Not buses and trains and soot and oil, but a transport of delight, in Ellie's company. Yet the dark forests are still there, on either side of the valley.

'So what's it going to be this evening?' she asks as they pause to consult the map. Ahead, in the depths of the forest, there's a place called Titisee beside a lake. A green delta symbolises a campsite. 'Your bloody tent again?'

'Unless we can afford another luxury hotel.'

It's strange that they should be back to their old relationship. Almost as though the events in Strasbourg have not taken place. But they have. He sees her in a different light now, the soft light of the Black Forest evening and the harsh light of her vulnerability. She is scarred; possibly scared. And yet she is still Eleanor, with her assumed self-confidence and her caustic tongue. And she has let him make love to her. The very thought of what has been and might be again almost brings his heart to a halt. Or makes it beat twice as fast. He can't tell which.

She hoists her rucksack onto her back and walks on ahead of him. 'About what I was saying at lunch,' she calls back.

'What about it?'

'Forget it, just forget it, okay? I was babbling on. Just forget it and it'll be like it was before.'

'But it's not like before, is it?'

She looks round, sharply. 'Of course it is.'

'No, it's not. For Christ's sake, Ellie—'

She stops, her face tight with anger. 'Look, I don't want sympathy. Still less do I want pity. I'm not a head case, so don't try and treat me like one. Just take me on my own terms and we'll see what happens, OK?'

He hesitates, not knowing whether to argue back. And that

is the moment when the car – a Volkswagen Beetle – clatters past them and slows to a halt.

Whatever the circumstances there is a small thrill of apprehension about a successful hitch. The vehicle – car, van, lorry – waits, anonymous and indifferent but pregnant with possibility. Where will it take you? Whom does it conceal? What secrets does it hide? It puts your own momentary circumstances into perspective.

They hurry to find out.

Inside the car there's a disparate couple, a young man driving and a middle-aged woman in the passenger seat. The man appears tall, folded awkwardly into the seat behind the steering wheel. He's good-looking in the rather daunting way of blond, blue-eyed Germans, while the woman is smaller, with grey hair scraped back into a bun and inquisitive, beetle-bright eyes. Perhaps she writes detective stories. Perhaps she is actually an amateur detective, a Miss Marple of Germany.

The man climbs out and asks, in English, 'Are you looking for a lift?'

They are, of course they are. He holds the door open for them to climb in. 'Is there room? It is a small car and there is not much room.'

But they manage, squeezing Ellie's pack into the exiguous space behind the rear seat while James sits with his own on his lap. Ellie crowds against him, thigh against thigh in smiling complicity.

'I hope you are not too uncomfortable,' the driver says as they set off. 'Where are you going? I am afraid we are not going far.'

James takes charge of their side of the conversation, happy that, amongst other things, Ellie no longer has the language advantage. 'We're heading towards Austria. Lake Constance, somewhere like that. But we need somewhere for the night. We've got a tent.'

'Ah, you are looking for a camping site. There are camping sites where we are going. Titisee, you know Titisee?'

'We've seen it on the map.'

'It is very pretty there. A lake. There is boating. There are water sports.' It sounds as though he has learned phrases from a guidebook and polished them into a simulacrum of fluent language. His passenger half-turns to see what species of beast they have caught. Her face is serious, as though they may have committed some kind of transgression. 'It says GB on your pack. Does that mean you are British?'

James wonders. Thoughts of the war come to mind. Resentment, rancour, enmities festering beneath a superficial gloss of liberal progress. His tone is almost apologetic. 'Yes, it does.'

'Are you students?'

'Yes, we are.'

'Are you at university?'

'Yes.'

'Which one?'

'Oxford.'

'Which college?'

The question is a surprise. James names his, with the faint feeling that he is handing over some kind of secret code.

'Ah,' the woman says. 'Do you know Professor Hubert?'

Professor Hubert. A tall, stooped figure who paces the quad with his gown billowing and his hair awry. Professor Hubert who smiles benignly on one and all. 'Yes, I do. I mean, not personally. But I know who he is. Maybe I've said good morning to him a couple of times.'

'Professor Hubert is a great friend of mine,' she announces. 'He is a fine musicologist.'

Memories of the war – folk memories, mediated by films and War Picture Library comics – fade. James nudges Ellie. 'I just thought Hubert was an old codger who dispensed sherry at his tutorials.'

'How do you know that?'

'I heard someone say.'

'Actually, he's a leading authority on Monteverdi.'

'How do you know *that*?'

'I went to a talk he gave at the Bach Festival.'

The woman looks round sharply, as though they have been caught talking in class. She has a kind of haggard beauty, like a cliff face eroded by weathering but still full of grandeur. 'You mention the Bach Festival,' she says in her measured, clipped English. 'It is there that I know Professor Hubert. I am playing there many years now.'

'Playing?'

'I am a cellist. I am Birgit Eckstein and this is my nephew, Horst von Eberhafen.' There is a rapid exchange of words with her nephew. She turns round again. 'We are thinking that maybe you can erect your tent in our garden, if you would like. We are having a big garden. And you may use our facilities – for shower and wash – so that will be like a campsite, no?'

'That's very kind of you,' Ellie says. 'I'm sure it would be much better than a campsite.'

'And maybe you can have dinner with us. Would you like that? I have a simple house, but interesting.'

The car has left the valley and is winding up forested slopes, stuttering across a high, wooded plateau. The sun catches the tops of the hills, imposing a dangerous flush of pink on the black trees. After a while they turn off the road and up a gravel drive. The house – simple but interesting – lies against a wooded slope at the back of an expansive lawn. It is like something out of fairy tales, a Hansel and Gretel house built entirely of wood, clad in wood, even tiled in wood – 'It is called Schindel,' Horst informs them, adding that he believes the word also appears in English, as 'shingle'. The roof slopes down almost to head height. There are dormer windows like startled eyes. Quaint benches guard either side of the front door, while pots of pelargoniums illuminate the window ledges. A doorbell hangs on a spiral spring.

Frau Eckstein almost apologises as they climb out of the car. 'It is perhaps not as ancient as your Oxford colleges, but it is old, perhaps the oldest in this area. The sixteenth century. You may look if you wish.'

They dump their rucksacks on the edge of the lawn and follow the woman into her domain, feeling more and more like Hansel and Gretel in thrall to their captor. Inside there is the resinous scent of wood, the murmur of flexing floorboards, a sensation of quiet, considered age. They duck beneath beams and edge around posts. The stairs are like companionways, the floors like decking. The whole building creaks and shifts around them like a sailing ship under way through the tides of history. Occasional gaps between the floorboards give glimpses into the room below. 'That does not make it a very private place,' Frau Eckstein observes, laughing to signal the little pleasantry. 'But the bathroom is at least of the twentieth century.'

And indeed, amongst all the woodwork, the bathroom gleams like a pathology lab. There is a white bath, and a bidet with its vague suggestion of sexual impropriety, and a shower cabinet that might be suitable for beaming you up to some orbiting star ship. But when they return to the ground floor it is to the *pièce de résistance*: the music room.

They stand at the door and peer in. The interior is redolent with beeswax. A grand piano stands at the centre like a coffin on a catafalque. Cellos, half a dozen cellos, some cased, some naked, gather round like solemn mourners. Photographs of the dead decorate the walls like saints in a chancel. One shows a balding, stout figure and is inscribed with a flourish *de Birgit con cariño, Pablo*. 'Casals,' Frau Eckstein remarks with a careless wave of one hand. Another frame encompasses the austere, aquiline face of Paul Tortelier. 'We were very close,' she explains, picking the picture up and gazing at it fondly. 'At the conservatoire in Paris.' She replaces it with loving care and indicates another, which shows a younger version of herself, rather stern, rather beautiful, sewn into a long, flared dress and standing beside a moustachioed man with piercing eyes. 'Toscanini.' And another – 'Furtwängler' – before she looks at Ellie and James with careful eyes, as though measuring them up for something, the cooking pot perhaps. 'Do you enjoy the cello?'

'I love the cello,' Ellie says. 'I saw Jacqueline du Pré playing the Elgar at the Royal Festival Hall. She was wonderful.'

The woman sighs, a fraction impatient. 'Ah, Jackie, dear Jackie. Great talent but rather too much emotion, I fear. Emotion will always find you out in the end.' She touches one of the instruments. 'This is my Guadagnini. Perhaps I will play it for you after supper. Would you like that?'

Of course they would, even if, in James's case, they really wouldn't, because the whole stuff of classical music, the seriosity of it, the long gowns and stiff collars and tailcoats, bores him. Guadagnini? What the fuck does that mean?

'But first you must make yourselves comfortable. You must pitch your tent, must you not? Before it gets dark. I am sorry I cannot offer you a room, but with Horst here, you see we have no place. It is not a big house. But it is a bit like being children again, no? Pitching your tent on the lawn, I mean.'

Ellie seems delighted at another little point of contact. 'I used to do that with my brother!'

'Of course you did. Everyone does.' Which somehow makes it less remarkable. 'And you must use the bathroom if you wish. This, I remember, is the bad thing of camping, that you often have no bathroom.'

So they pitch their tent in the dusk, keeping their voices low to avoid being overheard, giggling like children as they crawl around inside the tent and try to sort things out. What do they think of their hostess?

A sharp old witch.

Rather beautiful. A kindly witch.

Did you see her fingers? Lobster claws. All that cello-playing.

And what was that Gwadaninny business?

Guadagnini. The cello maker. Second only to Stradivarius. Don't you know *anything*? It's probably worth hundreds of thousands.

Not as much as Horst, I'll bet. *Von Eberhafen*, no less.

Prussian?

Nazi?

What was she doing during the war, do you think?

Playing to the troops, I suppose.

And Horst? Strutting around eastern Poland shooting Jews in the neck?

He'd only have been about ten.

Hitler Youth, then. Longing to get into action and shoot Jews in the neck.

They take turns to use the bathroom. The kindly witch has put out towels for them. 'Make yourselves at home,' she says, seeing James climbing the stairs. 'Dinner will be ready in half an hour. Is that all right? Just come in and find us in the dining room.'

The dining room is on the opposite side of the hall from the music room, a wood-panelled cigar box of a space with a tiled stove in one corner and wall lamps that mimic gas lights. They sit at a polished slab of wood while a small, silent woman – 'This is Frau Weber' – brings food in from the kitchen. Conversation is awkward and incidental – how lovely the house, how beautiful the dining room, how fine the setting.

'We had only gas lighting until after the war,' Frau Eckstein

171

explains, 'but when my husband came back we decided to move finally into the twentieth century.'

Her husband? Suddenly there is a human shape amongst the inanimate shadows in the corners of the room. Where is her husband? And where has he returned from, with his ideas of finally joining the twentieth century?

'Your husband?' James asks.

'My husband is not alive now. He was sent to the Eastern Front and the Russians took him prisoner. He did not come back until 1952 and then he was no longer' – she pauses and considers carefully what words to use – 'the same. Physically. So he did not live many more years. But at least he died in freedom.'

Horst reaches across the table and takes his aunt's hand. In his precise, perfectly enunciated English, he explains. 'Onkel Julius was a courageous man. A doctor of medicine of great learning who did not like the National Socialist ideas of science. That was why he was sent to the Russian front.'

'But it was also why he survived being a prisoner,' his aunt adds. 'Because it was a skill that the Russians valued. So he survived in the camps as a doctor and at last he came home.'

There is a silence while they contemplate this, the kind of silence you wish someone would break. James offers himself up as a sacrificial lamb: 'My father was in the army. During the war. The Royal Army Service Corps. RASC.'

'I am sure he was also a brave man.'

'I don't know about that. They used to say Run Away Someone's Coming.'

Frau Eckstein looks puzzled. 'I do not understand. Did your father run away?'

Ellie giggles. Lamely, James explains. 'Royal Army Service Corps, R-A-S-C. Run Away Someone's Coming. It's a joke.'

'Ah, an English joke.'

'Ironic English humour,' Horst adds.

172

Frau Eckstein does not attempt a smile. 'I expect he did his duty,' she decides, 'just as my husband did. That was all that most Germans wanted to do. The sadness is that now their courage cannot be acknowledged by the nation, only by their families and friends. Do you see what I mean? Great Britain can celebrate in public while we can only weep in private. Both my husband and my brother—'

'That is, my father,' said Horst.

'—they died for what? A country that no longer even exists.' She thinks for a moment, then looks as though she has made up her mind. 'Do you know what my brother did? Of course you do not. How could you? My brother was a member of the so-called *Kreisauer Kreis*. How would you say that? The Kreisau Circle? This was a group which met to plan for a Germany after National Socialism, for when the country would be finished with the Hitler regime. They were arrested, many of them, after the . . . ' She hesitates. For the first time her otherwise impeccable English lets her down and she glances at her nephew for help. '*Das Attentat vom zwanzigsten Juli.*'

'The plot of July against Hitler,' Horst explains.

'My brother – Horst's father – was brought before the *Volksgerichtshof*—'

'—the Nazi People's Court.'

'And was sentenced to death. But he cheated them of that.'

Horst wears the expression of a mask – unwavering, as though his face were pressed out of papier-mâché and glued in place. 'He hanged himself in his cell,' he says. 'I was six years old. My mother told me he had died in the war. It wasn't until I was fourteen that I learned the truth.'

Frau Eckstein puts her knife and fork to rest as though to bring the discussion to a conclusion. 'While Frau Weber clears the table, I think I will play something for you,' she says, rising from her chair. Solemnly they follow her to the music room, like mourners going to view the deceased. One expects flowers round the coffin, relatives in black, guttering candles. Horst sits at the keyboard while Ellie and James take two chairs as instructed and wait in dutiful silence. Frau Eckstein hitches up her skirt and sits down, pulling the cello – the beloved Guadagnini – into the open embrace of her legs. Her nephew gives her a note on the piano and there is a moment of strange discord while she tunes her instrument. Then she settles. 'Bach, of course,' she announces. 'The cello suite in C minor. The prelude.'

And she begins, making exact, articulate movements of hands and arm, like a craftsman assembling something out of intricate pieces of wood. But what emerges from this complex labour is not a *thing* but an ephemeral sound emanating from the body of the instrument like a human voice from the depths. The woman's eyes are closed. Her head, her whole body, sways to the tempo of the music. It seems to James, who is entirely ignorant of these things, that she is drawing her bow across the raw, exposed surface of her nerves. And the whole room resonates to the cry.

When the piece comes to an end there is a silence louder than any of the extraneous sounds, louder than the shifting of a chair or the breathing of any of the listeners or the faint touch of her bow on the floor as she lays it down. She opens her eyes and looks at her audience. Ellie is in tears. 'That was wonderful,' she whispers, and it was, full of wonder even to James's untutored ear.

'How do you *do* that?' He feels foolish as soon as the words are uttered, but the woman smiles kindly on him.

'You know the Oxford joke about lawns? Professor Hubert told it to me when we were in your college: a tourist from America sees the lawn in an Oxford college and asks to the gardener how he can have a lawn like that. He would like one

174

at his house back home. What is the secret? And the gardener says, well, you plants it and you waters it, and then you rolls it and you mows it for two hundred years ...'

She does it quite well, even an attempt at the gardener's accent. You rolls it and you mows it. They laugh.

'So, it is almost like that with playing the instrument,' she says. 'Not two hundred years, of course, although this instrument itself has more than that, but many years and much playing. Every day for, perhaps, eight hours. It is not practice, it is study. Like you study the subject you do at university. Only for a lifetime.'

Attempting irony, James says, 'That counts me out, then.'

'You play no instrument?'

'I fiddled about with the guitar for a bit. Strumming chords, not much more. R&B, pop, you know the kind of stuff.'

But she doesn't really. She doesn't know Rhythm and Blues. She knows of the Beatles – 'some good harmonies' – she knows about Elvis Presley. But not the Rolling Stones or the Animals or anything of that kind.

'I think,' Horst decides, clearly bored with the conversation, 'that we go back to the dining room where Frau Weber has presented one of her excellent *Apfelkuchen*.'

And over the apple pie they talk of other things, of where Ellie and James are going, both in the next days and in life; and where Horst is going – into politics, as a member of the SPD and a devotee of its leader, Willy Brandt – although in the immediate future he is accompanying his aunt to Prague.

'Prague?'

'Tomorrow we are going.'

'I have some master classes at the conservatoire,' she explains. 'And then a concert with the Czech Philharmonic Orchestra. It is something I have done for years now. This time it will be the Dvořák. Maybe' – she smiles – 'maybe it is always the Dvořák. But I will also play the Brahms Double

Concerto with a young Russian violinist. The conductor will be Gennady Egorkin. Do you know Egorkin?'

'By name,' says Ellie.

'He is celebrated,' she says reprovingly, as though mere recognition of the name is not sufficient, 'both for his conducting and his piano. One of the great musicians of our age. But he is known also for his – how do you say it? – outspokenness against the system. At the present time he cannot travel to the West, I believe, but to Czechoslovakia this is possible.'

'Only yesterday we met some other musicians going to Prague,' James says.

'Who are these musicians? Perhaps I know them?'

'I don't think so. A group called the Ides of March.'

'A chamber group?'

'A rock group.'

Her face falls.

'American,' James explains. 'Four of them. Long hair, Mexican moustaches, torn jeans. Guitars and drums.'

'Oh.' For a moment she looks downcast, but then she manages a glimpse of optimism. 'Yet Prague is still a beautiful city, even with such people. One of the most beautiful cities in the world. And what is happening there now deserves our support, do you not think? Even the support of your Ides of March.'

Of course they agree. It is wonderful, really, the way the people are having their say. And how they are all behind Dubček and his allies. Even Ellie, who hasn't yet worked out a way to brand the reformers as bourgeois lackeys of the capitalist world, agrees. Indeed, she waxes positively lyrical about Dubček's socialists as she and James eat their strudel. Perhaps Czechoslovakia is showing the way to the future. Socialism with a human face. Isn't that wonderful? An ideal. Something to believe in.

'I don't think so,' says Frau Eckstein drily. 'I think I have

176

already seen too much of idealism and belief to have any faith in either.'

They leave the house into a night that has the chill of high places beneath a cloudless sky. The moon casts a bleak, monochrome light as they blow up their airbeds, lay out their sleeping bags and struggle to undress within the narrow confines of the tent. Ellie seems changed both by her confession in Strasbourg and by Frau Eckstein's playing. There is something fragile about her, something tearful and dependent which is quite unlike the girl he thought he knew. They cling together like a couple adrift after a shipwreck. 'Isn't she wonderful?' she says, speaking of Frau Eckstein. 'Isn't she just the most beautiful woman?' Her head is nestled against his neck. For the first time ever, he feels that she has some kind of dependence on him.

'You're in love with her.'

She punches him lightly in the ribs. 'With her music.'

'It was all right.'

'*All right*? The music was judging you, you weren't judging the music.'

'I said it was all right.'

'It is not enough to find it all right. You've got to find it,' she pauses, considering, 'transcendent.'

'I don't even know what transcendent means.'

'Uplifting. Outlifting. Is there such a word? Taking you out of yourself, out of the world. Transporting you out of the material world and into something beyond.'

'That sounds like religion. You don't have religion.'

'It's just a feeling. Like getting high.'

'Maybe you shouldn't have sold that weed.'

She laughs softly against his shoulder. What has happened? Metaphors pile up in his mind. A dam has burst. A wall has been breached. Something, some hard carapace has at least

177

been cracked. He bends his head and buries his face in her hair.

'Maybe we should go,' she says thoughtfully.

'Go where?'

'Go to hear her play. In Prague.'

'For God's sake, we've planned on Greece, haven't we?' He imagines olive groves, parched hillsides, cool wine and hot nights. Not some godforsaken city in Eastern Europe. 'We can't change our ideas now.'

He feels her shrug. 'It was just a thought,' she says.

20

The next morning, after breakfast, there are fond farewells at the house. 'You are like my children,' Frau Eckstein confesses in a moment of surprising sentimentality. She kisses James on both cheeks, hugs Ellie to her like a daughter. 'You must keep yourselves safe,' she admonishes them, as though safety were a thing one could choose to have or not.

Horst drives them the short way to the nearest main road. He is full of instructions and information, delivered in the manner of the academic, as though what he says is an enormous joke if only you can see through the solemn façade. Apparently Donaueschingen is not really the source of the Donau, the Danube, at all. Instead the geographical honour ought to lie with the town of Furtwangen, a full 48 kilometres further upstream. There a stream called the Breg rises and runs down into what the whole world recognises as the Danube. So, is Furtwangen the true source of the river? And should the river be renamed the Breg, causing consternation and chaos amongst cartographers the world over? 'This important matter has never been resolved,' he tells them as he drops them at a convenient lay-by. 'Another curious thing is that here we are only about thirty kilometres from the Rhine. The Rhine going one way, the Danube going the other. Ships that pass in the night, isn't that what you say?' He looks up at them from within the prison of his own car. 'It is perhaps a metaphor for life. *Auf Wiedersehen, meine Freunde.* Perhaps in Prague.'

'Perhaps,' says Ellie.

'I am a bit envious,' he calls out, 'of your freedom.'

That paradox once again. The freedom and the restriction – they can go anywhere they wish, but unless a vehicle stops for them they can go almost nowhere at all. Thus the journey resumes – short lifts (a van, a car) – eastwards out of the Black Forest towards ... where? All around them is a vast expanse of southern Germany. James has never seen such size, the forests and fields going on to the horizon, seemingly unmarred by towns or cities. And the immaculate nature of the land, the roadside verge manicured, the fences polished, the woods perfectly trimmed. How is all this possible? The places he knows – Yorkshire, Derbyshire, Oxfordshire – shrink in memory to small, scruffy domains, while this, the map tells him, is only a fragment of Germany, called, apparently, Baden-Württemberg, which name evokes memories of model soldiers in shakoes and bearskins, fighting for statelets – the Grand Duchy of Baden, the Kingdom of Württemberg – that no longer exist outside of the history books.

A lift drops them at a junction where a signpost points right towards Konstanz, Lindau and Austria, or left towards Memmingen, Ulm and München. Ulm seems familiar. A treaty? A battle?

Ellie unfolds the map. 'So we go right,' James says. 'To Austria.'

What does Austria mean? The Alps. Vienna. The Waltz, the Blue Danube, which is this same river whose source, nothing more than a stream, is fought over by two neighbouring towns. Ellie turns the map thoughtfully. 'Or we change plans ...'

'Change plans?'

She points, to München and beyond. 'Why *not* go to Prague?'

180

'What?'

She smiles encouragingly. 'Wouldn't it be great? We'd see her perform. Frau Eckstein, I mean. And we'd see what it's really like there.'

'But we've planned—'

'And the Ides. That'd be cool.' She is bright and excited, suddenly enthralled by her idea. 'We're free, for Christ's sake. We don't *have* to do anything. And this ... it'd be a bit of history, the kind of thing we'll regret not having done. Italy we can see anytime, or Greece. But Czechoslovakia is now!' She waves the map as though that might conjure lifts out of the air. 'How far can it be? A few hours.'

'It's the other side of the bloody Iron Curtain.'

'So what?'

'Are you *serious*?'

But of course she's serious. Her eyes are alight with a brighter fire than James has ever managed to ignite. He looks around. To the south are distant hills, with the Alps beyond them, out of sight but not out of mind. He has never seen the Alps. The biggest mountains he has known are in the Lake District and North Wales. When you are that ignorant novelty becomes the norm.

'Let's toss for it,' he decides. 'Heads we continue as planned. Tails—'

'What's tails?'

He shows the coin. A Deutschmark. 'The eagle.'

'So, eagle we go to Prague.'

'If they'll let us in.'

'If they don't, we just carry on as before.' There is no further argument. Tossing a coin resolves everything. The coin sings in the air and falls at their feet. The eagle.

21

'What about a trip to Munich?' Sam asked her.

Lenka's eyes widened. '*Munich*?'

How do you measure distance? Munich was a mere two hundred miles away, yet beyond imagining. It was just over the border yet it was beyond the Pale. He might as well have suggested visiting the far side of the moon.

'I've got to deliver diplomatic bags to the consulate and there'll be plenty of room in the car. I'll have to take the security man along, but he's a mate and he'll turn a blind eye. All you need is your passport. You do have a passport, don't you?'

Her eyes glistened. Behaving as you please was a new experience, doing your own thing something that you needed to practise. But yes, she did have a passport, issued for a student conference in Budapest the previous year. The only time she had ever been out of the country. But she'd need an exit visa, which would take a few days and three hundred crowns. Something like that. She made a face.

'You're my guest,' Sam assured her, and felt a strange, erotic thrill at the idea of giving her the money.

They travelled in an embassy car, a large, sagging Humber Super Snipe designed to demonstrate the importance of British manufacturing in a world of Tatra and Škoda. The two of them sat in the back while Derrick, ex-police sergeant and head of security at the embassy, drove. 'They'll think we're the ambassador and his wife,' Sam said.

Lenka giggled. The trip had transformed into something like a school prank, vaguely illicit yet harmless enough. They sat close together in the back, their hands intertwined in her lap, below the sight line of the driver's reflected eyes. Sam experienced a terrible intensity of sensation, focused on the touch of her thigh against his, the grasp of her strong fingers, the warmth of her body. He wanted to make love to her, there and then, on the hot leather of the back seat of the embassy car as it swayed and lurched round corners and over switchbacks through the Bohemian countryside towards Pilsen. And he even wondered whether it might be possible to do it without the sergeant, with his tired, suspicious eyes, ever noticing.

Perhaps not.

As always there was barely any traffic on the roads, and after Pilsen they entered a landscape almost empty of people, as though war was imminent and the inhabitants had been evacuated. Warnings were posted along the road.

POZOR!
HRANIČNÍ PASMO
VSTUP JEN NA POVOLENI
Warning! Border Zone. Authorised entry only.

Sam felt Lenka tense beside him. But the embassy car drove blithely on into the no-man's-land that cut a swathe right through the centre of Europe. The first line of fencing appeared, running north and south away into the distance, over fields and through woods.

ZAKÁZÁNE PASMO
VSTUP ZAKÁZÁN
Forbidden zone. Do not enter.

But they entered with sublime indifference, confident in their diplomatic plates, their diplomatic immunity from all interference. Watchtowers appeared on either side, marching above double fencing that was twice as tall as a man. Ahead was the checkpoint itself, with striped barriers like barbers' poles. A few vehicles had collected against the gates like detritus in a stream. The Humber came to a halt in the reserved lane. Lenka's grip tightened.

'They know we're coming,' Sam assured her. 'All diplomatic cars have to cross at this point. We inform them we're crossing and more or less at what time. It's all perfectly normal. They probably won't even look at our papers.'

But they did. One of the guards, a mere child, leant in at the window and took the driver's passport and diplomatic pass and called something out to his colleague behind him. Sam could hear Lenka's sharp intake of breath, feel the tension in her body. She held her breath and waited. Sam got out of the car. 'Is there a problem? Do you want to see the bags?' The boot was opened and the guards peered in at canvas pouches with their diplomatic seals. Sam smiled, proffering documents. The senior guard refused the offer and told the younger one that he should have just waved them through. 'No bother at all,' Sam assured him. He reached into the boot, picked up a carton of two hundred cigarettes and proffered it to them. *Players Please.* 'Here, split it among your mates.'

There were smiles all round now. Even laughter. One of them tried out his English. 'Beatles, you like Beatles?'

'Beatles are great,' Sam assured him. 'But Rolling Stones are better.' More laughter. He got back into the car, then leant out of the window as though struck by a thought. 'Just so you know,' he told them, 'we'll be back tomorrow evening.' The guards grinned and nodded. Derrick slipped the car into gear and allowed it to run forward, down the slope towards the bottom of the valley.

Lenka let her breath go. 'Why,' she asked in a whisper, 'must I be afraid of them?' And then a hint of panic came into her voice, like the fluttering of a warning flag in the wind: 'I don't have an exit stamp. They didn't give me an exit stamp. If I don't have an exit stamp they won't let me back in.'

'Of course they will. At the worst it'll be another carton of cigarettes.'

'Is that right?'

'Of course it's right.'

They crossed the bridge and drove up to the border post on the West German side. The black two-headed eagle flew in the warm breeze. There were more uniforms, a cursory glance at the driver's documents and a salute from one of the guards. An American soldier watched from afar, leaning on the steering wheel of his jeep, chewing gum. The Iron Curtain had been crossed.

A day and a night in Munich. Their hotel was decked out in wood panelling and wrought iron and enough *Gemütlichkeit* to satisfy a multitude of American tourists. After they had settled in, they wandered through the narrow streets of the Altstadt. Sam suggested visiting the Frauenkirche and the Neues Rathaus, but Lenka demurred. 'We have,' she pointed out, 'many grand buildings in Prague.' Instead she wanted to see the shops, where she marvelled at the superabundance of goods on display. Sam followed her, trying to read her mood. It took him time to understand that the reason she looked but never considered buying was that she simply didn't have the money. The few deutschmarks she had changed from Czechoslovak crowns were enough to buy little more than a few cups of coffee.

'I'll buy you a present,' he suggested. 'A dress. Is that what you'd like?'

'You don't have to.'

'But I want to.'

She considered the matter as she considered many things, with a faint frown of concentration, as though she were facing some kind of political or moral dilemma. 'All right,' she said eventually. 'But only because you want to.'

They decided on a department store on Marienplatz, a building from the 1930s that nestled, and nestles still, against the neo-Gothic absurdities of the Neues Rathaus. The interior was heady with perfume and lit by crystal chandeliers. It was as though they had wandered into a piece of elaborate and tasteless costume jewellery; amidst all the glitter Lenka seemed like an uncut diamond, plain of dress and manner but clearly more beautiful than any of the treasures on display. Beneath the obsequious eye of a shop assistant, she tried things on – skirts of varying shortness, dresses with differing necklines, trousers, trouser suits – finally settling on a halterneck dress printed in squares of primary colour.

Very Mondrian, the shop assistant told her, producing scarves, necklaces, handbags that involved further expend-iture but would, she assured her hesitating client, bring the whole ensemble to some kind of perfection. 'These things are very swinging London.' A thoughtful pause. 'Although Madam is not English, I think.'

'Madam is Czech,' Lenka said.

There was a moment's hesitation in the woman's flow of superlatives. 'Czech is very interesting,' she said.

Later they had lunch at a café and afterwards strolled in the English Garden. The afternoon seemed trance-like, suffused with sunshine and pollen and the strong scent of anticipation. The agonies and excitements of Prague were matters affecting other people on the far side of the world. 'Can we stay here for ever?' Lenka asked. She knew the answer but at that moment all things seemed possible. One might for ever stroll hand in hand over landscaped lawns and think only of the forthcoming evening and the intense and humid night to follow.

Next morning they shopped for those items that could accompany them as part of the diplomatic bag – deodorants, soap, all the things you couldn't find on the other side. Stockings, silk underwear, an Hermès scarf. To Lenka it seemed both a subject of amusement – 'That is the trouble with everyone in the West: they are obsessed with *things*' – and a source of bitterness – 'Why is there so much, and yet we have so little? Didn't Germany lose the war? and yet here they are, like victors.'

After lunch Sam left her at the hotel and took their haul to the consulate to pack it away in the boot of the Humber, sealed in those canvas bags inscribed with HBM DIPLOMATIC SERVICE. There was the feeling of end of holiday, of bathos, of anticlimax. With Derrick driving, he went back to collect Lenka. Derrick got out to put their luggage in the boot while Sam held the door open for Lenka to get in. There was that manoeuvre of long legs, a glimpse of thigh that reminded him of saying goodbye to Steffie. That moment seemed ages ago, part of another world that he had inhabited. In just a handful of days this woman had strolled into his life with her particular mixture of innocence and recklessness and taken it over. He could hear the tut-tutting from senior diplomats, smell the scorched odour of disapproval among the office staff, see outrage and betrayal in Steffie's face. He wondered whether he cared and decided that he didn't because – this was the disturbing thing – beside Lenka they all paled into insignificance.

Once settled back in the car, Derrick's eyes glanced in the mirror at the two passengers in the back. 'You owe me one, Sam,' he said.

'Two. And a packet of crisps.'

22

It takes them two days. Two days, five arguments, one night in the tent somewhere in the environs of Regensburg. From Regensburg they follow the haphazard path of lifts through forested hills and open farmland. The size of the country dwarfs the two of them, reduces them to figures in a landscape, ants crossing the vastness of the place. By the afternoon of the second day a swathe of forest lies across their path as they plod through the empty heat. Occasionally a car goes by but no one stops. An American army jeep passes them travelling in the opposite direction, followed by a German military vehicle. A helicopter chutters in the sky away to the south. And there is something else in the air – a sense of threat, of fear, of moment, the kind of feeling you might have approaching the edge of a precipice. Iron Curtain. The phrase dominates their progress. On their map it is marked in a forbidding red, a serpentine line without obvious rhyme or reason, marked *Staatsgrenze*. *Staatsgrenze* is, they discover after thumbing through a phrasebook purchased in Regensburg, State Border.

What goes on beyond that line is as unknown as the blank spaces on a medieval map. Here be dragons. Ellie looks accusingly at the empty landscape ahead, the hills and woods, a winding valley with its occasional and indifferent farmhouses.

'I suppose we just walk,' James says.

'What's the choice?'

The choice, he almost adds, is to give up this fucking idiot idea and continue south as they originally intended, to Italy and the sunshine. But Ellie holds the ultimate card, the one that trumps every argument, the one she deployed with such devastating skill in the damp camp in Regensburg when they argued about it – you go to Italy if that's what you want, but I'm going to Prague. By myself if necessary.

The fact is, he doesn't want to lose her. Fando is held in thrall by Lis.

So they walk on towards the border with the stolid plod of soldiers tramping, while indifferent cars go past, a few in their direction, more the other way, westwards, away from whatever it is that lies ahead. A sign says *Waidhaus, 3 Kilometer* and warns *Staatsgrenze*. They walk again, and again no one stops. Waidhaus is a collection of dull, stolid houses around a central square with a blue and white striped maypole. Outside the town a sign commands

US Forces
Personnel
HALT.
1 KILOMETER TO
Czechoslovakia
DO NOT PROCEED
WITHOUT AUTHORITY

But ironically it is the American army which comes to the rescue, a jeep that draws up alongside them. The driver leans on the steering wheel and regards them with amused curiosity. He's chewing gum. His face has an open all-American smile, a farm boy used to vast fields and a huge sky. Perhaps at home here in Bavaria. He wears khaki fatigues with sergeant's stripes and a shoulder flash showing a fleur-de-lys with the motto *Toujours Pret*.

189

'Where y'all goin' then?' he asks.

'Why d'you want to know?' Ellie says. 'Are you going to arrest us or something?'

He laughs. 'Thought you might need a ride somewhere, ma'am. I passed you a while back and you sure haven't moved on a whole lot. 'Course, I can always leave you at the roadside if that's what you want.'

She bridles. Is that the word? It conjures up horses and struggling riders and reins. The sound of whinnying in the air. Police horses in Grosvenor Square. She shouted Pigs! at the police and chanted Ho! Ho! Ho Chi Minh! and tried, rather ineffectually, to get through the main doors of the American embassy – behind which, so the rumour went, armed marines stood ready to open fire on any intruders. 'Why aren't you in Vietnam?' she demands, her tone laden with sarcasm.

'Because I was lucky.'

'So what are you doing here?'

'With the Second Armored Cavalry, supporting our German friends and allies. Look lady, I can't stay here all day talking with you. If you don't want a ride then I'll have to move on—'

'We're going to Prague,' James says.

Amusement steps down the alphabet, as so often, to bemusement. 'Is that right? Well, I'm sorry to say I can't take you quite that far, but I'll take you to the border if you like. No one else is gonna give you a ride around here.'

Ellie looks enquiringly at James. As far as he is concerned there is no question to answer. They climb into the vehicle.

'We're not meant to carry civilians,' the sergeant explains as he shoves the jeep into gear, 'but if I found you in the border zone I could log you as an AVI. That's Avoidance of Incident.' There's a radio in the back of the jeep. As he drives he reaches over for the handset and talks to someone in that peculiar, truncated language the military use: Echo Foxtrot found two

190

Civs near the border and is escorting them to the checkpoint. A disembodied voice squawks back at him through the earphone. 'Affirmative, Echo Foxtrot,' it says.

The driver is called Chester. Chester B. Falk, Sergeant First Class. From Tennessee. 'Along with Davy Crockett,' he says. 'You folks been to Tennessee? No? That's no surprise. No one ever has but everyone has heard of it, because of Davy Crockett. Ain't that a thing? What about you folks? Where you from? England, I'm guessing.'

'I'm from Sheffield,' James says.

'Hey, we have a Sheffield in Alabama.'

Ellie is in the back of the jeep, with the rucksacks. She didn't deign to sit with the soldier in the front. 'I daresay the English one was named after it,' she calls out.

'I don't think so,' the sergeant replies. 'England's a whole lot more historic than the US.'

'I was being ironic.'

He laughs. 'We simple folk don't do irony.' Which seems to James pretty ironic in itself. They pass a further sign warning of the approaching border. Sergeant Falk glances round at his passengers. 'You wanna see?'

'What?'

'The border. The goddam Iron Curtain. 'Cause I'm meant to have picked you up there, so we had better make an alibi, hadn't we?'

The jeep decelerates and turns off the main road onto a farm track between fields of wheat. They bump over potholes, pass through a collection of farm buildings and come out onto the side of a shallow valley. A tractor is at work, dragging a plough through the heavy loam of the nearest field. As the machine turns at the end of the furrow, the driver catches sight of the stationary jeep and raises his hand in some kind of salute. Falk gives a jaunty wave in return.

'That's it, folks. The border between East and West.'

'Where?'

'Stream at the bottom of the valley.' A concrete road runs parallel with the stream on their side of the valley; the far side is forest, implacable ranks of black pines stretching away in both directions.

'Is that all?'

Sergeant Falk smiles. He's done this before. Same view, same laconic remarks. 'Pretty regular we get folks straying across the border. Step over the stream and you're in the CSSR. Sometimes even our own patrols. But you can't go far because it ain't quite that simple.' He turns the jeep onto the concrete road and drives south to where there is a break in the trees on the far side, a gap about a hundred yards wide where you can see through the forest into the world beyond, into the East.

'There's also that.'

Drawn across the far end of the break is the Curtain. More wire than iron, it cuts across the space about five hundred yards away, a barrier of fencing apparently as fragile and translucent as gauze. Beyond the fence is a watchtower, a spider creature supported on slender legs with the sky glinting on its several eyes. It might just have paused in its progress across the countryside in order to examine the jeep and its three passengers.

The engine of the jeep ticks as it cools. The tractor groans in the background, arguing with the heavy loam, while birds sing, as they will whatever the geopolitical circumstances. Far away the helicopter flies higher than most birds. Sergeant Chester reaches below the dashboard of the jeep, takes up a pair of binoculars and hands them to James. 'Have a look. The Reds usually build the fences about a mile back from the actual border, but just here it comes closer. Something to do with the lie of the land, I guess. So we bring visitors here to have a look-see.'

James puts the binoculars to his eyes. The spider's body leaps towards him as though he's examining it under a microscope. The beast is peopled, two figures moving vaguely behind the windows, watching him watching them. He pans down the creature's stick legs to the ground. In front of it there are two parallel lines of fencing, flattened together by foreshortening. He can pick out barbed wire coiled along the tops of both lines and guess at about fifty yards of cleared soil between the two. Beyond the watchtower is a parallel road to match the one that they are on.

Wordlessly, he hands the binoculars to Ellie.

'The question is,' Chester muses, 'what's it for? If it's to keep us out then it sure ain't gonna work. A Patton tank'd go through that like a tractor through a picket fence. They know that and we know that. So what's it for?' He glances round at his audience as though looking for an answer. 'Easy, really. It's to keep their people in. If you'll excuse ma French, lady, you're looking into the biggest fucking prison camp the world has ever seen.'

There's a significant pause before Ellie summons an answer. 'It's not as simple as that. Look at what's happening in Czechoslovakia at this very moment. There's freedom. They've abandoned censorship. They're allowing political meetings. And foreign travel.'

The soldier looks doubtful. 'When you're in the military you see the world through military eyes, ma'am. All I see is the Russkis just waitin' on the borders to pay a fraternal visit to their Czechoslovakian brothers.' He puts the jeep in gear and they move slowly along the track, away from the implacable gaze of the watchtower. 'And when that happens, it's game over.'

They reach the main road. Falk waits for a tourist coach to pass and then pulls out and turns left to follow the coach towards the border. The road dips down towards the bottom of the valley, but just before the stream there's the German customs post. It has the look of a railway station about it, with most of the trains delayed or cancelled. There are barriers striped like barbers' poles and German police standing around doing not very much. A concrete building flies the black, red and gold of the Federal Republic, while a signpost holds up a black eagle like a medieval shield on the end of a lance. In an adjacent car park are half a dozen cars and three lorries. Over to the right another building flies the stars and stripes and the union jack as well as the German flag. Beyond the border post the road dips down to the bottom of the valley, crosses a narrow bridge, then climbs up through the trees and disappears into the East.

'There we are,' the sergeant says. 'I don't go any further than here. Once you're over the border Czechoslovak border control is about one K further up the road. So they tell me.'

James and Ellie climb out of the jeep. 'You kids look after yourselves,' the sergeant says, 'and give my regards to Mr Dooby Check if you see him.' He turns the jeep round, waves jauntily to the German border guards and drives off.

James and Ellie contemplate the possibilities. As they watch, a single car appears on the Czechoslovak side and crosses the bridge towards the West German barriers. A border guard examines the driver's documents while his colleague walks round the car, inspecting it with scant respect.

'A Škoda,' James says.

'What's a Škoda?'

'The car is. How can you tell a Škoda from a Jehovah's Witness?'

'No idea, but you're going to tell me.'

'You can close the door on a Jehovah's Witness.'

Gratifyingly, she laughs. They watch the border guard complete his inspection and allow the car to clatter its way past them into the West. Then they sling their rucksacks onto their shoulders and walk down the slope to the barrier.

The German border guard is indifferent, taking their passports with barely a glance at the owners, flicking through the documents like a cardsharp before handing them back as though they are tainted. 'You are to Czechoslovakia going? They will not let you pass – you have no visas.'

They haven't thought of visas.

'Don't they issue them at the border?'

'Who knows? At the moment anything is possible.' He points up the hill on the other side. 'Seven hundred metres, Czechoslovak control. Stay on the road or ...' He makes a gesture, a pistol firing.

'This is stupid,' James protests to Ellie. 'You heard. We need visas. We haven't got them so we'll not be able to get in. We should turn round. There's no point.'

'Of course there's a point. We'll blag our way in. A bit of a smile, a bit of bullshit. It'll be all right.'

The barrier – a barber's pole, a jousting lance – rises for them and they walk down the slope towards the bridge, Ellie first, James half a pace behind. Notices are everywhere – warnings, exhortations, threats.

STAATSGRENZE
Das Überschreiten der Grenze ist eine
GRENZVERLETZUNG

Across the hollow boards of the bridge the language changes into one that means even less to them:

POZOR!
STÁTNÍ HRANICE
PROBÍHAJÍ HRANIČNÍM
VODNÍM TOKEM

Ellie leafs through the pocket Czech dictionary they bought off someone at the campsite in Regensburg. *Probíhají* doesn't feature. 'Looks like prohibition of some kind.' *Vodni tok* is 'stream'. *Warning!* she decides. *State border. Forbidden to cross the stream.* Which, despite James's protests, is precisely what they have just done, and are now stumping up the slope beyond, into no-man's-land, between ranks of silver birch that stand like sentinels forbidding trespass into the pine forest beyond. It's a long walk in the afternoon sun. A few cars pass them going out, the passengers staring through the windows; more cars pass going in, Volkswagens, Borgwards, NSUs, loaded with camping equipment. The Czechoslovak border post approaches, shimmering out of the hot air from the tarmac. Signs shout at them.

POZOR! POZOR!

Border guards observe their approach to the barrier with indifference. There's a queue of cars warming up the summer air. Rows of parked cars to one side. Coaches drawn up like ships at a quayside. People line up at a concrete building with small windows whose blurred glass panes have never been cleaned. From the open door of an office music emerges as though from the throat of a tin man, something vaguely Beatles, vaguely Beach Boys.

One of the guards snaps his fingers. '*Pas,*' he demands.

They hand over their passports. Ellie smiles. Smiles appear to be a newcomer to the border guard's repertoire of expressions. He attempts one with scant success. He is no older than they, a pale youth with a prominent Adam's apple and a scattering of acne pustules across his cheeks. He examines the documents with curiosity. 'English,' he says.

'English,' Ellie agrees. 'Anglický.'

'Beatles,' he says. 'Liverpool.'

196

But there's a change in the music emerging from the transistor radio inside the office. No longer approximately Beatles, it is now plainly and excruciatingly 'Puppet On A String'. In Czech. Ellie begins to sing along with the music, in English.

The guard smiles. This is a real smile, displaying a graveyard of teeth. 'Přenosilová,' he says. 'Loutka.'

'Sandie Shaw,' Ellie responds, guessing.

A second guard joins in. 'Foots. Naked foots.' And then adds something in Czech – a tripping, splintered sound like the snapping of bones – which makes his colleague laugh out loud. 'No vísum,' the first guard points out, handing the passports back with something like a hint of regret. He gestures towards the customs house where already people are crowding.

They join a queue. German is spoken all around. Someone tries to explain in English and they hear a story of displacement and desolation that they only half-understand. 'Once we live here,' the man tells them. 'Now we are as tourists coming.'

They edge forward along the pathways of bureaucracy. Inside the building is the smell of old concrete and stale sweat, and perhaps, lurking in the background, a hint of urine. Glum men sit at desks and administer the stamps of acceptance and authenticity with a device like a miniature guillotine. The mechanism descends, and there, on the page marked 'visas', is a new imprimatur: ČESKOSLOVENSKÉ VÍSUM. A few endorsements, a flash of a pen, a date stamp against VSTUPNÍ and all is done. Money changes hands through a metal grille. For their traveller's cheques they receive bundles of used notes denominated in Czechoslovak *koruny*. Questions are waved away. They move on, through further passageways and out into the afternoon sunshine on the inside of the Iron Curtain.

Border

It is interesting to contemplate the border they have just crossed. A curtain of iron – well, chain-link fencing, barbed wire and free-fire zones – but at the same time a mere line on a map between forest and forest, between mountain and mountain, between farmland and farmland. Between states, yes, the old kingdom of Bavaria, once ruled by mad King Ludwig, and the Austrian Empire, but a border between German and German, created during wars of religion and wars of politics and power, and culminating in the final border to end all borders, drawn on a map at the château of Saint-Germain-en-Laye near Paris in the year of peace, 1919, when the state of Czechoslovakia, mainly an amalgam of Czechs and Slovaks (who almost shared a language but little else), was created out of bits and pieces of the Austria-Hungary Empire. But here, with brilliant historical irony, the border meandered down stream valleys and along watersheds and failed entirely to take into account the language on the ground, neatly separating German speaker from German speaker and thereby planting the seeds of the next war which would bring the whole of the continent, indeed much of the whole world, to its knees in the bloodiest and nastiest conflict of all time.

Shortly after the end of that war, in the month of October 1945, in what President Beneš of the newly liberated Czechoslovakia called, with fantastic insensitivity, 'the final solution to the German question', the German speakers on the eastern side of the border (approximately two million of them) were systematically driven over this border to join their cousins on the western side. Thus, in the last sixty years of its effective life, the border became a linguistic barrier as well as a political one.

In the autumn of 1989, with the collapse of the Soviet empire, the watchtowers were dismantled and the barbed-wire fences uprooted. Finally in December 2007 the Czech Republic signed the Schengen Agreement and the border entirely disappeared, one hopes for ever. No barbed wire, no customs posts, nothing more than an almost forgotten line drawn on the map. More than that, the crossing point where James and Eleanor entered Czechoslovakia in 1968 was, by 1997, bypassed by a new motorway a mile to the south, so that road traffic now flows back and forth with only a ritual road sign to tell the driver that he has moved from one country to another. And yet ... Czech and German biologists have discovered that the red deer that roam the Bohemian forest are still keeping to their respective sides of the border, Czech deer on the east, Bavarian deer on the west. These deer cannot have been alive during the period of the Iron Curtain, so it seems that they have been taught by their parents, perhaps their grandparents. Thus the last trace of the Cold War division lies only within the brains of *Cervus elaphus*, the red deer.

23

James and Ellie walk away from this border, into the world beyond. Emptiness strikes them. They see woods, and fields, some cultivated, some derelict, but no people. A scatter of abandoned houses. Little traffic except for the West German cars that have been queuing at the border and are now driving past, indifferent to the lonely plod of Fando and Lis towards an unknown Tar.

Finally a tractor stops for them. The driver is dark, weather-beaten, more like a sailor than a farmer. 'Rom,' he says, beating his chest. They have no means of communication with him but they presume that's his name. Frowning, talking volubly, Rom takes them as far as a hamlet where there are more abandoned houses and a few modern concrete ones, where loudspeakers on telegraph poles play music to no one at all. The tractor goes off up a track running through the fields, leaving them on the tarmac road with nothing to do but walk. Along the roadside are fruit trees laden with fruit – cherries, plums, apples. They walk, eating ripe plums. It's late afternoon and there's the matter of where to spend the night. No hotels, no pubs, no campsites in this desolate corner of Europe. The space around them seems to grow larger, vast and empty. 'Plenty of places to put the tent up,' James observes. 'Only danger will be being eaten by bears.'

'Is that a joke? I presume it is a joke. Anyway, I've had it with your bloody tent.'

He ignores her and keeps on walking. Perhaps one of those abandoned houses which they passed a while back? Perhaps the ditch beside the road? Perhaps that line of forest away to the right? They plod onwards ...

24

Afternoon sunshine on the forests and fields of Bohemia. The embassy car reversed the route of the day before, passing through the West German border post without let or hindrance, crossing the bridge over the stream and climbing the slope through no-man's-land towards the Czech customs post. The car slowed to a crawl. There was a queue of cars at the normal channel, a jaunty wave of recognition as the Humber moved towards the reserved lane. The barrier went up. Lenka relaxed her grip.

'Not even a carton of cigarettes,' Sam said. 'But a pint for Derrick.'

'Two, you said. And none of that fizzy Czech stuff. Watneys.'

The car cruised on. Ahead two figures appeared at the edge of the road. Long hair and jeans. The usual uniform. 'Hitchhikers,' Derrick said. His policeman's mind came into play. Regulations were regulations no matter where you were. 'Shouldn't be hitchhiking in the border zone. Could find themselves inside.' He slowed and pulled out to pass them. Sam glanced out of the side window. GB.

'Better stop, Derrick. Otherwise the police will pick them up and the consular department will have to deal with it. No end of a fuss.'

The car came to a slow and reluctant halt. Lenka looked

round. The two hitchers were shuffling forward under the weight of their rucksacks, looking bedraggled and grimy. A boy with a fledgling beard. A girl with chaotic hair.

'Bloody kids,' said Derrick.

Sam opened the door and climbed out as the couple approached. 'Going to Prague?'

They came to a panting halt beside the car. 'You're English,' the boy said. 'I wondered what a Humber was doing here.'

'Embassy car, actually. You're lucky. It's forbidden to hitchhike in the border zone. You could have got yourselves arrested.'

'So sir's come to tell us off, has he?' the girl said.

'Actually, he's come to offer you a lift.' Sam opened the boot of the car. 'You may put your packs in with Her Majesty's diplomatic bags as long as you can assure me that they do not contain any illegal substances. My name's Samuel Wareham, by the way. Sam to friends and associates, but you may call me "sir" if you like.'

Chastened, the pair climbed into the back seat. A faint smell of unwashed bodies accompanied them. Lenka edged up to give them room and Sam took his place in front. 'I'm Ellie,' the girl said. 'He's James.'

'From Oxford,' the boy added.

'City or university?'

'University.'

'Which college?'

He told him. 'And Ellie's at St Hilda's.'

'And you're going to Prague ... ?'

'To suss the place out, really. Spur-of-the-moment decision. And to hear Birgit Eckstein play.'

'Are you musicians?'

'We know her.'

'Do you indeed?'

The girl explained – hitching through the Black Forest, a

lift from a couple of Germans, one of whom was the cellist. 'So we thought—'

The boy interrupted. 'No thought involved, just the toss of a coin. Italy or here, that was the choice.' His accent was from the North. South Yorkshire, Sam thought. Other side of the Pennines from Derrick. Chip on his shoulder, but that was hardly his fault when he found himself confronted by Oxford.

'So you've opted for Slav drama, rather than Italian opera? Well, be careful. Prague's all very exciting at the moment, but if you want to avoid getting into trouble, be careful what you do or say.'

'Is that sir talking?' the girl said.

'Just a piece of advice. We don't want to be arranging consular visits and trying to contact your parents to explain that their little darlings are in Pankrác prison.'

'You didn't do that for me when I was arrested in Paris last May.'

'What were you doing there? Playing at revolutions? Here they have them for real – and that's why it's so dangerous. Ask Lenka.'

From her corner Lenka made a little moue of distaste. 'I don't want to talk about things. They're young. Let them enjoy themselves.'

'As long as it's not at the taxpayer's expense.'

'Aren't *you* enjoying yourself at the taxpayer's expense?' the girl said.

Sam laughed. She was a snappy young lady and would, he didn't doubt, make a shrewish woman. 'You'd make a good politician. Where are you staying in Prague?'

'No idea,' the boy replied. 'A hostel or something.'

'It's not easy, accommodation in Prague. There's a chronic shortage of beds, just like there's shortages of everything else. It's the result of a command economy. If no one has ordered hostels and hotels, hostels and hotels don't get built.'

'I can help maybe,' said Lenka. 'You can have my room.'
She glanced at Sam. 'For a few days?' She wasn't intending to
go back to her mother's exiguous flat, he could see that by her
look. Sam thought about Steffie and her reluctance to move
in with him. Just the occasional night. Perhaps a weekend.
'We have to recognise the proprieties,' she had warned him
whenever he'd suggested a more permanent arrangement. She
had sounded like someone in a pre-war drawing-room drama.
And now Lenka was looking at him with that knowing smile,
as though proprieties meant nothing.

VI

25

The girl called Lenka has, it seems, taken them under her wing. James had thought her cold and indifferent when they first encountered her in the embassy car with that stuck-up Wareham bloke, but it appears he was wrong. Under her wing, in hand, whatever turn of phrase you choose. She's given up the room she rents in a friend's flat in the New Town, an area of largely nineteenth-century buildings beyond the square that everyone has heard of in the West, the square that isn't a square, named after the king who wasn't a king – Václavské náměstí, Wenceslas Square. 'There you are,' she says, handing them over to their new hosts. 'You will be happy.' Which is unlikely but full of good intent.

The flat is cramped and, despite being up under the roofs, cave-like. The ceilings slope, things are stacked in the awkward space where the ceiling meets the floor, the doors are low enough to catch out those unwilling to bow their heads. An upright piano occupies one wall of the living room, a poster by Alfons Mucha another. There is a family photograph – my grandparents, Jitka says – of a couple staring disapprovingly out of the Austria-Hungary Empire into the People's Republic of Czechoslovakia. A violin case stands against the wall beside a gramophone and a cabinet of records. Their hosts are musicians, a violinist with one of the orchestras of the city and a composer. Jitka is the violinist's name. She's a sharp, nervous woman with a fine face that hasn't quite discovered how to be beautiful but is instead merely trying to be interesting. Dark eyes and a sharp nose. A mole like a small blackcurrant above the corner of her mouth. Jitka is what everyone calls her, but her given name is Judita, the Czech version of Judith, she explains. Then she looks faintly embarrassed, as though such things don't really matter. 'You call me Jitka.'

Jitka's English is good. Not as fully developed as Lenka's but more colloquial. She spent six months in America, on an exchange, playing in a youth orchestra in New York. She knows the West ... and now, she says, we will become like the West. If the Russians allow us.

Zdeněk, her husband, mutters something that Jitka translates. 'He says I should have stayed there.' She laughs to show it's a joke. 'It was just before we married. I guess he means I could have stayed there and gotten him to join me. Or maybe that he is not happy being married to me.' More laughter, weaker this time, which makes it even less convincing. Zdeněk scowls. Composing seems to involve great anguish, because he wears an expression of grim disenchantment – they call him *Bručoun*, Jitka says, which is the name for Grumpy, the bad-tempered dwarf in the *Snow White* cartoon. 'But he is also very political,' she says. 'Maybe we are all political these days.'

The room that Lenka has vacated for them is a contrast to the rest of the flat – strangely feminine, like a teenager's bedroom. A painting of horses galloping on a beach, family photographs on the dressing table, one of them showing a young couple holding aloft a baby that may be Lenka herself, another showing her as a young girl dressed in some kind of uniform. Apart from these, an older photo shows a solemn couple standing amongst the props of a photographer's studio – a classical column, a bowl of flowers. On the bed a teddy bear sits waiting for an owner who has surely grown up and gone away. The bed itself threatens more than it promises.

After unpacking their things Ellie and James discuss the price of the room with Jitka. She wants payment in dollars. 'We need the dollars. For when we go abroad.'

'It'll have to be pounds. We've only got sterling.'

Pounds will do. Hard currency is what matters. Jitka apologises, as though renting the room to them is somehow wrong. On the occasional street corner in the centre of the city touts offer *koruny* for dollars at four times the official exchange rate. 'Be careful doing that,' Jitka warns. 'Police often pretend to do it in order to catch you. If you want, it is better if I do any exchange for you. This,' she adds in parenthesis, 'is what we're reduced to.'

Her husband smokes, thin, dark cigarettes with a powerful smell that seems to have been absorbed into the fabric of the flat. He works in the living room at the upright piano on which he plays figures while scribbling the spidery signs of musical notation on sheets of manuscript paper. His wish is to compose symphonies and concertos; his job is to write jingles for television. Ellie and James try to talk music with them. Ellie is better at this of course, but they both have the connection with Frau Eckstein to relate. Does Jitka know Birgit Eckstein?

A squeal of delight. Of course! Birgit Eckstein is giving a concert. Jitka plays in the orchestra. She can get tickets if they want. 'Here in Prague there is much music. More than in New York or London, I think. The government puts money into music because you cannot see the politics in music.'

James asks how much the tickets will be and Jitka laughs, embarrassed. 'No, a gift from me to you.'

At night James and Ellie can hear Jitka and her husband through the thin partition walls making love in the next room. 'Making love' seems a misnomer: it is an urgent, painful sound, like people at manual labour of some repetitive kind,

211

working in a factory making useless products for a socialist command economy.

Next morning they venture out into the city, with an agreement to meet Lenka for coffee at the Kavárna Slavia. 'It is where all writers get together,' she explained when they made the arrangement. 'Everyone argues. It will be interesting.'

So James and Ellie wander the streets of Nové Město, the New Town, finding them drab and dusty. The few shops have plain windows and sparsely packed shelves. The buildings, nineteenth-century most of them, appear tarnished and battered, like pieces of forgotten family silver found behind a locked door. Advertisements seem half-hearted, as though there is little point in making much impact because no one's really buying. Trams packed with people clang and grind along the wider roads. In Wenceslas Square there's some kind of public meeting: a speaker harangues a small crowd. Flags fly. Perhaps it's a celebration of some kind, but it's impossible to tell. As they walk away a man darts out of a side street and tries to sell them something. James assumes it's sex of some kind; Ellie imagines stolen goods. But it's just money he wants to sell, Czech crowns for hard currency. 'Good rate,' he says, presumably the only English he knows.

The café where they are to meet Lenka is on the corner of National Street, overlooking the river and immediately opposite the proud but grimy bulk of the National Theatre. Inside there is noise and the smell of coffee and cigarettes. People come and go, greeting, talking, arguing, ordering against the shrill percussion of china against metal. Waiters patrol between the tables with trays held high. Surreptitiously Lenka points out one particular table that is full of discussion or argument, it is hard to tell which. 'There they are,' she whispers, as though they are specimens – rare birds, perhaps – that might be frightened away by any sudden movement on the part of observers. She mentions names that mean nothing – Collage, Herschel, Cherney – while James and Ellie watch discreetly but uncomprehending. 'It is like Paris,' Lenka explains, without admitting that she has never been there. 'Writers and philosophers discussing in the cafés.'

The idea appeals to Ellie. She wants to know all about it, about the writers and the philosophy, about the demonstration in Wenceslas Square and the arguments all around them. There's the frustration of not being able to decipher a single word. Shop fronts, newspaper headlines, protest banners, all equally opaque. 'What's going on? What's happening?' she asks.

Lenka looks helpless. 'The Russians want one thing, we want another, and so there are meetings to talk. Meetings, meetings. Words, words, words. They speak of fraternal comrades and all kinds of *kec*. What's *kec*? Rubbish, nonsense. But everyone knows that Brezhnev holds a gun to Dubček's head and Dubček dares him to pull the trigger.'

'Russian roulette.'

Lenka manages a dry laugh. '*Ruská ruleta*. You see it is not so difficult we say the same thing. But this is true, that Dubček understands Russians – he lived many years in Russia, he speaks perfect Russian – but Brezhnev understands nothing of us. So, you see Dubček wins. That, at least, is what we hope.'

Jitka joins them at their table. Both women seem excited by the presence of these visitors from the West. There are things to discuss – what Ellie and James should see, what they should do. There are so many sights in this city. An English guidebook has been found. Plans have to be made. It is so exciting. Even Ellie is excited. If she has been in a bad mood in the last few days, all is now changed with this experience of her first socialist country, the one with the human face.

When James asks why they are being so helpful neither woman is the least bit disconcerted by his question. 'Because we want to make you love our city,' Jitka says. 'We want to make the whole world love our city.'

Lenka interrupts. 'In the West no one knows anything about Prague. They try to *forget* Prague after they betrayed us in 1938. Do you know about 1938?'

'The Munich accord?'

'*Accord*? Does accord mean agreement? But we did not agree to anything. *Mnichovská zrada*, that is what we call it. The Munich *betrayal*. And because of this betrayal we are forgotten, our country is forgotten, Prague is forgotten, and who cares that it is most beautiful city in Europe? So we need people like you to help the world rediscover our city and our country. And to protect it against the Russians.'

One of the writers, a short, gingery man in a leather jacket, gets up and walks past their table. He gives a toothy smile, pausing to greet Lenka in the way that you do when you're not certain whether you recognise someone or not. There's a brief exchange in Czech, a blizzard of consonants. Lenka agrees with something said, laughs and offers a comment that clearly refers to English students rescued from the streets.

'*Ahoj*,' he says to them, sounding bizarrely nautical in this landlocked country. 'Here is good,' he tells them and they agree, it is good. 'Very interesting.'

But he has to go. Clearly something calls him. '*Čau*,' he says, the Italian *ciao* borrowed just to show how bright and carefree Czechoslovakia has become. They watch him leave, going out through the door into the street and glancing back at the last minute to give a jaunty little wave. 'He is a writer of plays,' Lenka explains. 'Very important.'

Ghosts

That writer of plays is a ghost now, just another of the city's many ghosts, for Prague is a truly haunted place. You can feel them around you. Some of them are just that, mundane ghosts that the tourist trade loves – golems, headless knights, wronged women, all that kind of thing – but there are others, there are others. The ghosts of the tens of thousands of Prague Jews killed by the Nazis, for example. Or the ghost of Franz Kafka, that anxiety-ridden man with the beady eyes and the sharp, inquisitive features (a rodent? a bird?) who pinned humanity to the pages of his fiction like so many insect specimens.

Although he was a Jew, Kafka escaped being murdered by the Nazis by dying of TB in 1924 (his three sisters were not so lucky) but his ghost still haunts the city, along with the spirit of his greatest novel, the one he never finished and never wanted published, the one he called *Das Schloss*, *The Castle*. But when people here refer to the Castle, they are not talking of Kafka's masterpiece, which in Czech goes by the title *Zámek*, 'Château', but rather the seat of the president, as one might talk of the White House in the USA. And there it is, on the far side of the river as seen beyond the arguing writers through the windows of the Café Slavia: *Hrad*, *Das Schloss*, The Castle, dominating the town beneath, whose resigned inhabitants accept every complex, tortuous, irrational, absurd edict generated by the various organs of bureaucratic power – Federal Assembly, Party apparatus, Ministry – but signed off by the principal inhabitant of the Castle. Indeed, in his novel Kafka might almost have been prophesying the state that has come to pass in his home city less than three decades after his death, where fear is integral and endemic, where bureaucracy shuffles the cards and then loses them, where you are what the files say you are, where all is happy because it is decreed to be happy, and all is successful because that is what success is.

Other ghosts in the shadow of The Castle? Jaroslav Hašek for one, father of the Good Soldier Švejk. Hašek's lifespan coincided almost exactly with Kafka's (both were born in 1883; Hašek died one year before Kafka), but in every other way, both literary and personal, they occupy the opposite ends of any spectrum you care to invent. Drunk against teetotal, riotous extrovert against diffident introvert, bigamist against celibate, hilarious against sombre. Czech against German. Gentile against Jew.

But now all has changed. It is the summer of 1968 and the man in the high castle is a genial and white-haired war hero who goes by the name of Svoboda, which, in one of those coincidences of meaning that make one sure there is an ironist in heaven, means 'Freedom'. And the man more or less in charge of the Party and therefore holding the reins of power in the country as a whole is some kind of interloper, a tall and gangling Slovak with a long nose and a warm smile and a tendency, dangerous amongst rulers, to consider the true feelings of the man and woman in the street. So now the writers and philosophers are talking at the café tables, writing freely at their desks, publishing in *Literární listy* and *Reportér*. A mere Two Thousand Words – the journalist Ludvík Vaculík's famous June manifesto – has shaken the foundations of the socialist state. People can say what the hell they please and there is tacit concordance between the Party and the Castle because the Švejks are, for the moment, no longer in the ascendancy. Instead it's *socialismus s lidskou tváří*, socialism with a human face, while the Soviet Union gathers the fraternal parties together on the banks of the Danube, in Bratislava, for a conference where they all swear that, while claiming 'unwavering loyalty to Marxism-Leninism, each fraternal party may decide questions of further socialist development in a creative way, taking into account specific national features and conditions'.

It was during this Bratislava conference that a letter from five anti-reformist members of the Presidium of the Czechoslovak Communist Party was passed to a member of the Soviet Politburo to be handed directly to Leonid Brezhnev. This letter, the so-called 'letter of invitation', implored Brezhnev to intervene in Czechoslovakia 'with all means at your disposal' in order to save the country from the 'imminent danger of counter-revolution'. So that there would be no misunderstanding, this invitation was written in Russian, with a plea to treat it with the utmost secrecy (prior to 1992, when it was released from the Russian State Archives, its existence was no more than a rumour). This treacherous missive, the excuse that the Soviets needed to give an aura of legality to their invasion, was passed to the intermediary in exactly the place where shit and piss is always passed, in the gents' lavatory of the conference building.

What, I wonder, do the ghosts of Kafka and Hašek say to each other about all this as they meet on the ghostly Prague streets? Or do they merely nod and pass by on the other side, the one off to haunt his favourite brothel, the other to the pub?

26

Things to see, places that live on in postcards sent to parents and friends – Tyn Square with the stiletto spires of the church of Our Lady standing over it, the Charles Bridge where musicians busk until moved on by the police, the Art Nouveau marvels of the Municipal House just near the medieval Powder Tower which has Gothic needles at the brim of its tall, pointed hat. Even the building and the room where Vladimir Ilyich Lenin founded the Bolshevik Party of Russia. Lenka will write about their visit, a piece for *Student* on how the Prague Spring is perceived by two students from the famous University of Oxford.

'You will be famous in Czechoslovakia,' Lenka tells them. It's unclear whether her tone is ironic or not.

Another place that she wants to show them is something unique to her city. 'You must take the memory of this back with you to England,' she says. 'This is very special.'

The building is a squat, secretive place hunched below the level of the pavement as though endeavouring to sit out the harsh storm of the twentieth century. A synagogue. They follow her inside only to discover that the storm is within, a blizzard that stings the eyes and batters on the mind. Not snow or sleet but names. Names everywhere, names on the walls, names on the arches and the alcoves, ranks of names like figures drawn up on some featureless *Appellplatz*. Names and dates: given names and dates in black, surnames in blood. Dates of birth and dates of death. Seventy-seven thousand seven hundred and ninety-seven of them, names so crowded that they appear to merge one into the other and become just one name, which is the name of an entire people – all the Jews of Bohemia and Moravia who died in the camps.

Lenka speaks very quietly, looking up at the rows and rows of careful lettering. Ellie and James stand beside her, neither of them understanding what to do with this. They have both read about the camps in books, seen them in photographs, watched the horror on film, of course they have. They know the facts and the figures. But this is none of those things – this is just a list of names.

Lenka peers upwards, pointing. 'My grandparents are there.'

There's a shock of the unexpected, like a physical blow. 'Your *grandparents*?'

'Vadinský Elias and Vadinská Sára.'

They try to follow her finger and make them out, as though the sight of the names will somehow mean a sight of the couple itself, her father's parents, who stare out of the photo frame on the dressing table in her room in Jitka's flat.

'Yes, I can see them,' James says, but he can't. It's just that he doesn't want to disappoint her. He tries some mental calculation, guessing at her age. 'How did your father ... ?' The question fades away but, of course, Lenka understands what he intends.

'How did he survive? He was part of the communist underground. For the first years of the war he was in hiding, then things got too difficult and he escaped to Moscow.' She's still staring up, perhaps so they cannot see her expression. 'My mother was already pregnant with me by then, but she was a Christian so she was as safe as anyone could be. But the rest of my father's family stayed in Prague and they were not safe.

His sister, my cousins, all of them' – looking hopelessly round the white space and the myriad of names – 'they are all here somewhere.'

Here and not here. The fleeting nature of presence marked only by shadows on photographic paper and names inked onto the wall of a synagogue.

'Perhaps he always had – what do you call it? The guilt of the survivor.'

Later they make their way outside, into the old cemetery where a narrow pathway leads through a chaos of tombs and headstones to nowhere in particular. The air is ripe with the smell of earth and mould and weathered stone. 'This is just a historical cemetery. There is also a very big modern Jewish cemetery in Žižkov.' A pause. The sound of birds in the trees, traffic in the street beyond the walls. 'But of course now there are no Jews.'

No Germans in the border areas, no Jews in Prague, dissidents dead or in prison or relegated to menial work out of the public eye; a country defined by its absences. Until the last few months, that is, and these moments of strange, frenetic freedoms.

That afternoon, after the synagogue, she takes them to a political meeting in one of the many theatres of the city. The auditorium – black stage, black curtains and backdrop – is packed with an audience as vocal as the people up on the stage. Jitka's husband is there behind the microphone, his voice as sharp as a blade, while Jitka herself is in the audience. Lenka provides some kind of summary translation of the speeches. There is argument, debate, laughter as well as shouting. Her boyfriend from the embassy is there as well. James has forgotten the man's name. 'Samuel Wareham,' Ellie whispers. 'His father's at New College. A physiologist.'

How does she know these things? Physiology is more in

James's line than hers, and yet he hasn't made the connection. He feels stupid and naive, possessed only of limited knowledge that is useful to no one. Then, as they watch the proceedings on stage, the focus of the whole theatre shifts, rotates, swirls giddily round in a vortex until, absurdly, they have become the centre of attention.

'Representatives from English University of Oxford,' Jitka's husband cries over the loudspeakers, pointing at them. Lenka is telling them to stand up and take a bow. Voices in broken English are all around, urging them on. Zdeněk, that's his name, is calling them to come up on stage, to speak on behalf of the famous University of Oxford.

'I can't speak on behalf of anyone but myself,' James protests. People laugh. People applaud. People stamp their feet and cheer. Lenka has him by the hand and is pulling him down the aisle. Ellie is quite happy with the whole thing, as though this is some ridiculous revolutionary drama put on by the Oxford Revolutionary Socialist Students. But for James they are Fando and Lis, clambering onto the stage, finally arriving in the fantasy city of Tar. They are bathed in light. Zdeněk is showing them where to stand.

'Greetings from Oxford!' Ellie yells into the microphone. Her voice is edged with nerves but the audience cheer appreciatively. 'Greetings from the students of Oxford and greetings from the workers of Oxford.' More cheers. She's growing in confidence, standing small and indomitable before the crowd. 'Socialism has a human face!' she shouts, and those that do understand explain to those that don't. The cheering grows. 'Nothing,' she cries, 'is more powerful than an idea whose time has come! You can resist the invasion of armies but no one can resist the invasion of an idea!'

James has never seen her like this, doing her Pasionaria thing. The audience cheer and he stands there reflected in the light that falls on Ellie. They both smile and wave. In the wings Lenka is there to congratulate them and lead them back to their seats with the audience watching and still applauding and the English guy, Sam Whatever, smiling wryly at them and saying 'quite a rabble-rouser', in that nasty, sarcastic manner that people like him possess. Schoolmasterly. It gives James the shivers.

27

The building is close to the river, close to Kampa with its ancient waterwheels and historic flour mills. With conscious reference to the club in Liverpool this place is called *Kaverna*. It consists of brick-lined storerooms, like an ancient vaulted church of three naves with arches leading from one to the other. Each nave is packed with worshippers heaving and gyrating as though in the throes of religious ecstasy. The walls are painted black, so illumination is limited to small pools of light. The air is rank with sweat and smoke. At one end of the central nave is a wooden stage raised two feet from the floor. On it, bathed in the uncertain light from three spots and flanked by speakers, are the musicians. Their name is blazoned on the bass drum: **THE IDES OF MARCH**.

The leader, John, stands centre stage like a preacher in a revivalist meeting, his mouth almost enveloping the microphone, his voice booming round the vaulted ceiling: 'I don't understand what the fuck anyone is saying!'

His audience cheer.

'Y'all off your heads!'

They cheer some more.

'Just a couple a days ago we crossed our own Rubicon – the Iron fucking Curtain!'

Laughter from those who have understood.

'That's' – he glances at a scrap of paper in his hand – '*Shelezna-shoustani-opona* to you.'

More laughter. Cheering and laughter.

'An' we find you cats all spaced out here on the far side, just like the kids back home. So now we gonna sing about it.'

More cheers. Those who understand make some kind of translation for those who don't. The drummer – it's Archer, isn't it? – begins a thumping beat, the bass guitar adds a grating undercurrent of threat and they launch into their signature song, adapted for the occasion:

> *'We're gonna cross the Rubicon,*
> *We're going to be free.*
> *We're gonna cross the Rubicon*
> *And choose democracy.*

The audience cheer like a football crowd, singing along with the chorus. Democracy they understand. Rubicon, as well. Free, they comprehend free. There is a guitar solo with Elliot, all teeth, long hair and ragged beard, playing his instrument as though it's a girl's body laid out across his hips.

> *'Let me cross your Rubicon,*
> *Let me hold you tight,*
> *Let me cross your Rubicon,*
> *Girl, it's gonna be all right.'*

Ellie is dancing, smoking and dancing, her arms above her head, her hair loose, eyes glazed, mouth pulled into some kind of smile. From the small stage Elliot points her out and ejects new words into the microphone:

'I went down to her Rubicon,
I bent to taste it fine,
I crouched beside her Rubicon,
It had the taste of wine.'

People circle Ellie, clapping in time with the beat, while James watches from the sidelines, nursing a beer. He feels trapped, by circumstance, by language, by the girl even now gyrating in the midst of her little circuit of admirers. The temperature of the place rises. Jitka is there – they persuaded her to come, although, thank God, her husband refused the invitation. She is spiky and angular and strangely awkward with the tempo, but at least she is enjoying the gig, laughing with Ellie, circling round her while beyond them the music thunders on.

James goes over to the bar, where the beer is cheap and if you like you can chase it down with hard, white plum brandy. He finishes a beer and rejoins the crowd, feeling detached as he always does in this kind of setting, wondering where the ecstasy lies. Ellie grins at him out of her mop of unruly hair but barely seems to recognise him. They're playing an Animals number now – 'We gotta get outta this place,' John screams into the mike – followed by something slow, a piece of blues with the guitarist, Elliot, wringing pain out of his guitar and John bemoaning the fact that she, whoever she is, has been gone fourteen long days and he's praying to the Lord not to take his love away.

Later, James is out in the cool night, wandering along the water's edge. The sound of the concert comes to him dulled by heavy walls – a drumbeat from the bowels of the earth. Beside him the river flows past, a great dark weight of water shining like obsidian. Lights from the other side reflect off the surface, but the impression is that they are immersed deep

225

within the liquid, gleaming from the depths, shimmering with the passage of waves overhead.

Someone, a mere silhouette, approaches and says something in Czech. *'Prominyte,'* James replies helplessly. *'Anglitzky.'* I'm sorry. English. That's almost all he knows, along with a few other stock phrases that Lenka has taught him. He's sure the pronunciation is wrong but he doesn't really care. And anyway, why the fuck is he apologising for being English and not being able to get his tongue round this impossible language?

The figure – a male of indeterminate age – stands looking out across the river. There's the glow of a cigarette. 'Where you from?' he asks.

'You speak English?'

'Little.'

'Sheffield.'

'Ah.' The man smokes, one can imagine thoughtfully. Perhaps he's trying to marshal his knowledge of English geography. 'Student?'

'Yes.'

'I work three years in London.'

'Really?'

'Czechoslovak embassy. Kensington Palace Gardens. You know Kensington Palace Gardens?'

'Not really.'

'Is very beautiful. Very private.'

'And now what do you do?'

The man pauses and takes another drag on his cigarette. 'I watch people. You perhaps.'

At first James feels only bewilderment. 'You *what*?'

'And your girl. And these Americans, what are they called? Ides of March. And all these kids.'

'You *watch* us? Are you some sort of pervert?'

The man laughs. A faint gleam of teeth. 'Maybe you could say perversion, but it is my job. To watch people.'

226

'Your *job?*'

'In London it was important people. Cabinet ministers, members of your parliament, civil servants. But now? Students like you.'

'What the fuck are you talking about? Are you police?'

'Police, yes. Something like that.'

'Why should I believe you?'

'No need to believe. Not at all.'

'So why are you telling me this?'

The man pauses. The dull beat of music comes from the building behind them. Light leaks out across the grass as a door is opened, letting out a sudden flood of sound. There's a shriek of laughter and two shadows running. 'Perhaps I am warning you. You're having fun. It's an adventure, isn't it? Lots of good kids, lots of cheap beer and laughter. Music, all that kind of stuff. Girls. But don't make mistake. Here can be, *will* be, very dangerous.' He flicks his lit cigarette end into the darkness, so that it spins over and over, a small, angry fire, and vanishes into the river. And then the shadow, like its cigarette, has gone.

Bewilderment is overtaken by a kind of nausea. James walks back to the lights and the noise. Inside the sweltering space, recorded music is being played. The Ides' instruments lie around the stage like the debris after a fight. Some of the audience are dancing but most are just waiting for the next set. There's Jitka talking with some people.

'Have you seen Ellie?'

She grins. 'You wanna meet my friends?' Wanna. Her American intonation is exaggerated. There's an exchange of greetings, smiles, nodding, the fumbling of language. Hi. *Ahoj. Nazdar.*

'I want to find Ellie,' he insists.

'She's around some place. I saw her going out.'

He excuses himself and pushes on through the crowd

227

towards the far door. Archer, the drummer, is there with his arm round the waist of a whey-faced girl, his free hand clutching a bottle of beer.

'Where's Ellie?'

The drummer's eyes are clouded. 'Who's Ellie?'

'You know. The English girl. You gave us a lift in France, remember?'

'Oh, yeah.' A vague gesture, a grin. 'Saw her with Elliot, man. Out back. The van.' He squeezes the girl and she emits a little shriek of delight, like a doll that cries out when tipped over.

The van.

James pushes through the door. Beyond there's a courtyard where people stand in groups smoking, talking, drinking. Parked against the far wall is the van. The Ides of March, it says on the side panel. Childlike flowers – daisies, buttercups – are painted across the corrugations. There's something of the cash box about the vehicle. Riveted panels, doors closed and sealed, the sum inside unknown.

Ellie and Elliot. An assonance of names. James can imagine an assonance of bodies. Possibilities crowd in on him. He wants to know and he doesn't want to know. He wants to see and yet he doesn't want to see. He crosses the courtyard and goes round the back of the van and peers in through the single rear window. Within are variegated shadows and a chaos of stuff – boxes, blankets, sleeping bags, clothes – in the midst of which an octopoid creature writhes, tentacles spread, in the throes of ecstasy or death.

He looks away. If he looks away maybe nothing has happened. If he looks away, maybe everything will be as it was before. Behind him guitars clash and drums sound like thunder. Feedback screeches through the building and out into the night and a voice calls over the sound system, 'Elliot? Hey, can you hear me? Where the fuck is Elliot?' The name booms out into the night. 'Calling Elliot! Come in Elliot!'

228

There's noise inside the van, animal scrabbling. He waits, watching, until the side door of the van slides opens and Elliot emerges, all teeth and beard and seaweed hair, swearing and pulling at his trousers. He slides the door shut behind him and hurries across the courtyard. James runs forward and grabs him. 'Who's that in there?' he demands.

Elliot stumbles, looks confused.

'In the van. Who was in the van with you?'

The man shakes his head, eyes clouded. 'A chick, man, a chick. What the fuck's it got to do with you?' He throws off James's grasp and disappears into the building. All around people are pushing their way back into the venue while James stands there against the stream, wondering. Cowardice confronts him. To know or not to know. Ellie or not Ellie?

Spin a fucking coin. Heads, you open the door. Tails, you walk away.

He doesn't even dare trust the decision to the coin. Instead, he goes back inside the Kaverna, where the audience are clapping and cheering expectantly and the Ides are on stage again, strapping on their guitars, John fiddling with his microphone – 'How y'all doing folks?' – and Archer hitting the cymbals, sending splinters of sound crashing around in the narrow space. Elliot is there, his fingers snaking across the strings of a Fender Stratocaster as they snake across James's fevered imagination. John throws out his arms. 'Beware, The Ides of March!' There's cheering, even some screaming, and the band breaks into 'Mr Tambourine Man', jingle-jangling its way through the specious phrases while James pushes amongst the crowd looking for Ellie, the Ellie that isn't in the van, the Ellie who doesn't pull her knickers down for stoned guitarists, the Ellie who, so her father warned him, has a mind that lives on fantasy. Jitka's there but where is Ellie? 'Take me on a trip,' the Ides sing, 'upon your magic swirling ship' and Jitka lifts her arms and puts them round his neck.

229

'Haven't you found Ellie?' she mouths against the sound of the band.

'No idea where she's gone.'

She casts her dancing spell his way and they move in some kind of harmony, for a moment pressed hard together. She is small and sharp and surely she wants to be kissed. There's that mole on her upper lip. He leans towards her and for a moment their mouths touch before she pulls away laughing, tapping his lips with her agile, violinist's forefinger. 'Bad boy,' she mouths. He turns and sways, careless of what he does, indifferent to whether he is or might be a bad boy. And Ellie's there in front of him, dancing with the pair of them, her eyes glazed, her hair a disordered cloud. Jitka laughs silently. James leans towards Ellie's head and shouts against the noise. 'Where have you been?'

She mouths the words: 'A walk. Fresh air.'

He knows it's not true, hopes it is. 'I was looking for you.'

'I had a smoke.' She pulls him closer so that her voice booms in his ear. Laughing and talking at the same time: 'I'm stoned.'

'Where did you get the stuff?'

'You want some?'

'No.'

She moves her head in time with the music like some kind of automated doll. The music jangles on, replete with all the platitudes of the age – magic swirling ships and smoke rings of your mind and all that stuff – while the crowd sways and waves, for the moment quite indifferent to the threats that encircle them. Music, they feel, can overcome anything – the Vietnam War, the Warsaw Pact, all hate, all violence, all the grim realities of life.

After the gig comes the sad, post-coital let-down. People hanging around outside the venue, their ears still singing. Others drifting away into the night. There's calling and fractured

230

laughter. Equipment is being carried out of the side entrance
into the group's van. And on the footpath alongside the river
James and Ellie have a seething row.

'What the fuck were you doing?'

'I was doing whatever I please.'

'You were with him in the van.'

'And if I was, what's it got to do with you?'

'I just want to know.'

'You mean you have some kind of rights over my body?'

'Of course I don't.'

'Well, then.'

It's the kind of argument that goes nowhere, just turns
round and round with only occasional forays into a dangerous
world outside the circle. 'So what do you want to do? Go off
with him?'

'He's a hell of a lot more interesting than you.'

They make their way back to the flat, walking through the
ancient empty streets that might belong to any European city.
Jitka went earlier – something about Zdeněk expecting her.
She reminded him of the address and how to get there. 'Half
an hour to walk,' she said. 'It's easy. Or maybe you can find
a taxi. But beware – they cheat foreigners.'

Still arguing in a desultory fashion, James and Ellie walk
back across the river, past the now shuttered café where they
met Lenka, through streets he does not know to an address he
can barely understand. There are few pedestrians around and
less traffic. Shops shuttered, bars closed. At one point a police
car slows down beside them and a pallid face looks them over
before deciding that they are what they seem to be, just a couple
walking home. No threat to the Socialist Republic, at least not
for the moment. At first Ellie is acquiescent, but later, as the
walking goes on, as they wander back and forth through streets
already visited, she begins to complain. Complaint is a relief.
He can tell her to shut up and not care whether she is offended

or not. So, snapping at each other exactly as in the play, Fando and Lis walk on, unobstructed and unchallenged, turning past corners they maybe recognise, and buildings perhaps they've seen before, until James finally identifies the one they have been searching for and manages to open the street door with the key that Jitka gave him. Together, his arm round Ellie, they climb the stairs to reach the crouched landing on the fifth floor. As silently as he can he opens the door to the flat and they creep inside. But still they have to pass the tiny room where Jitka and her husband sleep, where a figure with Jitka's dimensions emerges from the shadows, saying something in Czech. 'It's just us,' James whispers. 'Sorry we're late, we got lost.'

There's a murmured acknowledgement, some further whispering, a collision with a piece of unseen furniture and a suppressed oath from Ellie before they gain the sanctuary of the bedroom. He feels for the switch. The light, when it comes on, is the colour of piss. Ellie is a ragged, morose figure standing resentfully at the foot of their bed. 'Turn that fucking thing off.'

He kills the light and plunges them back into a deeper darkness than before. It's easier in the darkness, easier to creep to the bathroom and back, easier to undress in total darkness not knowing what will happen when they come together in the bed, easier to slide beneath the sheet from opposite sides and lie on their backs in the dark.

He wants to touch her but doesn't dare. 'Ellie?' he says softly.

'What do you want?'

'Were you with Elliot?'

'Elliot's a creep. Why the hell would you think that?'

'Were you with him?'

There's a little breath of sarcastic laughter in the darkness. 'You're jealous.'

He remembers her words, snapped at him impatiently: you're jealous of what you already possess; envious of what someone else has. 'Of course I'm jealous.'

'That's very bourgeois of you. But sweet.'

'But were you? There was someone in the van with him.'

'How do you know that? Were you spying? How pervy. What did you see?'

'Never mind what I saw—'

'Well *you* obviously do.'

He thinks of her father, the barrister, cross-examining a witness to expose the truth. 'I saw him with a woman, in the van. Fucking.'

'And you think it might have been me?'

'You weren't around anywhere. Someone said you were in the van.'

'Someone said,' she repeats, her tone laden with sarcasm. There is a silence. And then her voice in the darkness: 'Anyway, if it *was* me, what would you do?'

It's a good question. What would he do? 'I just need to know, that's all.'

'I don't think *need* has anything to do with it. You *want* to know. You want to know what I do with my body.'

'Don't be daft.'

'It's ownership, isn't it? You want to own my body, and the thought of my sharing it with other men – Elliot or whoever – makes you think you've been robbed of something that's yours. But it's my body, to do with what I like.'

'You're putting words into my mouth.'

'I don't think I am. I think you are a typical bourgeois male chauvinist.'

And with that she turns away from him and goes to sleep. James lies beside her in the narrow bed. Still he doesn't know. Was that her in the van with Elliot, or not?

In the morning she claims to remember little of the evening before. 'What happened?' she asks, sitting up in bed, her hair in chaos, her face pale and drawn. As she looks round the cramped room she gives strange glimpses of her mother. 'God, I feel awful. Did I behave badly?'

'You weren't at your most charming.'

'You say that just to get your own back.' The sheet has slipped from her shoulders. Her small breasts look limp, like discarded balloons after the party. 'The music was good. I remember the music.' A sudden, sideways glance. 'Did I do things I have to apologise for?'

'If you don't remember them, I don't think they count.'

'How very Jesuitical of you. Did we . . . ?'

'No.'

'I thought not. I remember a long walk, going round and round in circles.' She slips out of bed and roots around amidst the mess for a T-shirt. 'God, I feel awful.'

Watching her, James feels intimacy alloyed with indifference. It's how he imagines a marriage might be after many years, when love has died and familiarity has taken its place. While she goes to the bathroom he gets dressed and finds Jitka in the tiny kitchen making coffee. Her husband has gone out early. Something to do with his work. She looks at James with quiet, thoughtful eyes. 'Did you have a good time last evening?'

He smiles at her and wonders, thinking of how he danced with her, pressed up hard against her for a moment, touching his lips on hers.

'It was fun. The music was good, wasn't it?'

She laughs. 'The music was bad. But it was still fun.' She pushes past him in the narrow space, resting her hand on his waist for a fraction of a second longer than one might expect.

28

That evening there is the Birgit Eckstein concert, in a nineteenth-century auditorium named after a prince of an empire that no longer exists. The orchestra – the sharp figure of Jitka is there in the first violins – is flanked by gilded columns and backed by the façade of a Greek temple. Overhead is a ceiling of plasterwork in blue and gold, while all around are fluted pillars and pilasters. Into the focus of this comes first the conductor, the Russian Gennady Egorkin, a sharp, anxious man with a receding hairline that makes him look older than he is. He stands on his little podium and faces the applause with something like apprehension. Then the fragile figure of Birgit Eckstein appears in the wings, looking a little like a cleaning lady who has just found a cello lying round the place, picked it up and wandered onto the stage to find the owner. But she *is* the owner, and Egorkin holds her hand aloft to display the fact while she gazes round with faint bemusement at the audience. The applause engulfs the pair of them. It echoes from the nymphs and satyrs, thunders on the boards, resonates in the instruments. As it slowly dies away Frau Eckstein takes her seat, hitches up her skirts and pulls the cello to her. Her Guadagnini, an Italian gigolo clutched between her legs.

There follows an intense silence. One thousand people anticipating the moment. Egorkin bows faintly towards

Eckstein, then turns to the orchestra. Maybe everything is to his satisfaction. If so, he raises his baton to start, like an artist putting his brush to canvas, and with quiet care paints the first notes – solemn, pensive strokes, a theme played back and forth between woodwind and strings while Birgit Eckstein sits immobile on her plinth, as though cast in pewter. It is only when the orchestra seems about to reach some kind of conclusion that suddenly, almost unexpectedly, she moves to strike her cello. That act brings about a kind of miracle, something strangely organic, a fusion between the sensuous curves of the instrument and the sharp angles of Birgit Eckstein's small frame, the two contrasting shapes becoming one sonorous body resonating throughout the auditorium, crying out in tones that are almost human. Is it a lament for something innocent that is lost for ever? James tries to cling to the notes as they circle round him, but they are ephemeral, evanescent, each following the other and all dying away before he can work out what to do with them. It is the totality that matters, not the fragments; the whole complex wave equation, not the individual terms. And as he listens, emotion creeps up on him without his being aware of it, like a thief in the night coshing him from behind. His nose stings and his eyes smart. Frau Eckstein's small figure clutches at the body of the cello, grips its torso between her legs, sways with it, senses – you can tell, from the body of the auditorium you can tell – the vibrations of it with her thighs and her belly as she draws her bow across the strings as though fingering the flesh of a lover. He had never imagined that anything to do with classical music could be so blatantly sexual. And he senses Ellie beside him feeling the same thing. What she cannot experience with sex she can capture here – possession, surrender, the absorption of self into something greater than the individual. Perhaps she knows it. She grips his hand with tight talons while the crescendos, the climaxes, the agonising slides into the depths, the slow, meditative passages work their way through the hall and into the thousand listening minds.

After the performance there is applause and bowing and a bouquet of flowers. While the orchestra stands, the indomitable soloist leaves for the wings before being called back to further plaudits, a strange ritual that takes on some of the qualities of a dance, the conductor holding high her hand as though leading her in a gavotte, Birgit Eckstein carrying her cello with the other, the orchestra players making their own little gestures of applause, the whole thing choreographed by obscure tradition. People call for an encore and on her third re-entry Frau Eckstein offers a faint smile and steps back onto the podium. There is immediate silence. She sits, composes herself for a moment, then lifts her bow, and from the first chord James knows, with the sudden thrill of arcane knowledge, what it will be – the Prelude from Bach's C-minor cello suite. When the piece comes to the end amidst the storm of more applause, he is in tears.

A novel experience, that, to be moved to tears by the abstract sounds of music. In fact, a first for James. Something to do with the instrument itself, so close to the human voice in tone and timbre, but also something to do with the shock of familiarity, that he knew the player and also that he *knew* what she was going to play as an encore and recognised it as soon as she struck the first note.

29

After the Dvořák came the interval. All the usual milling around, people not knowing exactly what to say about what they had just heard and what was to come. Sam wondered whether to try and find a drink, but Eric Whittaker was somewhere in the auditorium, and Madeleine with him. And Lenka had brought along those bloody hitchhikers she seemed to have adopted, which made things that bit more awkward. The girl was fine but the boy had seemed out of place in a concert hall. He had even started to applaud after the first movement of the Dvořák until the girl – Ellie, wasn't it? – hushed him to silence.

'So why the hell don't people clap when it's so good?' he was demanding as they stood around in the aisle, stretching their legs.

'Because they don't,' the girl retorted.

Sam noticed the Whittakers and couldn't avoid catching Madeleine's eye. He excused himself and made his way to the back of the auditorium where there was a fraught conversation in which Eric extolled the virtues of the Elgar Cello Concerto above the Dvořák while Madeleine strained to see who Sam had brought with him.

'What's next?' Eric asked, trying to read the programme. 'The Brahms Double Concerto, is it?'

Sam translated for him. 'A Russian violinist called Nadezhda

Pankova. Can't say I've heard of her. Apparently studied at the Moscow Conservatory under Igor Oistrakh. Second place in the 1966 Wieniawski Competition in Poznan and third place in the International Tchaikovsky Competition, 1965.'

'Hardly a star,' Eric remarked. 'Studied under Oistrakh? How many thousands?'

A bell rang; people filed back into the auditorium. Madeleine touched Sam's wrist. 'Who is the lovely lady, Sam?'

'A friend.'

'The friend looks very attractive.'

He feigned indifference. 'And a couple of hitchhikers she's taken under her wing. I think I'd better get back ...'

They filed back into their seats and settled. The orchestra was returning, followed by Egorkin himself, who now faced the audience with clenched hands held aloft in some kind of demonstration of solidarity. A Russian saluting the Czechs. The applause rose appreciatively, a tide of enthusiasm borne on their awareness of his reputation, his public protest over the trial in Moscow of the dissidents Daniel and Sinyavsky and the subsequent withdrawal of permission for him to travel to the West. They knew well enough where his sympathies lay.

Further applause greeted the soloists, Birgit Eckstein leading the way as befitted the senior player, followed by the young violinist, bringing with her a small reputation, promising abilities and a condescending smile from Birgit Eckstein. Yet, as the pair acknowledged the applause, the young woman's flame-red evening dress quite consumed Eckstein's charcoal grey.

There was that collective settling before the music began. And then the conductor raised his baton and launched the piece, the Brahms Double Concerto, a complex interplay of orchestra, violin and cello in which the young Pankova fenced

239

with the more experienced cellist and matched passage for passage, thrust for thrust, always keeping her opponent at bay, all of this without either looking at the other, as though they were two swordsmen fighting blind. Except towards the end of the final movement when the women glanced at each other for a moment, and smiled.

Applause. A tumult of applause. Catharsis.

Afterwards, in a pillared room with views over the river, there was a reception in honour of the musicians. The conductor was there with a small escort from the Soviet embassy to keep him company, while the Soviet ambassador himself, stout, bespectacled and grim, watched in disapproval. Beside him stood the minister for cultural affairs and the mayor of Prague, beaming on everyone as though they were to take the credit. Guests, journalists, photographers clustered round the soloists. Glasses of Moravian wine were raised in salute. Flashbulbs popped like bursts of summer lightning. Thankfully, Eric and Madeleine had gone, in the name of duty, to some diplomatic event or other on the other side of town.

Sam led Lenka towards the Russian group. 'I don't want to speak with them,' Lenka protested, but Sam only laughed. 'You can do what you please, but if diplomats applied that criterion we'd never talk to anybody.'

Reluctantly the conductor's guardians edged aside to let them through to the great man. There was a shaking of hands. Lenka was introduced. Surprise was expressed at Sam's fluent Russian and at Egorkin's near-fluent English. 'But my friends here do not like it when I speak in English. They fear I am saying dangerous things.' He laughed, slipping back into Russian to the obvious relief of the escort. They discussed the performance, the emotional impact of the Dvořák, the technical difficulties of the Brahms. It was hard for a young violinist to perform the Double Concerto with a cellist of such standing as Frau Eckstein, but Nadezhda Nikolayevna had achieved it with brilliance, didn't Mr Wareham agree?

Of course he did.

'You must come to one of our recitals,' Egorkin said. 'I will accompany Nadezhda Nikolayevna on the piano. We play in Brno, of course, and Ostrava, but also Marienbad. Perhaps you will make it to Marienbad? It would be good to have a sympathetic ear in the audience.' There was a sudden and surprising tone of pleading in his voice. 'Please come. Perhaps there we can speak more freely. I will give you tickets so you cannot refuse.' He glanced round and summoned the violinist from where she was talking with a journalist. She came obediently, more like a secretary than a principal performer. 'We will have tickets for Marienbad sent to this gentleman. Mr . . . ?'

'Wareham.'

Further introductions were made. Hands were shaken. Pankova's were small and slender but with a sharp grip. She wrote the name *Wareham* into a little notebook in careful Latin characters. 'Mr Wareham is at the British embassy,' Egorkin explained. He glanced at Lenka. 'Two tickets, of course.'

'Yes, but I'm not sure—'

'You cannot be sure to come?' The Russian made an expression of exaggerated disappointment. 'But you *must* come, Mr Wareham. We will be playing the Kreutzer Sonata, which everyone knows, but particularly the Janáček, which no one knows but everyone should. Do you know it? It is very beautiful and deeply mysterious. Full of the soul of this wonderful country.' And then one of the Russian embassy people had stepped in with an approximation of a smile and the suggestion that Comrade Egorkin and Comrade Pankova had other commitments to meet and could not spend too much time talking to just two guests.

'I would be most sad if you cannot make it,' Egorkin said, giving a jaunty salute as he and the violinist were encouraged away.

30

They wait while the diminutive grey figure of Birgit Eckstein sips mineral water and talks to someone from Czech Radio. James feels awkward and embarrassed but Ellie is determined. Jitka has managed to get them this far, into the room where Frau Eckstein sits and brings her mind back from Dvořák and Brahms to focus on the commonplace and the trivial. 'We've come all this way in order to hear her,' Ellie insists. 'We can't just walk away.'

When the interview is over Frau Eckstein looks round vaguely at the two of them, saying something in German. Even without knowing a word of the language, James can tell what she is saying. Who are these people? Are they students?

'Hello, Frau Eckstein.'

She doesn't recognise them.

'Frau Eckstein,' Ellie says. 'It's us. Eleanor and James. We stayed at your house a few days ago. We came to Prague, just as you said. To hear you play.'

A vague smile, as though she is tolerant of things the young will do, absurd things like cross the Iron Curtain on a whim. Somehow James expected more – an explosion of surprise, an embrace, a motherly welcome. 'I remember. Yes, I remember.'

But perhaps she doesn't even really remember them – just two hitchers picked up on the road and given a place to pitch their tent for the night. Nothing much. 'The Bach,' he says, as though to give her something on which to fix her memory. 'You played that for us. In your music room.'

'Of course I did. That is always my encore piece.'

Always my encore piece. Understanding dawns that, far from being spontaneous, an encore may be something practised, anticipated, given out like sweets to adoring children.

'Ellie and I thought you played wonderfully.'

The woman shakes her head. She's tired, bothered by all the fuss. 'What do you know? I played poorly but only I know it.' A bitter laugh. 'I play poorly and the people applaud just the same. What do they know? Dvořák himself disliked the cello as a solo instrument, do they know that? He said the instrument's middle register is fine but the upper voice squeaks and the lower voice growls. Did you know that? That maybe should be a lesson for you – it is quite possible for an artist not to understand his own art.'

She turns. There's a photographer trying to get her to look his way. Flashes bounce around the room. She looks peeved. No she will not pose with her cello. The cello is for playing, not posing. 'These people,' she says, with a tired and colluding smile towards Ellie and James, 'they are vulgar and they know nothing. '

VII

31

Meetings in the embassy safe room are daily. Rumours abound, throughout the city, over the airwaves, from one embassy to another. Leaders from various Iron Curtain countries drop in on Prague without notice. Troops are reported to be gathering in Hungary, East Germany, Poland and Ukraine. There are stories of late-night phone calls between Prague and the Kremlin, between Brezhnev and Dubček.

'The Czechoslovak leadership,' Eric Whittaker said yet again, 'is walking a knife-edge.'

Someone asked, 'What's our own position, Eric? If it should all go wrong, I mean. If the Soviets decide to move in. What the devil do we do?'

Eric winced. 'Heaven forfend. Of course we just keep our heads below the parapet. Strictly their own affair. Just like Hungary in fifty-six. We'll get everyone into the embassy and batten down the hatches.'

'And HMG?'

'The official government position is that any such escalation would be a strictly internal matter for the countries concerned – in this case, Czechoslovakia and the Soviet Union.'

'It seems like another betrayal, doesn't it?' Sam said. 'Munich 1938 and now Prague 1968. Do you see the pattern? Nineteen eighteen the state is created. Nineteen thirty-eight it is betrayed by the Great Powers, 1948 the communists grab power. And now here we are in 1968. It looks ominous.'

'I didn't know you were a numerologist, Sam.'

'Just a pessimist, Eric.'

'Well, let's have a bit of optimism. Hope for the best and prepare for the worst.' Whittaker would have liked that lapidary sentence to be an end to the meeting, but someone – the head of consular services this time – was always there to ruin a good ending: 'But *are* we preparing for the worst, Eric? What about the evacuation of British nationals in the event of an invasion? Since the place has become a magnet for every trendy socialist Tom, Dick and Harry we've got hundreds here. There's even a bloody pop group due in a couple of days.' He glanced at a typed sheet in front of him. 'Apparently they call themselves The Moody Blues, although, God knows, it's me that's moody. And blue.'

Sam fell in beside Whittaker as they left the safe room. 'I've just received this from the Russian embassy.' He held out an envelope with his name written on it.

Whittaker glanced inside with a look of surprise. 'Lucky you. That'd be a hot ticket in London.'

'They're from Gennady Egorkin himself. He seemed very insistent that I go.'

'So what's keeping you? Are you taking the young lady we saw you with? Madeleine was most intrigued. Found it better entertainment than the Brahms. I could barely drag her away at the end.'

'I hope she doesn't go shooting her mouth off to Stephanie. Not before I've had a chance to tell her myself.'

'Is it serious then?'

'It's all a bit sudden, really. Not quite what I expected.'

'Well, be careful. Playing away from home is not easy in these parts.'

'Of course I will.'

'And I won't breathe a word of it to Madeleine. Mind you, she already thinks you're a two-timing bastard.'

'It's not that simple, Eric.'

'My dear fellow, it never is. Speaks an expert.'

32

It's no longer Marienbad, of course, any more than Karlsbad is still Karlsbad. Once again, those are the German names lurking in the collective memory behind the Czech. Now the world-famous spa towns are Mariánské Lázně and Karlovy Vary. Karlovy Vary/Karlsbad may be the more celebrated of the two, but there's no doubt which is the more beautiful. Mariánské Lázně is a baroque jewel set in green velvet, a belle époque fantasy couched among wooded hills, a courtesan reclining in her bed. This is where Goethe came to take the waters and found his last and unrequited love, Ulrike von Levetzow; where the King-Emperor Edward VII failed to lose weight, chased tail and also encountered fellow emperor Franz-Josef I. Here Chopin stayed with his fiancée Maria Wodzińska, Winston Churchill spent part of his honeymoon with the lovely Clementine Hozier and Franz Kafka passed ten agonising days with his fiancée Felice Bauer. Finally, this is where General George Patton, he of the ivory-handled revolvers and a tendency to slap combat-fatigued soldiers, turned up with the US Third Army in May 1945, a fact conveniently forgotten by the government of the Czechoslovak Socialist Republic, which acknowledged the liberation of Czechoslovakia by the Red Army alone.

*

The hotel Sam had chosen was in need of refurbishment, but beneath the faded paint and crumbling stucco you could see the elaborate wedding-cake decoration that had made the place so famous in its time. He parked the car in front of the main entrance. The Škoda that had followed them throughout the two-hour journey from Prague stopped fifty yards behind them, but he didn't say anything about it to Lenka.

The receptionist checked them in with as much grace as the desk sergeant at a police station. 'Chopin suite,' he said, handing over a key that might have opened a prison cell. The lift was out of order. They carried their suitcases up the main stairs, out of the faded grandeur of the foyer into the drab functionalism of the upper floors where socialist ideals of uniformity and parsimony had long ago chased out any luxury that the nobility of Europe might have recognised. The door to the Chopin suite was marked with the composer's name, framed by a treble clef and a selection of crochets and quavers. Within there was a sitting room with a plasterwork ceiling that gave only meagre hints of what once might have been, and a bedroom with a fanciful portrait of the composer himself over the bed. Full-height windows overlooked the spa gardens.

'Did you see?' Lenka asked as they unpacked. Already there was a kind of familiarity about their relationship, as though matters had been speeded up and domestication was the next step. It wasn't an unpleasant sensation.

'Did I see what?'

'Of course you saw. The car that followed us, the same as before. The same as we saw when we went swimming. They follow you everywhere.'

He watched as she hung her Munich dress in the wardrobe. 'It's always like that. You get used to it.'

'I hate it. It is worse than we had before Dubček. At least we weren't followed everywhere.'

'But *we* were. Anyway, what does it matter as long as they haven't booked into the room next door?'

251

She looked round and ambushed him with that smile – a flash of white teeth, a glimpse of naked gum, a creasing of her eyes. 'I don't care what they hear,' she said.

Later they strolled in the spa gardens. Classical pavilions were scattered amongst the lawns, hiding within them the fountains that spurted life-giving waters whose details were specified at each spring – urinary diseases, locomotory diseases, gastrointestinal problems, gynaecological conditions, infertility, all were treatable. 'If all this were true,' Sam remarked, 'you wouldn't need doctors.' He took photos, posing Lenka in the pavilion of the Karolina spring and snapping her as she walked through the arcade, alternately in shadow and out. One or two people paused to watch. At the Kolonáda a threadbare band played waltzes and polkas. On either side of the musicians the faces of Gennady Egorkin and Nadezdha Pankova stared out from posters as though expecting less levity, but Lenka ignored their disapproval, taking Sam's hand and pirouetting with laughter while the musicians smiled and nodded. Sam took photographs of her spinning, her hair thrown out, her skirt billowing.

The recital that evening was held in a marbled hall decked out with neoclassical columns and naked goddesses. Just the two performers at the focus of the lights: Egorkin, dark and tense at the keyboard, and Nadezhda Pankova like a small, live flame (that crimson evening dress) beside him. As Egorkin had said, they'd chosen a demanding programme, opening with the Kreutzer Sonata and, after the interval, moving into the Slav world with Prokofiev and Janáček. The Prokofiev, vivid and melodic, was straightforward enough, but it was in the strange rhythms and echoes of the Janáček violin sonata that the Russian duo found their true métier, piano and violin throwing Janáček's musical motifs back and forth, sometimes like children at play, sometimes like warring creatures snarling at each other, sometimes like lovers caressing. Melodies initiated by the violin were cut to pieces by the staccato piano, and then the roles were reversed, a lilting piano theme chopped apart by buzzing violin notes. At the end the whole piece reached a taut climax before drifting imperceptibly away into silence, like a person dying.

There was a stillness in the auditorium, breathing suspended, hearts stopped. Then a blizzard of applause. As the storm engulfed them, the couple stood, holding hands aloft, bowing in careful unison. It was only then that Sam noticed something, a glance between the pair, shared smiles hastily suppressed, a second glance that lingered after the smiles had been extinguished. It was that in particular that convinced him, the held glance like a hand clasp that neither wanted to break. The maestro and his protégée were in love.

Dutifully the two musicians settled down to play an encore – a quiet, melodic piece by Tchaikovsky – and while the second round of applause was filling the auditorium Sam and Lenka slipped out and found their way towards the back. At a gilded door, an attendant blocked the way in the impassive manner of a palace guard.

There were a few moments of one-sided argument – only authorised personnel were allowed through – before Sam gave up and took one of his visiting cards from his wallet. He scribbled on the back: *Brilliant!* And then on an impulse added the name of the hotel where they were staying. 'Can you see it gets to Maestro Egorkin?' he asked the attendant, adding a ten-crown note to help the thing on its way. 'He invited us here and we want to show our appreciation. Do you understand?'

Did he understand? He seemed far beyond understanding anything much, viewing the card with rank suspicion before opening the door behind him and speaking to someone inside. The card disappeared. So did the ten-crown note.

'Thank you,' Sam said. 'Thank you very much.' Beside him, Lenka swore softly.

At dinner that evening they sat amongst workers who had exceeded their quotas, managers of farming collectives who had manipulated the figures to create an impression of surplus, factory managers who had passed their targets on paper if not in reality, party officials who had kissed the right arses. The men wore ill-fitting, shiny suits, their wives clumsy floral dresses. A pianist played Chopin remarkably well and a master of ceremonies commandeered the microphone to welcome a fraternal delegation from Poland to 'our Bohemian beauty spot, in the hope that mutual respect and cooperation might always be the bond that ties our two peoples together'. There was scattered applause, but the Polish delegates really wanted to get on with the meal. Soup came and went, the usual thin broth with a dubious liver dumpling floating in it like a turd in a lavatory pan. It was followed by pork and duck weighed down with bread dumplings, each portion carefully defined in grams as though parsimony ruled in the kitchens and every ingredient had to be accounted for.

It was as they were starting their main course that someone came over to their table from the Polish party. Sam half-rose from his seat but the man had eyes only for Lenka. 'Lenička,' he called her. 'My dear Lenička.'

She looked surprised and faintly embarrassed at his attention, but she accepted a kiss on one cheek. 'This is my friend, Samuel,' she said. There was a shaking of hands and an exchange of names. Pavel Rovnák, he said. He was slight of build with dark hair and a sallow complexion. He wore a moustache that might once have been a homage to Joseph Stalin but was now trimmed to suit the times. 'I am an old family friend,' he explained, 'but Lenka and I haven't seen each other for some time. Isn't it strange how even in a small country such as ours it is still possible to avoid someone' – he looked accusingly at Lenka – 'and then to meet up in Mariánské Lazně of all places?' He paused, as though expecting some matching remark from her, perhaps an explanation of what she was doing there with this foreigner who appeared to speak such excellent Czech. 'You look well,' he said to fill the void. 'And your lovely mother? How is she?' And then when Lenka had offered her scant information, he turned back to Sam. 'You are American, perhaps?'

'English. At the embassy.'

'Ah, the embassy.' Rovnák pursed his lips – the moustache twitched – and looked again from one to the other as though searching for further clues. 'You speak good Czech for a foreigner.'

'Not as good as Lenka's English.'

'She has been studying the language at university. I'm glad you have done so well, *zlato.*'

Lenka shrugged, as though it was of no account. 'Are you staying in the hotel?' she asked.

'Sadly I have to get back to Prague this evening. In fact' – he glanced round – 'I must get back to my table. These Poles cannot be left on their own for too long. It has been good to meet you, Samuel. And Lenička, you must keep in touch.'

Lenka said nothing and went back to her meal. An outburst of laughter greeted the man's return to his table. Sam waited. Lenka drank some wine then carefully replaced her glass. 'That's him,' she said quietly. 'I told you about him. The *aparátník*. Pavel Rovnák.'

Sam had always perceived her as tough – smiling, delightful, but tough. Yet now it was as though he saw her through a magnifying lens. He could glimpse her insecurities, imagine her as a vulnerable young girl, a lumpish fifteen-year-old uncertain of the vagaries of her body, possessed only of a distant memory of her father and subject to a rancorous mother. And there was this man with his amiable and enticing ways, a guarantor of present comforts and future success.

'I hated that moustache,' she said, reaching for her glass again.

Rovnák was as good as his word and left when the meal had more or less come to an end and toasts were being drunk. He passed their table on his way out and lifted Lenka's hand to his lips, renewing his exhortation to keep in touch. But he was very sorry, he just had to be back in Prague by that evening. Otherwise he would have asked Lenka for a dance.

'His wife keeps him on a tight lead,' she suggested when he had gone. It was difficult to interpret her tone. Was there some hint of regret there amidst the bitterness? The pianist had exhausted the possibilities of Chopin and begun to feel his way into a few popular numbers – 'Smoke Gets in Your Eyes', 'The Continental', that kind of thing. The Polish trades unionists and their wives took to the floor. Sam and Lenka followed. For a while they shuffled round amidst the insidious smell of sweet floral perfume and sour body odour that hung around the dancers before Sam suggested they take a breath of fresh air.

The spa gardens were beautiful at night, touched with a glimmer of their former glory. You could almost imagine the ghosts of the pre-war demi-monde encountering phantom crowned heads amongst the fountains and the colonnades. 'I thought you might be angry to meet my first lover,' she said as they walked. 'I have heard that Englishmen can be very jealous.'

'Not at all. He seemed very polite.'

'He was wondering if I have become a prostitute.'

'Don't be silly.'

'I could see it in his eyes. And he was calculating what my price might be.'

*

256

It wasn't particularly late when they returned to the hotel but the Polish group had gone and the dining room was shut. Only the disgruntled receptionist remained on duty in the foyer. As Sam took the room key the man handed over an envelope with grim ill-will, as though even passing on a letter went far beyond the call of duty. Sam pocketed the envelope without giving the receptionist the satisfaction of seeing him open it. Through pools of feeble light they climbed the stairs to the first floor. Sam unlocked the door to the Chopin suite and pushed it open for Lenka to go through into the sitting room.

'What is it?' she asked.

'Probably the bill. Just the kind of thing they'd do, in case we go off tomorrow morning without paying.'

But the envelope did not contain the bill. It was a simple one-line note, written in English. *Perhaps a stroll to the Kolonáda tomorrow morning? Eight o'clock?* It was signed Egorkin.

He smiled. In the more relaxed atmosphere of Mariánské Lazně the man clearly had a way of evading his escort. Lenka had gone into the bathroom. 'It's nothing,' he called to her. He went into the bedroom and looked round, as though hidden microphones might reveal themselves to his gaze. Hotels in which foreigners might stay were notorious for being bugged. You didn't wonder about it, you assumed it. But all he saw was the broken plasterwork of the ceiling, the heavy velvet curtains, the wardrobe with its poorly silvered mirror, the chest of drawers whose veneer was lifting away at the corners. He waited for her to come from the bathroom, her face scrubbed of makeup and as vulnerable as a young girl's, before handing her the note and putting his finger to his lips.

She looked at him enquiringly. 'You will go?'

'I think so.'

She reached behind her to unzip the dress, the outfit they had bought in Munich, and let it slide to the floor. Then she

257

dropped her slip around her feet and stepped out of it as though stepping out of a pool of water, holding his eye and smiling. 'Do you like what you see?'

'Of course I do.'

'And are you thinking of that man, Pavel Rovnák? Are you jealous of him?'

'You asked me that already. I'm jealous of what he took from you. But more than that, I'm angry that he used you.'

She unfastened her brassiere and dropped it as carelessly as a child discarding sweet papers. 'And I used him. So it was on both sides. And it was a long time ago. The past.'

But their love was entirely in the present, a slow, deliberate act, as though they had been lovers for years rather than weeks; at her climax convulsions racked her body in ways that couldn't be contrived, couldn't be anything but the ecstasy of the moment. He'd never known this with Steffie, never this intensity, never this incontinence. Anything else might be a lie, but this was not. Yet in the aftermath he looked at her lying there, spent, damp with sweat, and wondered about the hard core of her, that part which had accepted, even welcomed, the attentions of Pavel Rovnák.

Things were different in the morning. The morning was fresh and cool – the town lies six hundred metres above sea level, out of the smog and heat of the lowlands – and Lenka was lying on her back in the chaos of sheets. Sunlight from the open windows caught the froth of dun-coloured hair between her thighs and turned it the colour of honey. She smiled at him, and seemed, with that smile, entirely and delightfully vulnerable – and part of him in a way that he had never imagined a woman might be.

That moment could stand for ever, preserved in the fixative of memory.

*

At breakfast she seemed put out at the idea of his meeting Egorkin. 'Why does he have to steal our time?'

'I can't very well ignore him. Maybe you should come as well. To offer your congratulations on his performance.'

'I'll wait for you here.'

'You're going to sulk.'

'Sulk? What is sulk?'

'What you're doing now.' He made a face, pouting.

She laughed. '*Trucovat.*' And her laughter meant that she wasn't. So she went back to the room to wait, while Sam, with that morning's copy of *Rudé Právo* tucked under his arm, took a stroll in the spa gardens. A few drab figures wandered the paths, but it was early for the crowds and the magnificent wrought-iron Kolonáda was almost empty, like an elaborate stage set waiting for players.

What, he wondered, did the Russian want? Surely not just to thank him for coming all the way to his recital in Mariánske Lazně. He chose a bench and sat to read the paper, a task he had every morning at work, to deliver a digest of the morning's news for Eric Whittaker to review. Today's front page announced that the East German leader Walter Ulbricht was visiting Karlsbad with his sidekick Erich Honecker – an unforeseen event that stirred the commentators to a frenzy of speculation. Sam scanned the reports, pausing to read whatever caught his eye – in this case, Dubček meeting the unexpected guests at the airport and a young girl from the Pioneers dutifully presenting the East German leader with a bouquet of flowers and receiving an ill-aimed kiss on the neck in return. There had been a stony silence from the crowd that had gathered to watch. Ulbricht was hated in Czechoslovakia just as he was hated in his own country. But the question uppermost in Sam Wareham's mind was, what was the man doing here? Leafing through the pages and loathing the newsprint that stained his fingers, he felt like a soothsayer trying to read the entrails of some sacrificial animal and thereby foretell the future. One thing he knew for sure: a visit from Ulbricht was like a knock on the door from the grim reaper himself.

'Dobrý den.'

He looked up with a start. Egorkin was standing over him. Seen close and in the clear light of morning he looked older than previously. There were hints of acne scars on his cheeks. He'd cut himself shaving and there was a dab of cotton wool on his neck. Sitting down, he glanced at Sam's newspaper and said, in Russian, 'It looks as though we made the right choice to come here rather than Karlsbad. Of course, I am joking. I have no choice in such matters. They decide for me.' He took out a silver cigarette case and held it out. 'They're American,' he said reassuringly.

'Thanks, but I'm trying to give them up.'

That seemed to amuse the man. 'That is exactly what I am doing – converting to American cigarettes after a lifetime of *Belomor* is as good as giving up.' He blew smoke away towards the vaulted ironwork overhead.

'The recital,' Sam said, 'was wonderful. You played so well together.'

Egorkin nodded. 'We are, what do you say in English? In harmony. But I didn't come here to talk about my music. What I want to do is to explain my situation.'

Sam sat back on the bench and looked out across the gardens. He noticed inconsequential things. A woman walking a poodle. Two children running and laughing ahead of their parents. A fountain shattering sunlight into a thousand fragments. Quotidian events impressed on his retina and, perhaps, his memory. 'Tell me.'

Egorkin hesitated, as though he had not really thought this through. But he must have. Whatever it was, he must have thought about it long and hard. 'You perhaps know something of me by reputation.'

260

'I know something.'

'For example, that I have been outspoken about matters in my homeland and so I have been forbidden to travel to the West. My being here in Czechoslovakia is considered a great concession, almost a prize for having accepted my fate with good grace.'

'I've heard something about it.'

Egorkin nodded. 'And I am only here now because it is early morning and my escort is lazy. Like the whole Soviet system, they watch only when they know they are being watched.' He laughed. 'It is not quite as simple as that, however.'

'I didn't think it would be.'

'I expect you to act in an entirely professional manner over this.'

'Of course I will.'

'So. There is also the matter of Nadezhda Nikolayevna.' The Russian seemed to gather his thoughts, or perhaps, his courage. 'She is, you understand, in love with me. And I' – he hesitated as though he were not so clear on the matter – 'I am in love with her.'

The man paused, smoking and looking out of the colonnade. The woman with the poodle had gone, so too the children. An ancient couple, who perhaps had come to the spa to find the key to eternal life, walked past. They looked at Egorkin as though they recognised him.

Sam asked, 'What does this admittedly awkward state of affairs have to do with a British diplomat?'

Egorkin nodded thoughtfully. Finally he said, 'I would like your advice. You see' – another draw on his cigarette – 'I want your assistance in getting us to the West. We wish to claim political asylum.'

'You and Nadezhda Nikolayevna?'

'Exactly. Does that surprise you?'

'Not entirely. But I don't see how I can help you. The very

best you could expect is to gain entry to one of the Western embassies. You might be granted asylum of some kind, but that might mean the two of you becoming prisoners in the embassy itself. Like Cardinal Mindszenty in Budapest. Twelve years so far. Unless the Czechs would agree to your leaving.'

The man frowned. Dark eyebrows, pockmarked skin, a mouth clamped into a line of disapprobation, as though he had heard discord in the strings. 'Did you know that the London Symphony Orchestra offered me the post of principal conductor when they got rid of Kertész? I was not able to take the post because my country did not allow it. That is what I have to deal with.' He fidgeted another cigarette from his case, snapped at the lighter, drew sharply in. Sam continued, dredging up his knowledge of consular affairs.

'Whether an embassy would give you shelter is entirely at the discretion of the ambassador. You understand that, don't you? Most countries, including my own, do not recognise the legality of what is known as diplomatic asylum – sanctuary in one of its embassies. Legally a refugee cannot apply for political asylum until he is actually in the receiving country's territory.'

'But isn't an embassy—?'

'—an extraterritorial possession? That's a popular mis-conception. Under international law an embassy remains the territory of the host nation. It's just that the agents of the host nation may not enter the embassy without the express permis-sion of the ambassador. So you, or anyone else seeking refuge, would be relying on the goodwill of the ambassador. His job would be to consider what risks you might run if he were to insist that you leave his embassy, but above all he would have to consider the best interests of his own country. I'm afraid I'm beginning to sound like a textbook. Or a lawyer. Maybe I *will* have one of your cigarettes.'

There was a pause for the little ritual of lighting up. Sam attempted a smile. 'There go my best intentions. Up in smoke.'

He glanced at his watch and wondered when he could politely extricate himself from this conversation. It wasn't difficult to feel sympathy for Egorkin, a talent put at the mercy of the Soviet state, but the matter was hardly his concern. 'In your case there would be a further complication because the host country in this case – Czechoslovakia – is not hostile to you, so it is difficult to see what danger you would be in if you were asked to leave the embassy. In Moscow you would clearly be in jeopardy, but here, as things are at the moment . . . ' He shrugged.

The man digested these unpleasant facts, smoking and looking out across the gardens. Suddenly he seemed very vulnerable, crushed by the situation. Sam thought of Russia and what it did to its children. The largest country in the world, yet as claustrophobic as a prison cell; lives trapped and stifled; genius smothered. And how the contagion spread to its neighbours. He thought of Lenka, orphaned and shamed by the state, trading her body for the hope of education. He thought of hope itself, the violinist's name, *Nadezhda*, and how for the moment hope flourished here in Czechoslovakia, at least. Hope against hope.

'I can have a word with people in the embassy but I can't promise anything.'

Egorkin nodded, as though weasel words were only to be expected. 'Tell me, Mr Wareham, how is it that you speak Russian so well?'

It was a relief to shift the conversation on to firmer ground. 'Two years of intensive Russian during my national service, followed by a three-year degree.'

'So you loved our language.'

Was it a question? 'I still do. The poetry and the prose. But particularly the poetry.'

'And you will know that our writers have had their creative lives crushed. Pasternak unpublished in his own country and forced to refuse the Nobel Prize. Mandelstam killed in the gulag. Akhmatova banned for decades. Soul-destroying, Mr Wareham. Surely you understand that. Surely you *feel* it.'

'I don't see how my feelings come into it.'

Egorkin gave a dry laugh. 'That is because you are not yourself. You are just a representative of a government. A functionary. But I am an artist, representing no one but myself. I deal with the emotions and the soul. You heard us play yesterday evening. Didn't that speak to your soul? And to the soul of the woman at your side?'

'I'm sure it did.'

'Are you in love with her?'

He thought of Lenka, waiting in the hotel room, and then of Stephanie in her parents' house in England. He thought of loyalty and betrayal, of passion and affection, of desire and love, all those abstract nouns that were so difficult to pin down and were so inimical to diplomacy. The trouble with diplomats, Steffie had once told him, is that you never know what they're thinking. He made to get up. 'As I said, my feelings have nothing to do with it.'

Egorkin put out a hand to restrain him. 'Listen to your soul and help us, Mr Wareham. I am begging you.'

Sam stood, trying not to give the impression that he was abandoning the man. 'I will do what I can, Mr Egorkin, but I cannot promise anything. You have my phone number if you need it. Where are you staying in Prague?'

'At the International Hotel.'

'If I have anything positive to tell you, I'll contact you there.'

'We are watched. All the time, we are watched.'

'Then maybe you can phone me. At the embassy. Give me until Wednesday next week. But as I said, I really cannot promise anything.' He smiled, sympathetically he hoped, and walked away. Lenka would be wondering where he had got to.

33

A reception at the ministry of foreign affairs, to celebrate the fraternal visit to Prague of Nicolae Ceauşescu. Tito had paid a flying visit a few days ago and been greeted by ecstatic crowds. Now it was the turn of the enigmatic leader of Romania.

The British ambassador had been invited and so had Eric, but the Whittakers were away in Austria for the weekend and Eric was damned if he was going to ruin his break for some tiresome duty bash. Sam would stand in for him, wouldn't he? Wave the flag alongside His Excellency?

Sam rang a contact at the protocol section of the ministry and got Lenka's name added to the guest list in place of Madeleine Whittaker. 'You can write a piece about it for one of your journals,' he told Lenka, and she appeared delighted at the possibility. These days anything seemed possible, even someone like her, with her family history, being admitted to the purlieus of power. They shunned driving and instead walked up the long slope of the Castle Hill. Lenka was once again wearing the dress and shoes they'd bought in Munich. She appeared excited at the prospect of even being in the same room as Dubček. 'I might even get a chance to talk to him,' she said with childlike enthusiasm.

In Hradčany soldiers were on duty at government buildings and policemen were marshalling the traffic. Sam and Lenka joined a queue shuffling forward to be admitted to the portals of the Černín Palace. Sam could feel Lenka tense beside him as their names were checked against the guest list, but then they were in, wandering past gilded columns and Flemish tapestries with the other milling guests. There was no receiving line – apparently their hosts were still in private discussions in the Hrad, but the ambassador was already there, in conversation with a South American counterpart. He detached himself and came over to be introduced to Sam's guest. His bright, beady eyes didn't miss a trick, either at bridge, which he and his wife played mercilessly, or in the complex social intercourse of the diplomatic world. He was, he claimed as he smiled on her, delighted to make her acquaintance.

'Lenka's a student,' Sam explained.

The ambassador's smile was benign. 'Everyone seems to be these days. Surprised there's anyone left to do any work. How's Stephanie? Sorry she had to leave us.'

'I haven't heard from her for a while. I believe she's fine.'

'Belief is a great comfort, Samuel. I think it is what is sustaining our hosts at this very moment. One wonders' – glancing round pointedly – 'where they might be.'

'I believe they are still locked away in talks.'

'There you are again. Belief. What would we do without it?' He laid a hand on Sam's shoulder. 'But please don't let me bore you with my prattle. Go and circulate. Show Miss Konečková what fun we in the diplomatic corps have.'

'I don't think I like that man,' Lenka said as the ambassador moved away.

'He's all right. He's just a Wykehamist, that's all.'

'A Wykehamist?'

'It really doesn't matter.'

'Anyway, whatever he is, he did not have to mention Stephanie.'

Sam laughed. 'Oh yes, he did.'

They moved through the crowd, nodding greetings here and there. An American diplomat whom Sam knew came over. He was part Czech in origin, part Czech, wholly Jewish and every bit American, his family surname Růžička translating into Rose when his grandfather passed through Ellis Island in 1888. Harry Rose. He looked approvingly at Lenka. 'A real live Czech? As rare as hen's teeth at an event like this. Where did Sam find you?'

'*I found *him.''

'Touché. You know what?' That was how he always started his stories. You know what? 'Believe me, this is true. East German intelligence just reported American tanks crossing the border from Austria. Yesterday or the day before, this was. Invasion! Outrage! Claimed it was NATO belligerence, for Christ's sake. Tried to get the Soviets interested in starting World War Three. The reality? They were old World War Two relics, props for some damn war film they're making at Barrandov, can you believe it?' He basked in their laughter. 'It's true, it's true. We've got the whole lot here – Ben Gazzara, Bradford Dillman, Robert Vaughn. Half of Hollywood. You know these guys?'

'I know the man from U.N.C.L.E.'

'That's him.'

'What is uncle?' Lenka asked.

'It's some James Bond-type TV show.'

'United Network Command for Law Enforcement,' Harry said with glee.

'There is such a thing?'

Harry laughed, entranced by Lenka's credulity. 'You mustn't believe everything you see on TV.'

'James Bond fights SMERSH, and there is such a thing as SMERSH. *Smert shpionam*, death to spies. In Czech we say *smrt špionů*.'

'Well, this lady sure knows her stuff. You'd better watch

your back, Sam. Hey, and we even have Shirley Temple, would you believe it?'

'Shirley Temple's in a war film?' Conversations with Harry lurched from the improbable to the unbelievable and back again within a couple of sentences.

'No, she's here for some convention or other. Probably singing "The Good Ship Lollipop" to a plenary session. I'm surprised she didn't get an invite to this party – she has political ambitions, apparently. Wants to be a senator, wants to be president. Film star for president? Who the hell knows? Weirder things have happened. I mean, here we are meant to be representing the free West and our main concerns when the balloon goes up will be what the hell to do with half of Hollywood.'

A disturbance at the entrance announced the arrival of the hosts. People scurried to see. Svoboda came first, white-haired and red-faced, then Dubček, tall and awkward, like a heron in a stream worried about fish. Beside him was the dapper figure of Nicolae Ceaușescu. The trio came though the press of enthusiastic guests, smiling and nodding, pausing briefly for Dubček to exchange words with someone. In the background, observing all through horn-rimmed spectacles, was the Soviet ambassador Chervonenko.

A member of the ministry staff came over. 'Mr Samuel Wareham,' he said, 'I am so sorry that Mr Whittaker could not be present but it is good to bump into you again. That is the right expression, isn't it? To bump into someone?'

'It certainly is.'

'And this lovely lady is ... ?'

'Miss Lenka Konečková.'

'Ah, yes. I know about Miss Konečková.'

Lenka's embryo smile died. 'You know about me? What does that mean, exactly?'

The man pondered her question for a moment. All around

him there was the press of guests, reaching for the buffet. 'I have read some of your articles, of course. That student newspaper, what is it called?'

'*Student.*'

'Ah, yes. Not very imaginative.'

'The name of the paper or my articles?'

'Oh no, your articles are very imaginative.'

'We are all imagining a world where you may speak your mind, aren't we?'

The man turned to Sam with a wry smile. 'Your lady friend is very beautiful, Mr Wareham. But she bites. You must keep her on a tight lead.'

'I'm not on anyone's lead, thank you.'

Sam took her arm and eased her out of the crush. Lenka's fury heightened the colour in her cheeks yet turned her eyes glacial. It was a disturbing combination. 'I don't think picking a fight with a senior functionary in the interior ministry is the best way of passing the evening,' he said. 'Let's go and find ourselves something to drink.'

'What is that man's name?'

'Kučera. Petr, Patrik? I can't remember.'

'How do you know him?'

'You meet all sorts in my line of work.'

'What a horrid job.' She looked round the crowded room as though to get her bearings. 'Now let's go and speak to the First Secretary.'

'The First Secretary? Don't be daft. They won't let you near him.'

'Daft? What is daft?'

'Silly, stupid.'

'It is not silly. Or stupid. He is meant to represent the people, is he not? I am the people.'

'Actually he represents the Communist Party, which is a very different thing.' But she was already away across the room, pushing amongst the crowd to where the Czechoslovak and Romanian officials were making a little festive scrum. Sam hurried after her. He reached the edge of the group just as she achieved the middle.

'Comrade Dubček,' he heard her say. Someone tried to move her back but Dubček put up a hand to stop him. 'I just wanted to tell you that we are all behind you,' she said. 'You are surrounded by all these officials who keep you from mixing with the ordinary people, so I thought you ought to know.'

He smiled benignly on her. 'And what is your name, miss? You appear to know mine – I feel I ought to know yours.'

She hesitated. She was normally decisive, but this time she did hesitate. And Sam knew exactly what she was going to say before she even uttered a word.

'I am Lenka Vadinská.'

There was a terrible stillness. The name sounded in the silence like a funeral bell. People shifted away as though leaving space at a graveside. Lenka and the awkward, smiling Dubček were left alone.

'The daughter of Lukáš Vadinský,' she added, just to make things clear.

If it had been a common name, a Novák or a Novotný, perhaps, maybe nothing much would have happened. Perhaps Lenka would have been forced to explain, and thus the potency of the name would have been dissipated among the words. But she didn't have to explain. Vadinský is not a common name and Lukáš Vadinský was beyond any confusion or doubt.

Dubček spread his hands helplessly. 'He was a good man. He didn't deserve what happened. No one did. I want to ensure that such things will never happen again.'

'No one doubts your sincerity, Comrade First Secretary. The question is, will the Russians let you?' She waited for a moment as though for an answer, then turned away. People stood aside and let her through. Behind her there was a sudden outburst of talk, random things said about the splendour of the rooms in which they found themselves, the magnificent Flemish tapestries on the walls, the excellence of the food, the quality of the wine and, of course, the eternal friendship of the Czechoslovak and Romanian peoples. While the Russian ambassador watched impassively.

Sam caught up with her as she reached the door. He grabbed her by the arm. 'What the devil was that all about?'

'Did I offend your diplomatic sensibilities?'

'You treated him as though he were to blame.'

'He *was* to blame. They were all to blame. Dubček himself believed in the whole system. He used to think that Stalin was wonderful, the father of all working people.'

'But he's a man of goodwill, you know that. He wants things to change.'

She pulled away from him. They went down the stairs into the pillared entrance hall. Uniformed staff watched them go. Outside, where the fleet of diplomatic cars waited, she finally stopped and turned to him. 'That's the first time I've ever used my father's name. The first time.' Her expression hesitated between defiance and tears. He put his arms around her. The hard bones of her shoulders seemed suddenly fragile, as though they might snap if he squeezed too hard. 'All my life I was made to feel ashamed and now I feel proud.' She blinked tears away, looking directly into his eyes. 'Will you get into trouble?'

'For what?'

'For introducing a subversive into the halls of power.'

He laughed softly, breathing in her scent, that mixture of things that he still couldn't fathom. 'The ambassador will probably summon me to his presence and give me a ticking off. Rocking the boat, he'll warn me about rocking the boat. They don't like people rocking the boat. Very nautical, the British.'

A policeman came over and told them to move on. The strange thing was, he did it politely, with a smile. That's what had happened in the last few months. People had learned how to smile, how to be polite, how to be helpful. Service with a snarl, so characteristic of the past, had been given a facelift. They walked along towards the Hrad and then down the hill into the Malá Strana, into the soft glow of gas lamps and the weight of history that pervades the streets of the Little Quarter. That whole ancient part of the city seemed to have its breath held as they went down towards the river and the modest Renaissance building where his flat was.

Once safe inside, she asked if she could use his typewriter. 'What is the expression? Make iron while it's hot.'

'You mean you're going to *write* something?'

'A *fejeton* for *Literární listy*. They'll take this, I'm sure.'

Fejeton, feuilleton. He'd never taken her writing seriously, in fact he'd never seen her write and had only glanced at one or two pieces that appeared under her by-line in the student magazine. But now he watched her sitting at his portable, hammering at the keys, cursing when she couldn't find diacritical marks and had to reach for a biro to ink them, and he found himself convinced by her energy.

WHAT'S IN A NAME? Lenka typed.

What's in a name? Juliet wondered, seeing Montague
as her enemy but Romeo as her love. That which we
call a rose, she observed, by any other name would
smell as sweet. These days we have other, less poetic
concerns than Juliet of the Capulets. It is not so
much a matter of whom can we love but how can we
circumnavigate the obstacles of bureaucracy and
oppression when burdened with a name that offends

272

the powers that be. So for years my name — the
one appended to this article, the one that I have
employed throughout my school and university days,
the one that my friends know me by — has not been
my name but my mother's maiden name, borrowed from
her for the sake of convenience and deception. It
was only today, for the first time in my conscious
life, that I used the name that my father bequeathed
me, a name that throughout my childhood and youth,
like a deranged self-loathing Juliet, I attempted to
cancel from my life just as surely as my father was
cancelled from the life of the Czechoslovak Republic.
That name is Vadinský. Lenka Konečková is really
Lenka Vadinská.

What's in a name?

When I was at university — always under my borrowed
name of course — I spent some time in the archives
of Terezin for my thesis on the role of the Party
in the antifascist struggle. Within the sad lists
of those admitted to the ghetto I found some thirty
Vadinský/Vadinskás, all of whom died in the ghetto
or were taken away in one of the transports, some to
Treblinka, some to Auschwitz. Amongst them were my
paternal grandparents whose names are even now to be
found on the wall of the Pinkas synagogue in Josefov.

'You never told me.'

'It was obvious, wasn't it? A Jewish father, you know that.
Therefore Jewish grandparents. Therefore dead at Auschwitz
or somewhere similar. That is what happened here.'

He left her side and walked over to the window. The strange
medieval shadows of the bridge towers were a contrast to
the clatter of keys behind him. He thought of what he didn't
know about Lenka, which was almost everything. And then

273

wondered how much you need to know about someone before you fall in love. Probably, he supposed, almost nothing. What did Romeo know of Juliet? Just enough to get both of them killed in the most idiotic way imaginable.

What's in a name?

At least those grandparents have a memorial of some kind, even if their ashes were scattered to the winds or blown away in a puff of smoke. But my father? After much complaint my mother was eventually given a death certificate by the authorities, and, this year, even a medal of some kind. The death certificate stated baldly the date on which he was killed, but there is no mention of what happened to his body. However, there's a story going round that the ashes of all the principal victims were dumped secretly in a lake in the Sumava region.

Then there's another story, that on the way to that lake, the car carrying the remains actually slid off the icy road some kilometres before reaching its destination. It was midwinter and everyone knows what a Tatra is like on slippery roads — it's that rear engine that does it. So there they were, two members of the security service — let's call them Švejk and Brouček — stuck in a snowdrift in the middle of the countryside in the middle of winter. It is getting late, the snow is coming down and the rear wheels are spinning uselessly. So Švejk (or was it Brouček?) has the brilliant idea of shovelling the ashes of the people's enemies under the rear wheels to give some traction in the snow. Thus, in a cloud of flying bits and pieces did Slánský, Clementis, London and all the others, including my father, contribute to the extrication of two members of state security from a snowdrift.

274

Which story do you believe? The lake or the
snowdrift? And which would you like to believe? And
which — because this is the key to everything —
sounds more perfectly Czech? What is certain is that
the whole disposal was done in secret and is unlikely
to be properly documented even in the archives of
our beloved StB where they keep all the other files,
including those of my mother and me ... and, no
doubt, you.

Except that I changed my name so that Lenka
Vadinská would not be stigmatised by being denied
access to a university education but instead Lenka
Konečková would sail into the faculty of literature.
Still — ask my boyfriend — I smell just as much of
roses as if I were called Vadinská, or, as I'm sure
the authorities would have it, just as much of shit.

He looked over her shoulder at what she had written so far
and laughed. 'Will they allow "shit"?'

She shrugged. 'We'll see.' And went back to her typing while
he went back to watching her. Her hunched figure of concentration over the typewriter. Her bare legs. The way her toes moved
as though they had life of their own. Things like that.

And then the phone rang. He went out into the hallway to
answer it and at first he didn't recognise the voice on the other
end. 'Mr Samuel Wareham?' it asked, almost whispering. He
might not have known the identity of the caller but he did
know the whisper. It was the natural instinct of someone who
fears the line may be tapped, as though lowering the voice
might make it less easily heard.

'Sam Wareham here, yes.'

'This is your pianist friend,' the voice said. Suddenly the
Russian accent was obvious. 'I would like to meet, is that
possible? Immediately. At Stalin?'

'What is this all about?'

'Just a meeting, Mr Wareham, at Stalin, you know? As soon as you can.'

It was there in the voice, an urgency and a sense of panic just beneath the surface calm. Sam said, 'It'll take me fifteen minutes or so. Is that all right?'

'Of course.' And then the line went dead.

He stood for a moment trying to make sense of the call. Stalin was clear enough, although Stalin was no longer there, hadn't been ever since they blew him up in 1962. Until that moment he had been the largest monumental statue in Europe, a fifteen-metre granite representation of the great leader standing on the edge of the Letná escarpment over-looking the city. All that remained now was the massive stone plinth on which the monument had been erected, but they had called the place *u Stalina*, 'at Stalin', ever since. Tourists went there during the day for the view over the city; couples went there after dark when the view really didn't matter very much.

'I'm going to have to go out for a while,' he told Lenka. 'Half an hour maybe.'

The typing stopped. She looked round. 'Now? On your own?'

He considered. Motives clashed against each other – loyalty and betrayal and some ridiculous sense of professional pro-priety, but also plain fear, fear for her and fear for himself. What if? What if this were all some complicated entrapment? Should he get hold of the SIS man, Harold Saumarez? Backup of some kind? But as far as Sam knew Harold didn't have a team of heavies to give him help. He'd only panic.

'On my own.'

She didn't ask anything more, that was what impressed him. 'Is it about the same dog as last time?'

He smiled. 'It's Egorkin. The conductor. He wants to meet me at Stalin.'

'Letná Park? Is he a queer or something?'

He laughed, looking for a pen and scribbling Harold's phone number on a scrap of paper. 'If I'm not back by midnight, ring this number and tell him. He's Harold.'

She looked at him. She appeared entirely composed, neither concerned nor fearful. 'Why are you afraid?'

'Not afraid, just cautious.'

She nodded. 'I remember cutting a lecture to see Stalin being blown up. We watched from the other side of the river and we cheered when it went BOOM! The police tried to clear us away. People were meant to stay indoors.'

'It won't be as dramatic as that this evening.'

'I hope not.' She turned back to the typewriter.

```
What's in a name? The man I was introducing myself
to, using my original name for the first time,
happened to be the First Secretary of the Communist
Party of Czechoslovakia, Alexander Dubček. There's
a name with import, a sturdy Bohemian oak* (which is
ironic because, as we all know, Comrade Dubček is
actually Slovak). 'You appear to know who I am, dear
miss,' he said. 'Perhaps I might know to whom I am
speaking?' And so I told him.
    Recognising my name, the Bohemian (and Slovak) oak
seemed to sway in the wind for a moment ...
```

* *Dub*, an oak. *Čech*, Bohemian.

34

The vast Letná parade ground, where the Party gathered to celebrate May Day, appeared deserted; across the road, the Sparta Prague stadium was a mass of darkness. Sam parked the car as inconspicuously as possible, hiding it beneath trees with its number plates masked by bushes. There were people around in the dusk, young lovers looking for somewhere to be alone, a group sitting in a circle on one of the lawns around an apology for a camp fire. A guitar was being strummed. There was laughter, some singing, the glow of cigarettes. A crescent moon was just rising – barely enough light to follow the paths through the trees towards the edge of the plateau where steps led down to a paved esplanade overlooking the river and the Old Town.

Moonlight glimmered faintly on the great curve of the river below. Beyond the water the Old Town buildings were picked out in lights. He could make out the needle-like spires of the Týn Church thrust upwards into the belly of the night sky. Behind him the wall at the back of the esplanade seemed huge, the bastion of a fortress. It was up there that the great monument had once stood, the largest group sculpture in Europe – a gaggle of workers, farm labourers and soldiers all pushing and shoving behind the solemn figure of Joseph Vissaryonovich Dzhugashvili, better known as Stalin, who stood at the front and looked thoughtfully over the city.

With bitter irony they nicknamed it *fronta na maso*, the meat queue. Constructed of seventeen thousand tons of reinforced concrete and clad with thirty thousand blocks of granite, it was an exercise in posthumous sycophancy, because by the time it was finished Stalin had already been dead two years. On the orders of Moscow the grandiose monument was demolished in 1962.

How do you demolish such a monstrosity without getting egg on your face? You first attempt to hide the whole construction behind wooden fencing before blowing it up with a total of one thousand eight hundred pounds of high explosive and hoping that no one notices. As it was built in the most prominent place in the entire city, that is rather difficult.

It is said that President Novotný wept when the monument vanished in a cloud of concrete bits and granite chippings. What is certain is that the original designer of the thing did not shed a tear over its disappearance – he was long dead, having committed suicide a month before it was officially unveiled.

And now? Now there was nothing. Elsewhere in the night sky there were stars, but not there. It was as though the vanished presence of Uncle Joe still cast a kind of shadow, a void that seemed vaster and more frightening than any material monument to the man.

Sam stood close to the wall, feeling happier with his back to the stones. It was like standing on an ill-lit stage, waiting for the lights to come up and the performance to begin. There were others already there, mere blots in the uncertain light: a couple sitting, apparently wrapped in each other's arms, on the low wall that would be the apron of the stage; a solitary male figure standing apart, smoking. Was that Egorkin?

Shadows played tricks with perspective. Doubts crowded in. This was idiotic. What the hell did the Russian want? He thought of Lenka back in the flat, typing away at her *fejeton* and thinking of bed. He thought of the bed itself, a place that only had meaning with her couched within it.

Meanwhile on the esplanade a second figure joined the solitary one. The two exchanged a few words and went off together into the shadows. Sam almost laughed out loud. Queers. A world of secrecy and evasion existing below the surface of everyday life just as surely as the world of spies and traitors. Was this, he wondered, Egorkin's idea of a joke? He lit a cigarette and glanced at his watch. The luminous minute hand crept on. A cigarette seemed as good a measure of time as anything. He'd finish this cigarette and then go.

He took a last drag, dropped the butt on the ground and stamped it out. As he was about to walk away the fused couple on the wall divided amoeba-like into two individuals. One of them walked across the esplanade towards him, leaving the other seated, watching, her face a smudge of white against the shadows.

'I'm sorry to have kept you,' Egorkin said. It was hard to make out his expression – just shadows, an abstract combination of dark and light. But his voice was unsteady, as though there was a fracture somewhere deep within it.

'What the hell's going on?'

'It's ... there's been a problem.' He glanced behind him at the lonely figure. 'We are in trouble.'

'Trouble?' It sounded ridiculous, the kind of euphemism used to cover teenage pregnancy.

'We're being sent back to Moscow. Our programme for the next week has been cancelled. Tomorrow, that's what I've been told.' His hand darted across the shadows and grabbed Sam's wrist. 'We have no time, that's the truth. We must go now.'

'Now?'

'I'm asking you for help. We are. Both of us. Now.'

'Are you serious?'

'This is not the moment for jokes, is it? We need to be taken to the British embassy.'

Sam had a moment's vision of the chaos and confusion were he to knock on the embassy gate at eleven-thirty at night on Friday night with a couple of renegade Russians in tow.

'Look, I haven't spoken with anyone yet. Haven't had the opportunity, and now it's the weekend. I can't just turn up with you. They'd have to get the ambassador out of bed. I'm in his bad books already this evening. Me trying to deliver the two of you into his care would be the last straw.'

'But there is no time. They will soon see that we are both missing. It won't take them long to realise we have left the hotel.'

'And if I do get you into the embassy, the story will be in Moscow by lunchtime tomorrow. You'll end up trapped there with no way of getting you out and Mr Brezhnev demanding satisfaction from the Czechoslovak government.'

'You have no secrecy?'

'Locally employed people. Maids, stewards, even some secretaries in the consulate. They all report to the StB.'

'So what do you suggest?'

It was ridiculous. The whole situation was ridiculous. He could, of course, offer his apologies and walk away. That would be the safer option, at least for Sam Wareham, First Secretary at the British Embassy; not for Gennady Egorkin and Nadezhda Pankova, though. 'I'll take you to my flat,' he said, 'at least for tonight. Then we'll see.'

The girl came over, a small figure with the stolid face of a Russian peasant. Very different from the slight, fierce figure he had seen in concert. 'Nadezhda Nikolayevna,' she said, shaking his hand. She seemed sullen rather than frightened. What, Sam wondered, was her particular talent as far as Egorkin was concerned? But then the man took the girl's hand

and she looked up to give him a sudden, fleeting smile and Sam thought maybe, just maybe, it was love.

'Don't you have a suitcase or anything?' he asked. 'Clothes? Washing things?'

'Nothing. Not even Nadia's violin. It would have been suspicious. We were rehearsing for our recital tomorrow and we stepped out of the hotel for some fresh air. That's it.'

The sheer idiocy of their action crowded in on Sam. No planning, no preparation, just acting on the spur of the moment. Like children. Here I am, please sort it out. Was this the artistic nature Egorkin had talked about? You are a functionary, he had said accusingly. But at least functionaries plan ahead.

They made their way to the car, walking slowly – that was what Sam suggested – as though strolling through the park in the evening was the most normal thing to be doing. Ahead where the campfire flickered through the trees there was something else flickering – the blue light of a police car. Egorkin stopped.

'It's just kids being moved on,' Sam said.

They walked forward until the patrol car was visible. Familiar white door panels and the letter VB in black; the blue light sparking on the roof; a cluster of figures gathered round it, arguing. The kids argued with the police these days. As big a change as you could imagine. Egorkin and the violinist followed Sam past the scene and a few moments later they were climbing into the Mercedes and feeling safer. Not safe but safer. As he started the engine Sam wondered a dozen things but the most immediate was, what the hell was he going to do about these people? What would Eric Whittaker say? What would the ambassador say? What the fuck would the Foreign Office say when one of their officers had picked up a couple of stray Russian musicians and offered them sanctuary? Embarrassment, that was the great fear. If you want to make it to the top, a senior diplomat had once told him, never, ever embarrass the Office. Embarrassment is the one unforgivable crime.

There was something funereal about the drive back down to Malá Strana. Egorkin and Sam sat in the front like two undertaker mutes while the girl sat alone in the back like a principal mourner, sniffing quietly to herself.

In the square outside his apartment building there was nobody about, no watching policemen, no waiting cars, no sign of anything out of the ordinary. A light showed behind the curtains at the windows of his sitting room, which gave him some kind of comfort. He ushered his passengers from the car into the building. The hallway was silent and empty. They crept up like thieves to the first floor. His door key grating in the lock seemed loud and intrusive, an alarm to waken the dead.

'It's me,' he called into the interior of the flat as he opened the door. 'I've got people with me.'

There was a moment when he thought perhaps she had gone. And then she was there at the door to their bedroom, bare-legged with a towel held to her front, her face pale with anxiety, her eyes wide.

'Go back inside,' he told her. 'I'll be with you in a moment.'

The Russians had followed him in. They stood now, a disconsolate couple, in the middle of the hallway, like refugees from the outbreak of war. Egorkin seemed diminished in size compared with the man Sam had encountered in the gardens in Mariánské Lázně. And the woman beside him, who had appeared proud and vigorous on stage, was now seen in the hall light to be a mere slip, a bewildered child looking at him with horror, as though the full import of what she had done was only just dawning on her.

Sam pushed them past the bedroom and the living room, past the kitchen and bathroom to the spare room at the back.

There was nothing there beyond some of his old clothes. The bed wasn't even made up, hadn't been touched ever since his mother had come to stay the previous year. He found some sheets in the bottom drawer of the wardrobe and tossed them to Nadia. 'You'll have to make the bed,' he said in Russian, and she smiled at hearing her own language in a foreign mouth. 'Towels, soap, but I haven't got anything else. Not even a spare toothbrush. We'll have to get stuff for you in the morning. I can find you something to eat if you want.'

They wanted nothing. Frugal was the watchword for Russian defectors in the hands of their hosts. Egorkin sat on the bed, bent forward with his elbows on his knees and his forearms hanging slack between his legs. He wore the expression of someone who has jumped over the cliff and suddenly understands that there is no way to go but down. It was the girl, Nadezhda Pankova, who started to do something. She shoved him off the bed and into the only chair in the room. Then she began to make the bed, as though housework was the solution to all their problems.

Sam closed the door on them and went back to his own room where Lenka waited, her face set against the world. 'What are they doing here?' she asked.

Sam began to undress. 'They are guests for the night.'

'They are Russians. Perhaps they are musicians, but they are Russians. Why are they here?'

'Because they have just run away from Russia.'

She considered this, looking at him with suspicious eyes. 'Who can blame them?'

35

A brief telephone call, first thing next day. Sam tried to picture Eric Whittaker in his pyjamas, yawning and scratching his head and trying to work out who this might be disturbing him so early on Saturday morning. And Madeleine lying in bed beside him, wearing, presumably, some exotic French nightdress. 'Guests? What guests?' Eric asked irritably.

'Perhaps if you were to come round. I'd rather not talk over the phone.'

Whittaker was round in fifteen minutes. Sam opened the door to him and ushered him into the sitting room. 'It's Gennady Egorkin,' he said before Whittaker could utter a word.

'What about him?'

'He's here, in the spare room.'

'*Here?*'

'He called me last night. Threw himself on my mercy, more or less. Him and his girlfriend.'

'Girlfriend?'

'Nadezhda Pankova, the violinist. You saw her playing the Brahms. And then I heard them in Mariánské Lázně, and—'

'What the hell's going on, Sam?'

'They're looking for asylum.'

'*Asylum?* And you've done what exactly? Taken it upon yourself to grant it to them?'

'Not exactly. I just thought we ought to consider it. There's nothing wrong with putting them up for the night, is there? And then we can go from there.'

'Nothing wrong? For fuck's sake!' Eric Whittaker's face seemed about to explode. There was something almost geological about it, his whole countenance trembling under the onslaught of internal disturbances like the surface ripples from an earthquake buried deep below his crust of elegant complacency. Occasional eruptions broke out along the fault lines. A twitch, an open mouth, a grimace. 'What do you want, Sam? A row with the Soviet Union just when they're looking to pick a fight with the Czechos? Jesus Christ!'

'I just did what any human being would do – tried to help them.'

'Human being? But you're not a human being – you're a bloody British diplomat!'

He turned away and went over to the window, stood there looking out at the dunce-cap towers of the bridge gate rising over the neighbouring roofs. 'What the hell is H.E. going to say? I've no idea but I tell you one thing, whatever the final outcome, this is going down on your annual report as a pretty black mark.'

Sam smiled, grateful that Eric had his back to him because he would only have interpreted the expression as mocking or smug or something, whereas really it was relief. 'My annual report against two artists desperate for freedom? It doesn't really balance, does it, Eric?'

Whittaker turned. 'Do you know how pompous that sounds, Sam?'

'You *know* Gennady Egorkin, Eric. You've been to one of his concerts—'

'Two, actually. Heard him playing Beethoven at the Royal Festival Hall a couple of years ago.'

'So you understand his importance. And Pankova. We're

talking about artists here. I know it doesn't fit in with polit-ics or economics or whatever it is that occupies the Foreign Office mind at the moment, but it's every bit as important. I mean, look at Ashkenazy, for example. Or Nureyev. Not only a triumph for art but also—'

'A triumph for politics.'

'I wasn't going to say that. I was going to say, a humani-tarian act.'

'But it's the political side of things that London appreciates. And anyway, the wretched man is here, not in London.'

'So we get him out.'

'That, my dear Sam, is easier said than done.' Whittaker shook his head despairingly. 'Look, I'll have a word with him if you like, but I don't want to give him the impression that this is official, is that clear? Not until we've got some kind of clearance from head office. Or at least from H.E. So the story is, Egorkin appealed to you and you took him and his girlfriend back to your flat as nothing more than an act of kindness. A private decision. Is that clear?'

It was clear. It was precisely what Sam had told them. 'I'm not a bloody idiot, Eric.'

'That, dear fellow, remains to be seen.'

Egorkin was duly summoned to the sitting room to meet with the Head of Chancery and be told the hard truth, that his appeal would be considered but that it put Her Majesty's government in a very difficult position at this crucial time in relations with Czechoslovakia and the Soviet Union. For the moment he and his companion could only consider themselves private guests of Mr Wareham – after all there was nothing wrong with that – but they could not themselves rely on any official diplomatic protection from the British embassy.

'Perhaps,' Egorkin said, with solemn pride, 'you can contact Mr André Previn of the London Symphony Orchestra.'

Whittaker smiled. 'Mr Previn could not tell me anything I

do not already know, Mr Egorkin. No one doubts your standing in the world of music, but it is the broader political picture that we have to consider in a case like this. I'm afraid it will take some time and I can by no means guarantee the outcome.'

'We don't have no time,' Egorkin replied. It wasn't quite English but the sense was plain enough. The violinist had appeared behind him, watching the discussion with blank incomprehension. 'Now we have gone and they will be looking for us. We have made our move, Mr Whatever-your-name-is, and it is your duty to protect us.'

Eric inclined his head, as though acknowledging applause. 'So what I suggest is that you remain here – if that is all right with Mr Wareham – and keep strictly out of sight. And in the meanwhile, I will expedite my enquiries on your behalf.' He had the unnerving ability to talk in the language of official memos and draft accords. 'For the moment you are on embassy property, which gives you a degree of security, exactly as though you were in the embassy itself. The local authorities may not enter the embassy or any of its official properties such as Mr Wareham's apartment under any circumstances without the express permission of the ambassador. However, given the circumstances, and should they demand it, we might find it necessary to hand you over to representatives of the host country.'

Egorkin shook his head. 'It is not the Czechs I have to worry about. It is my own countrymen. Let me assure you that if the KGB discover we are here, they will take no notice of diplomatic property or the status of this apartment. They will break in, take us both and that will be the end of it.' He seemed about to add something, then thought better of it and remained silent.

'In that case, I am afraid there would be little we could do beyond express our outrage through the official channels. But let's hope that you remain hidden and nothing untoward occurs.'

With that Whittaker excused himself, leaving nothing behind him but the vague words expressed and equally vague hopes invoked. Sam ushered the guests back into their room, trying to reassure them. 'We'll sort things out,' he insisted. 'In the worst case, I'll drive you to the border myself.'

Back in the bedroom Lenka was getting dressed – shorts, a battered old shirt, walking boots. There was some plan to meet up with Jitka and her husband, to get out of the city to go hiking. Very Czech. An overnight stay at some place that she wanted to show him, an old castle or something. And those two English kids they seemed to have adopted, they'd be coming along. But now he'd have to remain behind, to keep watch over the Russians.

Couldn't they go somewhere else? Lenka suggested. The embassy? Why here? Why disturb our lives? For the first time she sounded petulant and proprietorial, as though possessing rights of ownership over Sam, his flat and his life.

'I'm sorry but that's not possible. I'm afraid you'll have to go by yourself, Lenička'

'You never wanted to go anyway, did you?' she said.

'Of course I did.'

'No, you did not.'

'I did. Really.' One of those stupid arguments that come out of nowhere, a storm on a summer's day. And to make matters worse, he had to get her help doing some shopping. Food and cigarettes of course, but Egorkin and Nadezhda Pankova needed other things – clothes, toiletries, even reading material. Could she help him get some items? A couple of pairs of knickers, a bra, a couple of blouses, anything you might need for a weekend away. And some sanitary towels.

They drove round to the nearest Tuzex and shopped bad-temperedly for the various items like a long-married couple.

'They won't fit you,' the saleswoman said, holding a pair of knickers and looking Lenka up and down.

'They're not for me,' she snapped back, as though she were being forced to shop for her husband's mistress.

Sam drove her round to the railway station and left her with all the usual admonishments: 'Give Jitka and, what's his name – Zdeněk? Give them my regards. And tell them next time for sure. And Lenička—'

'Yes?'

'Not a word to anyone about our guests. Please remember. No one must know. For their own sakes.'

'So what do I say?'

'Something came up, that's all you have to say. The embassy, work. They'll understand. But nothing more. Absolutely nothing more.'

She walked away towards the station entrance. As he watched her go, he felt the anxiety of separation like something tearing deep inside. Never with Stephanie, never that deep, organic pain. For a moment he contemplated the possibility of getting out of the car and running after her, but then he dismissed the idea, shoved the car into gear and drove away.

VIII

36

The main Prague railway station, echoing to the sound of trains and people. They push and shove to get onto the train and keep up with the others. The entire youth of the city seems to be here, crowding onto these carriages at this moment, although Jitka says that they are already late, that they should have been on one of the earliest out of the station – that way you can get into the countryside when it is still fresh from the overnight cool. But Lenka has only just joined them, apologising for being late. She had some shopping to do. 'Samuel cannot make it', is all she says by way of explanation for his absence.

They crowd into a compartment where four of the places are already taken. Jitka has to sit on Zdeněk's lap and the rucksacks are piled in anyhow, some on the overhead luggage racks, others on James's lap. There is laughter, some broken English, much splintered Czech. Jitka has brought her violin; her husband has a guitar which he holds across Jitka's front and manages to pick at while she laughs and wriggles. The train slides out of the station and traipses through the Prague suburbs. Lenka sits opposite James, a hint of anger lying behind her smile. She's wearing shorts like something out of the army, except these shorts were probably hers when she was a thirteen-year-old and went on camping trips with the Pioneers or whatever, so they are disturbingly tight, folded in at her crotch in ways he can barely comprehend. And her legs. Blonde, strong, dusted with golden hairs that catch the light from the window as the train rounds a cliff above the river and the sun glares in at their crowded compartment for a moment. He hopes she doesn't notice his eyes straying down there, but probably she does. You notice the direction of people's eyeline, don't you? Exactly where they're looking, precisely where their glance strays, to the nearest millimetre.

What does she see in that diplomat bloke? What's he got that James Borthwick doesn't have?

Almost everything, including her.

Anyway, thank God he's not here.

Jitka is still full of the wonders of the concert, the thrill of working with Gennady Egorkin and the brilliance of Pankova's violin-playing. And Eckstein, of course, but the whole world already knows Birgit Eckstein.

'I didn't,' says James, and they laugh.

The conversation slips back into Czech for Zdeněk's sake. But he's reading the newspaper – RUDÉ PRÁVO the masthead announces – leafing through the pages, throwing out critical comments here and there. He says something that includes the musicians' names, Gennady Egorkin and Nadezhda Pankova. Jitka translates: 'It says the couple have disappeared from their hotel and no one knows where they are.'

Zdeněk adds something. Jitka protests. 'He says the man is doing indecent things with his violinist. He says all violinists are like that.' She blushes. 'Which is not true.'

The train trundles on, through the countryside now – fields, farms, forest, glimpses of a river through the trees. They finally leave it at a halt somewhere on the edge of a small town whose name seems impossible to pronounce, all consonants and no vowels.

The group sets off down a rough lane and into the woods. It's like a childhood adventure, walking in the forest, along paths that are hard to follow, in directions that James can't understand. And it is quite unlike anything in Britain, where almost always you walk and climb in open country, on the fells, on the moors, on the bareback mountains; but here there are miles and miles of forest, holding in their shadows something Slavic, something mysterious and mythic, echoing with birdsong as though it's a cathedral dedicated to some ancient sylvan deity.

They walk on, talking, laughing, occasionally diverting from the path to forage for berries or mushrooms. These are city people suddenly revealed in different guise, in forest-ers' garb, at ease in this strange world that seems so distant from the city. Above all, Zdeněk appears truly at home here, identifying plants and mushrooms, pausing to listen and point as, silently, deer cross their path like shadows in the half-light beneath the canopy of leaves. He smells the scent of a fox, points to cones gnawed down by squirrels, shows where boar have been rooting, identifies polecat droppings. There's an unreal quality to the whole expedition, going from a place Ellie and James have never heard of to a place they don't know, that is spoken of only in vague, allusive terms by their hosts. You will see. A strange place. An old ruin. A place whose name, if it has a name, is uncertain. We just call it *Hrádek*.

It isn't long before they break out of the trees onto a bare promontory and there it is, *Hrádek*, which means little castle, and that is what it is, the mere bones of a place, the skeleton of a structure that has long since died – a broken circuit of walls, a tracery of outbuildings, a roofless inner keep and a shattered tower. A metal notice, peppered with shot, warns visitors – *Pozor!* – of unspecified danger. Far below the battle-ments a river winds through a narrow gorge. And beyond that is a view, a sudden, startling view of miles and miles of wooded hills running away to the east. How far does it go?

Because it seems endless, this procession of forest, as though it will not end until it has become other places whose names James barely knows – the Tatra, the Carpathians, the great Russian steppe, the Urals. He thinks of the Pennines rising up behind his home town. How small they seem in memory.

The group sits for a while in the afternoon sun, amongst the ruins of a castle that once belonged to a Boleslav or a Vladislav, Duke of Bohemia, listening to birdsong and the soft movement of the breeze through the trees. Zdeněk sits apart, his face without expression. Jitka is her usual animated self, like a small, sleek rodent. Occasionally she looks directly at James for a moment longer than one might expect. He remembers the touch of her mouth when they were dancing and wonders whether she remembers too, and if she does what she thinks about it. Ellie sits beside Lenka, who is cool and distant.

'This is very kind of you,' Ellie tells her. 'To bring us with you. It's lovely here.'

Lenka's smile is tired, as though there are other things on her mind. 'It is *Čechy*. What you call Bohemia. It is right that you see it. Everything is not Prague.' And then she does what to James seems a curious thing: she puts her arm round Ellie. And Ellie moves towards her, puts her head on Lenka's shoulder, seems, for that moment in the sun, a close friend. Perhaps more. Is that the kind of friendship that women may have and he has never understood? A kind of idyll. Manet might have painted it, or one of the Impressionists. The viewer might ponder the relationship between the various figures, the two men sitting apart, a dark girl who moves between them, laughing at something, two women who sit together, one with her arm round the other.

The tableau is soon broken by the arrival of others on the scene, three men and a woman who come blundering through the trees and are greeted with cries of surprise and delight, as though their coming had not been planned. There are introductions, a bit of fractured English. Lenka translates: these are old friends of Zdeněk and Jitka, childhood friends of Zdeněk, in fact. It is a kind of tradition for them to gather here at the Hrádek in August, something they started years ago when they were all at the local school and have kept up ever since. So for a while the castle is theirs. They gather wood and make a fire against the wall of the inner keep where the stones are soot-blackened beneath the shaft of an ancient chimney. They forage for mushrooms, with Zdeněk's friends showing remarkable mycological knowledge. And then, as the sun goes down and the evening sets in, they cook sausages and bake potatoes and open the beer that everyone has brought. Afterwards they sing songs round the campfire like an advertisement for the Boy Scouts from the 1930s, Zdeněk and Jitka playing guitar and violin. Some of the music is familiar – American folk songs, Peter, Paul and Mary stuff with a bit of Joan Baez thrown in – but some is quite foreign to Ellie and James. Zdeněk strums the guitar well enough, but it is Jitka's playing that captivates, the classical violinist transfigured by the flicker of her bow and the shadows of the castle ruins and the uncertain firelight into something elemental – as though she has been revealed in her true form, which is Romany, Gypsy, Cikánka.

One of Zdeněk's friends – James has forgotten the names – has a bottle of *slivovice* which he passes round. Cigarettes are lit; someone rolls a joint, about which there's a heated discussion between the girl and one of the boys. But still the joint goes round while Zdeněk strums his guitar and Jitka sings now about going to San Francisco and being sure to wear some flowers in your hair, which James has always thought a bloody silly idea but which appeals to him at this moment, especially as when she has finished singing she comes over and sits close to him on the edge of the shadows round the fire, close enough to touch, shoulder to shoulder. He can smell her in the cooling air, the heat of her, her faint, tart scent.

'I was in San Francisco,' she tells him, as if that somehow justifies the song. 'With the youth orchestra. It is an interesting place.' Her husband and two friends are singing some kind of comic, call-and-response song. Everyone laughs. The joke is plainly that everyone knows the joke in advance.

'Why did you come back?' James asks. 'Why didn't you stay there?'

In the darkness he can see the gleam of her teeth as she smiles. 'Why does anyone do anything?'

'There must be a reason.'

'Reasons, many of them. Because of Zdeněk. Because things were changing here. Because I missed my home. All those reasons. Anyway, my scholarship was for six months, so when it finished I just came back.'

Lenka is trying to teach Ellie the words of the song. Words without comprehension, an eternal problem. They laugh over the difficulties.

'And now?'

'Now I am trapped.'

The fire burns down, the singing becomes sporadic. Mummified in sleeping bags they lie down amongst the castle ruins, Ellie beside Lenka, talking with her in the dark, a soft, earnest sound. James wanders away, round one of the walls, feeling detached from the expedition, indifferent to Ellie, thoughtful about Jitka. He finds his place away from the others, out of mind. The moon, a half-moon, is rising above distant trees. Shadows shift in the darkness. A darker shadow comes round the end of the wall and coalesces above him.

'Are you all right?' Jitka asks, kneeling down. 'I saw you go. I don't want you to be left out.'

298

'I'm all right.'

'With Ellie, everything isn't good is it?'

He feigned indifference. 'We're friends. We get on well enough.'

'Not lovers?' Perhaps it's the dark that makes it easier to ask direct questions like that.

'We were. Maybe not now.'

There's a silence between them. The sounds all around – the shifting of leaves, the creep of nocturnal animals, the hoot of a tawny owl, the muttered talk from the other side of the wall – do nothing to erode this particular silence. Her shadow comes closer to his face until he can feel the warmth of her breath and then that same touch as in the Ides' gig a few days ago, lips soft like mushrooms with the taste of her saliva now – beer, grilled sausage, *slivovice*. He puts up a hand, perhaps to hold her off because her husband is there, just the other side of the wall. Yet whatever he intends is not what happens because he finds only the loose edge of her T-shirt and her naked belly beneath, and then – her mouth on his, their tongues intertwining – her breasts hanging loose. He cups one, feels its ripe softness and the hard nub of her nipple, and for a moment they are like that, mouth on mouth, hand on breast. Then she pulls away and is gone, back to the other side of the ruined wall, back to the dying embers of the fire and her marriage to Zdeněk.

That moment of communion is something James will remember for the whole of his life, an instant of intimacy in the midst of a Bohemian forest transfigured into something almost eternal. As eternal as events can be in a human existence. He'll remember it when other, not dissimilar moments are long forgotten, when Ellie is no more than a fond memory, when Jitka herself, entirely unbeknownst to him, has left Zdeněk, left her country, gone to America and found work as a teacher of violin and occasional orchestral player in New

York, to be knocked down and killed by a car when crossing a street in Chicago in 1978.

That's the way things work out. There's no plan, no narrative thread. They just happen. You may as well roll a die.

37

Dawn light leaks into the ruins of the castle. Figures emerge from sleeping bags, yawning and stretching and pulling on clothes with scant regard for modesty. There's the chill of early morning, the faint sensation of the evening before not having been worth the discomfort of the present. Someone kicks the embers of the fire to let them burn out. Others make their way down a precipitous path into the gorge below the castle, to the edge of the river where they wash approximately. The water is cold, as though it has come from high up and far away. Apparently indifferent to her audience, Lenka strips off completely and walks into the water until it's up to her waist. The others watch, laughing and calling and daring her to go right in. On an impulse Ellie pulls off her own T-shirt and shorts and stumbles in to join her. For a moment they are close together, squealing and splashing, their two bodies a vivid contrast, the one tall and languid, the other small and quick. James watches with a peculiar, embarrassed focus, thinking how incongruous they seem in this wild place, and how far away from nature the human body has evolved to become pallid, almost hairless, awkward and vulnerable.

'Stop staring!' Ellie calls. There's laughter.

Later the two bathers find a place apart to dry in the sun. James catches a glimpse of them through the trees, Ellie lying on her side with her hand on Lenka's shoulder, then moving down out of sight, obscured by Ellie's own body, Lenka laughing and lying back. And Ellie leaning forward.

He moves away hurriedly, fearful of being seen, fearful of the damage it might do.

38

They throw earth on the fire to extinguish it, look round their makeshift campsite for any scraps left behind, then shoulder their rucksacks and begin the return through the forest. Jitka walks with James; Zdeněk with his three friends; Ellie walks behind with Lenka. Ellie and Lenka are holding hands, which James notices as he turns to call something. He wants to hold Jitka's hand. He wants some recognition of what happened in the dark the previous evening, a further moment of contact that can mean something to the two of them. It comes when she stumbles on a boulder and he grabs hold of her to keep her from falling, a squeeze of her hand that no one but she would ever notice, holding her up a moment longer than is necessary. 'You saved my life,' she says, and laughs.

The train back to Prague is less crowded than the one that brought them. It's the holiday month, so who wants to be going back to the city? They talk about their plans, or their lack of plans. 'I guess we'll be moving on next week,' James suggests, but Ellie disagrees. Sitting close to Lenka she looks at her with eyes that hint at something more than affection. Revelation, perhaps. She has been captivated by a constell-ation of things – the country, the spirit of place and Lenka herself. 'Lenka thinks I could find work here. People want help with English now that so much is changing.'

Lenka shrugs. 'It would not be legal. But for a few weeks ...'

James remembers the two of them naked in the river, splashing and laughing, then lying on the bank to dry. He wonders about Lenka and about her boyfriend, the supercilious guy from the British embassy. What are her motives in all this? What does she *do* in the privacy of her own life? That evening, crushed into their bedroom in Jitka's flat, he and Ellie talk about matters of the heart and the head, Ellie hovering on the edge of confession. 'She's so beautiful,' she says. 'Don't you think so?'

'You do.'

'And you don't?'

'She's all right.'

'But you prefer Jitka?'

There's a silence in the darkness. 'Why do you say that?'

She laughs softly. 'Because of the way you look at her. Because of the way she went to find you when we were at that ruin. What did you two get up to?'

'Nothing,' he said. 'Nothing at all.'

IX

39

Lenka returned from the weekend in the country burnished by the sun, stained with sweat, smelling of crushed grass and earth and wood smoke. He watched her undress, walking naked round their room, flaxen and honeyed and entirely lovely. Like some half-wild animal returned to him.

'A couple more days,' he said when she asked about Egorkin and Pankova, 'that's all. Just pretend they're not there.'

'How can I pretend they're not there? I can *smell* them.'

Sam laughed. 'I can smell *you*.'

She'd brought a newspaper from the station. The main pages were filled with reports on the political scene, the coming and going of various foreign leaders, debates in the Party Presidium, rumours of the Russian leadership applying pressure on Dubček, on President Svoboda, on Prime Minister Černík. The Čierna nad Tisou accord, the Bratislava Agreement, all these vows of good intention were dissected and analysed. But on one of the inside pages, there was the story about the pair of missing Russian musicians. Various theories were voiced. Perhaps they had fled to Hungary with the intention of getting to Yugoslavia, or maybe they'd got across the border to Vienna.

Egorkin was delighted with the journalist's stupidity, as though his hiding in Sam's flat were all his own doing. Yet once the novelty wore off he went back to complaining as he had from the start. One of his first complaints was circumscribed by the very matter he complained about, so he had voiced his objections by holding Sam close and whispering in his ear, an angry whisper like the exhalation from a steam engine. 'The room will be bugged. We cannot live here. The room, your whole damn apartment. There will be microphones.'

Despite Sam's assurances to the contrary the Russian had carried out his own ridiculous search, hushing Sam and the girl to silence, while he went over the room inch by inch, passing his fingertips over the walls, lifting pictures, moving furniture, even examining the glass in the window panes. Finally he put the radio on and tuned it to Radio Moscow, turning the volume up and speaking more normally but still softly, as though he had a throat infection: 'I wish to register my protest at not being held in the embassy building itself.'

The violinist appeared better adapted to their current circumstances than her man. She was happy to lie on the bed reading one of Sam's Russian books, a copy of *Chyotki*, 'Rosary', Anna Akhmatova's second collection of poems that he had found years ago in a sixpenny tray outside a book-shop in the Charing Cross Road. It was one of the original Giperborei editions, but more than that, it was pencilled (he had struggled to contain his excitement as he had handed over his sixpence to the bookseller) with the poet's monogram on the title page, the letter *a* struck through with a dash. A small but perfect treasure. This book, taken from a bookcase in the sitting room, created a small point of contact with Nadezhda. Her eyes came alive as she turned it over in her hands, touch-ing it with her tough, violinist's fingertips. It seemed that Akhmatova was some kind of idol for her, the poet's death two years ago an event with almost religious significance. 'We thought we were beggars,' she murmured, quoting. 'We thought we had nothing at all.'

She was even more astonished to discover that Sam had actually met Akhmatova in Oxford when, after years of obscurity and persecution, the poet had finally been allowed to travel outside Russia to receive the plaudits of the West and an honorary degree.

The violinist's eyes widened. 'Tell me, what was she like?'

He hesitated. The truth was he had loved the legend that was Akhmatova, the woman of the early poems, the woman of the Nathan Altman portrait, all bony shoulders and languid legs and hidden treasures; the woman whose irregular lifestyle and courage in the face of Stalin's oppression had elevated her to the heroic. But there, in that reception in Oxford three years ago, amidst the chatter and the jabber and the clink of glasses, he had found only the ruin of that ideal, a stout old dear who looked incongruous in academical robes, more like a school dinner lady than a great poet. 'She was like an old warhorse,' he told the girl. 'Unsteady on her feet and a bit bewildered by all the fuss, but bright-eyed and curious. It was the first time she'd been allowed to travel outside Russia in fifty years.'

'But you *met* her? Spoke with her?'

'Shook hands with her. Told her, rather inadequately, that I was a great admirer, that I had been reading her poems since I was eighteen and it was through them that I first *felt* the language. I felt a bit stupid, to be honest. What do you say to someone like that?'

'And what did she reply to you?'

Sam laughed. 'She said, "How strange."'

'How strange,' Nadezhda repeated, as though this portentous phrase were a newly discovered work by Akhmatova herself. From that moment she looked at Sam with wonder, as though maybe, by proximity, some of the spirit of the poet had been transferred to him. Later, when he was leaving the room and he addressed her formally as Nadezhda Nikolayevna, she cast her eyes downwards and quietly invited him to please call her Nadia. It was a Chekhovian moment.

40

In his office Sam scanned the newspapers for any further hint of the news breaking. There were small items in a couple of the dailies – *Concerts Cancelled, Russian conductor rumoured to be unwell*, that kind of thing. But clearly no one had any idea of what had happened, that the whole world of Gennady Egorkin, conductor and pianist of international fame, and his violinist mistress had shrunk to this, the spare room in Sam Wareham's flat where they lived in artificial light, like creatures in a vivarium.

'The wheels are in motion,' Eric Whittaker assured him. 'But as you know they grind with almost glacial slowness at times.'

'What does H.E. think?'

'He's not exactly over the moon, Sam. I'm afraid he thinks what all ambassadors think – don't rock the boat if you don't have to. And in this case, we didn't have to. Except you did.'

That afternoon Nadia came quietly to the sitting room and presented him with a single sheet of paper taken from a notebook he had provided. Lenka was at the desk, revising the piece she was preparing for *Literární listy*. She stopped her typing and watched as Sam read. Nadia had written in pencil, a poem in the careful, concise, allusive style of early Akhmatova entitled 'How Strange', about a stranger who meets her in a foreign country and talks to her about the world from where he has come and to where she might go. Ambiguities informed the piece. Who was the poet – Nadezhda Nikolayevna Pankova or Anna Andreyevna Akhmatova? And where was the encounter – here in this flat in the Malá Strana, or in New College Oxford three years earlier when he had met the great Russian poet; or two decades earlier than that, when another English diplomat with the curiously un-English name of Isaiah Berlin had encountered, stumbling slightly over his Russian greeting, the great poet in her Leningrad apartment? And what exactly was the gulf of misunderstanding that separated the two protagonists?

Nadia blushed as Sam read it. 'It's just a small thing.' But it wasn't a small thing at all. It was rather good. That's what he told her. Rather good. She thought he was damning her poem with faint praise, whereas of course it was typical British understatement.

41

The inevitable call to the ambassador's office was delivered by Eric Whittaker. 'I'm afraid the Old Man wants to see you, Sam. He's not in a good mood. Remember, whatever you do, don't argue with him, do you understand? Don't argue with him even if you are right.'

The Old Man. It was like a summons from the headmaster, but then so much of the Foreign Office was like that, like the British public school with its rewards and its punishments, its fearsome jealousies and absurd rituals, its guilt and its triumphs. The ambassador was sitting behind his desk, which was a bad sign. Just as you might expect in the headmaster's study, on the wall behind him was a reproduction of that portrait of the Queen, the Annigoni portrait that depicts her as a young and desirable Renaissance monarch against a Tuscan landscape. Beneath this symbol of regal beauty the ambassador looked up from whatever he was pretending to work on and motioned Sam to sit down. That was another headmasterly trick, to keep the interviewee waiting while you completed the previous task.

'You've been a bit various recently, Sam,' he said finally, putting down his pen and looking up with a tight smile. It was an accusation dressed up as a pleasantry. Being various was not a good thing – constancy was what diplomacy demanded.

'Tell me about these refugees whom you've taken in from

312

the street. What's that all about, eh?' His expression was mild but the headmasterly threat lay beneath it.

'Gennady Egorkin, ambassador. And a protégée of his called Nadezhda Pankova.'

'So Eric told me. I've heard of him, of course. Quite a reputation. The question is, what the hell are they doing in your flat, almost as guests of HMG?'

'That's not exactly the case, sir. Both Eric and I have made the unofficial nature of their presence very clear to them. They more or less threw themselves on my mercy on Friday evening. After the reception, as a matter of fact. They'd escaped from their hotel when their minders weren't watching – I certainly don't have to tell you how it is with the Russians. Egorkin probably saw this as his last chance of getting out.'

'With your connivance.'

'No connivance at all, ambassador. Absolutely none. But what else could I have done? Told them to throw themselves on the mercy of the Americans?'

The ambassador gave a little grunt. Maybe that was the moment when the tide turned, that small grunt at the mention of possible rivalry by the Americans. 'I don't want them brought into the embassy, is that clear? I've been on to the P.U.S. and he's adamant. Hasn't spoken to the minister yet, but I'm sure he'll be in agreement too. We don't want a word of this to get out. We haven't seen them and we haven't given them shelter. If so much as a whisper gets into the embassy, the news will be all over Prague in half a day. You know that as well as I do. Chervonenko will be issuing diplomatic protests left, right and centre and we'll be accused of kidnapping two of his citizens and trying to destabilise a fraternal socialist country. For all I know he'll claim we're trying to start World War Three. The waters of Prague are muddied enough at the moment – we don't want even more shit stirred into them.' The word was shocking on the ambassador's lips. He gave a wry smile. 'And in the meantime, you and Eric had better work out how to get them out of the country without anyone knowing.'

'We'll sort something out, sir.'

'I suppose Saumarez will be involved, won't he? He usually is in this sort of thing.'

'He is the expert, sir.'

Another grunt, this one tinged with displeasure. Sam shifted in his chair but the ambassador clearly hadn't finished. 'And then there was that business at the reception.'

'Yes, I'm sorry about that.'

'Made a bit of a scene, didn't she?'

'I suppose Miss Konečková did speak with First Secretary Dubček in rather frank terms. But the circumstances . . .'

'We're all very tense at the moment, I know. Still, you're a diplomat, aren't you? And she's, well, she's a local, isn't she? Not a good idea, really. You bring a local gal to a diplomatic bun fight and it causes all sorts of trouble. Believe me, it's always better to play at home. Especially here behind the Curtain, you never know what you're letting yourself in for. Or us, come to that.'

'I can assure you that I am most sensitive to security issues.'

'Of course you are, old chap. Of course you are. I wouldn't think for one moment you'd—'

'And I've had Harold Saumarez check her out.'

'Have you, indeed? That's a good thing. Clean as a whistle, I expect. But still, you don't want to let her take your eye off the ball.' He looked faintly embarrassed. 'If you see what I mean.'

'Of course I won't. But as a matter of fact, I'm going to ask her to marry me.'

For a moment the ambassador looked startled. 'Good lord.' Then diplomacy papered over the surprise with a broad smile, as though the idea of marriage changed the whole complexion of the affair. A bit of casual sex with a local girl was suddenly

314

transformed into an aspect of statecraft. 'Oh, that's wonderful news, Sam. Wonderful.'

'For your ears only at the moment, sir. I haven't even asked the lady yet.'

Suddenly all smiles, the ambassador came round the desk with his hand outstretched. 'I must congratulate you, Sam.' Angling metaphors replaced cricket metaphors with note-worthy fluency. 'I'm sure you'll land the catch successfully, old fellow. Let me know when you've popped the question and we can celebrate properly. Meanwhile, what about a glass of sherry?'

'That's very kind, sir. A small one.'

The ambassador busied himself with decanter and glasses at a side table. He'd got an amontillado or a fino. Which would Sam prefer? Had them shipped out by Berry Bros. & Rudd. Cut glass – Bohemian, of course – and amber liquid. They sipped.

'Now tell me about the girl. She seems quite a force of nature. I gather her father was a victim of the show trials.'

'Yes, he was. Lukáš Vadinský.'

'So I gathered. Can't have been easy for her.'

'She's certainly had a pretty hard time of it. Only got to university by taking her mother's maiden name. She's still a student but she also does some journalism. A bit of radio as well.'

'You must bring her round to the residence to meet Margaret.' He frowned. 'She docs speak English, doesn't she?'

'Very well.'

Relief. 'Good for her. And good for you, old chap. And good to know that in these troubled times it's still matters of the heart that rule.'

Sam returned to his office feeling that some kind of victory had been achieved, a diplomatic coup without having had to marshal arguments to support it. But marriage to Lenka? He'd voiced the idea before he'd even thought about it. Did that mean the idea had already been there, lurking beneath the level of the conscious? So did he mean it? And if he did mean it and if he were to ask her, what the devil would she say? The phone rang. It was somebody from the consular department with some damn-fool story about a TV programme they were making on the Charles Bridge – a British pop group or something. Was he interested in watching? This afternoon. The Moody Blues. He recalled that Lenka had already mentioned it. She knew someone in television who was organising it. Was he interested in taking part? Of course he wasn't.

'Of course I'm not,' he told the person from the consular department. 'Isn't it economic affairs? Exporting British pop music to the world, or something?'

Then a messenger came in from communications with a telex from London that had just come through, something about a report of troops being moved up to the East German–Czech border. Did the embassy have any confirmation of this?

He sighed. There had been reports of troop movements both inside and outside the country ever since the spring manoeuvres. Half the bloody Warsaw Pact had been sniffing round Czechoslovakia for months now, like dogs round a bitch's arse. He passed the telex on to Eric Whittaker, along with a suggested anodyne response that mentioned neither dogs nor bitches. Then he went through whatever else there was on his desk and closed down for the day. He was taking Lenka out for dinner, to the restaurant overlooking the river at Barrandov where they had had lunch on their first date. There was a certain tension between them over the Russians and over that weekend jaunt to the castle that he'd been forced to miss. He'd make it up to her, tell her that he loved her. Maybe, if things went well, he'd even propose to her. The idea shocked him. Could you shock yourself? Apparently it was possible.

Mrs Lenka Wareham. How did that sound? Of course, here she'd become Paní Lenka Warehamová or something equally hideous. But it wouldn't be here, would it? It'd be a posting to somewhere undistinguished, as a counsellor probably; or if he got lucky, something good for the curriculum vitae, such as Washington or Paris. Moscow would be the obvious one, with his knowledge of the language, but surely they'd not post him to Moscow with a citizen of a Soviet Bloc country in tow.

Was this all nothing more than idle daydreaming brought unexpectedly out into the open when confronted by the ambassador's enquiries? Perhaps. But the idea had brought with it a strange, physical sensation, a blend of warmth and contentment and blatant sexual arousal. Mrs Lenka Wareham.

42

A pop group on the Charles Bridge. There's something feminine about them, something effete. Long, waved hair. Blouses with puffed sleeves. Skintight trousers. They call themselves The Moody Blues and are the soft side of the hippy craze, come across the Iron Curtain to bring some glimmer of psychedelic beat music to the benighted inhabitants of the Soviet empire. Television cameras peer at them while a dapper little man bobs around with a microphone, telling people in French where to go and what to say. No one understands. He slips into German, which everyone pretends not to understand either. Someone from Czech television translates and the technicians do more or less what is asked of them as though it was obvious from the beginning if only he'd said. The audience – a gaggle of girls in short skirts and beehive hairdos, boys in jeans and open-necked white shirts – sit along the parapet of the bridge trying not to look bored. This is television, this is exciting. They clap because someone tells them to and the anchor man explains to an imaginary audience that *nous sommes sur le très très vieux pont Charles. Die schönen Karlsbrücke*, he adds for an imaginary German audience. 'Who is your spokesman?' he asks, in English now, of the hapless musicians. He pushes a microphone in the face of the volunteer. 'How do you depict your musical style?'

The musician looks perplexed. What to say? 'Well, it's still beat,' he decides. 'But the way it's progressing now, it's getting very classical.'

The anchor man translates these gnomic words into French and then German. The song they are about to sing is well known to all aficionados of such music, and the artificial audience clap once again as though having something to do has at least aroused them from their summer torpor. The members of the group begin to strum dead guitars, finger a dumb keyboard and tap a muted drum kit while a recording of their number comes out over a pair of speakers so they can pretend to sing. 'Knights In White Satin' is the title. James imagines Lancelot and Guinevere, in white satin both of them, just the kind of image conjured up by the fantasy worlds of *Camelot* and *Jesus Christ Superstar*.

Ellie giggles. 'It's *night-time*, you idiot, not men in suits of armour, *nights* in white satin *sheets*.'

For a moment they're reunited in barely suppressed laughter. Lenka looks at them askance, in case their noise intrudes on the soundtrack. She has arranged their presence there, through someone she knows in TV, so she feels responsible for their behaviour. But their laughter doesn't intrude on the soundtrack because the whole thing will be dubbed over later in the studios in Paris.

The song, vaguely mysterious, vaguely evocative, seeps into the hot afternoon air. Whatever their merits, James thinks, The Moody Blues are not the Ides of March.

43

Dinner on the terraces at Barrandov, in the humid evening. The darkness was punctuated by candlelight and laughter, as though there was not a care in the world. A jazz quartet played 'Take Five', the saxophone wandering off into the vagaries of improvisation.

'One thing about Prague,' Sam said. 'You can always guarantee the music.'

Lenka smiled. 'Every Czech a musician. That's what they say.'

They talked about the weekend, his imprisonment in the flat with Egorkin and the violinist, her trek with Jitka and the others out to the *hrádek*. 'It was fun. The girl, Ellie. I like her.' She added, still with a hint of accusation in her tone: 'Perhaps you should have been there.'

'I'm afraid my life is like that. The unexpected happens all the time.'

'If it's all the time, it's not unexpected, is it?'

One of her sharp retorts that he still could not fathom. He wondered whether and how he should pose the question. Confessions of love did not come easily to him, perhaps because love, promising so much yet threatening disaster, seemed the very antithesis of diplomacy. Feeling something akin to panic, he reached across the table to take her hand just as 'Take Five' came to a thoughtful end and the quartet segued into some Miles Davis. People got up to dance. Lenka too, taking Sam with her. She was strong and sinuous, drifting softly to the music, moulding her shape to his. 'What,' she whispered in his ear, 'do you want?'

And so, dancing slowly on the Barrandov Terraces in the warm evening, he told her. And for a while – that dance, her whispered reply, the rest of the evening together – happiness seemed possible.

He woke from nightmare into nightmare. Lenka slept undisturbed beside him, breathing softly. For a while he lay on the borderline between the two states, between the sleeping nightmare and the waking nightmare, the dream fading from his memory to leave only a vague sense of dread and the ringing of the telephone that didn't fade. He fumbled in the dark for his watch and read the luminous hands. One-thirty.

The phone continued to ring.

No good ever came from a telephone call in the middle of the night. He thought of his parents. He thought of Steffie. What had happened and what might have happened. There was the temptation to ignore the damn thing and return to sleep, but the ringing continued and now there was the sound of aircraft, unusual in the night. The whine of turboprops. The roar of jets.

Lenka's voice in the darkness: 'What is it?'

'Planes. The phone.'

The fragmentary nature of disaster – a telephone ringing; the sounds of planes in the night sky; a sense of unreality. Surely this was a dream of some kind, a phantom created at the edge of sleep? Then came a flutter of panic at the knowledge that it wasn't a dream, that nightmare had turned real, like a fog freezing into hard black ice. The Russian winter. The phone was still ringing and he stumbled out into the hall to pick it up. A bleak voice on the other end of the line said, 'It's Eric.' There was a moment's bleeping and whirring on the line and then Eric's voice continued: '... should be here in a couple of hours,' it was saying.

'Who'll be here? I missed what you just said.'

'Who the fuck do you think? Ivan the Terrible. The fucking Red Army. The duty officer's just phoned me. It seems they're all over the airport. The main force crossed the Polish and East German borders just before midnight. They'll be with us any time now.'

Sam took a deep breath, as though he might stop the hope draining out of him. 'Are you sure?'

'Of course I'm sure. What sort of stupid question is that? President Svoboda has issued a statement telling the Czech armed forces to remain in barracks and show no resistance. We're calling all diplomatic staff into the embassy, Sam. Can you come round as soon as possible? There are new chaps on the gate, so make sure you've got your papers. At least there'll not be a Hungary if the Czech army units do what they're told. But still, be careful in the street.'

'I'll try, Eric.'

'You'll succeed, old fellow. But you'll have to leave your guests for now. We'll have to work something out later. Just get them to keep their heads below the parapet for the moment. Oh, and ... damn, I'm afraid I've forgotten her name. Your girl.'

'Lenka. What about her?'

'Is she with you? You see, it seems they're keeping their own nationals from seeking refuge in foreign embassies. They must have been planning this for months. Why the hell didn't we know? Anyway, the point is, you can't bring her with you, Sam. They won't let her through. Sorry about that, but that's how it is, old chap. Look, I must go. Place is in an uproar.'

Sam put the phone down and stood for a while, not knowing what to think, not even knowing *how* to think. He went back to the bedroom. Lenka was sitting up in bed, prepared for disaster, her face sketched in chalk against the dark frame of the headboard. 'What is it?'

'They're invading,' he told her. No need to say who.

She got out of bed and began to pull on her clothes. 'The radio, turn on the radio.'

He fiddled with the tuning to find the state radio. Recorded music was playing, the Czechoslovak national anthem, which was the separate Czech and Slovak anthems jammed untidily together just like the country itself. And then the music ceased and there was an announcement in solemn tones addressed 'To all people of the Czechoslovak Socialist Republic'.

Lenka stood still, her jeans pulled halfway up.

On Tuesday, 20 August 1968, at approximately 11 p.m. the armies of the Soviet Union, the Polish People's Republic, the German Democratic Republic, the Hungarian People's Republic and the Bulgarian People's Republic crossed—

Then the thing went silent. Just the rush of static. He looked round. Lenka pulled her jeans up and fastened them, then grabbed an old shirt, yesterday's shirt, the first thing to hand. 'That was Vladimír Fišer,' she said. 'I know his voice, I *know* him. Try another frequency.'

He turned the tuning knob, but there was nothing from any of the state radio frequencies, only at 210 metres a different voice announcing Radio Vltava and explaining that 'personalities of the Czechoslovak Communist Party requested military aid from the Soviet Union because our republic was threatened by counter-revolution and anti-socialist elements ...'

'Radio Vltava? I've never heard of it. And the voice – it's not Czech, not native, I mean. It's Russian or Ukrainian, something like that.' Lenka's tone was contemptuous, but there was despair in her eyes like the first symptoms of a terminal disease. 'It's true, isn't it?' she said, as though, hope against hope, it might have been a gigantic hoax. 'Are they here already?'

'Apparently some units have already landed at the airport.'

'What will happen?'

'You're asking questions that I can't answer.'

'Will there be fighting?'

'I shouldn't think so. What would be the point? Eric – that was Eric Whittaker on the phone – says that Svoboda has called for the army not to resist, but maybe some hotheads—'

Sam went through into the sitting room and opened the curtains a fraction. The tiny square outside was barely illuminated by a single street lamp, just enough to show a lone car parked there, a black Tatra lying like a shark in the depths of a pool. He went back to Lenka. 'They want me at the embassy.'

Then he went to the spare room and knocked on the door. There was movement inside, hurried whispering and a call to come in. Egorkin was sitting on the side of the bed in pyjamas. Nadia had the sheet drawn up to her chin, looking wide-eyed. 'What's happening?' Egorkin asked.

'Your lot are invading the country, that's what's happening.' For a moment he felt anger. It was an untidy emotion that could encompass almost anything, even Egorkin and his woman. But the Russian seemed confused, as though the whole world was suddenly not working to his command. 'What will happen now?'

'God knows. For the moment you'd better just stay as you are. I have to report to the embassy.'

'Will this mean war?'

'Of course it won't. No NATO country is involved. It'll be treated as an internal affair of the Soviet Bloc.'

'And what about us? What about me and Nadezhda Nikolayevna? Your people will say, we don't want to be making trouble with the Soviets at this delicate moment, so get rid of them. Let them – what is the English expression? – stew in their own juice, is that it?'

Sam drew a calming breath. The instinct of a diplomat: think before you argue; never commit to anything you cannot deliver; choose, out of the large range of evasive expressions at your disposal, the appropriate one. Not exactly what he has done in his private life. 'That remains to be seen. For the moment, may I suggest you are even more careful than before about keeping quiet? We are being watched outside and apparently they've tightened things up at all embassies. It is in your best interests to keep as low a profile as possible.'

Low profile. A good phrase just then starting to worm its way into the lexicon of the diplomatic world.

'I will,' he assured the Russian pair, 'keep you informed.'

While Sam showered and shaved, Lenka spent most of the time on the phone – someone she knew in radio, her mother, Jitka, other friends. The phones were still working, which seemed a miracle, and rumour diffused through the wires faster than if it were shouted from the rooftops: the airport had been occupied, tanks were on the move from Hungary, from Ukraine, from East Germany; the country was being crushed in the jaws of the Russian bear just as it was crushed in the jaws of the German wolf thirty years ago.

There's a pattern in Czechoslovak history: 1918, 1938, 1948, 1968.

The phone rang again and once again it was Eric wondering where the hell he was.

'I'm coming, I'm coming. I've got to sort things out here first.' He turned to Lenka, knowing there was no point in trying to keep her there. 'What are you going to do?'

'I'll try and find Jitka. Find out what's happening. Maybe go to the radio station, I don't really know.'

'Listen.' Sam wanted to keep her for a moment longer. 'How will we keep in touch?'

'I'll phone.'

'I'll probably be at the embassy.'

'If you want to find me you can try Jitka's. You have her

325

number?' Hastily she scribbled it and the address on a scrap of paper beside the telephone. Then they embraced, wordlessly, except that he said, 'Be careful', that useless advice you give people when you don't know what else to say. And then she had gone, closing the front door behind her, her footsteps sounding on the stairs as she ran down. He went to the window to see that she was safely past the Tatra and part of him hoped that she might look up and see him watching her, wanting to watch over her but helpless to do anything. She didn't. She passed the car unimpeded and turned the corner that led to the bridge and went out of sight.

X

44

There's a noise in the city, an undercurrent like the coming of a flood. And then the immediate fact of someone knocking on their door and calling them to wake up. The phone is ringing in the other room. James can hear Zdeněk answering, speaking rapidly in Czech to whoever's on the line.

'Something's happening,' Jitka calls. She edges the door open. Her face, pale with anxiety, hangs in the shadow of the opening. Beside him Ellie emerges from the cocoon of her sleeping bag, looking confused. 'What time is it?'

'Early.'

'What's happening? What's going on?'

'The barbarians,' Jitka says. 'The barbarians are coming.' Which seems uncommonly dramatic, poetic almost, words from the hand of Cavafy. But in Cavafy's poem the barbarians didn't come and everyone in the city was left in a kind of limbo, not knowing what to do. Here it is different. The barbarians have actually come and still no one knows what to do. 'Russians,' Jitka explains more coherently. 'They've invaded the country. Soldiers, thousands of them, tanks, planes.'

In the next room Zdeněk puts the phone down, calls out something and leaves the flat, slamming the door behind him. James and Ellie are scrabbling for their clothes. Disaster is in the air, or in the ground, shaking the foundations. What do the tremors presage? Earthquake or tornado? Jitka is on the phone now. *Rusi*, she says to whoever is on the other end, *rusi*.

Then she's asking if they're ready because she has to go – unless they want to stay here. Maybe that would be better. But no, they'll go with her. So, barely understanding what the hell's going on, they follow her downstairs and out through the main door onto the pavement.

Dawn paints the street in the pallid colours of panic. There are people around, walking in the same direction, as though drawn to the epicentre of an earthquake, perhaps to rescue people from the rubble. Words are exchanged with passers-by. The tone is an untidy mixture of panic and anger. They feel like children being barely tolerated by an adult.

'Where are we going?' Ellie asks.

Jitka is distracted by what she has heard and what's rumoured, saying things they half-catch and don't understand. '*Václavské náměstí*,' she says, and then, a concession to foreigners: 'Wenceslas Square.'

'But what the fuck's going on?' James demands. Then, turning a corner, they discover what the fuck is going on because it is there, a presence across the end of the street, a metallic alien thing amongst the nineteenth-century façades of the New Town. A tank. James thinks of *The War of the Worlds*, of Martian tripods tramping through London streets. Another part of him thinks *arthropod*, then *reptile* turning its empty gaze (half-blind, peering through small openings in the carapace) up the street and pointing its proboscis straight at them, the muzzle forming a perfect O. Then T-54, he thinks. This from another part of his mind, the part that used to play wargames. Surely it is not about to fire. That would be ridiculous. But still he shouts 'Move!', grabs Jitka's hand and pushes Ellie in the back. They run across the street and press themselves into a doorway while the turret turns and the proboscis shifts back and forth as though sniffing the air, perhaps even trying to work out where the humans have gone. Then a remarkable

330

thing happens: a hatch on the top of the machine opens and a head emerges, cased in a black leather helmet. The head looks round at the buildings and the watching people, then takes a moment to consult a map before looking back at the buildings and then down to the map. The man, the arthropod itself, the reptile, the T-54 battle tank and all who travel in her, has lost its way.

People gather, some just to watch in sullen silence, others to shout. The smell of diesel exhaust and despair fills the air. The figure in the turret takes no notice and after a moment drops back inside. With a roar and a cloud of black smoke the beast shifts, its tracks screeching on the tarmac and pavement. Figures emerge from a side street and run round it, like dogs at a bear-baiting. From somewhere out of sight a glass bottle arcs through the air and smashes against the flank of the beast. A blossom of flame erupts below the hull with a low wumph of exploding petrol. The machine bellows in anger, grinds kerbstones to dust and roars out of sight.

Václavské náměstí, Wenceslas Square, with dawn leaching between the buildings and flooding the space. The great sloping boulevard is filling with people. Trams are stopped, while crowds gather, talking, wondering what the hell is going on when what is going on is plain for all to see as tanks gouge their way up the slope and arrange themselves as though for battle. Saint Wenceslas dominates the scene from his pedestal in front of the museum at the top end of the square, but even he, at the moment of greatest need, when he is meant to emerge from the Blaník mountain, is powerless before the armour. There is the stench of diesel, clouds of black smoke as the tanks manoeuvre, the awful clangour of their tracks. A kiosk sells bread rolls and sausages while young men and women argue with soldiers.

'Why have you come here?'

'What do you think you're doing?'

'Do you even know where you are?'

The soldiers have stock answers to hand as though they've been on a language course and have painstakingly learned the phrases without a glimmer of comprehension:

We are here to maintain order.

We are here to suppress the counter-revolution.

We are obeying orders.

We come as friends.

A whole litany of platitude.

A youth appears with a sheet daubed with the slogan идите домой! and manages to drape it on the rear of a tank. People cheer.

'What does it mean?' asks Ellie.

Jitka provides the translation. '*Idite domoy.* Go home. But they won't, will they? They're here for good.'

The air is stained with sound and fumes. From somewhere comes a sharp burst of gunfire. The crowd utters a collective gasp, as though there is a sudden shortage of oxygen. Some people run, others stand still. Perhaps a moving target is easier to spot than a motionless one. But the shots aren't repeated, just the grinding of the tanks and the gruff sound of their engines. Others come into the square bringing news, so Jitka says, of the Central Committee headquarters under siege, of leaders being rounded up, of Dubček himself being led away to be shot. Someone places a transistor radio on the ground and a small crowd gathers round to hear the news. Ellie and James stand to one side, not wishing to intrude. It's like a traffic accident where you can feel the horror but don't know any of the victims, a tragedy that belongs to other people. Lenka is there. They don't see her arrive, but she's there, talking with Jitka, talking with others, giving a distracted wave of acknowledgement to Ellie and James.

More tanks appear, scouring the cobblestones up the slope

towards the museum at the head, followed by a cry of 'Radio!', and people begin to move up the slope, fragile humans following the iron beasts. 'The radio station is still broadcasting,' Jitka explains. 'It's on Vinohradská beyond the museum. Who knows what will happen?'

There is noise from beyond the museum, the sound of metal, the rattle of machine-gun fire. A helicopter flies overhead, a great locust-like thing without markings but painted dun brown. Incongruously, the transistor radio on the ground nearby is broadcasting exactly the same sound – the gunfire, the clash of metal and the helicopter all sounding behind the calm voice of the announcer. Jitka attempts to translate – the studio is under attack and may be invaded but for the moment the staff will continue broadcasting the news as long as possible. When you hear unfamiliar voices on the radio, the announcer says, do not believe them!

Lenka hurries over. She's distracted, as though they are unexpected mourners appearing at a family funeral, irrelevant to the real drama. 'You must go,' she tells them. 'This is no place for you. People are killed.'

'We want to show solidarity,' Ellie replies, and suddenly Lenka is angry, as though the wrong thing has been said at the funeral, the wrong friendship mentioned, a previous relationship referred to, a hidden embarrassment exposed to the explicit light of day.

'Just go! This is not student protest. Not banners outside the American embassy in London. Not even tear gas and throwing stones in Paris. This is rape and you must not be here. It is disgusting to watch. So now go. Go to your embassy and ask for safety. Go and speak with Sam Wareham and tell him Lenka sent you. But go!'

She turns and hurries away, half-running towards the museum at the top of the square where the tanks are lined up, leaving Ellie smarting as though she has been suddenly and unaccountably struck in the face. As if to confirm the words of warning a battered lorry roars into the square from the direction of the river. The vehicle is crowded with young men and on the bonnet sits a youth holding aloft a flag, a Czechoslovak flag smeared with blood. The watchers make noise, something between a cry of despair and a shout of triumph, as though spilt blood is a catharsis of some kind.

'Go,' Jitka says. 'This is not safe. Go back to the flat and get your things. If they find English here . . . ' She gestures helplessly and turns to follow Lenka.

When Ellie moves to follow James grabs at her. She shakes him off. 'I'm not fucking running away,' she yells. The moment of indecision is over: she hurries after the other women. James follows as well. Pushing through the crowd up the sloping boulevard, there is the sensation of things moving out of control, of chaos blundering onto the scene. Lenka is ahead of them, taller than others around her. From somewhere a shot rings out but no one falls, nothing happens, the people just move on up the square towards the national museum whose soot-blackened façade is pitted with white scars. Tanks stand like boulders in the stream of people. There's shouting. Stones are thrown. People are running around the side of the museum into Vinohradská. Further on, buses and lorries have been parked across the roadway as a barricade. Smoke and dust drift over the scene. Flags wave, a nation of flags, used to being called out in unison on patriotic parades but now jeering and derisive; the unison is in the chaos. A Soviet flag burns. Careless crowds confront tanks before the dull concrete building that bears its name across its façade: *Československý Rozhlas.*

There's Lenka, pushing past a bus. Jitka runs towards her, and Ellie and James follow, blindly, not knowing what to do. A tank grinds and turns, its tracks screeching on the paving stones, its gun sweeping in an arc. Lenka looks back at them, then falls. Jitka and Ellie don't see it – they're watching the tank – but James does. A moment acid-etched into his memory, cut into the neurones and the synapses even as the rest of the morning fades into a uniform blur of movement and noise. Lenka pushing between the bus and a car, then falling.

There are screams. But there are screams everywhere. People huddle round. The tank moves forward and rams into the bus, like a spoilt child fed up with his toys. The smash and tear of armour against thin steel as the bus pitches over. People are lifting a figure out of the way, screaming at the smashing tank, scurrying with their burden to the side of the street to some kind of safety in the lee of a building. There are flames at the barricade now, a truck on fire, its fuel leaking out and blazing. Soldiers, civilians scatter away. A tank, engulfed in flames, smashes forward in some kind of animal panic, then reverses to back out of the fire. And Lenka lies on the pavement with people crowding round her and Jitka on her knees beside her and Ellie and James standing by helplessly.

There's blood. Someone tries to staunch a wound behind her ear. Someone else folds a coat and eases it beneath her head. Words fly around. James makes out *ambulance* and *doktor*. A siren sounds and someone appears with a stretcher. They bundle Lenka onto the stretcher and carry her down a side street to where an ambulance is waiting, its rear doors open. Jitka follows, turning to Ellie and James and shouting, 'Go! Go back to the flat! I'll telephone when I can.' She climbs in after the stretcher, the doors slam and the vehicle moves off, its siren wailing.

Ellie and James make their way through the city, a frightened city, a city with the air sucked out of it by the vacuum of Wenceslas Square and Vinohradská. They ask themselves pointless questions – Was she alive? How did it happen? Did she hit her head? – questions with no answer. The occasional car drives by with people waving flags from the open windows. People run, going nowhere in particular. The barbarians have actually come and nothing anyone has expected has come to pass. The occasional sign of normality – a man sweeping the pavement, two women arguing about something, a queue at a shop beneath a sign that says *potraviny* – lends an air of strangeness to the morning, as though all these people are playing a part in a film and merely waiting for the cameras to roll. From the queue someone shouts out to them. James spreads his hands helplessly. '*Anglický*,' he calls back.

English? What are English doing here? People in the queue stare after them as they hurry past, Fando and Lis hurrying through the streets of Tar, trying to make sense of it all. Somewhere they take a wrong turning and emerge onto the embankment of the river, into sudden sunlight with a view across the water to the Malá Strana and the wooded hill of Petřín. A convoy of army lorries grinds past, filled with soldiers. Their features are vaguely Mongol, as though they might have come from the further reaches of the Soviet empire, the endless steppe of central Asia rather than the crowded buildings of a European city. Passers-by shout abuse but they take no notice. Further on three armoured personnel carriers are parked on the pavement surrounded by a group of young men, arguing with the crew members. A tram rattles by, passengers staring out at the parked armoured vehicles and the arguments while Ellie and James stand on the other side of the road, on the other side of the gulf of language, understanding nothing. But they understand well enough when the argument round the armoured car becomes heated, a protester climbing on the front of the vehicle and gesturing with his fist. A Russian soldier lowers his rifle and points it at his tormentor's head. Is it an empty threat, a piece of absurd bravado? Theatre, perhaps, the one actor shaking his fist, the other pointing his weapon. And then these things happen.

They seem to happen simultaneously, although logic says that there is a sequence of cause and effect. But still they appear simultaneous: the report of the gun, a deafening crack close to James and Ellie, the sting of stone beside James's head, a scream, people scattering away from the shooter. James grabs Ellie's hand and pulls her round the corner into the cover of the buildings. He feels a sense of detachment, as though none of this is happening to him. Yet when he touches the side of his face his hand comes away with blood on it.

Ellie gives a cry of alarm. 'God almighty. Are you all right?' Her voice sounds muffled to him, as though she is speaking underwater.

'What the fuck's happening?' he asks, bewildered. He's shivering now, as though with cold. First Lenka and now him. Ellie's being motherly, reaching up and moving his hand away so she can see better, producing a handkerchief and dabbing at his cheek. 'It's just a graze. A bit of stone or something.'

His right ear sings in protest at whatever has been done to it. In the distance there's more gunfire, the rapid rattle of a machine gun, while out of sight round the corner the armoured cars have started their engines and are driving away, people shouting after them.

She takes his arm. 'Come on, let's get back to the flat.'

45

The embassy was in an uproar. Phones rang incessantly. Teleprinters chuttered out reams of paper. Secretaries scurried from office to office with flimsies to be read, to be acted on, to be contradicted within minutes. Meetings were called one moment, to be cancelled the next. London wanted to know everything when there was nothing to know beyond what Czechoslovak radio reported. Furthermore – insult heaped upon injury – the embassy lay at the head of a short cul-de-sac and access was now blocked by a Russian armoured car lying across the entrance like a beached boat across the mouth of a harbour.

'This sort of behaviour is intolerable,' the ambassador decided, on being told of the offending vehicle, and ordered the Head of Chancery to demand that they leave at once.

Eric Whittaker put his head round the door and cut short Sam's efforts to write a situation report for London. 'Do be a dear and go and tell them that they aren't really welcome. H.E. feels a point must be made and you're so much better with the languages than anyone else.'

'You mean he asked for me by name? How flattering.'

'Not exactly. But you did seem the perfect man for the job.'

So Sam went down into the courtyard, duly had the gates opened and stepped out from the enclave of Britishness onto the cobblestones of the Malá Strana. Under the iron gaze of

Russian guns he walked down the cul-de-sac to the armoured car.

There were two soldiers sitting on top of the vehicle. They wore no identifying insignia and neither did their vehicle, but it was plain enough what they were.

'*Chto zdes' proiskhodit?*' he asked.

They showed no surprise at being addressed in their own language, just watched him with a gaze as indifferent as the stare of the assault rifles they levelled at him. Like a puppet appearing on stage, a grim-faced official from the interior ministry came round the vehicle. What did the Englishman want?

The Englishman smiled. He wanted to know what was going on here. It appeared that the embassy was under some kind of siege by the Russian army, and Her Majesty's ambassador would like to see matters revert to how they had been before. It was the duty of the Czechoslovak authorities to protect diplomatic premises in their country.

The official didn't smile back, for this was plainly not a smiling matter. The fraternal allies were here to protect the embassy from counter-revolutionary troublemakers.

'But there *are* no counter-revolutionary troublemakers,' Sam said, looking round as though curious to see if counter-revolutionary troublemakers were skulking around the nearest corner.

'That shows how efficient our fraternal allies are.'

It sounded like the punchline to a joke. There followed a moment of stasis, each waiting for the other to make the next move. Sam offered a cigarette and waited for the moment of temptation – he could see it in the other man's eyes – to pass and the offer to be declined. 'Look, my ambassador's on my back,' he said, in a confidential tone that suggested they both knew what a pain in the arse such senior people could be. 'Couldn't you just move round the corner, out of sight? The guards could be here, of course. Just move the vehicle.'

The man's expression did not change. 'We have our orders. They' – he meant the Russians – 'have their orders. Your ambassador will have to talk to the relevant authority.'

Sam nodded. 'That's the problem, isn't it? Who exactly *is* the relevant authority at the moment?'

He glanced regretfully at the packet of cigarettes, slipped it back into his pocket and turned to walk back to the relative security of Her Majesty's domain, all the while conscious of eyes and assault rifles levelled at him. Back inside the fortress of the British embassy he looked in at Whittaker's office. 'The Russians aren't going anywhere for the moment, Eric. Sorry about that.'

Whittaker looked resigned. 'We made the effort.'

Sam went back to his own desk. Through the window he could see smoke rising over the Old Town, in the area of Wenceslas Square. That's where the radio reports were originating, in the street behind the National Museum, with the sound of gunfire coming across the transmission as background to the announcer's voice. Was Lenka there? The agony of uncertainty, of hope pitched against likelihood. She'd be there, in the thick of things. He tried to recall the moment of her leaving. How had the mood been? What had been said? Not just the words but the emotions that informed them. But memory was a deceptive thing, an unreliable witness.

He picked up the phone again and rang the flat. The two guests sounded more or less all right. They wanted to know what was going on but he couldn't give them much information. The Red Army is occupying the city. That was about it. And what should they do? Just sit tight.

He put the phone down and went back to drafting the report for Eric to send to London. It was a chaos of changing news and unconfirmed rumour. One of his contacts said Dubček and his lieutenants had been arrested. Another report even said they'd already been spirited out of the country. Yet the

National Assembly was in continuous session and the radio was broadcasting Dubček's words appealing for people to go to work as normal. And the president? The old man, silver-haired and pink-faced, a general who had fought alongside the Red Army during the Great Patriotic War, had delivered an address over the radio calling on his fellow citizens to show calm and dignity. 'A complicated situation has arisen in our country,' he had told them with magnificent understatement.

Sam came to some sort of conclusion, took the draft report to Whittaker's office and handed it over. 'That's as good as I can manage for now, Eric. If you don't send it in the next half-hour it'll be out of date. Now I think I'll go out for a while, if you don't mind.'

Whittaker looked startled. '*Out*? But I need you here.'

'I've spent most of the time listening to the radio and the rest trying to ring people who won't answer the phone. Anyone can do that. I'd be better employed finding out what's really going on.'

'Well for God's sake be careful. We don't want a diplomatic incident to go with the rest of the mess.'

He walked out of the embassy and down towards the armoured car at the end of the cul-de-sac. Was there a flicker of recognition from the soldiers as he edged past? Probably not. He dropped by his flat to see how the musicians were doing and found them in the sitting room with the television on with the sound turned down, and the radio tuned to the BBC World Service. They had the look of refugees in the middle of a war, sheltering from the bombs, fearful of rape and murder.

'What's happening?' Egorkin asked.

'Your guess is as good as mine.'

Nadia seemed to have been crying. She shook her head in disbelief as images flickered across the television screen of civilians throwing stones at tanks. 'It is terrible,' she kept repeating. 'Just terrible.'

Egorkin said, 'The phone has been ringing, but I didn't answer it.' His expression was anxious, as though he hoped to curry favour.

Sam closed his eyes in something like despair. 'It might have been important.'

'But then they might know we're here.'

Anger flared. Sam almost shouted, almost lost his temper. No one gives a fuck about you now! he almost yelled. Instead he said, 'You're right,' and picked up the phone to dial Jitka's number. The only lifeline he had. But the phone at the other end just rang and rang in an empty flat that he couldn't picture.

46

They climb the stairs, out of the noise and confusion and fear of the streets. Somewhere above them a phone is ringing. Is it Jitka's? But as they pass the floors it stops, and when they reach the flat it is a haven of peace and quiet with only the distant sound of a siren breaking the calm. They close the door behind them and turn the key. Through one of the dormer windows James can see smoke rising over the roofs. He and Ellie don't discuss what to do. Somehow it has been decided by a kind of communication that operates beneath the level of conscious thought. She begins packing her things away, rolling up her sleeping bag, collecting her stuff from the bathroom, while he rings the embassy and asks to speak to Mr Warcham. In placid tones – the British in a crisis – an embassy voice asks if he is seeking consular advice, in which case he should phone the consulate on—

'I don't want the consulate. I want to speak directly to Mr Warcham. Samuel Wareham,' he adds, suddenly remembering the posh guy's first name. 'My name's James Borthwick. Tell him Lenka told me to contact him. It's about her.'

There's a moment's hesitation. He can sense the operator wondering about the importance or otherwise of this unknown voice with its Northern accent. 'Hold the line please.' There's a pause. Silence on the line, just the rush of static in the earphone. Then the sound of the operator again. 'I'm afraid Mr Wareham is unavailable at the moment. May I take a message?'

47

At the entrance to the Charles Bridge there was a Russian checkpoint. Only the day before TV crews had been filming that British pop group, with everyone basking in the fiction that the country was in the process of joining Western pop culture; now half a dozen Russian soldiers were rifling people's bags and searching them for offensive items. But the procedure was less to do with security, more plain highway robbery: they were taking cameras, pens, wristwatches, anything that might have pecuniary value. A young soldier – a mere boy – advanced on Sam as he moved to go through. Sam waved his diplomatic pass. '*Britanskoye posol'stvo,*' he said. British embassy. The soldier hesitated. Standing downwind of him Sam caught the sour scent of stale sweat. There was a brief conversation between the soldier and his officer before Sam was waved through onto the bridge.

The bridge itself was already daubed with graffiti. Red stars and black swastikas in intimate conjunction, BREZHNEV = HITLER chalked on the parapet in case you'd missed the point. In one place a Cyrillic scrawl exhorted the Russians to ИДИТЕ ДОМОЙ! GO HOME! On either side of the bridge the embankments had become a tank park, Soviet armour lying like a great, articulated reptile alongside the water's edge. Gunfire punctuated the morning, while from the crowded buildings of the Old Town came a noise like the roar of a football crowd. Sam went on, past the statue of the emperor Charles IV, hung now with a Czechoslovak flag, past the incurious gaze of soldiers, towards whatever was happening in the heart of the city. The streets, the squares were rancid with the smell of the occupiers – diesel fumes, hot metal, unwashed bodies. The act of walking, hurrying, almost running, distracted him from his feelings, which were visceral, a sensation of vomit, a feeling of fear lying just below the sternum and spreading up the spine to his brain.

Memories of that walk became confused in retrospect, so that he could no longer plot the exact route he took through the streets of the Old Town. There was the incongruity of tanks in narrow streets, of armoured vehicles confronting trams, of soldiers ringed by arguing men and women. Roads were blocked. Trams tipped over as barricades. A bus driven into a shop front. Smoke and dust eddying in the narrow spaces. Groups of youths waved banners while a motorbike drove past distributing copies of *Rudé Právo*. Bullets pockmarked buildings. Façades were smashed and broken stonework lay on the pavements. The National Museum at the head of Wenceslas Square, dark grey with urban soot, bore white spots where shells had hit. On Vinohradská there was a litter of overturned vehicles blocking access to the radio station. Tanks had ground their way through the debris, spewing clouds of exhaust fumes. Guns fired. Boys argued with tanks. Flags waved. Girls screamed.

At one street corner an argument was going on between a dozen youths and a young Russian officer. Their common language was an amalgam of Czech and Russian. 'What are you doing here?'

'We came to help.'

'We don't need your help. You can see that. So go back home.'

'We were invited.'

'By whom? Not by the people.'

'By your leaders.'

'Dubček didn't invite you. Císař didn't invite you. Svoboda didn't invite you. So what are you doing here?'

'We came to help.'

So it went on, a circular litany with no end in sight.

As he stood in the midst of this chaos, Sam's fear gave way to a curious sense of detachment, as though the ferment all around were happening in some other, parallel world. These tanks, these soldiers, the blunt fact of their presence had all been inevitable. What had people expected? What had Lenka and her friends, with their fifteen minutes of freedom, imagined would happen? This was reality. The last eight months had been but a dream.

A group of protesters walked past chanting Dubček's name. They parted and flowed round him like water round an obstacle, like the river that had flowed round Lenka as she stood there in the stream. A gunshot rang out. People flinched and scattered, but Sam had learned from his national service basic training that you never hear the report of the shot that hits you, so that particular bullet, echoing between the buildings, was safe for him at least. He had never felt so indifferent to risk.

He walked on. The steel rasp of tank tracks ground paving stones to dust. Sunlight through smoke. The smell of oil. A fire blazed beneath an armoured car while the crew tried to beat out the flames, just as people would try to beat out the flames of Jan Palach's body in five months' time in more or less the same place. A passing motorcyclist shouted, 'Take these!' and thrust a bundle of leaflets at him. He walked on, handing the leaflets out to anyone he passed, not really caring what the leaflet said – the simple act was enough. Was this what combat was like: fear transcended to become something close to euphoria? He came across a young man also distributing leaflets. There was an absurd hiatus during which they compared leaflets and found them to be different. 'That's good, then,' the youth decided. He wore a black leather jacket and jeans. His hair was down to his collar. A badge of some kind. 'You German?' he asked.

'English.'

'You speak good Czech.'

A lorry roared past filled with kids yelling and waving the Czechoslovak flag, chanting Dubček, Dubček, Dubček! 'Oh, one thing. You don't know a girl called Konečková, do you? Lenka Konečková?'

A frown. 'I've heard of her. A journalist?'

'She writes a bit. And speaks on the radio sometimes. Have you seen her?'

The youth shook his head, indicating the chaos all around. 'I wouldn't know her by sight anyway.'

'Blonde, tall.'

The youth laughed. 'Aren't they all?'

Sam walked on, handing people leaflets until his supply vanished. What else to do? On the embankment there were groups of people arguing with the tank crews. Slogans had been chalked on the steel hulls – swastikas, hangmen, the exhortation to 'go home' in Russian, in Czech, even, presumably with an eye on the news media, in English.

'When's that guy from the embassy going to ring back?'

'Why don't you ring him again?'

'Because he's too busy to take my call.'

'You don't know that.'

'That's what she said. Anyway, maybe he already knows.'

They have been bickering like this ever since they came back to the flat. What else is there to do? Once it was different. Once there was that mutual attraction of a kind, but it was always a fragile thing, and now they are kept together by no

347

more than the kind of tension that keeps oil droplets together in water – a shared reaction to the unintelligible world around them. Outside in the streets people argue with tanks in a language they cannot comprehend; here in the cramped living room the TV shows a serious young woman talking to the camera in a blizzard of incomprehensible Czech. Whenever the transmission goes off the air, James retunes it to another channel and the picture returns. The announcer appears to be sitting in a room with bare walls, except for the Czechoslovak flag that has been roughly draped behind her. Every now and again she is interrupted by poor-quality film of tanks in the street. A bus lies on its side and one of the tanks goes at it like a petulant child, bashing it again and again, trying to climb over. People jeer from the sidelines. The building beyond the fallen bus has *československý rozhlas* across the front. They wonder whether a figure, caught for an instant on the edge of the picture, is Lenka. They wonder where she is now.

Ellie says, 'We can't just sit here on our bums.'

But James perceives the world differently. On his bum is precisely where he wants to be. He has a headache and his right ear is still singing from the crack of the bullet that almost killed him. Sounds are muffled on that side, as though he might have a perforated eardrum. It's like observing the world from inside a glass tank, sounds coming to him deadened and occluded. 'The embassy said stay put.' He puts on an exaggerated accent, like the Queen doing her Christmas broadcast. 'We are recommending all British citizens remain indoors if they possibly can. We will inform you of developments as soon as we are able.'

'Well you can stay if you like. But I want a breath of fresh air.' She gets up decisively.

'Don't be stupid, Ellie. You can't go out by yourself.'

They argue about that, too. Why can't she go out? He could if he wished. Girls against boys. But he won't go with

348

her because he's got this ringing in his ear and this ache in his head and because he's bloody well going to wait in the flat until either Jitka or Zdeněk come back to tell them what the fuck is happening, or that guy from the embassy phones.

'You're frightened.'

'Of course I'm fucking frightened. I've seen Lenka shot—'

'We don't know that.'

'—and I nearly had my own head blown off.'

'Well we've got to get something to eat. There's that shop just round the corner. *Potraviny* or something. We can try there. It'll only take a few minutes.'

While they're arguing the phone rings. James picks it up gingerly, expecting more incomprehensible jabbering on the other end, but it's Jitka's voice that sounds in his ear, his good ear, the one that still works properly. 'Is that James? Is Zdeněk there?'

'No, he's not.' This is the woman who just two days ago let him kiss her on the mouth and cup her breast in his hand. He wants to use a term of endearment, to let her understand what he feels for her despite his being entirely unworthy of her interest. But only the banal comes to him: 'What's happening? Where are you?'

'I'm with Lenka. Tell him that. Tell him not to do anything stupid and to come round as soon as he can.' Stoopid. That American intonation to her English. 'Have you spoken with Sam at the embassy?'

'I couldn't get hold of him.'

'Well try again. Tell him about Lenka.'

'What do I tell him? Where are you? Where should I say?'

There is an edge of impatience in her reply. 'Na Františku. Didn't I tell you?'

'What? No, you didn't.' He scrawls *nafrantiskoo* on the pad beside the phone, not knowing whether he has got it right or what it means. 'Can you repeat that?'

There's silence on the line.

'Hello? Are you there?'

Her voice comes back. Perhaps the line is faulty. 'I thought I told you. I'm sorry, it's been difficult.'

'People have been ringing but no one spoke English. What did you think you'd already told me?'

'*Nemocnice na Františku* – it's the hospital. I thought I already told you. I've been ringing round.'

'How is she?'

'I can't talk now. There are others that want the phone.'

'How is she, Jitka?'

She speaks rapidly, quietly, almost whispering. As though telling it softly might mollify her words. 'She's unconscious. It is not certain. Here it's chaos, like war zone. I must go.' And the phone goes dead.

He puts the receiver back on the cradle. Ellie is staring at him. 'How is she, James?'

'She's unconscious.'

'Still unconscious? How *serious* is it, James? Didn't you ask her?'

'I don't know. I don't know how serious. She was in a hurry. Jitka, I mean. She was in a hurry because others wanted the phone. She didn't say how serious.'

'You should have asked!'

'I didn't have a chance. She rang off.'

She screams, her face contorted as though with pain, 'But you should have *asked*!'

They're trapped in a strange flat a thousand miles from home and familiarity, with people dying around them, and she's screaming: *Why didn't you ask? Why didn't you ask?*

48

The nearest bridge was blocked to traffic by armoured vehicles, but people on foot could pass. Across the river, Kampa island was an oasis of quiet, but there was more armour in the wider streets of the Malá Strana and tanks in the square around the church of Saint Nicholas. He wondered whether to check on Egorkin and Pankova but decided against it and instead crossed the square and made for the narrow road leading to the embassy.

Little had changed there. The armoured car still blocked the cul-de-sac, soldiers still stood on stolid duty, the grim-faced official from the interior ministry was still there, the Union Flag still flew over the gatehouse. One of the soldiers moved to block his way, but the Czech official muttered something and the Russian stood aside. At the end of the cul-de-sac the gates opened just as he reached them, as if someone had been watching his progress up the alleyway through a peephole. Inside the gate was the reliable face of Derrick, the security man.

'You made it back.' He made it sound as though Sam had just been through the front lines of some kind of trench warfare. 'What's it like out there?'

'Chaos. The Russians have come looking for a fight but all the Czechs want to do is argue. It's a rather uneven contest.'

'Who's winning?'

'The moral conflict or the military one?'

Derrick sniffed. He was a straightforward sort of man. 'Not much point in winning the moral one if you've lost the battle.'

'I'm afraid you're right.'

In the courtyard there was activity round the embassy cars and talk of a convoy being organised to evacuate non-essential staff. A story was going round that the transport ministry was arranging a train to get foreign visitors out to Austria or Germany. Sam looked in at Whittaker's office and gave a brief account of how things were in the Old Town. Eric listened with feigned patience. 'You haven't heard the latest,' he said when Sam had finished. 'It seems the powers that be have finally pulled their fingers out.'

'Out of what?'

'Their arses, Sam, their arses. It seems they're sending us a plane.'

'A *plane*?'

'Apparently it's those bloody pop singers. The Moody Men or whatever.'

'Blues.'

'That's right. The ministry of defence has got permission for an RAF aircraft to fly in to evacuate them along with our non-essential staff. Unbelievable, isn't it? First they give the Beatles the MBE, then they lay on a special plane for this Moody Blues lot. Next thing they'll give Cliff Richard a knighthood.'

They laughed at the incongruity of it all. A plane, from a NATO air force, flying into a Warsaw Pact country in the middle of an invasion. It seemed absurd. 'What about our musicians – Egorkin and Pankova? Can we get them out that way? Or by the road convoy?'

'One way or another, I suppose we'll have to try. We don't really need an added complication, do we?'

'But we've got one whether we like it or not.'

He went to his office and rang the switchboard. Someone

352

from the American embassy had called. A Mr Harry Rose. And there had been a call from England. The telephonist couldn't believe the system was still up and running, even for international calls. 'Someone called Steffie,' she said. But surely she knew exactly who Steffie was. His affair with Stephanie was hardly secret. 'She asked if you were all right and said she was thinking about you. I told her you were fine and awfully busy. She said, maybe you could give her a call back.'

'Thank you.'

'Oh, and there was a call from a Mr Borthwick. I think that's right. He said that Lenka told him to get in touch with you. I'm not quite sure what that means. It's probably some-thing consular, we've been snowed under this morning by that kind of call.'

Borthwick? He struggled to put a face to the name, and then he recalled the two hitchhikers. James, that was one of them. James Borthwick seemed likely – it had a Northern flavour to it. Or was it Scottish?

'Did he leave a number?'

'No, he didn't. He seemed quite agitated but he insisted that he didn't want consular assistance, just to talk to you. I gave him our standard message about staying safe and he rang off.'

Sam thought for a moment, while possibilities and probabil-ities chased themselves through his brain. Missed calls were some kind of reproach – calls for help, cries for attention, pleas for understanding. But if the youth hadn't left a number what was he meant to do? 'If he calls again, make sure you get his number. In the meantime, can you get me Harry Rose at the American embassy? Counsellor Rose, that is.'

It was a couple of minutes before the call came through and Harry's familiar voice sounded in his ear. 'Is that Sam? Good to hear from you. We're burning all our classified documents at the moment. What are you doing?'

'You're joking.'

'I'm as serious as Brezhnev himself. Aren't you burning your stuff?'

'We don't think it's that dangerous. Not yet, anyway.'

'Typical British phlegm. I wish you could send a bucketload of it over here. We're in need. Any news? Washington's on the line asking what the hell's going on, but the truth is they know more than we do.'

'Dubček and the others have been arrested, that's for sure. Černík, Smrkovský, Kriegel at least.'

'We know that.'

'Some reports say they've already been flown out.'

'That too. What a fucking mess. They never saw it coming, that's what's incredible. These guys were good communists – didn't they know the score? Tread on our toes and we'll stamp on your face. That's always the way. I'm mean, look at how we treat other countries, and we're the *nice* guys. Jeez.' There was a moment's silence while they contemplated the Harry Rose analysis of US foreign policy. 'Hey, don't go telling Ambassador Beam I said that.'

'I wouldn't dream of it.'

'Good fellow. So, what's our news? We're getting a road convoy organised to get people out. I told you about the Hollywood crazies, didn't I?'

'The Man from Uncle?'

'Napoleon Solo himself. And Shirley Temple. And a hundred participants at some damn conference.'

'We can't match Hollywood but we have got The Moody Blues.'

'The *whose*?'

'Some pop group. Sub-Beatles. Long hair and lacy shirts.'

'Guys?'

'So the girls inform me. Apparently we're planning a road convoy too.' They discussed how they might coordinate

354

operations for a convoy, the number of vehicles, the route out. And there was also the possibility of a train to Austria. At the moment one of Rose's colleagues was talking with someone from the transport ministry and it looked as though that might happen. They'd keep each other informed of developments. 'Nothing like an invasion,' said Rose, 'to bring the diplomatic community together.'

It was only when he hung up that Sam remembered. It was obvious really, but events had scrambled his mind: the hitchhikers – James Borthwick and Ellie whatever-her-name-was – were staying in Jitka's flat. Lenka had given up her room for them. The fortuitous event that had ended up with Lenka in his flat, in his bed, in his whole world. He rang Jitka's number that Lenka had scribbled down, and when the youth answered he thought how stupid he'd been not to make the connection before.

'It's Sam Wareham here,' he said. 'I believe you phoned earlier.'

A small fragment of his mind wondered why Jitka or her husband hadn't answered. What was his name? Zdeněk. He could imagine him out in the streets, confronting the tanks in that grim, fanatical manner that he had. The kind of fellow who would end up doing something foolish – throwing a Molotov cocktail or hitting a soldier with a brick or something.

'Yeah. Look . . .'

'Is everything all right with you? The best thing to do is just sit tight for the moment. I think you've been told that already. Don't expect anything much until tomorrow, do you understand? Things are being organised to get foreign nationals out of the country, but it takes time. We have your number – I'll make sure it has been passed on to the consular department – and they'll get in touch. But for the moment it's best to keep out of trouble and off the streets.'

355

'Yeah. Look – sorry, my head's buzzing – we were out earlier. You know, Wenceslas Square and that.'

'Were you? Well, discretion's the better part of valour at the moment. Just stay where you are—'

'And we saw what happened. To Lenka, I mean.'

'*Lenka?*' It was as though all the air had been sucked out of the room and he had to struggle against some kind of vacuum merely to breathe. 'What happened to her?'

'She was injured. At the radio station.'

'Injured? How?'

'I don't really know. She fell. They took her off to hospital.'

'Hospital, which hospital, do you know which hospital?'

'Jitka told me. I was just going to phone the embassy when you called—'

'*Which hospital?*'

The youth hesitated. 'Something like *nafrantishkoo*. I tried to write it down.'

'It doesn't matter. I know it. When was this? When did it happen?'

'Couple of hours ago, I reckon. I'm not sure exactly—'

'It doesn't matter.'

Sam put the phone down. Overhead a jet aircraft tore through the sky, barely clearing the domes and spires. It passed away, reverberating round the ancient buildings, leaving behind only a distant murmur of its passage. He told the secretary that he was going out. 'Tell Mr Whittaker. I'll be back as soon as I can.'

Summer warmth greeted him in the courtyard. It should have been a pleasant sensation, but with it came something else, a sound, ill-defined and tuneless, as though the whole city was moaning with pain.

49

He walked as quickly as he could. He couldn't take the car because the bridges had been blocked to traffic, but as he had discovered earlier, it was still possible to cross the river on foot. It took him twenty minutes to reach the hospital.

The František Hospital was more reminiscent of a prison than a place of healing – a forbidding block of stone on the right bank of the river, with only a hint of *Jugendstil* decoration to alleviate its grim façade. Ambulances were coming and going. Sirens sounded. Soviet military vehicles provided the only elements of stasis as men in white overalls manoeuvred stretchers in through the doors. Most people moved on the edge of panic while Russian soldiers looked on with sublime indifference.

Sam pushed his way inside. In the entrance hall the familiar hospital stench of disinfectant papered over other smells – hints of ordure, the tang of blood, the scent of torn flesh and torn lives. At a desk he asked for Lenka by name but got nothing more than indifference. A passing nurse was more helpful, giving some sort of direction that he could try. He walked along corridors of institutional bleakness, past anonymous doors which gave an occasional glimpse of other lives, other problems, other disasters. Finally he knew that he had reached the right place when he saw a cluster of people gathered outside doors that said *Neurologie*.

Doctors and nurses hurried in and out. Occasionally a stretcher was wheeled through. Jitka was there, and her husband, Zdeněk. The others he recognised from that evening after the concert, and the political meetings he'd witnessed. Jitka detached herself from the others and came towards him. She had been weeping. He could see scorched eyes and flushed cheeks.

'How is she? Can I see her? What happened?' All questions that were easier to ask than to answer.

She gave a sketchy account. The barricades outside the radio building. Tanks, soldiers, vehicles blocking the way. Was there a gunshot? There had been firing. One moment Lenka was pushing past a wrecked car, the next she was on the ground with blood coming from her head. It seemed no one really knew.

A surgeon came out of the department, dressed in white and wearing an apron. Almost like a butcher. There was muttered discussion, talk of cranial trauma, of pressure on the brain. X-rays showed a foreign object – maybe a ricochet, maybe a shell fragment – lodged against the brain. After a while they were allowed in to see her, a few at a time, down the corridor into a bare room with two beds. Sam was next in line, after Jitka and Zdeněk.

Lenka was in the bed by the window, lying on her back. Her body, beneath sheet or shroud (it was impossible to say which), was preternaturally still. What is the difference between life and death? It seemed a debatable point. She was somewhere on the borderline between the two states, neither one thing nor the other, neither the lovely living *rusalka* wading into the flow of the river Vltava, nor yet a cadaver ready for burial. Her head was bandaged and her features were familiar in the way that the features in an indifferent portrait may be familiar – her and yet not quite her, recognisable but not convincingly lifelike. A bottle hanging over her dispensed liquid parsimoniously down a narrow tube into a vein while another tube came out from under the sheet and drained pale yellow liquid into a bottle on the floor. Perhaps these two flows, of liquid in and liquid out, were a sign of animation. A wider tube, held between her lips by surgical tape, emerged from her mouth and disappeared into the mechanical ventilator beside the bed. Although her chest rose and fell faintly, that was only in response to the black rubber bellows of the machine, which opened and closed repeatedly like a concertina playing the same notes over and over. But no musical sound came out, just a succession of sighs, as though the constant movement was infinitely tedious.

Sam stood beside the bed looking down on her and felt nothing. There's no training for this, he thought. No experience, no guidance, no special knowledge. There was just the sight of her lying between a life and an end, and the vivid sensation of the fragility of the border itself which was nothing more than a narrow line over which one might step or be pushed in a moment. He thought probably that his heart was broken and that this is what it felt like – not overwhelming grief or anything like that, but just this void, this absence of feeling, as though the very part of him that might experience pain and misery was, in fact, broken.

After a while he did some of those things that you do, pointless things that bring some kind of comfort to the visitor if not the patient. He called her name and saw no response, touched her hand and felt no answering movement. After a few minutes like that he turned away and went out.

'We have to be patient,' another doctor was saying to the sorry little group outside in the corridor. He had other patients to attend to but she was being closely monitored, he could assure them of that. They were doing their very best for her. Now, if they would excuse him ...

Sam stood with the others for a while, but it was too much like a gathering of mourners at a funeral. He had to go. He

359

had to do things, anything to get away from this feeling of helplessness. 'Let me know,' he said to Jitka. 'Any change at all. Do you have my number?' Just in case he took out one of his cards and wrote the telephone number of the flat on it below the number of the embassy.

When he got back to his apartment building the Tatra was still parked outside on the cobblestones. He stopped beside the car. A face peered out at him, like a creature inside an aquarium, something that lives on the bottom and grubs around in the detritus for food. He rapped on the glass and the man wound the window down. There was a release of rancid air, the smell of stale sweat and cigarette smoke.

'Why don't you fuck off?' Sam shouted. The man looked puzzled. 'You heard me. People are dying thanks to your bloody Russian friends and all you do is sit in your car and obey orders. You're just a couple of shits.' His Czech was approximate but the meaning was clear enough, yet the man's expression didn't change. He just turned to his companion and shrugged, then wound the window back up.

In the flat, Egorkin was whining. *This* wasn't right, *that* wasn't right, he shouldn't be cooped up like *this*, *they* shouldn't be cooped up like this, they should have been taken to the embassy, the Americans would have done it better. Sam tried to focus on Egorkin in order not to think of Lenka. Egorkin he could deal with. His complaints he could deal with. 'You don't understand my importance in the world of music,' the man insisted. But Sam knew full well that the embassy, the ambassador, the whole pyramidal ziggurat of the British Foreign Office right the way up through the ranks to the Permanent Under Secretary (who might sound 'under' and 'secretary' but was in fact lord high everything and Knight Grand Cross of the Order of St Michael and St George to boot), no one in this great artefact of state would actually *want* Gennady Ivanovich

Egorkin if they ever came to know of his existence. They wouldn't give a shit. The only people who would want him, presumably, were those worthy souls who commanded the cultural life of the country and politicians who would make a bit of political capital out of it. And the journalists who would work it up into a story.

'Listen,' he said to the man. 'André Previn might think you're the greatest thing since Toscanini, but at the moment, here in Prague, no one gives a toss about you. In fact, I'm the only friend you've got. So you'd better just shut up and play along to my tune.'

Egorkin looked as though he had been struck across the face.

'And at the moment,' Sam continued, 'the woman I love, the woman whom I am going to marry, is lying critically ill in hospital. So believe it or not, Mr Egorkin, you are not even high on my own list of priorities.'

The fire of anger had burned itself out by the time he appeared in the embassy. 'I needed you,' Eric said when he saw him, 'and you were nowhere to be found.'

Faced with his boss he felt no more than a kind of exhaustion. 'She's in a coma, Eric.'

'Coma? Who?'

'Lenka. The woman whose name you forgot. The woman I couldn't have with me because they weren't letting their own people take refuge in foreign embassies.'

Whittaker looked shocked. It was rare to see him disconcerted. He just had single interrogatives to deal with, like someone struggling with a new language. How? Why? When? He seemed sorry, he *was* sorry. And shocked and appalled and distraught and all those other emotions one lays claim to at moments of consternation, whereas Sam felt only the cold hand of anger descend once more.

'If you want to go home, old fellow ... '

But Sam shook his head. 'Brooding on my own is the last thing I need, Eric. Tell me what I can do.'

Whittaker considered. 'You are our Russian specialist. You can talk to them better than anyone else we have. Perhaps you can get on the phone to the Soviet embassy, to whoever you have some sort of understanding with, and explain to them that we are proposing to evacuate a substantial number of our citizens by road and we need their understanding and cooperation. Because with their little toy soldiers all over the place, trigger-happy and frightened out of their wits, this whole circus parade could go horribly wrong.'

Sam smiled. It was not a smile of amusement or even complicity. It was a smile of something close to despair. 'I can do that, Eric,' he said. 'I know just the man to talk to. But he'll not be able to guarantee that poor frightened Ivan won't pull the trigger of his Kalashnikov. After all, I doubt anyone was given the order to fire the bullet that hit Lenka. And yet there she is, unconscious in a hospital bed.'

Whittaker winced. Sam watched him for a moment, then nodded and went to his office.

Zdeněk has come from the hospital, come from seeing Lenka. Ellie and James try and talk with him, although it's not easy to communicate across the barriers of language and anger. But medical words are more or less the same in English as in Czech. That's the way with such vocabulary – an international language of disaster. *Kóma*, he says. *Trauma. Ventilátor.*

'I think,' he says, 'she die.'

Ellie weeps. It's a shock to imagine her broken like that. James feels sad enough but, hey, it's not the end of the world, not yet. Lenka's world maybe, yet she's still alive, isn't she? There's always hope. But Ellie weeps and somehow he envies her weeping, the fact that she can have access to a great well of feeling that seems denied to him.

362

Outside, the city drags wearily towards evening. Guns are fired in the gathering darkness, lines of tracer arcing through the sky like a blizzard of shooting stars. Perhaps this is to signify the beginning of a curfew imposed by the occupying forces and announced by posters plastered all over the city. Perhaps it is just the city weeping for its lost freedom and not to be comforted.

Jitka returns late, her face drawn in anguish. When asked how Lenka is she merely confirms what her husband has already conveyed, that Lenka lies on the borderline between the living and the dead, neither one thing nor the other, like the country itself, neither free nor captive.

Zdeněk leaves. There are things to do during the night. Posters to be made, plans to be laid, a petition to be composed and names of collaborators to be published in the streets: Kolder, Indra, Biľak, Jakeš, others. Names that will live in infamy. Jitka talks into the night, her sharp, frantic, mind jumping from one thing to another. 'What will you do?' she asks them. 'You cannot stay here. It is dangerous for you. And perhaps for us.'

James tells her about his contact with the embassy. 'Tomorrow, they told us, wait until tomorrow.'

'We don't want to leave you,' Ellie says.

'You have to,' says Jitka. 'You have to. There is nothing here to stay for.'

She might have been speaking for a whole people.

50

Sam spent the evening with Harold Saumarez, discussing how to deal with the Russian musicians. The SIS man had come up with a plan to get them out, a careful construct of cars and hiding places and false passports, with decoys and extras just to confuse the issue. Whisky made the whole idea seem plausible, but against Lenka's injury it seemed a kind of blasphemy to be talking of saving the Russians while she lay unconscious in hospital. When Sam explained what had happened, Harold offered a bluff sort of comfort: 'Don't you worry, old chap. The one thing these fellows can do is medicine. She'll be right as rain, just you wait and see.'

The whisky bottle was half-empty when he left after midnight, dismissing any suggestion that there might be a curfew or that he might be subject to it. From the sitting room window, Sam watched him cross the square in front of the building undisturbed, and disappear round the corner. The Tatra that had been there earlier was nowhere to be seen.

His bedroom – his and Lenka's bedroom – was a refuge of a kind, filled with her possessions as though she had been there for months rather than ... how long was it? Days or weeks? Time seemed distorted, both stretched and compressed by the gravitational fields of events swirling around him, by the shock and the misery, the fear and the hate. Disconsolately, he tidied up her things, scraps of underwear, her shoes, stockings, some books, pages of articles she had typed, including the last one about her encounter with Dubček, written but never submitted and no chance of publication now. He tried to put some items together that he might take to the hospital for her – toothbrush, soap, her hairbrush, a hand towel – but he really didn't know what might be needed. Her nightdress, still redolent of her presence, lay where she had tossed it over the back of a chair. He picked it up and held it to his face, breathing in her scent, remembering. He didn't put it aside with the other things but instead climbed into bed and tried to sleep, with the nightdress clutched to him like a comforter to a child.

Dawn seeped into the city, bringing with it the dashed hopes of another day. Tanks still blocked the bridges over the river. Armoured cars still guarded the offices of state. The radio still broadcast defiance, exhorting listeners to take no notice of the renegade Radio Vltava and listen only to those voices they could recognise and trust. Do nothing to provoke the occupying forces, it said, but give them no help. Deny them even a drop of water. Say only that if they come as peaceful tourists driving Ladas then you will happily show them round your beautiful city; but as they have come in uniform and driving tanks you will not even look at them.

Sam rang Jitka's number as early as he dared. Her familiar voice was almost a comfort as he struggled to betray no panic, no sign of the desperation that bubbled up inside him. 'Lenka? How's Lenka?' But there was no news. Jitka was going to the hospital as soon as she could. 'I'll try to get over there sometime today,' he told her. 'It's just that everything's happening here.' And he felt stupid saying that, because everything was happening everywhere at the moment, wasn't it? To Lenka and Jitka and her kind much more than to the pampered foreigners who had their safety nets, their diplomatic immunities, their escape lines, their ways out.

'Could you put one of the English kids on the line?' he asked as she was about to hang up. 'I need to speak to them.'

Words sounded in the background, and then the flat, Northern vowels of James's voice came on the line. ''Ullo. It's James here.'

'This is Sam Wareham. Are you ready to go? We did speak yesterday.'

'Yes.'

'Yes, you remember speaking or yes, you're ready?'

'Both those things.'

'Right. There's a road convoy being organised. There's also probably going to be a train, but we'd like to get you out by road, is that all right? We're going to send a van for you both, but we can't cross the river because the Soviet army is blocking the bridges. So you've got to come over to this side under your own steam. Do you understand? You're in the New Town, aren't you?'

'I dunno. I s'pose so.'

'Well you are. What you've got to do is make your way to the Palacký Bridge. That's the nearest one to where you are now. Cross over the bridge and you'll find our minibus waiting for you at the first corner on the right. It's a white VW. You shouldn't have any problem with the Russians, but if they do stop you, show them your passports and say *Britanskoye pos-ol'stvo*. That's British embassy in Russian. Can you do that?'

'I guess so.'

'Repeat it to me.'

There was a moment's farcical lesson in Russian pronunciation, with the boy floundering around amongst the unfamiliar vowels.

'Just saying "*britanskoye*" should get you by. And calling him "*tovarishch*" could be useful. That's comrade.'

'I know what *tovarish* means.'

'Good.'

'Why i'nt it a Transit?'

'Why isn't what a Transit?'

'The van. Transits are made in England.'

It was a joke. Sam laughed dutifully. 'I'll have a word with the ambassador. The driver's name is Derrick, by the way. He will want you to identify yourselves of course, but he knows all about you. Is everything clear? Can you be there in half an hour? Timing's important, we've got a road convoy leaving for the border at ten-thirty.'

'We'll get a move on.'

'Fine.'

'Just ...' A pause.

'What?'

'Why are you doin' all this for us?'

'Just part of the service.'

'I don't believe that for one moment.'

Not so stupid after all.

No traffic on the bridge, just as the Wareham guy promised, but half a dozen Russian soldiers standing by their vehicles watching pedestrians go past.

'Is it the right one?' Ellie asks.

'The bridge? 'Course it's the right one.'

The soldiers eye them but make no move as they walk past towards the Malá Strana. Behind them was an approximate farewell with Jitka, before she rushed off to the hospital. Now, suddenly, all that seems very remote – Jitka and Zdeněk, friends for ten days, have already faded into the past. The present is this, the rucksack on his back, the slog of feet against tarmac, the road ahead once again, with Ellie, for better or for worse, beside him. Ahead is their next lift, the Volkswagen minibus waiting as promised with a stern policeman type behind the wheel. 'Hop in the back,' the man says, once he's given their passports a cursory glance. 'You kids going home?'

'Haven't thought about it yet.'

'Out of this madhouse, anyway.'

The journey takes less than fifteen minutes, but it doesn't lead to anything resembling a British embassy. Instead the driver parks the vehicle in a side street not far from the river, across the entrance to a small alleyway.

'Where are we?' James asks.

'A couple of passengers to pick up,' the driver says.

There's movement outside the van. The door slides open and there's the guy from the embassy – Wareham, Samuel Wareham, standing there and giving a humourless smile while stating the bloody obvious: 'You made it safe and sound.' Which is fine, but why does he have to sound as though he's talking to children? 'Now I'm going to need your cooperation. And we haven't much time so I'd be grateful if you would do exactly as I say and ask no questions. Understood? We'll want you off the back seat for the moment. Have your rucksacks on your laps. We've got a couple of passengers coming and one of them' – as they move places he reaches forward and lifts the rear bench seat to show a coffin-like space beneath – 'goes in there. The other, a young woman more or less your age, sits between you, on top of him. He'll be all right. Don't worry about him. But she speaks hardly any English and she might be frightened, so you are going to treat her like she is your long-lost sister. Right? Smile and put your arm round her – not you, *her*,' he adds, pointing at Ellie – 'and generally treat her like a treasure. She's been briefed but still it'll be a bit of a trial for her.'

Ellie appears quite unfazed by all this. 'What language does she speak?'

'Russian. I'll be in the front so I can talk to her when necessary. For the moment we've only got to drive round the corner to the embassy. There'll be a control at the approach to the embassy, so get your passports out. They want to stop

368

Czechos seeking asylum so it's not a problem for you. Just hand your passports over when asked. OK? Any questions?'

'What's this all about?'

He pauses for a moment, as though this might be the one question he did not want to be asked. 'Look, you may recognise them, but if you do don't say anything, all right? They want out. It's a simple as that. And we want to help.'

'Why this way, with us involved?'

A hint of impatience in his expression. 'They're looking for a middle-aged man and a woman. Instead they'll see you three kids with rucksacks. Sleight of hand.'

Wareham steps back. As though at a signal things happen, more or less as predicted: two figures emerge from the alley, a man and a younger woman, both of them hurrying almost as though pursued by a third figure behind them. Except that James recognises them, that's the bizarre thing. He recognises them from that concert, the Birgit Eckstein one – the bloody conductor, all bow tie and tails then but nothing of the kind now, and the violinist.

'Bloody hell,' he says to Ellie, and he can see that she's recognised them too.

The man comes first, ducks into the van and dives into the space beneath the seat. Wareham slams the seat down on him. Then the girl, as frightened as a rabbit, clutching her own rucksack, sits on the bench on top of him and peers at James and Ellie as though they might be predators. Ellie holds out her hand. 'I'm Ellie,' she says. 'We heard you at the concert. We loved your violin playing.' She smiles warmly but the woman looks aghast and responds with a small torrent of words that make no sense. The door slides shut. The driver and the Wareham guy are climbing into the front. The engine starts and the van lurches forward.

'OK back there?'

'OK.'

Along with her rucksack the woman is clutching a passport, a battered British passport with the name *Miss Nicola Jones* written in the window.

'Nicola?' Ellie asks.

The woman looks helpless. It's not her name. It's not her passport. She opens the document and displays a photo of herself looking startled at the very idea of being documented.

'Just play along with it,' Wareham says, watching them from the front. 'She's just a friend of yours, someone you've joined up with. OK?'

The van turns onto a main road, turns again, bumps over cobbles and edges through tight alleys between buildings that are like something out of the Brothers Grimm. Finally it comes to a halt at a military roadblock.

'Passports ready,' Wareham calls back. 'Just act naturally, as though you don't have a care in the world. Should be straightforward.'

Should be. A whole world of uncertainty is subsumed under that innocent phrase. Their situation, a little while ago dangerous but more or less comprehensible, now seems completely mad. They're sitting in front of a Russian violinist pretending to be Nicola Jones yet speaking not a word of English and on top of – *on top of*, for Christ's sake! – an orchestral conductor of international fame, at this very moment lying prone within the stifling, claustrophobic box beneath their seats. James begins to laugh. Giggle, really, like in school assembly when something catches your attention and you cannot control yourself.

'For fuck's sake!' says Wareham.

There are soldiers at the driver's door. Wareham is suddenly transformed, speaking Russian to them, even laughing at something said. James's own laughter vanishes as a face peers in at the side windows, like someone observing exhibits in a vivarium. The door slides back to reveal the owner of the face,

370

a soldier in a khaki blouse and forage cap. There's a red star gleaming like a drop of blood on each of his collar tabs. Slung over his shoulder is an ugly piece of ironmongery that James recognises, because he knows this kind of thing, as a standard issue AKM assault rifle. The soldier has a scrubbed, youthful look, unblemished by stubble but marked instead by a small cluster of acne spots on either side of his mouth. 'Passport,' he demands. James says, 'Tovarich,' as he hands his over and there is, perhaps, the ghost of a smile from the Russian. He leafs through the documents, glancing up at the passengers, comparing with the photographs, sucking his teeth as though that might aid his concentration. Beneath his look the woman – Nicola? – tenses. Perhaps the soldier is an amateur violinist, perhaps he knows what's-her-name Pankova, maybe he's even seen her perform in Moscow or Leningrad or Kiev or wherever he comes from. 'What a bloody mess, eh Nicola?' he says to the woman and receives a frightened smile in response. She's trying to play the game, attempting, with the few tools at her disposal, to be Nicola Jones, student, born in London on 16 September 1946. 'Yes,' she says. *Yes*. At least she has got that right.

The soldier nods and hands the passports back. '*Ládno,*' he calls to the driver, sliding the door shut. The van moves forward up the short cul-de-sac towards forbidding fortress doors. Nicola – Nadezhda, James remembers – is breathing again. As though by magic, the fortress doors open at their approach, allowing them through an archway and into the courtyard of the Thun Palace, where cars are jammed and people are running around as though there's a fire to put out somewhere.

'Well done,' Wareham says, glancing back.

The van threads its way through the mêlée and edges into a narrow garage. In the sudden gloom James leans across to Ellie and whispers, 'What the fuck is this all about?'

Wareham turns in his seat. Is he about to give an answer to James's question? It's hard to see his expression in the low light. 'Any news?'

Ellie replies, understanding what he means. 'I'm sorry, no. Jitka was going off to the hospital when we left.'

He nods. 'I'll ring as soon as I get a moment.'

'No, it's *not* the responsibility of the consular department,' Eric Whittaker said sharply. 'For God's sake, Sam, you can see that this whole thing is bloody dangerous. Dozens of civilians driving their own cars through a countryside occupied by a couple of hundred thousand nervous Russians, all of them armed to the teeth and trigger-happy? What can possibly go wrong?' He was seeing himself as the soldier he used to be during his military service spent largely in Aldershot, standing at the window of his office with his hands clasped behind his back just like Montgomery. 'So I want a senior man present at all times. Which means you, Sam. I'm sorry but there's no question about it. Quite understand about your girlfriend and very sorry and all that, but I'm sure she's getting the best possible medical attention and there's nothing that you can contribute in that line of business anyway. I need you here, in the convoy, seeing that things are OK. You're a Russian specialist and a Czech speaker where those idiots in consular can only just about manage *Dobrý den*. So that's it, really.'

Sam had already phoned Jitka's flat once again and got no reply. The phones at the hospital appeared to be permanently engaged, or maybe they'd just been left off the hook. He felt the sickening of fear and the anger of resentment. All he needed was an hour to get over there and see how things were going, but instead he was stuck here being forced to play soldiers. He almost stamped to attention and saluted, just as he'd been taught during basic training. Instead, he managed a subdued 'Very well, Eric', and went back down to the courtyard where someone from the consular department was faffing around trying to instil some kind of order into the dozen vehicles manoeuvring there. 'If we don't get a move on,' he said, 'we're going to miss the rendezvous with the Americans, and then we'll have to do the whole thing on our own without any direct guarantee of safe passage.'

The vehicles finally left the courtyard of the British embassy at half past ten in the morning. Led by the ambassador's car flying the union jack, the convoy drove slowly through the narrow streets of the Malá Strana and up the hill towards the Castle. There were other vehicles from other embassies on the move in the same direction, and by the time they reached the outer suburb for rendezvous with the Americans over three dozen vehicles had come together, a great shambolic serpent straggling through the streets and along the Pilsen road.

The Americans had walkie-talkies. Of course they did. Harry Rose was standing in the middle of the street directing traffic and giving commands over the radio. 'Stole them from the marine detachment at the embassy,' he told Sam with glee, waving his walkie-talkie around. 'Always wanted to do this kind of stuff. How do you read me? Copy that. Over and out. Affirmative, negative, all the Hollywood crap. Hey, do you want to meet Shirley Temple? She's over there in the Buick, hiding behind smoked glass.'

'I just want to get the whole thing over and done with,' Sam said.

It was past eleven o'clock when the cavalcade finally moved off, a motley string of vehicles more like a bank holiday traffic jam than a military convoy, forty-two in all from most of the NATO countries, with the US ambassador's car flying the Stars and Stripes at the head.

*

Despite open windows, the air inside the van is thick with the smell of bodies. James's head is singing, that whining in the right ear like the insistent stridulation of an insect. Feeling faintly sick, he clings to the breeze that comes in from one of the open windows while the stout man in the front seat – Harold Summery is his name – tunes a transistor radio to the BBC World Service, which is how they learn, scratchily through the ether, what is happening in the city they are abandoning. Street signs are being taken down, the reporter says, protests are growing, civilians against tanks, a strike has been called for midday. The country's leaders have been detained by the occupying forces, their whereabouts are unknown.

'We should have stayed,' Ellie says.

'What good would that have done?'

They've been joined in the back of the minibus by one of the embassy secretaries, a sharp woman with a pinched Edinburgh accent. 'I think you're well out of it,' she tells them primly.

Once out of the built-up area Harold turns to speak. They can let the hidden passenger out for a breather. It's an awkward manoeuvre in the confined space, all four of them having to crowd forward so that the rear seat can be raised and the coffin opened. Gennady Egorkin rises, like Lazarus, from the dead. Middle-aged, balding, pallid, slick with sweat, he has the look of the hunted about him. For a few minutes he sits there in his coffin beneath the gaze of his fellow passengers while the girl leans over to minister to him, offering him water and words, presumably of comfort. The sight ought to be incongruous, perhaps even comic, but instead there's something disturbing about it, as though one is watching a nurse administer a slow and uncomfortable medical procedure.

'I need to piss,' Lazarus says. They're the first words he has spoken in English and they betray a surprisingly colloquial command of the language. Harold passes an empty plastic bottle back. While the passengers look discreetly away, the renowned orchestral conductor unbuttons his trousers and pisses into the bottle. You might evade the sight but there's no avoiding the sound or the warm smell of urine that pervades the enclosed space and wrinkles the Edinburgh woman's nose.

When the deed is done it is the young violinist who disposes of the urine, sliding the side door open a fraction and pouring the piss out onto the tarmac. Later, as they approach a built-up area, the man is closed back in his coffin, normal seating is resumed and the journey continues.

At Pilsen the column grinds to a halt. They wait, not knowing. The vehicle in front is a Karmann Ghia with West German number plates. In front of that an Opel, and then the British Embassy Humber. They can't see any further. After a while the Wareham guy walks back down the road and leans in at the driver's window.

'Some kind of roadblock. Don't know what the hell's happening but there are soldiers all over the place.'

Soldiers cannot be good. Wareham glances at his watch, then at the radio at Harold's feet. 'Can't you turn that bloody thing off?'

There's a sudden silence in the van. The wait goes on. It's stiflingly hot beneath the midday sun and people are getting out of their vehicles and wandering in the road, straining to see. When James pulls the side door open he's told to stay inside by Harold, but it doesn't take much to ignore him. He steps out into the sunshine and what little breeze there might be. Ellie climbs out after him, and then the embassy secretary and the violinist after her. It seems only a single move is needed to undermine the voice of authority. A haze of exhaust fumes rises above the snake of vehicles. The tarmac is hot, painted with a mirage of water.

Soldiers come nearer, going to each vehicle, checking documents, opening car boots.

Wareham asks of nobody in particular, 'What the fuck are they looking for?'

The embassy woman seems shocked by such language, especially from a diplomat. They don't behave like that in Morningside. James thinks of war films, of Nazi guards walking down a train, peering into compartments. What will happen? Will someone break and run? Will there be a sudden shout, the raising of a rifle, the crack of a bullet fired like the one that flew past him only the day before and smacked into the wall mere inches from his head? The singing in his ear still hasn't stopped.

As the soldiers get nearer Nadezhda scuttles back into the van. Ellie goes with her. Wareham is on the tarmac, saying something to the soldiers, offering a cigarette, even laughing with them. 'Passport,' he calls to his charges. 'They want to see your passports.'

Ellie and the violinist are ordered out of the van. They stand by the open door while the soldiers lean inside, pushing a rucksack off a seat, peering beneath the front bench, grunting when they find nothing. The violinist is shaking. Ellie holds her hand as the soldier examines her passport, flicking through the pages to find the entry visa before handing it back without a word. Then the same thing for the others.

Wareham glances at his watch and says something to the soldiers. They move on to the car behind, a Morris Minor Traveller with British plates. Everyone climbs back in the van. Wareham leans in through the window and says something to the violinist in Russian, then to the others in English: 'Well done.'

Ahead of them cars are starting their engines. With painful slowness the serpent begins to move forward, stretching its neck into the industrial smog of Pilsen and on to that empty border area which James and Ellie crossed only ten days ago. By the middle of the afternoon they come to a halt once more, but this time at the checkpoint where Czechoslovak border guards show scant interest in their documents. Foreigners getting out while the going's good? Who gives a damn?

Soviet troops watch with the indifference of conquerors.

The road goes on, cutting through the forest and slanting down into the wooded valley of the watercourse that the Germans call Rehlingbach, Fawnbrook, but the Czechs know simply as Hraničňí potok, Border Stream. The black eagle of the Federal Republic of Germany flies on the other side of the bridge while a crowd waits beyond the checkpoint – American military, anonymous black limousines, television crews with cameras levelled at the refugees like weapons. There's a festive air, the sense of release and relief.

'What were you doing in Czechoslovakia?' a voice asks Ellie as they climb down from the van. A microphone is pushed into her face. A camera aims at her. 'Tell our viewers what it was like.'

James follows her out into the afternoon sunshine. Behind them the van moves away towards a couple of black Mercedes where men in suits gather round. He catches a glimpse of the girl being hurried into one of the cars, and then the other passenger, the man in the coffin, being helped into the other.

'It was frightening,' Ellie is saying. 'Tanks, soldiers, shooting. The people were so courageous.'

'What do you have to say to the Russians?'

'They should go home. They're not needed and they're not wanted.'

As the cameras move on to other prey, unexpectedly the Wareham guy appears. 'Where are you kids off to?'

James looks uncertain. 'Haven't decided really.'

'How you doing for cash?'

'Got to get some, I suppose. We've still got koruna.'

'That won't be worth anything here. Look' – he takes out his wallet – 'here are some Deutschmarks to tide you over.' It's like handing out charity. One hundred D-marks in a mixture of notes. About ten quid.

'We can't,' Ellie says, but James has already folded the money away.

Wareham smiles that annoying, patronising smirk. He knows the one who has money plainly enough; by nothing more than their accents he can recognise the contrasts and conflicts between the two of them. 'Take it as a present from Her Majesty, to say thank you. You did very well. I just want to remind you that we'd rather you kept quiet about the details of this whole business. You'll read about it in the press, I expect – famous conductor flees the Russians, you know what I mean. But no one needs to know the details of how it happened. It does, as a matter of fact, come under the Official Secrets Act.'

'We haven't signed it,' James points out.

Wareham smiles pityingly. 'The Act is law, old chap. You don't have to sign it any more than you have to have signed the Homicide Act before you can be convicted of murder.' He glances round. The black Mercedes are driving away from the border. The VW van has already gone back to the East and the embassy Humber is waiting for him with its engine ticking over. 'I'm afraid I've got to get back.'

'Lenka,' Ellie says.

He blinks. A man with his emotions well under control, but he blinks at the mention of her name. 'What about her?'

'We're so sorry about what happened. And worried about her. Can you let us know how things work out?'

He paused, then took a visiting card from his pocket. 'A bit impersonal, but if you drop me a line when you're in Britain I'll get in touch with you.'

378

'And give her our love. I'm sorry I only got to know her for so short a time.'

'Yes.' He nodded, then turned and went towards the Humber. 'Good luck,' he called. The driver had been listening to the radio while he waited. 'Any news?' Sam asked him.

'The demonstration in Wenceslas Square. It's been called off. People gathered but then were asked by the authorities to disperse, not to provoke the Russians. It seems they did.'

'Which authorities?'

The driver looked awkward. Sam could see his face in the mirror. That was what someone looked like when they were wriggling on the horns of a dilemma. 'Just the authorities, sir.'

Sam attempted a laugh but it wasn't easy. 'Come on, let's go. I've got to be back in the city as soon as possible.'

51

It was dusk by the time he got back to the embassy. There were things to do, a meeting with the ambassador and Eric Whittaker, grudging congratulations over the success with Egorkin and Nadezhda, a report to dictate, a whole day of chaos and confusion to attempt to understand. There were reports that the Czechoslovak leadership had been spirited out of the country. Some said they had been taken out and shot, some that they were still in Prague being held incommunicado. But the best bet, Whittaker said, was that they were already in Moscow.

'Maybe you can find out something more concrete, Sam? You seem to have the best contacts.'

All this was the very stuff of his job, but utmost in his mind were other things, personal matters, matters of the heart and the soul. In his office he discovered a message from Steffie sent early that afternoon. She'd known how to get through by telex, using one of her friends at the Office. It was addressed formally *for the attention of Mr Samuel Wareham, First Secretary, Chancery* but the text was anything but formal. *Darling, darling Sam*, it read. She rarely addressed him as darling, never twice, and certainly not openly on something as public as a telex. *You can't imagine how distraught I am, worrying about whether you are safe. Please let me know as soon as you can. It puts everything else, our stupid uncertainties, in perspective, doesn't it? I love you, darling, and miss you more than I can say. More than that, I'm frightened for you ...*

He tried ringing Jitka's flat but got no reply. The hospital switchboard seemed perpetually engaged, so he took his car and drove round. There were still troops blocking the bridges, but now they were letting vehicles through one by one, slower than they had crossed the Iron Curtain itself at Waidhaus. He sat behind the wheel, his bowels eaten by anxiety, while he edged the car towards the barriers. Car boots were examined, bonnets opened. Someone was searching beneath vehicles with a mirror on a long handle. Having kept them at bay throughout the day, he allowed thoughts of Lenka to come pouring into his mind. There was a feeling of helplessness before the flood, boulders and rubble cascading through his life with a merciless inevitability, crushing him personally while all about him the Czechoslovak nation was itself being crushed.

Eventually the soldiers waved him through, and he turned towards the hospital. There were armoured cars outside the main entrance but it was always possible to find a place to park in this city that had so long been starved of cars. At the doors a sullen guard nodded him through when he showed his diplomatic pass; no one took any notice of one man in a crumpled suit making his way up the stairs and along the corridors. There was the clang of distant enamel basins being sluiced. Nurses and porters passed him by, always in a hurry to get somewhere else. The atmosphere was rank with that hospital smell that underlies the memory of so much personal tragedy. No one stood guard at the entrance to the neurology department, so he pushed open the doors and went along the corridor to Lenka's room.

Both beds were occupied now, two women lying prone beneath intravenous drips, one of them well into her seventies, the other some decades younger, neither of them Lenka.

People looked vague when he asked, as though Lenka Konečková might never have been in their care, but eventually he found a nurse who knew. 'Transferred,' she said, moving on.

He felt a momentary panic and put out his hand to stop her. 'Transferred where? Why?'

The nurse looked indifferent. 'The Střešovická Military Hospital. Neurosurgery department.'

'Military? Why *military*?'

'Only the best for the Party, isn't that the rule?'

'What do you mean, the *Party*?'

But the nurse just smiled pityingly, detached herself from his grasp and walked away to whatever problem she faced next.

He forced himself to breathe deeply and slowly, not to panic. He could deal with this. He knew where the military hospital was. He'd go there, blag his way in somehow, find out what was happening, get her out, maybe. All kinds of fantasy passed through his mind. He'd take her to England, have her seen to by some British surgeon who was at the summit of his profession, not one of these Czech medics stuck behind the Iron Curtain, underfunded and underpaid. He'd be the knight in shining armour riding to the rescue.

He drove back over the river, edged his car through the roadblock on the bridge once more, and took the road that wound steeply up between the Letná heights and the Castle itself. The hospital – he'd been there during an official visit six months earlier – was in one of the smart suburbs beyond the castle, the kind of place where the bourgeoisie had once lived, now populated by the new elite, members of the Party. The car rattled over cobbles and tramlines, overtook a tram that seemed to be blocking the way, emerged onto the road that ran along the northern perimeter of the Castle where he could pick up speed, catch a glimpse of the spires of the cathedral over to his left, lose himself for desperate minutes in a maze of narrow roads before picking up the boulevard that led past the villas and gardens of the great and the good. Although street signs had been taken down to confuse the occupying army he found the left turn easily enough.

It was getting dark by the time he drew up at the gates of *Ústřední Vojenská Nemocnice*, the CENTRAL MILITARY HOSPITAL.

Arc lights had been turned on, casting pools of chalky light in the dusk. There was a guardhouse, barriers striped like barbers' poles, flags flying, all the paraphernalia that he remembered from his national service. A young soldier flagged him down at the barrier. Sam explained the nature of his visit. He was looking for a patient, a civilian patient transferred from a public hospital yesterday sometime this morning. An emergency. He gave the name, showed his diplomatic pass, waited while matters were pondered and phone calls made. Almost he shouted. Almost he screamed, *I crossed the bloody Iron Curtain twice today! I went across to Germany and then back into your damned country and here I am, being held up outside a fucking hospital!* Almost he shouted these things, but he didn't. He sat there in front of the barrier, tapping his finger softly on the steering wheel, waiting.

The soldier came back, puzzled. 'This person is British?' he asked.

'No, she is *not* British. You can tell from her name. Lenka Konečková. I have just explained that. She is Czech, like yourself.'

'I am Slovak.'

For a moment Sam closed his eyes and saw a world in which there was no stupidity. 'I'm sorry. Like you, she is Czechoslovak,' he said, with careful emphasis.

'So if she is Czechoslovak, why do you want to see her?'

Because I am in love with her, he thought. Because I am

desperate to see her get well. Because I am frightened of what the future might hold for her and for me. 'Because she is a friend. I am a British diplomat and she is a friend.'

'Does she perhaps work for the British embassy?' the youth asked, as though that might explain everything.

Sam clutched at that particular straw. 'Yes,' he said, 'she works at the British embassy.'

The soldier seemed to relax. 'Then you may visit. You will park over there' – he pointed ahead where cars were drawn up in military ranks – 'and you will go with an escort.'

Military it might be, but the sensations were the same as the civilian hospital – the same long, uniform corridors, the same harsh lighting, the same smells and sounds. Eventually the escort brought him to the department of neurosurgery, where no one else waited under the plain, unshaded bulbs of *čekárna*, the waiting room. There were a dozen metal-framed chairs with plastic seats and backs. A framed photograph adorned the walls, a portrait of the president, white-haired and smiling and looking as though Spencer Tracy had auditioned successfully for the part. Two ashtrays on aluminium stands underpinned the room with the smell of stale cigarette smoke. The escort left. Taking the cue from the ashtrays, Sam lit a cigarette and waited. A nurse glanced in on him but disappeared before he had time to speak. Was he even in the right place? Somewhere a phone rang but no one answered and the ringing went on and on. He got up, went to the door and looked down empty corridors. Nothing. There was the feeling that he was actually in the final, never completed, never even started Kafka novel – *Das Krankenhaus*, The Hospital.

Samuel W. awoke one day to find himself in a deserted hospital ...

Finally a footfall sounded in the corridor and he looked up to find a doctor standing at the door. His white coat bore military tabs on the collar. A major. 'I understand you are asking after a patient.'

Sam stubbed out his cigarette. 'That's right. I was told she'd been transferred here.'

'And your name is?'

'Samuel Wareham. I'm at the British embassy.'

The major nodded. 'Come with me, please.'

They went up a floor and along further corridors. Doors bore nameplates with titles and ranks – *generálmajor prof. MUDr*; *plk. prof. MUDr* – and then there was yet another waiting room, only this one had a photograph of the president shaking hands warmly with Marshall Zhukov. Glass doors led to a balcony but it was dark outside and the windows did little more than mirror the room itself and the two people waiting there. Lenka's mother was one, standing in the centre of the room like a ruined reflection of her daughter. Beside her, with his arm protectively round her waist, was the same man Sam and Lenka had encountered at the hotel in Mariánské Lázně, the man who had once been her mother's lover and then, in a perverse succession, had become Lenka's own. Pavel Rovnák.

'*Paní* Konečková,' Sam said. 'I'm so sorry we have to meet again like this.'

The woman nodded, as though he was confirming something she had long expected, as if all this was the conclusion to some explanation she had been attempting in their previous encounter in her tiny, stained flat. *This is what happens. This is what belief does.*

Sam turned to the man. '*Pane* Rovnák.' The two men shook hands. No surprise registered in the mother's face that he and Rovnák already knew one another, so he assumed he had already been discussed, his presence here mulled over, explained, considered. 'What's happening?' he asked. 'I was told—'

385

'She's in the operating theatre,' Rovnák said. 'In the best possible hands.'

'I saw her at the other hospital. Why was she transferred? Why a *military* hospital?'

'It's the best we have.'

'Pavel arranged it,' the woman said, as though that explained everything.

'And she's being operated on now, you say?'

'That's right.' He glanced at his watch. 'Over two hours now.'

There was a strange abstraction about the scene, that they were here in this soulless room and Lenka was somewhere near, unknowing, lying prone beneath glaring lights with surgeons stooped over her like priests at a mummification.

'What do the surgeons say?'

Rovnák didn't answer immediately, but solicitously sat Lenka's mother down in one of the chairs; then he took Sam's arm to lead him away through the glass door onto the balcony. There was something paternal about the man's behaviour, as though it was his daughter rather than his former lover who now lay beneath the surgeon's scalpel. He lit a cigarette, offered one to Sam. They stood side by side in the cool evening air, smoking and looking out over the hospital complex. There were people moving along the dimly lit paths between the buildings, nurses and orderlies as white as ghosts. Sirens sounded in the distance. Ambulances drove in, blue lights flashing. Perhaps something had occurred in the city, some incident between the occupation forces and civilians. Presumably injured Russian soldiers would be brought here for treatment.

Rovnák spoke. His voice was level and emotionless, as though he were talking about the weather. 'The chances are about even, that's what I was told.'

'The toss of a coin?'

'If you want to put it like that. Even if they are successful, she may have suffered brain damage. When they spoke to Kateřina they appeared more optimistic and less precise. They talked of modern techniques, how so much can be done.' He pondered the matter of modern techniques as though he didn't believe it either. The burning end of his cigarette glared like an angry eye. 'I love her, you know that? Whatever she may have told you.'

Strangely, Sam found that he rather liked the man. There was something matter-of-fact about him, something honest. 'I can understand that. I love her too. And I'm sure she'll come through.'

'How can you be sure? As you said, the spin of a coin.'

'It'll come up heads.' He wondered whether his confidence in the ability of these unknown military surgeons was entirely misplaced. 'How did you get her admitted here?' he asked. 'I though it was reserved for the military.'

'And the Party.'

'But Lenka's not a member of the Party. And neither is her mother.'

Rovnák smiled wryly. 'But I am. And I've always looked after them.' He said no more, just smoked and looked at what passed as a view. Finally he asked, 'Do you know what happened to her?'

'Lenka?'

'Of course Lenka. Who else?'

'Only what I've heard from her friends. She was at the radio station yesterday morning, when they were barricading the place against the Russians troops. A stray bullet or something.'

The man turned towards Sam. His voice rose out of its flat calm. 'You could have stopped her.'

'*I* could have stopped her? What do you mean by that?'

Quite unexpectedly, absurdly really, there was anger in the man's face. 'She'd dropped those foolish friends of hers and moved in with you, hadn't she? You'd turned her head. Trips to Mariánske Lázně. Even to Munich. You had her that close and yet you let her go.'

'How do you know all this?'

Rovnák looked away again, as though something in the darkness had attracted him. When he spoke again it was tangential to Sam's question. 'She phoned me yesterday morning from your house. Wanted to know what was happening. I told her to keep away, but it's not easy to persuade someone on the end of the phone. But you could have stopped her.'

'Don't be ridiculous. She's an adult – she can decide what to do and what not to do. And she was determined to go into the city to see what was happening.'

The man drew on his cigarette. Sam watched his fingers, the same fingers that had known Lenka. How had they been? Probing, insistent, shameless. Rovnák shook his head. 'She had no business to be there in the Old Town.'

'*She* had no business there? For Christ's sake – what about the fucking Russians?'

He went back inside after that and sat next to Lenka's mother, while Rovnák stayed out on the balcony. They waited. The woman smoked. Her breathing was harsh, as though she had obstructions deep inside her chest. Time moved with glacial slowness. Noises beyond the room seemed to come from another world where people did things – calling, talking, hurrying along corridors, pushing trolleys – yet in the waiting room time appeared suspended. This gave each trivial movement an enlarged significance, as though it was observed through a magnifying lens. Such as when Sam reached across and took hold of Kateřina's hand and she grasped his in return. The faint smile she gave him. Her skin was tough and dry; her finger joints swollen by arthritis. She swallowed, moving her lips as though contemplating speech. She said nothing.

*

388

How many minutes passed before steps sounded in the corridor outside? Ten? Twenty? But then there was a footfall outside and a man appeared in the doorway. He was robed in white like a priest and wore a white surgical cap. A cotton mask was pulled down below his chin. Kateřina got to her feet. Rovnák came in from the balcony. The man looked at them with an expression that was curiously neutral, as though he had done this many times before and had become indifferent to the task, whether it was good news or bad.

'*Paní* Konečková?'

Sam stood up, watching the slow interplay of people – the man in white, the woman with the broad hips and brassy hair, the man with the moustache who had just come in from the balcony with a lit cigarette in his hand. Time seemed dilated by the gravitational fields of events around him, stretched out on a rack and close to breaking point, close to confessing all its secrets. One day, he thought, all this will be past. It will be consigned to memory, twisted into different shapes, given that patina of age that will hide most of the pain. Perhaps it will be taken out once in a while and wiped free of the dust of forgetting, so that for a few minutes it may shine bright again; but it will be past, whatever happens.

52

They've walked away from the border as far as the village. There was so much going on at the border – military, radio and TV crews, journalists all milling around like flies at an open wound – that no lifts were forthcoming. So they walked, and now they've found a *Gasthof* on the edge of the village – *Gasthof zur Grenze*, with *Biergarten* and *Gaststätte*, whatever that is, and rooms, a dozen of them, tucked under the eaves. The place is full of that slightly dodgy Bavarian cosiness, manifested in wood carving and wrought ironwork and paintings of lads and lasses dancing round the maypole, that they even have a word for: *Gemütlichkeit*. Ellie might not be able to speak German but she produces that word from somewhere. Enveloped by this *Gemütlichkeit*, they've been served beer and plates of pork and sauerkraut by a middle-aged woman in a dirndl. Enriched as they are by the Wareham bloke's contribution to their funds, they can afford it all. James's head has almost stopped singing and his hearing is less muffled, but still there's a sensation of unreality about the last ten days, as though everything happened to other people, Fando and Lis, perhaps. They discuss it all in the abstract – Jitka, Lenka, Zdeněk, even the embassy guy, Samuel Wareham – as if somehow the people no longer exist in the round but have faded into two dimensions, identified only by what they might have said or done. And in this bucolic beer garden, in the slanting

August evening sunlight, the whole vision of Russian troops in their helmets, their uniforms, their massive tanks, seems something of a fantasy.

'I just hope Lenka is all right,' Ellie says.

'She will be.'

'What makes you so sure?'

What makes him so sure is that he is too young to have witnessed much in the way of death. A couple of ancient grandparents, neither of whom he saw very often; that's about it. His beer finishes and is replaced by another. 'You fancied her, didn't you?' he says.

The conversation trips. Ellie's expression changes. She's suddenly caught between emotions, embarrassment and excitement in clumsy juxtaposition, battling for command of her expression.

James sips his beer through the foam. 'I saw you after the swim. You went off to dry and I saw you touch her.'

'What's wrong with that?'

'Nothing's wrong. I saw you, that's all. You touched her shoulder and then her tits and she laughed. And then you kissed her. On the lips.'

'You dirty pervert. Peeping Tom!'

He laughs at her embarrassment. 'You did, though.'

Ellie says nothing for a while, but she's still thinking about it. 'I've never touched a woman like that before,' she says eventually. 'Never really wanted to. But she ...' She gives a small, humourless laugh. 'Do you think I'm a lesbian, Jamie?'

'Does it matter?'

'It does if I'm going to start wearing tweeds and a collar and tie and cutting my hair short.'

'And smoking a pipe.'

'And wearing brogues and talking in a gruff voice and calling myself Elmer or something. One of our dons is just like that. Dr Sappho we call her. She's really Safford.'

'Somehow I don't think you'll be like that.'

'Have you ever felt anything for a man, Jamie?' She has never called him Jamie before.

'I haven't. But there's a bloke in college does. Fancies me, as a matter of fact. Asked me if I was interested.'

'And what did you say?'

'I told him I wasn't. But if I ever changed my mind, I'd certainly let him know.' She laughs. He has always been able to do that, make her laugh. 'And hey, what about the Russians? Egorkin, and what's her name?'

'Nadia Pankova.'

'Sam got quite peculiar about it. Official Secrets Act and all that. But it'll be all over the papers tomorrow, won't it?'

They speculate a bit, their ideas getting more and more absurd. They should sell their story to the highest bidder. They should write a novel. They should ... More beer. People at a nearby table ask if they are American. 'Everyone asks if we're American,' James tells them. 'But unlike the Americans, we speak proper English.'

There's laughter.

Ellie points at James. 'He doesn't. He's from oop North and speaks a strange dialect.'

More laughter. *Gemütlichkeit*, that's what it is. Jolly laughter and contentment. After a while the English pair bid their German interlocutors good night and make their way upstairs. The floors creak beneath their feet, the door creaks as they shut it, the bed creaks as they lie on it. 'Do you want to?' James asks.

Ellie hesitates, and then says, 'Yes, OK.' So they do it. It's brief and not very skilful, but at least it's companionship of a kind, and no tears.

Early next morning there's a feeling of renewal, that they still have a journey to make, although where they might go remains undecided. Tar has been dispensed with. Do they continue south as originally planned? Or?

Arguing about where and what, they sling their rucksacks and head towards the main road. There's little traffic but they expect that now. This border area is a wasteland. Empty fields and woods. Fences and military patrols. But after a short distance they do pick up a lift, a local farmer who speaks unintelligible German at them and laughs at what they say back to him. He and his battered NSU take them to a junction near his destination, where the road branches left and right.

Left is to Regensburg and München, right is to Nürnberg. They stand by the roadside and face the choice. Ellie takes a coin from her pocket and hands it to James. 'Heads left, tails right,' she says.

He flips his thumb. The coin sings as it climbs, spinning over and over, glittering in the morning sunlight. They watch it rise and fall.

About the Author

Simon Mawer was born in 1948 in England, and spent his childhood there, in Cyprus and in Malta. He then moved to Italy, where he and his family lived for more than thirty years, and taught at the British International School in Rome. He and his wife currently live in Hastings. Simon Mawer is the author of several novels including the Man Booker short-listed *The Glass Room*, *The Girl Who Fell from the Sky* and *Tightrope*.